MW00564739

LEVELED
SERENA J. BISHOP

EOS

PUBLISHING

I hope you enjoy the novel.
Much love,
　　　Serena J. Bishop

Serena J. Bishop — Leveled

Copyright © 2020 by Serena J. Bishop

Published by Eos Publishing
https://eos-publishing.com

First edition: 2020

All rights reserved. This book or any portion thereof may not be reproduced or used in any manner whatsoever without the express written permission of the publisher except for the use of brief quotations in a book review.

Cover art credit: May Dawney Designs
Editing credit: Eanna Robert at Penmanship Editing

ISBN

MOBI: 9789492935229
EPUB: 9789492935236
Paperback: 9789492935243

ABOUT THE AUTHOR

Website:
www.serenajbishop.com
Twitter:
twitter.com/SerenaJBishop
Facebook:
facebook.com/SerenaJBishop
Instagram:
instagram.com/SerenaJBishop

ABOUT EOS PUBLISHING

Website:
http://eos-publishing.com
Twitter:
twitter.com/eospublishing
Facebook:
facebook.com/eospublishing
Instagram:
instagram.com/eospublishing

Subscribe to newsletter:
eos-publishing.com/newsletter

DEDICATION

To the bond of sisterhood.
But since I don't have any biological sisters, this also goes out to
Julie and Jess. You're my chosen sisters.

CHAPTER ONE

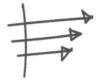

YOU HAVE A *roof over your head.*
You have food to eat.
You are safe.
Be grateful.

Perse realized her positivity mantra had progressively become less and less effective as she drove home from her shift at retail hell. It amazed her how much she had come to loathe khaki. She didn't mind the color when she had been researching in the Andes, but now her work clothes consisted of black-on-black garments that reminded her of the standard uniform of a concert crewmember.

But her clothes hadn't been the only drastic change in the past four months.

Her field notes had turned into a register. Authentic cultural experiences had turned into holiday sales. And the local Peruvian radio station that acted as a soundtrack as she visited home to home had turned into banal popular music piped into an establishment of commercialized mass production.

God, it was depressing.

With the late afternoon sun shining down upon her and her hair blowing freely from the open car window, she made the familiar turn down the suburban street to her sister's home. Perse got along well with Missy and her family, which was fortunate since she had been living with them since she had arrived back in the states.

Her happiness grew as she saw her niece and nephew playing in the fenced backyard with the other neighbor children. As she pulled her Jeep alongside the curb, she was mindful not to hit the bicycles littering the street. Through her window, she heard the excited barking of Dandy and the kids' boisterous yelling.

"Aunt Erse's home!" Alec yelled as if he were a notification system.

She never once thought she would be called that, but the name was cute coming out of the mouth of that fair-haired little boy. He most definitely did not inherit that trait from Missy. Perse and her sister received most of their looks from their Brazilian father. Although Perse was the only one who had inherited his aquiline nose, much to her chagrin. Her ice-blue eyes, however, were every bit from her mother's Germanic ancestry.

"Hey, kids." Perse reached through the fencing slats of the suburban home to pet Dandy behind his floppy ears. "Is your Mom inside?"

Liz ran to her aunt. It never ceased to amaze Perse that while Liz looked like Missy, she accepted responsibility like Gary, Missy's husband. "She's making banana muffins and then is going to make her own juice."

"She's baking? It's eighty-five degrees out here." It really was unseasonably warm for mid-May.

"It's for the soccer team tomorrow."

"Ah. Well, in that case, I'll refrain from having any." Perse walked back to the front, waved to a neighbor, and entered the home. The aroma of freshly baked, spiced bread greeted her.

"Welcome home!" Missy shouted from the kitchen.

"Happy to be home." Before Perse engaged further, she needed time to relax in her basement sanctuary, which, as far as basement standards went, was well above average. Free room and board in exchange for help around the house and piano lessons for Liz was not something she could complain about.

Perse's decompression ritual consisted of replacing her work clothes with lounge wear and gathering her mane of hair into a messy bun. From there, she completed her favorite asana yoga series. The breath work calmed any creeping anxieties she may have. As she focused on her breaths and warmth filled her limbs, she felt

8

the gradual return of the energy that had been depleted by a week of mind-numbing labor. She knew there were worse jobs, but re-folding the same set of clothes everyday was not why she had spent so many years in school and over a decade traveling the world.

After she finished her final pose, she shook out her ponytail and scratched the mosquito bite on her shoulder. Her skin became pinker as she scratched the area around it, the color blending seam-lessly with the ink in her lotus flower tattoo.

With temporary relief from her bite, she rolled her mat, then sighed at the mess that remained from her morning epiphany. A map of the Andes was spread across the futon and three boxes la-beled *Mesoamerica* were open with some of their contents on her desk. Other boxes like *Japan 1 of 2* and *North Africa 1 of 3* were still stacked against the wall, but those resources weren't needed for the grant she was writing. No one had ever investigated or compared how the role of indigenous women had changed in the area now known as Peru and Chile due to Spanish invasion. Her research would incorporate religion, education, geography. Every-thing.

But, before she did that, she needed to catch up with her sister.

Perse checked her phone as she climbed the stairs. There were no messages for jobs. No notifications on her dating apps that piqued her interest. Although, the lack of news wasn't a surprise since the well had gone dry in both of those areas only a few weeks into her stay. It wasn't the lack of dates that got to her, though. It was the underemployment. Hence, the grant she'd initiated. If the powers that be wouldn't hire her, she would make her own mis-sion. Her own adventure.

As she reached the top of the steps and turned the corner for the kitchen, she saw Dandy eating scraps of fruit off the tiled floor and Missy involved in a unique struggle: a double-sided, curved blade in one hand and a plastic lid in her other. Missy clearly had not figured out how to use her new juicer.

"Tell me again why I'm using this fucking thing instead of just adding water to a mix?"

Perse sat at the kitchen island and folded her arms. "Because what you'll make is much more nutritious than what's in those mixes, and you love doing things that make other parents feel inferior."

"That's true, but it's such a pain in the ass!" Missy, with a look of concentration, reached inside the larger unit and snapped the blade in place. Then, she filled the inside with a colorful assortment of cut apples, celery, kale, and lemon. "You're right though. I do love one-upping the soccer mom society, and I want my children to grow up strong and free of deformities."

"You're a very conscientious mother."

"That's what I keep saying." She locked the lid in place and pressed the blend button with gusto.

Missy really was a great mother, but never fit into any of the stereotypes of one. From her penchant for profanity, to her current outfit of fashionably distressed jeans and a genuinely distressed, and very familiar, Nine Inch Nails t-shirt, great mothers came in all shapes, wardrobes, and personalities.

The time Perse had spent with Missy had also reestablished that Missy was, and always would be, her best friend. They were three years apart, had different interests, professions, and lifestyles, but Missy understood her better than anyone else.

Which, on occasion, was incredibly aggravating.

Missy carefully poured juice into two cups, one of dinosaurs and the other of purple flowers. She held the remainder of the green, liquid-filled pitcher up to Perse, who shook her head to pass. "Perhaps after your week you'd prefer something more fermented? Or maybe a birthday brownie? I have one left. It can thaw in the microwave like *that*." She snapped her fingers to indicate how fast.

While the birthday brownies did have the perfect strain of weed baked inside, she wasn't in the mood and wanted a clear head for when she returned to her grant. "Wine will be fine, thanks. Also, you're wearing my shirt."

"Consider it part of your rent," Missy said as she leaned out the open window. "Kids, your juice is done, and you have thirty more minutes outside! Liz, you're on the timer!" Missy directed her attention back to her younger sister. "White or red?"

"White. Okay, for starters, my day started with"—she leaned forward on the granite island—"*him*."

Missy reached into the refrigerator for a bottle. "The pervy guy?" When Perse nodded, Missy grimaced and poured them each a glass. "Please tell me security tased—"

Perse's cell phone vibrated on the counter, and she read the digits. Her eyes widened. "That's an Annapolis number. That's CBU."

"Well, don't stare at the fucking thing. Answer it!"

Of all of the job prospects, this was the one golden opportunity. A starting professor position at Chesapeake Bay University was better than any six-month opportunity to study outside of Santiago. It really was too good to be true. "What if they're calling to tell me I didn't get it?"

"That's what email is for. Now, answer the phone."

Perse took a few breaths to relax her racing heart. Her anxiety had started to climb as each second passed by. Her skin started to hum and the air became thick. Once she closed her eyes and imagined the air thinning, she sat straight in the island barstool and willed herself to answer the phone with a confident and polished voice. "Hello."

A baritone and cheerful voice on the other end responded. "Hello, this is Christopher Jackson from CBU. Am I speaking to Dr. Persephone Teixeira?"

Perse's excitement and nerves wouldn't allow her to sit still. She slid out of the stool and began to pace the kitchen. "This is she. How are you, Dr. Jackson?"

"I'm doing quite well and, depending on your answer, I may feel even better. The reason I'm calling is because I'm extending an offer for the position of Assistant Professor of Anthropology and History at CBU."

She got the job. She got the job. The news overwhelmed Perse. So much so that she realized she hadn't spoken until her sister slapped her upside the head. "That's fabulous news."

"I was hoping you would think so," Christopher said. "However, before you accept or decline the position, you should know that an element of the contract could change depending on your situation."

As long as she didn't have to teach in a solid black uniform, Perse was sold, but she couldn't stop the apprehension from creeping into her psyche and taking control of what should be a joyous event. She shoved her inner villain away and focused. "What change is there?"

"The faculty member you would be replacing needs to leave earlier than anticipated and won't be able to teach a summer session course that already has significant enrollment. The registrar's office would rather not cancel the course and the provost doesn't want us to hire an adjunct. The course itself is on ancient Egypt, and it's in the second summer session, so you would have almost a month to prepare. I think you've already presented similar material elsewhere."

"Yes, in Toronto about five years ago," Perse said as her nerves quelled and her smile returned. The change wasn't a set back at all. She could start work sooner, move into her own place, and say goodbye to khaki pants. "If that's the only change, then I wholeheartedly accept the position."

Missy initiated a silent kitchen dance in celebration.

"That's fantastic! I'll notify HR who will make June 1st the official start date. They'll be in contact with you on Monday for the necessary paperwork, and I'll send you an email with additional departmental details early next week as well."

Perse was jubilant as Missy rushed to hug her from the side. "Thank you so much for this opportunity, Dr. Jackson. This really means the world to me."

"You're very welcome. We're lucky to have such a qualified individual join our department. But, please, call me Christopher, and I'll see you soon."

"Yes, I'll see you soon." Perse hung up after Christopher said his farewell and looked at Missy. "I'm a tenure-track professor!"

They both jumped up and down like when they had won the radio call in contest for New Kids on the Block tickets when they were kids, while Dandy ran in excited circles.

After their adrenaline rush waned and they were still, Missy raised her wine glass. "Now we can drink to celebrate! To my little sister, the newest and cutest badass professor at CBU."

"I don't know about the 'cutest badass' part, but I'll drink to it." Perse really didn't care for pinot grigio all that much, but this time decided it had never tasted so good. "Who would have thought that having my travel papers to India stolen would have led to this?" She sat back down in her island chair and drank again. "I can't believe it."

"Believe it! We always knew you could do it. And you also know what else this means?"

Perse shrugged.

"I get my basement back, so I don't have to drug myself to sleep when Liz has sleepovers anymore."

CHAPTER TWO

THERE WAS NOTHING that could have been done to eliminate the emotional and physical stress of moving. The hours of sitting in her Jeep caused Perse's internal monologue to place seeds of doubt that grew like weeds and started to cut off the energy for her positive thoughts. Not to mention the severe back compression and sciatic nerve aggravation. These were the same issues she always contended with when she found new work, and she had been through the process so many times, she knew how to fix her ailments.

Perse settled into the yoga class, listened to the teacher's calming, introductory words and set her intention: she needed to ground herself. It was the first time in nearly two decades she felt the chance to grow deep and extensive roots. She wasn't working on a six or twelve-month grant. Her time wasn't limited by being a foreign traveler. She was in her home country and had a job that, in theory, she could have until she retired. She could grow roots.

The idea of a regular routine with a "normal job" was exciting. And also terrifying. But she reminded herself that regardless of where she was or what she was doing, so long as she stayed focused and grounded, she would be fine. That was the key.

At the end of the class, another yogi kneeled beside her as she rolled her mat. The smell of musky essential oil wafted toward her. "I hope you enjoyed your first class in the studio, and if you don't mind me saying, you have excellent form. You should think about the advanced class I offer on Wednesdays."

Strangely enough, a new person approaching her in this manner was not one of her triggers. She was confident to speak about areas she exceled in and in her ability attract the eye of those who maybe wanted to do a little more than just talk. But, Perse had one thing on her mind—her new job. "Maybe after I get myself settled in," she said as she stuffed her mat into her bag. "Thank you for the compliment, but I think I'll stick to the basic flow classes for now."

As she left the studio, the air around her became less patchouli-scented and more perfumed with the delicious scents of a café that reminded her of Missy's kitchen. But here she doubted that some-one would slap her ass with a wooden spoon if she took the last slice of zucchini bread.

She detoured from her car in the direction of the mouth-watering aroma.

Perse's first thought as she peered through the large storefront window was that the café was more of a bakery. There were a few tables, but they were overshadowed by displays of baked goods in the front and along the walls.

When she opened the heavy wooden door, she was over-whelmed by the smell of buttery cinnamon and warm chocolate. While she hadn't been hungry moments ago, she was now. Her mouth watered as she anticipated her taste buds coming alive with rich and sweet flavors. She gladly took her spot in the lengthy line and tried to narrow down what kind of post-yoga treat she desired. Cookie or brownie. Pie or cake. Scone or muffin. It was a difficult decision.

She was so lost in her thoughts she hadn't noticed someone be-hind her until a muttered curse was uttered. Rather than turn around, Perse saw the individual's distorted reflection in the dis-play case. The agitated person was an athletically built woman in shorts and a tank top, with shaggy blond hair. She had a cute fig-ure, and based on her profanity, she either desperately needed sug-ar or she was in a hurry. Perse turned to learn that the face matched the figure. "You can go ahead of me if you'd like."

The petite woman looked at her with a sheepish grin. "I'm guessing my lack of patience is pretty noticeable. I just need to pick up a birthday cake, and my friend is circling the block since there's no parking. Sorry, that was more information than you needed."

Perse observed her more carefully. She had slight sunburn on her nose and cheekbones, tawny eyes with the faintest crow's-feet surrounding them, and at the bottom of her heart-shaped face, a chin cleft. There was only one word to describe her: adorable. "I've never been here before and have no idea what to order, so I don't mind if you butt in line."

"That'd be great! Thank you so much. And, um, everything here is pretty good. You can't go wrong. Well, maybe that's not entirely true. The brownies are too fudgey for my liking."

Perse laughed, not so much at the statement, but from the serious tone. "I don't think a brownie can be bad. Cookies on the other hand . . ."

"What's wrong with cookies?"

"They're hit and miss. I don't trust a baked good that needs dunking in milk or coffee to add moisture. The moisture should be there."

"I won't deny that moisture is essential to a quality cookie. Even different types of cookies can have the appropriate moist-factor if the math is calculated correctly."

Perse grinned. "Would you care to elaborate on this calculation?"

They barely acknowledged the movement of the line. Perse was surprisingly amused by the in-depth conversation, which made it more difficult to keep flirtatious notes out of her voice. She found it particularly entertaining that she heard the phrase "manipulation of surface area to volume ratio" come from the stranger.

"Next," the teenage cashier announced with a touch of impatience.

"Looks like it's your turn," Perse said.

"Thanks again for this. Picking up a birthday cake for Blake." The teen turned and retrieved a large sheet cake off the tiered stainless-steel cart behind him. "And before you ring me up, could you add on an iced chai with coconut milk and a salted toffee cookie for the woman behind me?"

The order brought Perse out of her current state of admiring the woman's short shorts. "Oh, you don't have to do that."

"I know I don't have to. I want to. Think of it as my way of paying it forward and, based on what you told me, I think you'll really like the combination." She paid, then picked up the cake, which brought out the definition in her shoulders and arms. "Thanks again for letting me cut in line . . . Ah. I'm sorry, I didn't get your name."

"Perse. And Blake, I presume?"

"That's me," she said, slightly dumbstruck. "I have to run, but hopefully I'll see you around. Maybe after your yoga class next week?"

This move intrigued Perse, but Blake hadn't offered her number, so Perse deduced she was either incredibly friendly or terrible at picking up women. Either scenario worked for her. "It could happen."

Blake smiled and left the bakery in a clumsy escape, almost running into an elderly couple with the pastry box.

"So, do you want that drink and the cookie or something else?" the cashier asked her.

"You know what, I think I'll have exactly what she suggested."

***

Perse stood triumphantly in the center of her new living room, surrounded by books: glorious notebooks that had been spread across her sister's home and texts that had been crammed into footlockers. The sheer joy of having them together in plain sight overshadowed the fact that she had no room in her studio apartment to reasonably store them.

Unfortunately, while the change to start teaching sooner was good for her bank account, it was not conducive to finding a place she was comfortable signing her name to a twelve-month lease. She could look more seriously at apartments or condos once she knew the area and her life had settled more. So, for now, most of her books could go in her new office.

Her new university office. The idea of organizing her materials there gave her a sense of calm, because the feeling of the walls starting to creep in had started. She had to organize her materials ASAP. That would calm her.

She debated on the best location for *Spiritual Pharmacology* when her phone rang. She didn't want to break her unpacking momentum, but she made an exception for her sister. She always made exceptions for her sister. "Hey! I thought you had Liz's soccer tournament today."

"I do, but I thought I'd check up on you."

Perse stifled a laugh. "You're trying to escape, aren't you?"

"Three games in one day! That's insane, and two games too many if you ask me. I really, really hope Alec hates team sports because I can't fucking take the idea of two kids both doing travel sports. Anyway, how's the move?"

Perse appraised what she had done with her new home. "The tricky part is finding space for all of my stuff, but it's going well enough. Thanks again for all of your help yesterday, especially stealing the cargo trailer from work."

"The stealing was nothing. What you really need to be thanking me for is sitting through beach traffic on a sunny weekend to move your ass. But, you're welcome, and unless you have Mary Poppins-like powers, I don't see how you're going to find enough space. You can't even slide your keyboard under that weird bed."

Perse looked over at the Murphy bed currently folded into the wall. "I think it's kind of cool. Besides, I'll get a new place soon enough. One where there's space for a bed I can hide things under. Maybe even an actual piano."

"That's dreaming big, sis. Were you able to find a place to work out your kinks? And I'm referring to your chi, not some ropes and bubble bath fantasy. Not that I'd ever yuck your yum."

Perse chuckled. "I was able to get one of the final spots at a yoga studio, which was great, and then I went to a bakery for a treat. Three treats, actually."

"My, my, my . . . Do tell."

"Well . . ." Perse slid her Spanish–English dictionary into the built-in shelf. Not that she really needed it anymore. "A charming woman bought me a drink and a cookie."

"*Please* be careful. You live really close to campus and do not want to accidentally fuck a student. I will totally yuck that yum."

"Are you kidding? I won't do anything to risk this job. I didn't even flirt back! And, just so you know, she was probably around my age, so she falls outside the traditional student age range."

"Hmm. That's better, I guess. Did she give you her digits?"

"You're a little old to be saying 'digits,' aren't you?"

Missy gasped. "You're a little old to be living in a pseudo-dorm room and taking weed gummies like every week?"

"There's no high with my CBD gummies! Plus, I'll be signing a new lease before you know it."

"Okay, I take it back. You're a grown up. You have a stable job with benefits, medical weed, and aren't picking up women with that herpes app."

"It's called HerPlease, and I've actually turned all of those apps off." As soon as she came within ten miles of campus, her phone sounded like a four-alarm event. "I need to focus on work, not my libido. So"—Perse's attention fell to her remaining stack of unopened boxes—"if you're done insulting me, I must focus my attention here. Goodb—"

"Say that you love me," Missy taunted.

It was something their mother always made them say after they fought as children. "Fine. I love you."

"I love you too. Now you can go. And good luck tomorrow at your first day. I know you'll kick ass."

CHAPTER THREE

CHESAPEAKE BAY UNIVERSITY was established in 1891 and had evolved over the years. The north, south, east, and west sections of campus had been built during different time periods, and their architecture reflected that. The science buildings were the newest, with sleek lines and technology integrated into the rooms, halls, and even roofs. Conversely, her department buildings, while renovated, still had slate roofs, brick sides, and stained glass.

Perse paused in the main history building's hallway to view the display cases highlighting the Chesapeake region. While her area of expertise was Mesoamerica, she acknowledged the drama of the Mid-Atlantic's past: There were the first European settlers and the subsequent genocide of many indigenous peoples. There were the Salem witch trials and women's suffrage. Slavery and its abolition. Various civil rights movements. The American Revolution, the French and Indian War, and the Civil War. Then, there were cities with stories that rivaled some countries: Boston, New York City, Philadelphia, Baltimore, and Washington DC.

Casually strolling past the displayed clothing, musket balls, yellowed and curled papers, and black and white photos was a thousand times more interesting than her time in the HR Department getting her paperwork completed.

For her first day in the department, Perse was mildly disappointed she wasn't able to meet with Christopher since they already had established a comfortable rapport. Instead, Perse was reassured she would meet his trusted second-in-command, Timera Vasquez, who could answer questions and show her the campus highlights. Christopher was a published author and regular figure on documentaries due to his expertise in the Union Army, but Timera had an impressive resume of her own. According to her bio on the school's website, in between writing essays about different minority experiences in America, she had recently become a videographer and often collaborated with the Film and Theater Department at CBU. Timera's interviews with different groups were initially for classroom use only, but interest had spread and now Timera posted them online.

Perse hoped she could create a way to distinguish herself from her colleagues. Part of her still wondered if she had what it took to even be considered a peer.

She followed the hall until the display cases shifted to professor offices, most with their doors shut, and continued walking until she heard the rapid clacking of computer keys. She knew as soon as she announced her presence that her new life had started. A life of changes. A life where unexpected things would happen. A life she didn't have a routine for yet.

Her skin tickled. Her windpipe constricted. Her pulse quickened and she fought for more air. An anxiety attack before she even had an office was not what she needed.

Perse pushed herself against the wall for an inconspicuous mountain pose. She stood tall and steady, and imagined looking down on herself. The picture in her mind manifested through her body to become more grounded. She was mindful of her breath and pushed her heels into the earth. As a single root sprouted from her barefoot, it split and spread into a dozen others until her heart and brain calmed.

Calm and collected, she waited until the woman stopped her feverish typing, then knocked on the door jamb. "Hello."

Timera turned and met her visitor with a smile. "Dr. Teixeira, we meet again. Hopefully under slightly less stressful circumstances."

Perse shyly smiled. During her final interview, she'd met one-on-one with several members of the department to discuss different topics that challenged liberal arts education, university policy, and the role historians have for the future. "While I enjoyed our talk, it is very nice knowing I'm not competing today."

"I bet. Pardon the mess in here," Timera said as she gestured to a seat. "I've decided to do some organizing now that finals are over, but clearly I'm failing miserably."

Perse averted her eyes from the paper explosion, and instead, observed the decorations in Timera's office, from diplomas to paintings, to the set of three small flags on her desk. There was the red, white, and blue of the United States and Puerto Rico, alongside the Pan-African colors of Senegal. "Your office certainly is eclectic."

"That's a nice way of putting it. Speaking of offices, would you like to see yours now or later?"

An office would provide her with a safe space if she had another attack, but the odds of that happening were low. "Later's fine. I know there are other items of business that need attendeing to first."

"That's correct, but I need to apologize for something. We were supposed to go to lunch with the department to introduce you to a few committees and whatnot, but I'm afraid not everyone is here."

The email Perse had memorized regarding the day's agenda hadn't mentioned lunch with the department. "I'm sorry, but what do you mean? The entire department?"

"Oh, God no! That'd be fifty people. Christopher extended the lunch invitation to anyone who didn't have a chance to meet you during your hiring process and are more on the anthropology side of the coin. So, probably like a dozen or so folks. I hope you don't mind."

Perse's stomach leaped into her throat. A dozen wasn't fifty, but she still hadn't mentally prepared for social interaction. Maybe she could see her office before lunch. "I don't mind at all," Perse said and was pleased her voice didn't quake. A lunchtime conversation with a new colleague was one thing, but all of those questions and comments from so many people at once was an entirely different situation. Why did she have to leave her gummies at home? "Do you suspect we'll spend the entire lunch discussing committees?"

Timera gave her a three-ring binder packed to the brim. "There are a few other things too."

The volume of the binder astounded Perse. She opened it to discover it wasn't just information about her summer and fall schedule, it was also interdisciplinary projects, clubs, department social media policy, library resources, and more. "Graduate Curriculum Committee?"

"Don't even get me started. On more than one occasion that meeting has prevented me from squeezing in all of my planned evening entertainment. I think somebody just hates going home and this is an excuse for them to stay late at work."

"You must be talking about the GCC. Completely daft."

Perse turned to the individual who had entered with a Scottish accent and saw a woman with extremely close-cropped red hair and an abundance of hoop earrings.

Timera looked at her watch. "Perse, this punctual lady is Gillian Duncan. Gillian, meet Perse, the newest member of our fine department."

Gillian vigorously shook Perse's hand. "Great to meet you. I hope you don't mind, I think I might be the only one joining you for lunch. I think Christopher forgot that today was the bus trip to DC."

"Damn," Timera muttered under her breath. "I'm sorry about that. I guess it'll just be the three of us then."

Perse contained her joy from dodging the forced socialization bullet. "It's not a problem, really. I'm sure I'll meet everyone in due time. Where are we going for lunch?"

"Where would you like to go?"

***

The three of them were taken through a bustling section of tables with built-in Zen sand gardens before being seated in the section that gave Big Mizu its name.

"That's a lot of water." Perse looked at the aquarium wall with wide eyes. The glass stretched from floor to ceiling and divided their section of the dining room and the bar. Through the slowly waving aquatic grasses, she watched the bartender on the other side mix a drink. As she studied the spectacle in front of her, she realized the soothing trickling sound she heard wasn't coming from the massive tank, but rather from across the room where a small fountain bubbled out of a polished gray stone. "This place is amazing."

"There's a lot of competition in and around CBU," Timera said. "That keeps the quality for everything pretty high."

Gillian scoffed. "Plus, they charge five dollars for a soda."

Perse's view of a colorful angelfish became obstructed when their hostess stepped to the table. After he summarized the lunch specials and gave them their individual order forms, Perse removed her reading glasses from her bag and checked the boxes for dishes she had never tried before. Her little adventure for the day. "I have to say I'm glad it's just the three of us for lunch. I have a touch of anxiety."

"Is that why you looked like you were going to pass out when I mentioned lunch with the department?" Timera asked.

Perse thought she had covered it better than that. "Yes."

"But"—Gillian's brow knitted together—"I heard that you've played the piano in concert halls."

"When I was an undergraduate, I did. It was part of my scholarship."

"How can you do that—or give lectures to hundreds—if you're so shy around others?"

Perse understood the question and had been asked it many times. "It's not about being shy. Starting from when I was a kid, I realized as long as I had a plan and practice, I didn't have anxiety." She also liked the sense of accomplishment when she met those challenges. She refused to allow her condition to dictate what she could and couldn't do. Modifications were sometimes necessary, but she would not give in.

"So, it's not so much the people, it's what you're going to say or do once you're on the spot," Timera summarized.

"Exactly. Just the idea of small talk at a party makes me nervous." Perse sipped her water and thought of an exception. "Small groups or one-on-one are not as bad because I don't feel so many eyes on me."

"That's fair. Luckily for you, Gillian and I talk enough for about five people."

"True. And hopefully by Friday you'll feel comfortable enough around us to see us as pillars of support in case you feel nervous."

Perse furrowed her brow. Of all the important events and steps she needed to take care of in her first week, nothing on that day rang any bells. "What happens Friday?"

"There's a reception for the new Dean of Students," Timera answered. "Unfortunately, attendance is pretty much required."

She could practically feel her vessels dilating and her blood pressure drop. She felt the seat under her. She was grounded. She would be fine.

"Are you okay?" Gillian asked.

Perse took a sip of water, but the constriction in her throat made swallowing difficult. "I'm good." Or at least she would be once she had the opportunity to process the event. "Now that I know, I can prepare and there won't be any issues." At least, she hoped that was the case.

"If it helps, the building has a lot of art. If you need to get away, you can check out the latest displays."

"Plus, you can always come find us," Gillian added. "We'll probably just be talking to each other or Stef."

Perse practically memorized the faculty bios and didn't recall reading about anyone with that name. "Is she in our department?"

"God, no," Timera answered with a laugh. "Stef's a friend of ours who's in the biology department. We met her during a campus wellness initiative and have been friends ever since."

"Total sweetheart for someone who used to do some batshit crazy research. But she's cool. Just don't get her started about anthrax or botulism. She'll talk your bleedin' ear off."

Those weren't topics Perse had ever brought up in casual conversation. Rather than question their friend's background, Perse politely nodded. "Well, if I meet Stef, I'll either try to stay clear of bioterrorist topics or stick to wellness."

***

Another reason to hate soccer.

Missy's neck muscles grew stronger by the second from all the nodding she had done during a "conversation" at practice. She didn't think of it as a dialogue between parents because that would have implied she contributed words, but no. She listened to a fellow parent drone on and on about school boundary changes and what that meant for her precious son's chance at starting on the basketball team.

She couldn't take it anymore.

"Oh!" She jerked her seated body up and pulled her phone from her pocket. "Sorry, I'm expecting a call." She turned on her screen and, to her amusement, viewed an actual message. Missy turned to the disgruntled parent. "Sorry, I have to take this. Sister needs advice." She hurried away from the sideline, glanced to see that Alec was still making his own fun, and dialed Perse. "So, what's this I hear about a university shindig?"

"Pretty much what I said in my text. You didn't have to call me so soon."

"Yeah, but then I couldn't have escaped the queen of privilege." She turned to the woman in question who was now griping to a new poor soul. "Besides, you used a worried emoji and you never emoji your feelings. I'm concerned. So, what gives?"

"There will be hundreds of people there. Important people too."

"You're important." She seriously didn't understand her sister.

"No, you don't get it. Like really important. The entire university staff will be there, which includes a Pulitzer winner, first and last authors for *The New England Journal of Medicine*, a former public radio host, someone running for the Senate, and—"

"You've made your point. This sounds like the worst party ever, but I still don't know why you're worried."

That was a lie. Missy knew exactly why her sister's anxiety had started to creep in. Over time, she realized if she forced Perse to vocalize, and therefore rationalize why she was so nervous, Perse could talk herself down from the metaphorical ledge.

"What if they talk to me?" Perse asked.

"I'm not going to lie, that's possible, but do you think they'll ask you anything personal about yourself?" Her sister's Achilles heel lay in anything remotely related to her personal life. But if she had the track record of family and relationship catastrophes Perse had, she might be wary of sharing too.

Perse laughed. "I think they'll pretty much want me to justify my hiring. So, they'll ask about my experience and publications, but then probably get distracted or bored and leave."

"Okay, one, you aren't boring. You're like Indiana Jones but without the stealing from other cultures. And who cares if they get distracted, it's a hobnob event with lots of shiny new people and humble bragging."

"I'm starting to feel a little better."

"Good." Missy tossed a stray soccer ball back onto the field. "Now, what are you going to wear?"

Perse groaned. "Such a good question."

Missy thought of possible outfit combinations while she watched Alec chase a rabbit. "Well, let me suggest—Oh!" she yelled with a grimace as Alec took an errant soccer ball to the back of the head.

"Everything okay?"

"Alec took a head shot, but he seems to be fine." She held the phone to her shoulder and yelled, "Are you okay, little man?"

He responded with his face in the ground and a thumbs up.

"Yeah, he'll be fine. Back to you and your situation. I would say to plan a few different outfits that incorporate layering, dark top—purple or navy—because you do not want to pit out among the big shots, and make sure you have a pocket to stash an emergency gummy."

"Okay, all that makes sense. Thanks for helping me put this in perspective. There's so much change and stress. I feel like I'm overanalyzing every little thing, which only makes everything worse, and—"

"Hey! You'll be fine." Missy watched Alec resume his rabbit chase. "You stumble sometimes, but you always get back up."

CHAPTER FOUR

HUNDREDS OF PEOPLE in business attire milled about in the cultural center for the dean's reception. Some on the first floor stationed themselves at cocktail tables and picked hors d'oeuvres off trays from the passing servers, while Perse stared at the massive, domed ceiling with dozens of flags hanging from it. "This is impressive. Is there more art on the second floor or is it all offices?"

Timera plucked a bruschetta spear from an offered platter. "All art. Offices are in the basement."

Perse scowled. She hated working in basements.

"You know, I thought you'd be more nervous," Gillian said. "But you seem very cool with all of this." She gestured to their surroundings.

"That's because I had time to prepare." She smoothed out her pencil skirt, and in doing so reassured she had one extra gummy if she needed it. "What do you know about the art here?"

Gillian hitched her thumb toward Timera. "Ask that one. I haven't a bloody clue."

"The upstairs has the permanent, donated pieces, but this floor rotates the art. They try to merge different styles of paintings, photographs, and sculptures to suit the theme of the year."

"What's the theme this year?" Perse asked.

"*War and Peace.* And I just found the new dean," Timera said with a shake of her head. "He's just as grown-up-frat-boy-looking in person as he was in the university newsletter."

"And I found more refreshments," Gillian announced. "Hungry? Thirsty? All of the above?"

The past few days had been both mentally and physically strenuous for Perse. She completed moving everything into her office, which had required the demanding task of transferring dozens of book-filled boxes from her apartment. While a glass of wine would provide her muscles with a faux-massage, mixing alcohol with her gummy was a poor plan. "I think I'll teetotal for now."

"Sounds good to me. Timera, I'll pick up the first round while you keep Perse company."

The last thing Perse wanted to be was a burden on her new colleagues. "No, you two go ahead. This place is immense and I'm really curious about what else is on display. I think I'll break off for a bit."

"By all means, explore and mingle. We're an easy group to spot."

Perse watched them leave for the bar, then focused on the sign above an arched entryway: *War and Peace*. She made a beeline for the exhibit hall and prayed that no one along the way stopped her for introductions. She was feeling steady, but there was only so much she could take before she would need to leave.

Perse kept her eyes forward and strode with purposeful steps until she reached the room of the exhibit. There were no windows, but the white walls and marble floor reflected enough light to illuminate the art in the room. One wall featured paintings that emoted pain, conflict, and fear, while the other showcased joy, harmony, and love, and at the far end of the exhibit was a hallway that featured a sign, which pointed in the direction of a memorial garden.

From that hallway, she heard a feminine voice become progressively louder and clearer.

"I'm sorry to tell you this, but it sounds like you ran the test backward . . . Yeah, you're going to have to do it again . . . No, you can't guess! This isn't creative writing."

Perse debated turning around when she heard the one-sided aggravated phone conversation, but once she saw the blonde turn the corner she decided to stay.

The annoyed woman's eyes were glued to the screen as her thumbs danced over her phone.

"You know, texting while walking can be dangerous."

"Yeah, well, I'm a rebel," she said sarcastically, then looked up from her screen. Her brown eyes widened and she smiled. "Hey! It's you . . . um, Perse! What . . . ? Do you work here?"

Perse was tickled by the transition of hard-nosed, focused professional to befuddled exuberance. "I just finished my first week here. I presume you work here as well . . . Blake, was it?"

She nodded vigorously. "Yeah. Stefanie Blake. My friends call me Stef."

That was too much of a coincidence. "Friends like Timera Vasquez and Gillian Duncan?" She watched Stef nod enthusiastically again while she searched Perse's face for an explanation. "They were talking about you over sushi my first day. Not too much, though. Only that you all met during a fitness initiative and you're in the biology department."

"Oh," Stef drawled. "Oh! Wait! Are you Persephone Teixeira?"

"One and the same. Let me guess, they mentioned me at some point too?"

"Yeah. They mentioned that lunch—Gillian hates overpriced soda. They were *really* happy you accepted the position here."

Perse was reassured that her initial impression of Stef from the bakery had been correct: her maroon Converse sneakers matched her sleeveless top, the bubbly personality was layered over a quiet intensity. Stef was very cute-sexy, and Perse had very little apprehension speaking to anyone with those characteristics. "So, Stef, why are you away from the party?"

"I had to rescue a student from wasting even more time on a botched experiment, so I needed a quiet place to hear her panicked summary of events. How about you? I would think you'd want to meet all the people. You know, get your name out there."

"I have a thing with social events and crowds. Plus, I love exploring new areas." She gestured to Stef. "Surprises around every corner."

While Stef grinned, her phone beeped rapidly. "Dammit, that's my timer. I have to head out so my samples don't overgrow. I tried to plan my experiment so I wouldn't have to rush out during the reception, but that wasn't meant to be."

Had they met a month earlier, Perse would have tried to convince Stef to let her samples wait. They had an easy banter and quick chemistry, which could lend itself to other entertaining activities, but Perse had other priorities she could not be distracted from. She'd have to settle for fantasy. "I don't want to keep you from something as serious as sample overgrowth," she said with a smile. "It was very nice running into you though."

"Would you like to run into me again? Maybe tomorrow evening over dinner?"

Perse giggled, then sighed. "I'm sorry, but I have a lot on my plate since I just started, and I don't want to make it uncomfortable between my colleagues—your friends. Plus, I still have that hour presentation about sexual harassment in the workplace embedded in my brain. I hope you understand."

Stef tersely nodded. "I completely understand, and that's why I'm only asking if you'd like to get together with me to learn more about the town and campus over tacos . . . from a food truck . . . on uncomfortable chairs that will probably give your ass splinters."

Stef had played that well, and Perse smirked at her persistence. "So, in other words, not a date?"

Stef shook her head as though the idea repulsed her. "This is a meeting for me to share tribal knowledge about the university and possibly discuss new interdisciplinary research topics between a microbiologist and history-type person. If, in the process, we learn more about each other, what's the harm in that?"

Perse's interest had been piqued. She crossed her arms and leaned against the wall. She knew better than anyone there were elements of a location one couldn't learn from reading a brochure or studying a map. In addition, the taco meeting could be handy to determine locations for apartment hunting. "Okay, I'll go. But only if we each pay for our own food and I meet you there."

"Deal. I'll meet you at six by the swings in Tubman Park. Do you know it?"

"I do."

"Great! Well then, it was a pleasure seeing you at this university-sponsored event." Stef gripped Perse's hand in a professional shake. "Okay, now I really have to go. See you tomorrow."

Perse watched Stef leave the exhibit hall. The pep in Stef's step almost distracted Perse from her damn near perfect ass. However, *Peaceful Protest*, a metal sculpture of olive branches, reminded her why she came into the room in the first place. She wanted to learn about the art at CBU.

She read the plaque adjacent to the artwork. It fascinated Perse that the metal was sourced from melted assault rifles and the artist was—

"So," Gillian's voice echoed down the hall as she came closer, "I hear you met Stef."

Perse was impressed by how quickly that news had spread. "Yes, I did. She seems . . . very friendly."

"Oh, she is, and is an excellent source of uni information. You'll be amazed how helpful she is. She rescued me when I started a few years back trying to figure out the campus when new construction was going on. But she's hilarious too, so your meeting should be fun."

"She told you we were meeting?" Perse asked and tried to make her voice sound casual despite the nerves that had suddenly appeared.

"Yeah. I think it's great, but she takes interdisciplinary projects very seriously, so don't be surprised if she shows up with a list of questions."

That was interesting. Maybe Stef really had abandoned the idea of a date and stepped into the role of a non-official welcoming committee. Perse did find comfort in knowing people outside of her immediate co-workers. Afterall, she was in a new city with no friends. There was safety there, especially if the new acquaintance-ship lacked any prospect of intimacy. Emotional intimacy and her anxiety didn't mix. Mostly because emotional intimacy led to abandonment and embarrassment, and those were terrifying.

Of course, since Stef and Gillian were friends, Stef could have told Gillian about more than just their meeting.

"Out of curiosity, did Stef say anything else to you?"

"Tacos."

CHAPTER FIVE

PERSE STARED INTO her closet once again and deliberated over what to wear for taco dining with a new colleague.

A sexy and charming colleague.

Despite the voice in her head that said the meeting with Stef was a terrible idea, her stomach also spoke to her. It was pissed for only being given reception appetizers and snack bars over the last few days. She knew better than that. Regular healthy eating and exercise helped keep her in control. The non-date would also assist with learning about the town and give her eyes a break from staring at a computer monitor. She could solve all of those problems while keeping her blood sugar stable. An hour of taco-talk in the least provocative outfit she could think of wouldn't kill her.

She pushed her clothes in the closet to the side, and pressed against the wall were the least sexy pairs of pants she knew of—khaki cargos. She traded in her work capris for the cargos and, as she reached for a black tank top rolled in a drawer, her phone rang. She put it on speaker. "I'm so glad you called me back."

"Yeah, yeah," Missy answered with a loud whistle in the background. "What's the emergency?"

She should have remembered Missy would be at soccer. "Do you remember which box my vintage black sandals were packed in?"

"Yes. They are in what is known as the trash box."

"What?" Perse shrieked. "Those shoes would have been perfect."

"Those shoes were terrible! Not fashionable at all. You should be thanking me for removing them from your life. How could they be perfect for anything?"

Perse sighed. "I'm meeting someone, and I don't want to look sexy." The other end of the phone was filled with howling laughter. "It's not that funny."

"Oh, I disagree. That's hysterical. But I can finally understand why you'd want them. Those shoes were so unsexy I think they gave virginity back to people."

"You've made your point."

"I think so too. Now, what in the hell is this all about? Yeah, three waters and three hot dogs."

"I'm not going for hot dogs. It's tacos," Perse said as she began to search for new shoe options.

"Not you. I'm in line at the concession stand for hot dogs. So, you were saying . . ."

"The woman who bought me that drink and cookie is also a microbiology professor at CBU. She asked me out, but I gave her the whole—"

"You have to focus. Yeah, yeah, I know. It's a boring but necessary conversation."

"Right." Perse picked up a pair of teal flip-flops, but tossed them into the back of the closet. "And she understood where I was coming from. So, instead of a date, she offered to give me insider CBU information while we talk about possible interdisciplinary topics over a food truck dinner."

"Wow. Now, that's a line! And you fell for it. You're either slipping as you approach the big four-oh or you're incredibly horny."

Perse was fortunate she was a hundred miles away and not beside Missy in the concession line to see the on-lookers' faces when her sister made that statement. "I'm neither slipping, nor . . . horny," Perse said while she slipped on an old pair of running shoes. "This is a good chance to learn about the campus, nothing more, so I don't want to send mixed signals."

"Interesting. So, no make-up or landscaping your downstairs?"

Perse was very grateful she was not in line with her sister. "No. It's just regular me. And I'm hoping Stef shows up with a similar idea."

***

Perse arrived at the agreed upon location in her unsexy outfit and looked around for signs of Stef, but saw no one, so took a seat in one of the swings. For several minutes, she swayed in the thin plastic seat and listened to the ducks quack from the large pond across from her. After an audible stomach rumble, she glanced at her watch. Stef was late. Perse exhaled a frustrated breath and kicked a stick by her feet.

"You seem really annoyed for someone who isn't on a date," Stef called out from an open car window.

"How long have you been sitting there?"

"About five minutes." Stef rounded her car and stood before Perse.

The first two times Perse saw Stef, she had a fresh-faced, girl-next-door appearance. Now, Stef's dirty blond hair had more volume, her eyes were more defined, and her lips shined. Then there was the issue of her clothes. Stylish jeans and an off-the-shoulder white t-shirt. Stef had dressed the sexy route. God, that was unfair. It was hard enough trying to keep a professional distance as it was without being teased. That was so frustrating, and also, in a way, enticing.

"The idea of you sitting in your car for five minutes watching me is pretty creepy."

"Agreed. You'll be happy to know I wasn't watching you. I was waiting for my audiobook to come to the end of its chapter while I studied maps. Shall we taco now?"

Perse gestured for her to lead the way. Stef walked slightly ahead and looked left and right. Perse didn't know what she searched for, but she knew her own eyes were drawn to the denim covering Stef's shapely rear. "How far is the taco truck?" Perse asked after a few moments of silenly watching Stef's hips sway.

Stef pointed to a red structure in between a grouping of trees on the other side of the park.

"That's not far at all. Part of me thought this would be an attempt to squeeze in extra conversion by dragging me across town."

"That wasn't part of the agreement. I figure if we want to spend more time talking, it should be at the end of tacos, not before, and near the agreed upon location."

Despite Stef's appearance, she wasn't acting like they were on a date. "You know, you're a little on the dressy side for this outing."

"I thought about that as I was driving. I didn't have time to change from my previous engagement."

"Were you showing another new professor the latest wine bar?"

Stef chuckled. "No. Most Saturdays I go visit a friend of the family at a retirement community that's nearby. Today I took him to a distillery that just opened. Harry loves his bourbon. Anyway, there was a tour and tasting. It was fun."

"Sounds like it."

A comfortable silence fell over them as they neared the food truck. Once they arrived, Stef, again, displayed very atypical date behavior. She jumped in line, ordered her food before Perse even read the offerings, and then left to watch the ducks. Once Perse collected her buzzer, she joined Stef on the Adirondack chairs that overlooked the pond. She could faintly hear Mexican pop music playing through the outside speaker. "So, what book were you listening to that you had to hear the end of the chapter?"

"*People of the Forgotten Plague*. Have you read it?"

"Can't say that have. What's it about?"

"The Black Death in Egypt. I know that Mesoamerica is your main thing, but most of their well-documented epidemics are virus related. Not my deal. So, I thought maybe you'd be willing to discuss a region outside of your expert wheelhouse as long as I could add something significant to the discussion. Is that cool?"

It fascinated Perse that Stef started their conversation with an actual interdisciplinary topic. The non-romantic subject caused her to relax further. "That is an interesting idea. Europe is so much of the focus of that time, people don't consider the Middle East, even though it was in the center of the trade routes. What made you think of the plague specifically?"

"That's my area of expertise. Well, I dabbled in anthrax, too, before I came to teach here."

Perse never heard someone refer to bioweapons like it was a hobby. "How does one 'dabble' in anthrax?"

"Honestly, I can't talk about it. Had to sign all kinds of non-disclosure agreements before, during, and after I left. Now, I do research with much tamer bacteria. Oh, tacos!" she said as both of their buzzers went off simultaneously.

Stef jogged the short distance to meet the food runner and, after she shared a quick laugh with the server, returned and handed Perse her basket.

"Do you know him?"

"Nope. Just being friendly." Stef held her taco out in a cheers-type gesture. "Bon appétit."

Perse reciprocated the motion and bit into her dinner. It was lightyears better than almond-cranberry bars. The handmade made tortilla, spiced meat, and fresh vegetables caused her to flashback to her time living in Texas. "Ay, Dios mío."

Stef grinned, a small amount of queso fresco on her lip. "I thought you might like it."

"I never in a million years would have guessed this was here. I may have to come here every day."

"Except that you can't. They're only here Tuesdays, Thursdays, and Saturdays."

"What's here the other days?" Perse asked, not caring that juice ran through her fingers and down her forearm.

"Um." Stef's eyes traveled lower and quickly moved back up. "Oh! A burger-hot dog truck, which is so-so. But on Sunday it's waffles, and not just the regular waffle kind. It's the fancy le—the kind I can never remember how to say."

"Liége," Perse said with perfect pronunciation.

"Yes! That's the one. How many languages do you speak?"

"Fluently? Four. But I try to know the emergency basics for every country I go to."

Stef appeared to listen with rapt attention as Perse detailed her travels in Central and South America, Europe, northern Africa, and southeast Asia. Stef's questions eventually led to her to tell the most recent story of how her travel papers were stolen and she was forced to abandon her plan to study cultures, past and present, of the Ganges River.

"That sounds like it would have been amazing," Stef said. "I'm really sorry to hear that you couldn't go, but I'm sure you'll be able to someday. If you like it at CBU and want to settle down, there are sabbaticals you can take."

Settle down. It was something she had never done and something she didn't think she was capable of. If she were honest with herself, she hadn't only moved to live what she studied, but also to escape. She wondered if it was time to start confronting her fears.

Stef allowed her to have her introspection in peace and appeared to be entertained enough by the ducks and her food. That was something Perse hadn't experienced in a while. Someone who was content to be quiet with her.

"Can I share something with you?" Perse asked, and then watched Stef put her taco down and rest her chin in her hands. Perse smiled at the comical pose. "I've traveled a lot. My dad was in the Navy, and we moved five times when I was a kid. During undergrad, I traveled during breaks and abroad during my senior year. I backpacked during grad school breaks. And professionally . . . I didn't stop moving until six months ago. I loved living the different cultures, not just reading about them. But the last few months have made me question certain things, like maybe I can reach professional excellence, travel a little, and have a permanent address?"

"What made you start to question yourself?"

Stef looked at her so earnestly, it didn't matter if her answer sounded stupid. "Dandy," Perse said with a chuckle, "my sister's beagle. I lived with Missy while I was trying to find work. I knew I loved my sister and her family, but that dog was a surprise. I never had a pet growing up, so when I heard that dogs love unconditionally, I didn't really understand it. But I get it now, and it'd be nice to come home to that."

"Dogs are awesome."

"Do you have one?" Perse asked with more excitement than she would have thought.

"No, I don't, but I'd like to now that I live alone again." Before Perse had a chance to question, Stef offered, "When I came here five years ago, I moved in with my aunt Carol to help her, but, um . . . she passed away four months ago."

"I'm so sorry to hear that."

Stef broke eye contact as she took a pull from her water bottle. She kept her eyes averted even as she twisted the cap back on.

Four months or not, Perse could tell the loss was still difficult for Stef. She scrolled through her mental files of comforting quotes, proverbs, and song lyrics but couldn't think of a thing. She just didn't know Stef well enough to offer comfort in that capacity. There was the universal language, though. Perse gently placed her hand on Stef's upper back.

Stef turned to her and her mouth upturned in a sad smile. "Hey, remember when we came here to talk about the plague and all that fun stuff?"

"I do. That was a bit more personal than the original plan." Perse understood the need to bring the topic back to work. She had essentially admitted that she was ready to put down her roots and Stef had revealed a recent family loss. "Although, I've never associated plague with fun."

"Not even 'Ring Around the Rosey'?"

41

"Okay, in that case I'll make an exception," Perse said with a chuckle. "The class I start teaching next month is about Ancient Egypt, so this suggested topic is a good way for me to test my knowledge. How much do you know about trade in and around Egypt?"

Over the music, their interdisciplinary topic of conversation organically shifted into other areas. They discovered that they both had soft spots for action-adventure movies of the 1980s and modern design. And, of course, tacos.

When the food truck's exterior lights turned off, Perse commented, "I guess that's our cue."

"Yeah, which sucks because I still want to know more about your musical past and if you have more tattoos. Unless you can tell me in the time it takes to walk to my car," Stef said as she stood and threw away her trash.

"Yes, I do have more tattoos." She lifted her hair to expose the back of her neck, showing a series of musical notes. "And maybe a few others. But my pianist history is a much longer story and it's already dark. I should head home."

Stef looked up as if to confirm the sun was gone. "If you feel uncomfortable walking home, I can give you a ride."

"Would you give a friend a ride home?"

Stef barked a quick laugh. "The way my friends drink, I'm always driving someone home. Especially Gillian."

"Then, I would really appreciate a ride." Without a hint of apprehension, Perse got into Stef's car and buckled herself in. "Do you know where the downtown laundromat is?"

"Yes, I do. Head in that direction?"

"Please."

Stef pulled out of the space and started toward her apartment. "So, why piano and not, say, guitar or tuba?"

"My mom was a professional pianist."

"Well, you don't hear that every day. Did she force you play?"

"Not really. More like she'd put me on her lap when I was little and told me which keys to press. Eventually, I hit that stubborn kid streak that demanded I know how to do everything, so she started to teach me."

"I take it you're pretty good."

"Good enough to get a half-music half-academic scholarship."

"Nice humble brag." Stef smiled and turned onto the main downtown road. "Let me ask you this: do you enjoy playing?"

"I do. I've lost a step now that I don't practice two to three hours every day, but it's fun and helps me focus on something if my anxiety is high."

"That's so cool. Sorry, not the anxiety part, but the ability to play an instrument so well," Stef said as she signaled to turn down Perse's street. "I don't play any instruments, but I enjoy live music. The university puts on great concerts that we get discounted tickets to."

"That's a nice perk." Once again, she learned an aspect of the college no one had considered telling her. "You can park behind the Jeep."

"You live here?" Stef asked, alarmed. "This is practically campus housing! If you keep going straight on this road, the apartments get much nicer."

"Really?"

"Yeah, once you pass the bend in the river it's a different zip code," Stef said and turned off the engine. "Here's your stop. Delivered as promised."

Perse returned the smile Stef gave her. Stef had shown that she was highly intelligent, funny, and sensitive. It really was one of the best non-dates she had ever been on, and she could see them continuing this friendly, professional relationship. There might be sexual tension from time to time, especially if Stef kept wearing pants like that, but Perse was an adult and could deal with feelings like that. "I had a really good time tonight. Thank you."

"You're just happy I introduced you to the taco truck."

"That is true, but I enjoyed our conversation a lot. You're very easy to talk to and have some interesting perspectives to go with your unique background. I'm hoping I didn't bore you."

"Are you kidding? If you were boring, I would have spent more time with the ducks."

Perse laughed, not out of politeness or mild amusement, but as an unrestricted release of happiness from her body. "I'm pleased to know I have more to offer than waterfowl," she said as she released her seat belt.

Stef looked on with a sweet grin. "Before you get out, can you do me a favor and grab the manila envelope that's on the floor behind me?"

Perse leaned slightly between the seats and saw it. She recognized the CBU Fighting Crab logo immediately, despite not wearing her glasses. "Is this an internal mail envelope?"

"It is. There's something for you inside, but do me a favor and don't open it until you're in your apartment. Instructions are inside," Stef said matter-of-factly.

"Alright." Perse was flummoxed by the odd request, but that did seem to align with Stef's character. "Goodnight. Thanks again for the ride home."

"And a good night to you."

Stef waited to pull away from the curb until Perse was safely in her building.

Once Perse was in her apartment she rushed to her desk, where her reading glasses lay. On the outside of the envelope was a description of where the contents should be sent: *Human Resources Re: Policy 75.*

Due to her recent employee orientation, she remembered everything about the university's sexual harassment and relationship policy, but that didn't stop her initial shock from reading the bold title across the sheaf of papers, *Dating and Relationship Agreement and Acknowledgment of a Harassment-Free University (Policy 75)*. The papers also had sticky tabs indicating where initials were necessary and a larger, bright pink note on the final page with Stef's phone number and the message: *No hard feelings if you really need to focus on work right now, but if you'd like to go out with me on a real date, here's our way without us risking our jobs. Could be fun. Best regards, Stef.*

Perse flipped through the document and noted that Stef already initialed and signed. "What the . . . ?" She closed the document in a huff.

She thought she made her feelings abundantly clear. She had no time for this. And she sure as hell didn't want to sign a document that notified her new employer she had decided to date a staff member after her first week on the job.

Who did Stef think she was?

Perse grabbed her phone to tell Stef exactly the kind of person Perse thought she was but then paused. What would she say? *"My instincts and my sister told me this would happen. And it did!"* Not only did that make her sound immature, but it also made her sound asinine.

She couldn't believe she had been so gullible. Stef had planned the entire outing. She had created the guise of a non-romantic outing, yet still laid on the charm, and Perse had fallen for all of it. She didn't know what was more infuriating, Stef's deception or the fact that she still found her attractive.

Perse put the phone down and took a deep breath. She needed to settle her emotions and organise her thoughts before she made her next move. All she knew right now was that Stef had gone too far.

CHAPTER SIX

THIRTY MINUTES OF yoga and forced meditation and Perse still didn't feel right. She hated it when her brain and her gut disagreed. Yoga should have given her mind and her belly the opportunity to balance, but the rocks in her stomach stayed. Her thoughts still tumbled, mostly because she was second-guessing her initial reaction.

Yes, Stef had crossed a line, and in doing so Perse questioned the respect Stef had for her boundaries, but she enjoyed Stef's company and found her attractive. Yes, once she simmered down and reread the note in the paperwork, it wasn't that bad. There were much worse ways to be asked on a date, and their time together was responsible for the most fun she'd had since arriving at the school. However, Stef was also best friends with her new co-workers. Co-workers who were helping her learn the ropes before her summer class started. That in and of itself should have been reason enough to say no and keep her conscience clear. But it wasn't.

As she rolled her yoga mat at the end of the class, she felt a small tap on her shoulder.

The yogi in harem pants and a man bun smiled serenely. "I'm sorry to trouble you, but I wanted to tell you that your dancer pose is gorgeous."

"Thank you. That's very kind of you to say . . ."

"Thom," he said and placed a palm to his bare chest. "Perse, right?"

She nodded politely despite the fact that she had a feeling she knew where this was leading. He was cute, but she already had one too many people with that description in her life.

"Well, if you don't have to run out right away, there's a café of sorts just across the street. I'd love to learn more about where you've done your practice."

"I'm sorry, Thom, but I have to go to work." That was true. She could at least avoid adding guilt to her list of emotions. "Maybe some other time."

"I'll look forward to it. See you next week," he said with a wave and left.

Perse stuffed her mat into her bag and headed to her car. Once inside she took a moment to collect her thoughts and create a strategy to deal with this ridiculousness. Her obsession over Stef's paperwork was an unnecessary distraction. She had to deal with the matter quickly and cleanly.

She took out her phone to text Stef. *Can you meet me at the smoothie bar in the student union building in two hours?*

The reply came seconds later. *Yep.*

***

The cold shower after her yoga workout did not assist Perse's attempt to appear cool. In the walk from her office to the smoothie bar, the hot spring day caused her shirt to cling to her skin and sweat to bead on her forehead and neck. She was almost certain there would be wet imprints of her palm and fingers where she carried the manila envelope.

Once she ordered from the counter and a tart kombucha was in her possession, she craned her neck to find Stef. It wasn't difficult.

Stef waved frantically in her seat by the large philodendron.

Perse was amused that after establishing eye contact, Stef's exuberate expression changed to one that was pensive. It was almost like she was being studied. Normally, that would have made her uneasy, but under Stef's gaze, she found it titillating. Avoiding the arousing sensation would have been easier had Stef not looked so fit. As Stef picked up her smoothie, the muscles in her arm flexed, highlighting a large bruise on her bicep. Then, her tongue quickly licked away a stray droplet.

I wonder if she's a top?

Perse reprimanded herself for the thought. She had a clear reason for requesting Stef's presence, and it wasn't so she could ogle her. "Thank you for meeting me here, especially on such short notice," Perse said as she sat.

"You're welcome, but I was already in the lab. I have a lot of data I need to collect before my conference this summer, so I come in on the weekends when I can."

Why did Stef have to be interesting? Perse wanted to ask, *What kind of research?* Or, *Where are you going?* Or even, *Why do you have a massive bruise?* But this meeting was to cut off any possibility of a romantic relationship. Stef, while devious, seemed too nice to lead on, and Perse was terrible at relationships. Or, more accurately, relationships had been terrible to her. She had promised herself that her last broken heart would be just that. Her last.

That's why she hadn't been in a traditional relationship in fifteen years.

"Are you okay?" Stef asked. "You kinda look like you have heat stroke."

Perse would go with that for now. She held her tea to her forehead and nodded. "I forgot how ungodly humid it can get around this area of the country and I don't think I rehydrated properly after yoga."

"Then you should drink up," Stef replied, then took a long sip from her pink smoothie. "I see that you have an envelope which resembles the one I gave you yesterday. Coincidence?"

Perse took a long drink from her refreshing beverage. She didn't want to stall, but the longer she waited, the less time there was for her to be the bad guy. "It's the same envelope, and for the exception of the papers being creased more at the staple, it's exactly the same as when you gave it to me." Perse watched Stef's mouth shift into a frown. "I know that's not what you wanted to hear, but I thought if you understood why, it would soften the blow, and I didn't want to tell you over work email."

"I really don't know if I want the details of my rejection. However, I do appreciate learning why my hypothesis was incorrect. Okay, tell me."

"I *have* to focus on my job. There's so much to learn here, and I have less time to work on my lectures than I initially thought due to additional responsibilities and the ridiculous number of meetings. It's not a good idea for me to date. Plus, I have to say, the pre-signed paperwork was a little underhanded and creepy."

"No!" Stef shook her head adamantly. "Not creepy. It's persistent and charming."

"Persistent, yes, but stalkers are also persistent."

"That's true," Stef said and her shoulders slumped. "I promise I'm not a stalker, and I'm sorry if I was too forward. It's just that I'm very goal-oriented, and after we had such a delightful time at tacos, I thought maybe you'd change your mind."

"Fair point, but if I had changed my mind, wouldn't it have been easier to just ask me out?"

"Well, there was the aforementioned rejection piece, and if you had said yes, then having the paperwork already there would have been very efficient." Before Perse could jump in to describe the selfishness of that tactic, Stef continued. "But you're right, I'm sorry I wasn't more direct. And I'm also sorry I didn't respect your initial answer."

That was an unexpected but welcome addition. "Apology accepted. You should know that I did enjoy your company last night and I think we had some excellent conversations. Do you think you can handle us only being friendly professionals?"

"Yes," Stef said, but the ponderous expression returned as Stef sipped her drink. "Sorry, not to beat a dead horse, but you not signing has absolutely nothing to do with finding me too nerdy or not being your type?"

"Oh no. I think you're a very interesting brand of nerdy and very attractive. But, as I've said, work has to come first, and there's the possible conflict between seeing you and being colleagues with Gillian and Timera. I'm afraid if we started seeing each other, I might have to bail because I was overwhelmed with the semester. I'd hurt your feelings."

"I could have a heart of stone," Stef retorted. "You don't know."

"Oh, please. Based on the look on your face when I told you I didn't sign the papers, somebody would have thought I gave away your puppy. And you opened up to me pretty easily yesterday. I can tell you're a sensitive person. Which isn't a bad thing, but I can see you wanting a type of dating relationship that I can't participate in. If I were to go out with you—with anybody—they would have to know they were way down on my priority list, and the time and place of dates would have to be decided by me. That's a lot to ask of someone. That's—"

"Perfect!" Stef slapped the table.

Perse arched a brow at Stef's reaction. "How is that perfect?"

"Because that aligns with level one," Stef said with glee.

She shook her head. "You lost me."

Stef skewed her mouth and raised her eyes to the hanging philodendron as she took a moment to collect her thoughts. "Okay, so after a serious analysis of my past relationships, I created a system that ensures perfect compatibility before moving into the next phase of a relationship. By definition, it slows the relationship down."

Perse wasn't sure if she was impressed or disturbed by Stef's announcement. "You designed a relationship system? Why?"

"Ever been married?"

She hated that question for numerous reasons. "No. I . . . haven't had the pleasure."

"Well, I have, and no matter how amicable, divorce sucks. The next person I marry will be my last. End of story."

"Why be married at all?" It was a question Perse often asked. There were various methods different cultures used to show commitment to one or more persons. Conversely, many individuals

50

from around the world practiced different forms of non-monogamy.

"For me, having that level of commitment means something extra, and I want that."

Perse opened her mouth to speak.

"I know what you're going to say, because it's the same thing Timera always says. 'You don't have to be married to show commitment.' I think that's theoretically true, but when you pledge yourself to someone for life it turns theory into practice. I dig that. Plus, there are tax and estate benefits, which is smart financial planning."

Perse thought about Stef's explanation as she sipped her drink. The idea was fascinating, which meant it should be scrutinized. "What if I don't believe in marriage? What if I think it's an archaic philosophy meant to enslave women and prevent natural sexual desires?"

"Seriously, have you and Timera established some kind of psychic link?"

Perse chuckled. "No. I assure you these are my own thoughts and I'm just playing devil's advocate. And you didn't answer the question."

"Well, the answer is simple. The levels naturally weed out someone who doesn't believe in marriage or during the course of the earlier levels would cause the woman in question to change her mind. Probably around level four."

Perse had become less concerned with her own possible role and was instead fixated by this approach. "How many levels are there?"

"Six. Dating, love, orgasms, family meetings, cohabitation, and marriage."

Out of the six, there was one which caused Perse's brow to knit and her lean back into her chair, arms folded. "Orgasm is a category? Not sex?"

"I'm glad you caught that, because it was sex for a while, but then I really thought about the whole 'what is sex?' thing. I concluded that sex has too many definitions, so I decided to base that level on a specific outcome. Do you have any more questions? Because I really like talking about my system."

"I can tell." And Perse liked hearing about the system. There was logic and she could see its organic progression, but she found elements impractical. "Why did you put love before orgasms?"

"I think it's romantic. Plus, this is where it's helpful to separate sex from orgasms. There can be some sex, it just can't cause an orgasm."

Perse could not stop the laugh that traveled its way from her belly to her mouth, while Stef directed a stern teacher-look in her direction. "I'm sorry. I didn't mean to laugh. It's just . . . you're completely serious. Don't you think that's unrealistic?"

"No. I think it poses a challenge, but just because something is challenging doesn't mean it's unrealistic. Haven't you ever been with someone, and even though things were getting hot, you stopped?"

Perse opened her mouth and shut it again. Had she ever done that? She scrolled through her memory bank of different sexual encounters and had to admit that she had. Many times. A roommate who came home early. A fallen candle that caught the carpet on fire. Someone who fell asleep while going down on her. And vice versa. "Okay. You've made your point. But still, I'm skeptical. Those particular situations had serious interruptions. It wasn't . . ." Perse sighed when she couldn't articulate her argument.

Stef smirked. "Let me ask you this. Would you give up the romance of a lifetime because of a little sexual frustration that, honestly, you could take care of yourself?"

Now masturbation was a topic? The entire conversation was utterly surreal for Perse, who had detached emotions from sex for the better part of her adult life. Her willpower when it came to sexual urges was being questioned—challenged, even. The temptation that resulted was unexpected. "So, for your levels, you won't give or receive orgasms until you love that person, because you want that moment to be as emotionally powerful as possible?"

"Yes!"

Perse viewed Stef suspiciously. "This has nothing to do with a perception that this gives you a moral high ground?"

"I don't judge others for how they have sex. But, if I'm involved with someone, I want to make it emphatically clear from the beginning where I stand. Especially, since, no offense, lesbians become attached very quickly after a sexual relationship starts."

Perse shrugged. "I'm not offended. I don't classify myself as a lesbian."

Stef's eyes widened. "Oh! What are you then? If you don't mind me asking."

"Most of my life I identified as bisexual, but after my experience with someone non-binary I've decided that pansexual is a more accurate description. I learned a lot about myself when I went to Thailand."

The slight pinkish hue to Stef's cheeks was adorable, but if she knew the details of her month in Nonthaburi, Stef's skin would be crimson.

"That sounds like one hell of a trip."

Perse laughed loud enough to draw the attention of the student worker behind the counter. "It was very educational." She unfolded her arms and shook her head. "How do you know when to advance to the next level?"

"I figured I'd assess it on a month by month basis. For example, after the first date—because after that it's pretty obvious to me if I want to continue seeing someone—if the dates don't evolve, then there's no way a long-term relationship is possible."

"What do you mean by evolve?"

"Well, different date activities start to reveal character, physical attraction, and, most importantly, emotional intimacy. If after a month of dating there hasn't been a conversation that goes deeper than party talk chitchat, then the relationship is bound to stay in the land of the superficial because there's some kind of barrier." Stef took a long slurp from her smoothie. "I think the orgasm bit is fairly self-explanatory, but family meetings are a little trickier."

Perse suppressed a laugh. "I'll agree with you there."

"Right? Because once you think you've exposed all of yourself to this wonderful person you love, you haven't! Because family members bring out different parts of us. They tease us. They get out embarrassing photos. And occasionally, they toss in family expectations you had *no idea* existed. Then, once that test is over, you can start to think about cohabitation, and I'm not talking about sleepovers or vacations. If two people can live in the same place, share responsibilities, and truly feel free to be themselves all the time for at least one year, then marriage is on the table." Stef frowned slightly. "Unfortunately, aside from my one-year cohabitation rule, the time is variable, which I hate, but I haven't figured out a way to quantitate everything yet."

At least Perse could understand that part of the rationale. "When did you make this?"

"Around two months ago. Timera, Gillian, and I went on a spring break cruise—even though I was still really depressed and didn't want to go—and that's when and where I started brainstorming. You're the first woman I've asked out since I invented it." Stef cleared her throat and took a long sip from her smoothie. "I feel that we've covered a lot of ground here, but do you have any other questions?"

Perse had dozens, but they were too personal to ask, like, *How long had she been married? Since her divorce, had Stef been in another relationship?* "As of now, I don't think I have any more questions."

"Great! You know where I stand, and I know where you stand. So, would you rather we remain professional colleagues and discuss the plague in Egypt? Or would you like to venture into level one and sign the papers?" Stef asked as she held the envelope in front of her and moved it in a dance.

#

54

The smell of wet dog lingered in Missy's nostrils as Dandy made an escape from his bath and ran out of the bathroom. "Gary!" Missy shouted down the hallway.

Her husband's head appeared in her son's doorway.

"Are you finished covering Alec with calamine lotion?"

"I don't know. What do you think, buddy? Are you covered?"

Alec jumped out in his dinosaur print underpants and covered in pinkish salve. Only the occasional light beige of his skin was visible. "I'm a cotton candy Ninja Warrior, Mommy!"

"You sure are!" Her surprise was genuine. Gary had gone way overboard on the treatment since Alec only had a few spots of poison ivy rash on his legs. "Can the warrior's daddy give me the lotion because my skin's on fire?"

Gary handed the bottle to Alec, who happily handed it over to his mother.

After she thanked her son for the lotion and kissed her husband for handling that portion of the poison ivy incident, Missy shut the bathroom door behind her, opened the tube of lotion, and proceeded to take off her clothes. Her shorts were at her feet when her phone vibrated. If the dipshit from the office was calling her on a Sunday, she thought she might go there and rub whatever poisonous oil was left on her skin all over his face.

However, it wasn't the office. It was Perse, so she put her phone on speaker. "Do you mind if I'm partially naked while we talk?"

There was a pause. "You're not about ready to . . ."

"God, no! It's the middle of the day on a weekend. Sex does not happen at that time when you have two kids." The burning of her skin and its accompanying itch almost caused her to forget why her sister might be calling when she wasn't at work or soccer. Missy's preferred time to talk. "Oh, how was the taco non-date?"

"I honestly don't even know where to start."

"Gary's on a yard project and the kids are watching a movie. I have time. Start at the beginning."

While she listened to Perse summarize dinner, the paperwork surprise at the end of the evening, and the subsequent meeting she'd had with Stef regarding her levels, she completely forgot about the itchy red blotches covering her skin. The tale she listened to as she treated herself with the lotion was easily one of the most entertaining stories she had ever heard.

"Did you fall asleep?" Perse asked suddenly.

"God no! This is fucking hilarious."

"It's not that funny."

"Um, have you met you? 'Hello, I'm Persephone, but you can call me Dr. Ayahuasca Three-Way,'" Missy said between fits of laughter and putting on her fresh clothes. "You never should have told me that story."

"That was a once in a lifetime opportunity for me. How many times am I going to be invited into a Peruvian shaman's home and be given the honor to share the same cup as him and his wife? And I published a fantastic paper after that."

Missy feigned a deep snore and closed the lid on the commode to have a seat. "Oh. What? I'm sorry. I did doze off that time. Get back to the levels part."

"I understand you might find it a bit odd, but it does have substantial logic behind it and to hear Stef explain it is so inter—"

"Holy shit! You signed the papers."

"I did. We're going out to dinner sometime this week. I decide when and where. But I made it clear that if Stef had control of the levels, I had control of the pace."

The situation went from being comical to worrisome. Missy sighed. "Are you sure you want to start this with her? This Stef person seems seriously invested in finding someone for a long-term relationship, and you haven't had one of those since Anthony, which was forever ago."

"Which proves that I am capable of having a relationship if I want one. And I'd say talking about the long-term is really jumping the gun. This is one date."

Missy couldn't criticize Perse for doing everything in her power to avoid relationships after what Anthony did—or what the others before him did—but Missy was concerned. She didn't like that Perse denied herself something Missy *knew* her sister wanted. However, she also didn't like any person being led on. "I can see your point, but what if you like Stef and you go on a second date, and then a third date . . . What about the sex-orgasm thing?"

"What about it?" Perse said, her voice impatient.

"That you like orgasms. A lot."

"Who doesn't?"

That was a fair question. "Okay, let me rephrase. Your lack of relationships has not hindered you in that department. Can you be with someone like Stef and not want to finish the deed?" *Or develop feelings?* Missy thought to herself. God knows if she talked about relationships and feelings Perse would have a panic attack.

"I'll be fine."

"If you say so," Missy added skeptically. "Okay, last question and then I have to put on a cold compress because my skin still feels like it's on fucking fire."

"Oh, did Dandy roll in the poison ivy again?"

"You know he did. Anyway, are you going to say anything to your new work colleagues about it?"

Perse had forgotten about that element. "I'm still working out the pros and cons."

***

Perse tossed and turned for hours. All night different scenarios played out of how Timera and Gillian would react when she told them about the date. Finally, she shoved the covers off, dragged her keyboard out, and sat down to play the piano. It wasn't until she was in the fifth song her brain finally stopped torturing her.

There was no risk to her job. She and Stef were adults. And people dated at universities all the time. Hence, CBU created paperwork for when relationships went awry.

But she still felt it best that she delivered the news face-to-face. Even Stef agreed.

Thoguhts settled, Perse eventually fell asleep, if only for a little while.

From the time she woke to her arrival in the building, she rehearsed what she would say, and any possible rebuttal or criticism they might have. Timera's door was still shut Monday morning; however, the sound of punk rock became progressively louder as she approached Gillian's office.

"Hello," Perse said, hoping to be louder than the Sex Pistols.

Gillian slowly turned from her desk. "Perse? To what do I owe the pleasure of this visit?"

Perse sat in the visitor's chair. The message she was about to deliver needed to be clear, short, and professional. "I want to tell you something face-to-face, but before I do I need to make it clear that my job is my first priority."

Gillian nodded. "So, this is about you going on a date with Stef, then?"

Perse's jaw dropped. "She told you! She said she wouldn't!"

"She didn't say anything, but I figured it out. Stef was way too chipper during our rugby game. Then, I asked how tacos went, and she went into unprecedented detail, which for her is saying a lot. Lastly, she sent Timera and I about two dozen texts yesterday telling us she had a date."

It was comforting to know that Stef hadn't violated her confidence, but Perse's larger concern still wasn't addressed. "And you're fine with it?"

"Fine with what?"

"The two of us going on a date."

Gillian stared back at her completely dumbfounded.

"You don't think it's a conflict?"

"Oh, God no! I think it's great. Stef's had a very bad hand dealt to her, and I want to see her happy. Plus, if you two don't click, I trust that you're a professional like everyone else. It's not like people within our very own department haven't given it a go." Gillian leaned forward and gestured for Perse to come closer. "Bjorn and Jin," she said in a whisper.

"Really?" Perse said in faux-surprise. After watching the two men squabble during her first meeting, she'd decided they made a perfect love-hate pairing.

"Mm-hmm. And it's not like you and Stef are going to run into each other here. Her building is on the other side of campus. Just relax, it's fine."

Being told to relax was never effective, but she appreciated the sentiment. "Thank you. Do you think Timera feels the same way?"

Gillian grimaced. "She likes her world compartmentalized. So, she'll be okay as long as you don't make Stef a topic of conversation while you're in the office, and, for argument's sake, let's say she does have her knickers twisted about it, she'll let you know in her own way. Feel better?"

"I do. I generally don't get so . . ."

"Anxious?"

Perse smiled. "Right. At least when it comes to things like this." She could get lost in the frantic, nervous energy that filled her when she had an attack. What she failed to comprehend was why a single date was sending her to a place where she had barged into a colleague's office to say that she was going out with her friend. That was fairly ridiculous. "I really appreciate your time and I'm sorry I bothered you with all of this."

"It's no bother. You're under a great deal of stress right now, and that can make anyone a bit off-kilter. Just focus on the job and don't worry about Timera. I'm sure she'll lighten up once Stef calms down."

***

By Wednesday afternoon, Perse was convinced she had read more Egyptian textbooks in the past two weeks than she had in an entire semester in graduate school. When she closed her eyes, she could see the white etchings in the dark gray rock of the Palermo Stone she'd worked on back then. But her efforts this week had been worth it. Not only had she created a solid syllabus that integrated newer literature, but she also had two weeks of class lectures planned. At that pace, she'd be done with her lectures by the time the course started and could then focus on grading and planning for the fall.

It was exhausting to think about.

A knock at her office door drew her attention away from a thick tome. She took off her reading glasses to see Timera more clearly. "Hello."

"Hi. Sorry for the pop in, but I wanted to ask if you were you able to upload your syllabus to the campus network?"

"Yes, I was. Thank you for your help with that. I'm sure I'll need your assistance again at some point."

Instead of leaving, Timera inched closer and regarded the office décor. Her eyes were drawn to the area of the bookcase that featuresd all of Perse's musical note-themed accessories. "I'm going to have to start calling you Treble."

Perse couldn't help but think that nickname sounded a lot like another word, but she disregarded her paranoia. "Ever since I was a kid my sister has been giving me this stuff. I finally have somewhere to put it." She tapped the top of the Elton John bobblehead, causing the icon to bounce.

Timera softly chuckled. "I have a second reason for my visit. I need to apologize. I screwed up the invite for the department meeting we had scheduled from three to five today, so I don't think you got the cancellation."

"Oh. Well, thank you for telling me. Although, next time I don't mind if you send me an email. That'll save you a trip."

Timera bobbed her head along with Elton as she stood in her office.

"Is there anything else?"

"Nope. I just wanted to tell you about the cancellation now so you had more time to plan what you're going to do with that extra time in your life. You could even leave a little earlier this afternoon if you wanted to. It's a beautiful day outside."

"Maybe." Perse glanced out the window. There wasn't a cloud in the sky and the spring heat wave had left for cooler, seasonal weather. "I have been averaging twelve-hour days for the past week."

"You definitely don't want to burn out. This is a marathon, not a sprint. If you like wine, there's a place called Vinos. You can walk around the vineyard and the wine-food pairings are to die for. I recommend the chocolate torte," Timera said, then left her office.

Perse didn't know her colleagues very well, but she knew them well enough that she found Timera's visit odd. With her, any question or comment was sent through email. But Timera had gone out of her way to deliver all of that information in person. It was almost like . . .

Perse opened a new tab in her internet browser and searched for Vinos. She quickly learned that it was a farm-to-table restaurant and winery noted for its romantic ambience.

Gillian was right, Timera had her own way of communicating her feelings.

Perse picked up her cell phone and then put it back down. Did she want to do this? She could use the extra time to start writing the course's first exam. Or, she could taste flavorful food and sip wine while she gazed across a candlelit table at a beautiful woman.

Perse picked up her phone again and texted Stef. *Busy tonight? My meeting was canceled. I could pick you up around seven for dinner if you're free.*

She turned her phone upside down so the glowing screen of an incoming text wouldn't distract her. She couldn't lose her focus. She had to—

Her phone buzzed on the desk, and she immediately flipped the phone over to read the response. *I happen to be free and will be seeking nourishment around that time.*

She should have guessed Stef wouldn't have sent a simple 'yes' or 'no'. *Send me your address and I'll see you then. I'm looking forward to it.*

She debated telling her sister the news, but knowing Missy, that conversation would take an hour, and she needed that time to prepared for her date.

CHAPTER SEVEN

STEF LIVED AWAY from the campus in a development reminiscent of 1950's suburban America. The houses were smaller than the monstrosity her sister lived in, most had carports instead of garages, and the yards were neatly divided by waist-high fences. She hoped for Stef's sake that if her home had been built in the 50s, the interior had seen some adjustments. Asbestos and lead paint were not quaint features.

Perse pulled into the carport and did one last appearance check in the visor's mirror: her eye makeup wasn't smudged, her upswept hair had the appropriate amount of loose tendrils, and the owl pendant at the end of her necklace fell just above her cleavage, further showcased by her summer dress's plunging necklace. She had to admit that she felt good. The yoga she did before she'd left helped ease first date jitters, and even if their date turned out to be a dud, she had at least been able to escape from her books and have a nice meal out. If their date turned out to be the opposite, at least there was no need to be nervous about how their date would end. A kiss at the door.

At least, a kiss at the door seemed reasonable for level one. She doubted Stef would permit more, but Perse could handle keeping the physical PG-rated. Stef was a culture in and of herself, and she needed to respect that.

The royal blue fabric of her dress swished around her as she walked up the brick path that led to Stef's door. As soon as Perse knocked, she heard footsteps scurrying from inside.

The door opened and Stef greeted her with a slack-jawed expression. "You look . . . way nicer than I do."

Perse smirked and craned her neck slightly back and to the sides to observe the exterior of the single-level home. "I can't agree or disagree. It's kind of tough to see you from all the way out here."

"Oh! Please, come in"—Stef stepped to the side—"I have several windows and lamps, so you should be able to see me much better from in here."

Perse had seen Stef well enough before, but completely out of the shadows Stef was striking. Small, drop earrings matched her golden-brown eyes. Her diaphanous, forest-green blouse allowed Perse to see through to the camisole that hugged her figure. And she wore khaki capris that managed to be sexy. Perse made a show out of studying Stef from head to toe. "I don't think I look nicer than you. Let's call it a tie."

"That's a pretty big compliment coming from you." Stef reached for the small bouquet of dark pink stargazer lilies on the console table beside her. "These are for you. It feels kind of weird giving them to you this way, but I didn't want you to miss out on them just because you're the one behind the wheel. It's a tradition of a first date I like," Stef added as she played with her hands.

Perse smelled the light fragrance and smiled. She found Stef's nerves comforting, and she tried to remember the last time someone had bought her flowers. She couldn't. "Thank you. These are lovely."

"You're welcome. Are you sure you don't want me to drive?"

"I'll learn the area better if I'm the one behind the wheel." She held the blooms to her chest and took a moment to study the interior of the home.

The room was furnished in a modern style that matched what Stef described during their taco outing. On each of the walls were framed pictures of mountains and coastlines. The couch's accent pillows and other knickknacks were bright, complementary colors that stood out from the light gray that dominated the room.

"This is nice."

"It's not my forever place, but it is home. Would you like a quick tour or are we tight on time?"

A few nervous twinges remained in Perse's stomach. However, each extra piece of information about Stef helped dissolve a knot. Whether it was knowing Stef was nervous too or seeing the more intimate details of how she lived. "I think we can spare a few minutes."

"Just enough time for me to show you my pride and joy." Stef took the flowers and laid them on a table, then led Perse through the small dining area and out a sliding glass door.

Perse saw a birdhouse hanging off a large oak tree and hummingbird feeders sprinkled throughout the yard. The brick-paved patio included a built-in fire pit with four chairs circling it. But the most impressive element of the yard was the water feature. There was a series of three half barrels that held hidden flowerpots, but also acted as water sources to create a miniature waterfall that flowed into a small pond. The fire circle was a clear invitation for socializing, but the sounds of the pond offered tranquility.

Perse was impressed. "Did you do all of this?"

Stef proudly nodded. "I did have help from Timera, Gillian, and her husband, Ian. I got the idea from the water feature where my aunt Carol lived—where Harry lives now. I think every time I visited her I took notes about their set-up. One time she yelled at me because she said I was harassing the groundskeeper."

Perse chuckled lightly. "I'd say your attention to detail paid off. This is really, really beautiful. It must be relaxing to come out here and listen to the water."

"It is . . . kind of. When I'm alone, I find it hard to relax. My brain just won't shut up." Stef tapped at her head. "I have a lot of thoughts."

"Care to share your thoughts right now?"

"Way to put me on the spot." Stef blew out a long breath. "Um. Beautiful woman in my backyard. Sweaty palms. Out of birdseed. Beautiful woman. I hope I have good lab results in the morning. Beautiful woman. Say something funny." Stef bobbed her head about as if she were thinking. "Those are pretty much my thoughts. How about you? Want to share?"

Perse considered Stef's admission and her continued hand wringing. "I think nervous babble is more charming than surprise paperwork, and that my date should take a deep breath, because I think she's funny without trying, created a gorgeous landscape, and looks amazing."

Stef smiled innocently. "I tend to overshare and have a busy brain."

Since they were on a date, Perse reasoned that some amount of physical contact was appropriate. She approached Stef and touched a freckle on her temple. "Maybe we can slow your brain down?"

Stef's pupils dilated in a field of amber. "Um. We should probably head out now."

"Okay." Perse was delighted she'd caused such an obvious physical reaction and was disappointed she couldn't continue. She smoothed down the blond strands that had blown astray in the slight breeze and reluctantly moved her hand away as she felt her own body temperature increase. Apparently, she was reacting too. "Lead the way."

"Would you like to leave your flowers here?" Stef asked once they were in the house again.

Perse glanced at the flowers Stef had laid by a family portrait. "Do I still get them even if our date doesn't go well?"

"Okay, two things. One, yes, you would, but it would be pretty awkward. And two, our date will be fabulous."

Perse liked the confidence. "Then, your chariot awaits."

After Stef made herself comfortable in the passenger seat, Perse watched her eyes dart around the backseat with interest. From memory, a box of maps, a collapsible shovel, and an emergency kit were in view.

"You seem prepared for the apocalypse," Stef said.

"I like to get away from crowds and travel off the beaten path, so I come prepared."

"Preparedness is very important, but some people don't appreciate that. People like Wayne."

"Who's Wayne?" Surely, a pissed off undergrad who received a lower grade than he thought he deserved.

"He's a mycologist in my department who forgets about ordering supplies for his classes and then 'borrows' them from my lab. I should mention that he's my nemesis."

"Nemesis is a pretty strong word. I'm guessing he's done a few things other than steal your supplies."

Stef huffed. "Um, yeah. When I first started at CBU, he treated me like a grad student, and his research is less than admirable. He doesn't respect statistics. To me—and the rest of the scientific community—a p-value means something."

Perse politely listened as she drove and it confirmed her impression that Stef was a highly intelligent, yet emotional person. It could be a volatile combination, but she was reassured that what you saw with Stef was what you got. Perse would take that over deceit any day of the week.

"How about you?" Stef asked. "Do you have a nemesis?"

"No one's ever asked me that question before." *Was there anyone in her life she'd consider her nemesis?* Certainly, there were individuals who had wronged her, but she wouldn't classify them as her enemies. "I don't think I do."

"No professional rivalries?"

Perse laughed. "Now, that's a different question. The anthropologist in India for the study I was supposed to lead has methods which I have substantial issues with. Their strategy is akin to a bulldozer to dig for information."

"What's your style?"

"Compared to a bulldozer? A spoon. Possibly a strong fan."

Stef chuckled. "You prefer a subtle approach. That's good to know."

Perse grinned wickedly. "Not always. I think being direct when it comes to certain things definitely has its advantages." She took the exit her GPS directed, which led to an open road bordered by farms.

"Oh!" Stef blurted. "Are we going to Vinos?"

Perse glanced to her right to see Stef's excited expression. "We are. I'm guessing you're a fan."

"Huge fan!"

Their conversation of nemeses forgotten, Stef provided the directions for the remainder of the short trip. Soon, grazing cows and silos sprinkled the landscape. As they crested a hill, Perse saw a large stone cottage in the distance. She followed the windy road Stef directed her down until she parked in the restaurant's gravel lot.

The hostess led them through a merlot-colored dining room and a new aroma wafted toward them as they passed each table. Garlic and lemon. Rosemary and butter. Warm chocolate and raspberry. They sat at a votive-lit table, lined on three sides by white, gauzy drapes. Only the silhouettes of other patrons and their whispered conversations came through the translucent material.

Stef looked around their private cocoon. "This is definitely a step up from tacos."

"I don't know about that. Those tacos were pretty damn good," Perse said with a grin and gave a nod of thanks to the server who placed the wine menu on the table between them. She spied the bottle she was most interested in, but Stef probably had a favorite. "What do you like?"

"I like your lotus tattoo."

Stef's answer amused Perse. "Thank you, but that's not at all what I meant."

"I know, but you threw me off by using a sexy voice. Then, just answering white or red seemed boring, so I went with my gut with what to say."

There was a lot to be examined. For one, maybe she'd lowered her voice a bit, but she'd hardly used a sultry tone. And two... "Your gut told you to compliment my tattoo?"

"I'm very bad at flirting; therefore, I default to compliments. I don't know how much flirting is too much. There's no scale."

Perse came to a realization about Stef. "You like to quantify everything, don't you?"

Stef sipped her water thoughtfully. "How do you mean?"

Perse tucked her glasses away and folded her hands in her lap. "Do you approach every question the same way?"

Stef shrugged. "Scientific method, duh."

Perse smirked. "I think people are far too complicated to approach with that one strategy. In this case, there is no single appropriate level or scale of flirting because people are so different. Showing an ankle could be just as scandalous or arousing as sweeping my finger through that whipped cream over there and licking it off."

"You're suggesting I have to try different things to find the area between ankles and finger sucking to flirt?"

"I said licking, but yes."

"That sounds a lot like an experiment to me. Very scientific method."

"Touché." Perse pushed the leather-backed wine menu toward Stef. "For your prize, you choose the wine, but I want to see some flirting out of you that's not giving me compliments."

"Challenge accepted."

They ordered their food and wine, and while they waited, Stef spoke about the vast amount of renovation she had done to her home. The information about the updated electrical work was more interesting paired with the candlelight flickering off Stef's polished earrings. The effect made her hair more golden. Perse also noticed while Stef spoke that she skewed her mouth in a comical way when she was in the process of answering a question that required considerable thought.

"You must get a great deal of satisfaction seeing your projects through," Perse commented.

"I really do, but there is a financial limit that keeps my projects shorter."

Perse tasted her risotto which embodied the freshness and salt-iness of the sea. "What if, hypothetically speaking, you had twenty thousand dollars. What would you do?"

Stef swirled her sauvignon blanc while her face held that pensive pose. Perse had no idea her renovation inquiry would be such a challenge.

"So, you just give me twenty thousand dollars?"

"Well, not me, but someone with the money just gives it to you. No strings attached, except that it can only be used on your house." Most would probably consider it a silly question, but it was interesting to learn people's priorities and thought processes.

Stef put her glass down and her eyes danced. "I got it! I would sell my current house and pretty much everything in it, and use that money to buy land. Then, I would use the twenty thousand dollars to build my own house."

"It takes a lot more than that to build a house."

"Not when you do it yourself," Stef said boldly. "It wouldn't be a big house, but I'd never worry about its infrastructure because I would learn how to make it solid."

Levels. Perfect statistics. Solid foundations. Stef appeared to make sure everything in her life had a sound structure before she built off it. "I have to say that's one of the more creative responses I've ever heard."

"Does that mean I win?"

Perse almost choked on her wine with laughter. "Yes, in the competition of this evening's game of house fantasy, you win first place."

Stef smiled and gave a small fist pump. "Now, I want to learn more about you. I know you play piano and are supposedly pretty good, but I don't know what you like to play."

Perse was amused by the 'supposedly' and that Stef's line of sight drifted down for a moment. "You could search for performances on-line and find out."

Stef grimaced. "I could, but then you made that stalker-persistence comparison and I felt weird."

"Oh, well, thank you for remembering that. But I would say pop or rock music that lends itself to piano. I play a lot of Elton John, Coldplay, Fleetwood Mac. You get the idea." She caught Stef's eyes lowered again. "Did I dribble wine on my chest?" Perse asked nonchalantly, and then sipped.

"I was admiring your owl," Stef said with confidence and a straight face.

"Who am I to deny you a good look, then?" Perse reached behind her neck and unclasped the chain. She passed it to Stef and then leaned back to allow their waiter to serve the entrée course. The aromatic steam of fresh seafood and herbs lifted between them.

Stef inspected the pendant. "I love sapphire."

"Me too. It's a recent gift from my sister, Missy. She said it would help me remember I'm a wise professor, but I think it's really because she feels guilty for throwing away a pair of my sandals."

"This reminds me of something my mom had. It's very beautiful." Stef stood and walked to the other side of the table to Perse. "May I?"

Perse gave the slightest nod and felt Stef's fingers graze the nape of her neck as she reclasped the chain. She wondered if Stef would linger by tracing the top of her musical note tattoo. But she didn't. As soon as the chain was in place Stef returned to her seat. A restrained flirt, but a flirt nonetheless.

"How was that?" Stef asked. "Too much flirting? Not enough?"

The questions caught her off guard. She wasn't entirely sure how to answer, but based on Stef's personality, Perse decided on pure, undiluted honesty. "Not enough. If I closed my eyes that could have been my mom or sister clasping my necklace for me."

Stef was crestfallen. "I promise to be more assertive next time. I'm really paranoid about overstepping my boundaries because of how this whole date started."

Okay, that was really cute. "Based on what I know about you, it's highly doubtful you'd do something this evening that would make me physically uncomfortable."

"That's very reassuring," Stef said with a smile. After a little pause, she took a deep breath. "Tell me more about your sister?"

"God, where do I start? Missy has given me so much in the past six months. I don't know what I would have done without her."

"I take it you get along with Missy pretty well," Stef asked as she twirled her pasta.

"We do now, but it was pretty rough when we were kids. A three-year age difference can take its toll."

Stef nodded vigorously.

"Once I was in college and she was in grad school, we'd get together for a concert or if there was personal drama because we were only a short train ride away from each other. That was when we really solidified our bond."

"That's really sweet. Are you close with the rest of your family?"

Perse waved her flattened hand. "So-so, but it's not because I dislike them." *Even though my mother has accidentally caused strife.* "I just haven't been around. My travel has really prevented me from developing relationships with them. I don't know if that'll change now that I'm here."

"How do you mean?"

"Well, in addition to the fact that I'm in a position that will hopefully last beyond twelve months, my parents found their retirement home a few hours away from here. Missy's house is in between, so we're going to try and do a monthly Sunday brunch."

"That sounds fun."

"I hope you're right." Perse wanted a better relationship with her parents, but she didn't know where to begin. They felt more like distant relatives than the people who had created and raised her. "How about your family? Based on your reaction earlier, I think you understand little sister syndrome."

Stef bit her upper lip as she formulated an answer. "Well . . . There's no easy way to say this, but, my parents and brother died in a car accident when I was twelve."

Perse dropped her fork with a loud *ting*. "Oh my God! I'm so sorry. I didn't mean to—"

"I know and I get it. Please, don't feel bad you asked. That would make me feel bad and then we'll just go in an awkward cycle," Stef said without a trace of a frown. "It's not something that breaks me. From time to time I will get sad about it, but I'm okay. My aunt and uncle took me in and treated me like I was their own daughter. They never had kids, so I kind of was."

As they finished their meal, Stef spoke more about her departed family. She shared a few of their personality traits and interests, and a few anecdotes. However, Perse noticed Stef hadn't included her aunt Carol in the reminiscing. After witnessing how Stef reacted the first time she discussed her in the park, Perse understood. She was perfectly content to watch Stef speak with animated flair and hear the adoration she had for the people who were once in her life.

Over dessert, they traded stories of what it was like being the youngest child. Perse insisted that compared to Missy she was a perfect angel.

Stef shared that her brother, Will, would dare her to do things when he knew she was scared. Stef enjoyed the dare and proving she was braver than her big brother thought she was.

Yes, Stef appreciated, and probably needed, people in her life to challenge her.

"Coffee or more wine?" their server asked when their dessert plates were clear.

Perse looked to Stef, who emphatically shook her head. "I think we're good, thank you. But, could I get a piece of the chocolate torte to go? Then, I'll take the check."

"Second dessert? I'm impressed, but I'm also concerned about your blood sugar levels."

Perse chuckled softly. She had done that often over the course of their dinner. "It's for Timera. She popped into my office and suggested this place."

Stef's brow rose to her hairline. "Timera's why we're here? You talked to her about our date?"

Had she said too much? Was she stirring up trouble between friends? Her pulse increased to the point where she imagined an owl bouncing on her chest. "No. I didn't say anything to her about it. I told Gillian that we may go out, and in that same conversation she told me Timera likes to keep her personal and professional life separated, and I would be fine as long as I didn't talk about dating you at work."

"Don't worry about Timera. Gillian has my back and can talk her down. You know, for someone who specializes in medieval warfare, she's a great diplomat." Stef brow suddenly furrowed. "Are you okay?"

Perse hadn't realized her breath had started to become irregular. When Stef rose from her seat, Perse held an index finger up, which kept Stef paused and hovering. She appreciated that Stef gave her space and took several breaths to calm herself. "I'm okay. Just a little panic attack." She took a long sip of water and focused on the cold liquid running down her throat.

"I apologize in advance if this question comes off as ignorant or judgmental, but what about that makes you anxious?"

"I'm concerned Timera would be so uncomfortable with us seeing each other Gillian would have to intervene. Maybe we shouldn't do this."

Stef's mouth crinkled, but her eyes softened. "I don't want to add any pressure to your life, so if this is it for us, then . . . I'll learn to deal."

"But . . . ?" She didn't believe Stef would give up so quickly.

"No but. Although you should know that I think Timera suggested this restaurant to you so you'd bring me. If that's the case, then she has absolutely no problem with us dating, and any lingering doubt she has will be erased with the chocolate torte. However, it's also possible that I'm wrong. Maybe she doesn't like the idea of us going on a single date, but then you have to ask yourself how important Timera's opinion of your romantic life is because it's not like what we're doing is morally or professionally wrong."

"Yes, b—"

"I'll add this and then I'm done. Timera doesn't even like Bjorn and Jin together, and those two are adorable! Have you seen their banter?"

"I have." Perse sat back and assessed all that Stef said. She was worrying over a problem that may not exist, and even if it did, it was more of an inconvenience than an actual conflict. As the logic seeped in, the room became cooler and her heart returned to its normal rhythm. "Have you ever not been completely honest and direct?"

"Nope. I came out of the box that way."

Perse smiled and reached for the check.

"No, no, no." Stef took the billfold away. "I got this."

"You're sure?"

Stef signed the check with a quick scribble. "You can pay me back with a post-dinner stroll." The outside air would do her good.

They exited the restaurant and found the dimly lit, pebbled path that led around the vineyard. The humid, but cooler air hummed with insects and the clouds that moved overhead left the moon playing a game of peekaboo.

Stef pointed at the night sky. "Found Cassiopeia."

Perse located the constellation in question. "There she is, alright. That's what happens when you make Poseidon mad." She closed her eyes with embarrassment. "Sorry, nerd moment."

"Um, hello! Which one of us completely made up a possible collaboration based on the plague?"

"That was the first time anyone used that move on me," Perse said with a laugh and glanced to Stef, who moved down the path with a sweet smile. It had been ages since Perse thought about seeing someone beyond a first date, but there was so much more about

Stef she wanted to learn. "Based on the photographs in your living room, I'm guessing you like to hike."

"I love to hike! Do you?"

"I do. Hence, the reason I asked."

Stef slowed their pace as they entered the cabernet franc section. "I know some really nice trails of various difficulties." She reached for Perse's hand and, with the other, ran her thumb lightly over her knuckles. "Interested?"

The light sensation traveled from Perse's fingers and up her arm, causing the slightest goose bumps. Stef had taken the flirting comment to heart. It was good to know she learned quickly. "Interested is a good word for it."

"I could plan a little outing. Whenever it works with your schedule, of course."

"I like the sound of all of that." What wasn't there to like about a no pressure approach to seeing new countryside and a charming woman? "Maybe we could go off the trail for some adventure? Or after dusk?"

"The rangers don't really like that. The paths and rules are there for a reason."

Paths, rules, and levels: Stef definitely liked structure. Perse had never met anyone quite like her.

While driving back, Perse entertained Stef with stories of some of her more accidental and exciting hikes. When she pulled into Stef's driveway, she finished telling the tale of inadvertently taking a pee break beside a well-camouflaged and coiled bushmaster, the largest venomous snake in South America. Stef countered by sharing that one time when she was drunk, she got off at the wrong floor at a hotel and was lost for an hour.

Stef led them to her door. "I had a fantastic time, and please don't take this the wrong way, but I'm inviting you in only so you can get your flowers."

After any other date which had gone that well, Perse would have been inside and pinned against a wall already. But not this time. This time she'd have to wait. Although, they'd basically already made plans for a second date. There'd be more physicality then. "I understand. I had a great time too, and I'm grateful to have my gift returned." She followed Stef to where her bouquet rested and studied the photograph near it. It showed a blond teenage boy dressed in jeans and a polo shirt. On either side of him was a man, almost identical to the boy, and woman of slight build. Even though Perse knew the answer to her question, Stef confirmed it for her.

"Yeah, that's my mom, dad, and Will. I took that picture just before they left for his first college visit weekend. He wanted to be a lawyer. I sometimes I wonder if my folks ever talked about where I might go to school or what I'd end up becoming." She passed the flowers to Perse.

What Stef shared went beyond the typical, superficial first date chatter, and it created an emotional charge Perse had never experienced so soon. Her heart ached for that pre-teen girl behind the camera, and for present day Stef, who would never have an answer to that question. "I'm sure they'd be proud of what you've become."

"What's that?"

"A thoughtful, successful, and stunning woman. I'm sorry if that sounds clichéd, but I hope you know what I mean."

Like in the vineyard, Stef took her hand, but this time she lifted it to her mouth and skimmed a knuckle with her lips before kissing it.

The move was ten times more erotic than being slammed against dry wall in a clumsy attempt to create friction.

Stef looked up from their hands with a familiar heat in her eyes. Just as she thought Stef was about to ask permission to kiss her, Stef brought her in closer and grazed their lips together.

She wanted to seize forward and capture Stef's lips in her own, but she knew it was up to Stef set that pace.

Stef's hand traveled to her neck, her fingers teasing the area where her clasp lay, before she pulled her in closer and deepened their kiss, taking her lower lip into her mouth and teasing the entrance with her tongue.

Perse parted her lips and moaned when Stef eased herself inside. Her body melted into Stef's. The restrictions Stef had placed on the physical level were more than made up for in quality. Still, it was a good thing she had to hold on to a bouquet with her other hand, or it might have traveled places.

When a soft moan escaped her throat again, Stef slowly retreated from their kiss. "I think we should stop. I'm starting to get pretty worked up."

She was worked up? Perse took a breath to redirect the blood that had traveled to her skin's surface. However, it was reassuring to see that Stef was also flushed.

"That *really* exceeded my expectations," Stef said, a bit dazed.

"Mine too."

"But it was good? No, not like that. Of course, it was good. What I mean was, that was the appropriate balance to show you that I'm interested and leave you wanting more?"

Perse didn't know if Stef planned on questioning her this way after every encounter they had. Or even what Stef'd say if she answered no, but at that moment, she didn't care. All she knew was she wanted to have that experience again. "Very good balance. I definitely want more."

"Excellent! Thank you for respecting my boundaries. I know my way of doing things is a bit different."

Perse took the offered lilies again. "Different isn't bad. Different allows us to adapt so we can thrive in our own individual microcosm."

"You talk so pretty."

Perse laughed causing the flowers to shake against her chest. "I have my moments."

"Do I get to hear more of those moments when we hike?"

"I think you will." Perse leaned forward and kissed Stef softly on the lips. "Goodnight."

"A very good night," Stef said with a grin and stayed at the door.

Perse smiled as she walked back to her car. The image of Stef's silhouette waving goodbye in the doorway stayed with her as she drove away. The conversation. The food. That kiss! Perse wouldn't have changed any moment of their date. It was flawless.

And now she was scared.

***

Missy waited all morning at work for Perse to get back to her with her text, *Did you sleep with her? Or did your vibrator make you pass out from exhaustion?* But Perse hadn't had the decency to respond. What was it with people? Her children had been exceptionally needy that morning, the "leader" for the project she was working on kept asking her questions he should have the answer to, and her only sibling ignored her.

She was already thinking she may need to indulge in her last birthday brownie once the kids were in bed. Maybe stream some music from college. That'd be real fun.

Finally, after several minutes of waiting, Perse responded to her text. *Why do you have to be so crass? I did not sleep with her & I will not answer the other question.*

Missy laughed and her cubicle neighbor glared at her. "Sorry, that latest email from corporate was hilarious. I'll try to keep it down." Once her coworker turned away, she got out her phone once more. *I'm crass because you hate it. All kidding aside, did you have a nice date?*

It was lovely. Excellent company and the scallop risotto was to die for.

Missy drummed her fingers on her desk. *Kiss goodnight?*

Yes.

Tongue?

A little.

"Now we're cooking," Missy muttered. *Which was better, the risotto or the kiss?*

Tough one, but the kiss was . . . toe curling.

"Oh my." She looked over her shoulder to see her neighbor's stern look again. "Seriously, corporate is on fire! Are you not getting these emails?"

"No," the plain brunette said slowly and sternly.

Missy shrugged. *Do you think you'll see her again?* It was a simple yes or no question that took longer for Perse to answer than she would have liked. Missy knew that she and their mother could get carried away when Perse vocalized finding someone attractive, but Perse was ready to be in a relationship again. Missy knew she was.

If I do, I promise I'll tell you. Is that fair?

Yes. Has anyone at work said anything?

Only that Gillian's jealous she didn't get chocolate torte. I worried for nothing. Like always.

"Mmm, torte." *Yeah, I want one of those too. Gotta go, I hear the clomping of my PM's cowboy boots getting louder.*

Missy turned her phone upside down and then maximized the presentation on her screen. She turned when she heard the faint knock at her cubicle. "Hi, Chris! Wasn't expecting you. What's up?"

"You know those numbers I asked you to send over to me?"

"Yeah, I sent those over yesterday afternoon."

Chris nodded unsurely. "Okay, but where are they? I didn't see them."

Missy bit her tongue. Screaming at the embodiment of nepotism would only give her temporary relief. She had to think about the end game. "They're in the sheet labeled *Final Statistics.*"

"Oh!" Chris drawled. "I keep forgetting about the tabs."

She heard his heavy steps travel down cubicle row and promised herself a nice chocolate birthday brownie later.

CHAPTER EIGHT

PERSE CAME TO the conclusion that Stef was a treat.

And like a treat, she knew if she indulged herself too much, it wouldn't be healthy. She would be left physically ill and disappointed because Stef couldn't give her what she'd want. But a moderate amount of time with Stef would enrich her soul and add joy to her life.

After taking into account her manageable weekend schedule, her shortened to-do list, and the perfect weather, Perse texted Stef Saturday morning about hiking later in the day. It was simply too gorgeous outside to spend her time apartment hunting indoors.

Perse checked her phone when she was in the middle of cleaning, putting away her groceries, and eating her lunch for a response. There was none. When pangs of disappointment began to set in, she reminded herself that this was a casual arrangement and she had started to obsess like a teenager. Stef had errands to run too and she had friends who were local. Stef interested her, and interesting people did things. They didn't have their phones tethered to themselves 24-7.

When Stef finally responded, Perse practically tossed her carrot stick aside. Stef said that she would love to but asked if Sunday could work since she had planned to spend part of her afternoon with Harry. Perse wished she could be flexible, but her family's first brunch conflicted with that. Luckily, Stef understood and only asked that they hike an easier path since rugby, even touch rugby, created aches and pains that hadn't existed in her twenties. Or thirties.

***

"I don't even want to think about how sore I'll be tomorrow," Stef said as she pushed her legs up the steepest section of their "easy" hike.

Perse shook her head in amusement. "What on earth would possess you to still play rugby?"

"I played in college, and from there in a few local teams, until I moved here. Then, I stopped because I had to focus on the whole new job thing, which I believe you're familiar with," she said with a mischievous smile. "Once I got settled at CBU, I met Gillian and Timera and hit it off. We try to join a league of sorts once or twice a year. When I found out about the touch league, I was so excited—so was Gillian. I feel like I can recapture some of my youth," Stef said with heavier breathes.

"How does Timera feel about it?"

Stef chuckled. "It's fun teaching her, but she still doesn't understand all the rules." She paused at the top of their ascent and looked down at where they had been. "I don't remember that being so steep."

Perse nodded and winced at the accumulation of lactic acid in her legs and glutes. "I've never, ever been athletic. Just your typical uncoordinated bookworm and theater-band geek, which I was teased at length for in school."

"Kids can be such assholes."

The venom with which Stef commented implied more than sympathy. "I take it you had some rough times too."

Stef nodded as they took the trail around a rocky outcrop. "When I was in elementary school, I skipped a grade, so I was very small compared to the other kids. Recess was hell. Then, when I moved to be with my aunt and uncle, the powers that be decided I should skip to high school since I was in a new school anyway."

Perse did the math in her head. "You were twelve when you started high school?"

"Yeah. What's worse is that it was common knowledge why I had moved to the school, but they teased me for being small and smart anyway."

She almost stopped in her tracks to give Stef a hug. Perse imagined being a twelve-year-old girl forced to change schools because her family had died and then being ostracized by her peers.

"Eventually, I made a few friends, but I'll tell you what, it never gets easier."

"What doesn't?"

"Making friends," Stef said and pointed ahead to a patch of pine trees, which looked like a drop off point. "There's the lookout. Would you like to take a break and watch the sunset? Should only be fifteen more minutes or so."

"I'd like that." Not only did her muscles need a break, but emotionally she was overwhelmed. Stef had shared so much intimate detail with her, yet kept restraints on what she would share physically. It was the complete opposite of what Perse had grown accustomed to.

Stef sat on a smooth boulder and patted the area next to her.

Perse joined her and casually stretched her hamstrings. Once she settled, she took in Stef's profile of her viewing the stream and trees below, and the waning, orange light of the horizon. Joyful and tired, she was stunning. Perse wanted the moment to simply pause, so when Stef asked for a selfie of the two of them, she obliged.

Stef directed how she should position herself, but Perse intentionally didn't quite move as Stef directed. The slight tease caused them both to laugh, but eventually Perse settled into the correct pose: cross-legged on a smooth rock, while she leaned back on her hands. It wasn't until the end of the theatrical photo shoot it occurred to Perse she hadn't had a photograph taken on a date since she and Isabella hit the photo booth along a New Jersey boardwalk.

That had been just a short time before the Christmas Eve break-up. The carefree, late summer day of fun had been followed by a sucker punch a few months later. That's why Perse experienced life to its fullest while she kept her guard up. She could enjoy her time with Stef and be prepared to block another gut-wrenching blow.

A hand came into Perse's view, taking her out of her introspection. "Sorry, I zoned out for a little," she said, and then accepted Stef's chivalrous hand.

"Then I should be trying harder to capture your attention."

Once she had both feet on the ground, Stef brushed her lips against Perse's, teasing her, before kissing her more deeply. Perse wanted to linger into the touch, but Stef cut the moment short.

Stef grinned. "You seemed pretty focused that time around. I'd like to stay here and try again to make sure it wasn't a one-time event, but we should head back or we'll be caught in the dark."

Perse could have stayed on the quiet overlook with Stef receiving her attentions for hours more. "Right. We don't want to upset the rangers."

When they traversed down the trail, they came to talk about the few men in their lives. Stef had several mentors from her post-doc and days working as a civilian in the military. But currently, the only consistent figure whom she loved was Harry. A Morgan Freeman look-a-like who was a retired journalist, veteran, and widower.

"So, how did you meet Harry?" Perse asked as she used the rough bark of a tree to brace herself going down the trail.

"Oh! Harry's wife was best friends with my aunt Carol. For the last few years, whenever I would visit her, he was usually there for part of the visit. When she died, having him there helped me grieve. I could keep part of my weekly routine by still going there and we could talk about how we felt."

"That sounds very cathartic."

"It was . . . still is. He's basically the only family I have left." Stef stumbled over a protruding root as she said it, but kept her footing. "How about your family? Tell me more about them, aside from Missy."

Perse didn't talk about her family often, so this posed a unique challenge. The version of her family she kept in her mind's eye was when she lived at home as a child, but that wasn't them now. How could she clearly articulate who her family was? She supposed, they were the same people with the same values, and the only element that had made their relationship more difficult was the distance between them all.

But she didn't know their favorite local hangouts. She couldn't say what the last movie they saw which they'd really liked was. Without knowing the details, Perse decided to keep her answer basic and start at the beginning. "Well, my dad immigrated to the US from Brazil when he was a boy and went into the Navy. My mom grew up pretty well off in New York City, which is where she stayed until she joined a touring company. That's how my parents met. My mom came to my dad's port."

"Aw. That's really cute."

Perse smiled. "Yeah, they have their moments. Overall, they're pretty good parents. To this day, I have to remind myself that even if it doesn't seem like it immediately, their intentions are good."

"Not to get too personal, but how'd they take the whole pansexuality thing?"

Perse chuckled. "I don't think they know what that terms means, but they don't have any issues with my attractions."

"Well, that's good to hear." They turned the corner into the parking lot. Stef looked at her watch and shot her fists in the air. "Three thousand calories burned for the day! I can sit down!"

The pure joy with which Stef announced her triumph caused Perse to burst into laughter. "We could have taken a longer break at the top."

Stef casually pointed to the sky. "But darkness."

"Right. I forgot about that." They walked back to Stef's car, but she paused at the passenger door. "Do your legs work well enough to push the pedals?"

"I'm good, but you can help by finding us music to listen to."

While they listened to the radio on the drive back to her apartment, Perse absently moved her fingers to the music. Stef called her out on her 'air keyboard' and asked if she could play a song for her. For Perse, performing for a single person was incredibly intimate, but again, she found herself saying yes.

For the first time since Perse had moved, she went to set up her keyboard.

"Do you need some help? I can't really feel my legs, but I figured I should offer."

Perse smiled as she kneeled on the floor to slide her keyboard out from under the couch. "Thank you, but it won't take me long. You can rest those gummy legs of yours by sitting on the couch if you'd like." She put her folding stand against the wall and began to lock the various pieces into place.

"This is much more elaborate than I thought it'd be. Is there also a smoke machine?"

Perse chuckled as she locked the frame in place. "No smoke for this performance. Just little ol' me."

"Still seems like one hell of a bargain."

Perse placed the keyboard on top of the stand. "Let's see if you still have that opinion after you hear me," she said as she pulled over a dining chair to sit. "But I need to do a few exercises first to warm up my fingers."

"Can't go in with cold fingers."

Based on Stef's serious expression, Perse doubted she caught her own double entendre. "I think it's safe to say warm fingers are always better." She started to play a simple, but favorite song: *Don't Stop Believin'*.

"Even your practice sounds really good," Stef said.

Perse grinned from the compliment. "Please remember that if I miss a note."

Soon, she found herself lost in the music and with a different kind of peace than she'd felt earlier at the summit of their hike. Her mind left while her muscle memory took over and she played her favorite classic rock tunes. She was in her own world where she was one with the notes.

What reminded Perse that she wasn't alone were two hands that came to rest on the tops of her shoulders and gradually slid down her arms during her rendition of *Tiny Dancer*.

"You know," Perse said as goose bumps rose and she turned to see Stef standing over her. "That's pretty distracting." *And also, very arousing.*

Stef kneeled so she was at eye level. "Maybe I wanted it to be."

Perse didn't know who initiated the kiss. But she did know that this time it was different. It wasn't tentative like earlier. Now, they were both comfortable. Very, very comfortable.

Especially when Stef took her hands, led her to the couch, and, to Perse's surprise, pulled her on top.

Her body molded to Stef's perfectly.

It wasn't as though Perse had gone without sex since she'd arrived back in the states, but this was the first time she had felt her skin flush and wetness build from touches that were fairly innocent. A tongue grazing her lip, delicate fingers teasing her abdomen. Stef may not have the boldest hands, but her touches were provocative. They encouraged Perse to explore.

When she dipped her head to Stef's neck and heard a sharp intake of breath, she felt the bottom of her tank top rise and her skin cool. Perse read that signal loud and clear. She reached down and stripped off her own shirt.

Stef kept her hands on Perse's ribcage and stared. But not at her eyes. Or the tattoo that peaked out from her pants.

Perse looked down. There was a generous amount of cleavage pouring out from her bra. "See something you like?"

"I have to go now," Stef said in a nervous voice and crawled out from underneath her.

Perse furrowed her brow and panted while on her knees. That was not the typical reaction. "Did I do something?"

"You took off your shirt!" Stef pointed at the garment wildly. "And it's still off!"

More than a little confused, Perse put her tank top back on. "I thought you wanted it off. You were tugging at it. That's the universal sign for 'take it off.'"

Now, Stef's brow crinkled and mouth skewed in thought until she had a moment of clarity and pointed at her watch. "My fitness tracker got snagged on a thread. I was trying to get my hand out because I had gone too far. This is only our second date. Clothing off is *well* beyond the second date."

Perse sighed. She thought she understood Stef's system, but clearly there was a disconnect. "Okay, for one, I'm sorry I misinterpreted your signal. I genuinely thought you wanted to get more physical."

Stef's tense posture relaxed. "Apology accepted."

"I'm glad. Number two, your system, while clear to you, is not clear to me. I was under the impression that we could fool around as much as possible just as long as we didn't take it to the point of climax."

"Oh," Stef said, a bit embarrassed. "Yeah, that's not what I meant."

Perse hoped for more of an explanation, but Stef stood, patiently waiting for her. "This is where you have to tell me what you mean, because I don't get it."

"Is it clear enough if I say follow my lead?"

"Meaning, if you do it, then so can I? Yes. I understand that."

"Excellent!"

"But we also have to consider that accidents happen, like when a watch gets caught on a thread, and if that happens, we'll have to talk about it instead of assuming the other overstepped intentionally. Okay?"

Stef sucked her bottom lip. "Okay, that's fair."

Okay, now they were progressing. Perse turned her sexual energy into cognition. She stood from the couch and paced with her arms folded. She wanted to head off any possible trouble which could come her way again. "How about sexy comments?"

"Like double entendres?"

"Sure, but also playful teasing? Words can be very powerful sexual tools."

Stef guffawed. "I know that. I have an entire bookcase shelf of lesbian erotica."

"An entire shelf?" Perse was just as surprised as she was impressed.

Stef shrugged. "It's not like I read it every day, but sometimes I get in the mood and that mood might be elevator shenanigans or dystopian survivalists or—"

"I get the idea. You like variety."

Stef smiled brightly at her conclusion, but still hadn't answered her question.

"So, how do you feel about word play?"

Stef bit her lower lip and began to mimic Perse's pacing of the room. They circled each other like competitors even though they were on the same team.

"I got it," Stef announced proudly. "At this point, word play can point out observable physical features with the intent of arousing the other person."

"Give me an example."

Stef lowered her eyes and gestured to Perse. "Your nipples are very hard right now."

Perse looked at her chest and saw two points straining against the fabric of her tank top. "So they are. And I could say that your ass looks amazing in those pants. Well, any pants, really."

Stef grinned. "That is very acceptable."

Perse stopped in front of Stef. Every part of this woman fascinated her. She was like no one she had ever met in her life. Frustrating at times, but that was the process when learning how to successfully interact with a new culture.

Stef gently touched a spot at Perse's temple, a mirror of their first date. "It's really cool watching your brain at work."

"Why? Do I look confused?"

"The opposite. You look confident, like you have a puzzle in front of you and you just know you're going to solve it. Which I happen to find endearing." Stef grinned and reached for Perse's hand. "And just so you know, I find you very sexy." She took a deep breath. "Especially that tattoo at your hip."

"I have other tattoos, you know," she said, but then winced. "Was that too much?"

Stef bit her lower lip. "I'll allow it since it aligns with my hypothesis. From what I've observed, most people who get a tattoo have more than one." She cocked her head toward the door. "I should probably head out."

"That's probably best, but I had a great time tonight and appreciate our discussion," Perse said as she walked Stef to her door. "Have fun with Harry tomorrow. What are you two doing?"

"Mini golf or bowling. It's weather dependent."

"Regardless of what you choose, I'm sure it'll be quite spirited."

"No doubt about it. And have fun at your family brunch." Stef rose on her tiptoes to give Perse one final kiss goodbye. The quick peck had no time to evolve into something deeper. "Anything more than that and I'll be in trouble."

Perse simply smiled and opened the door. She could tell she was in trouble already.

***

"I'm telling you, the current project manager might be the dumbest fucking person I've ever met in my life." Missy gave a bowl of batter to Perse on her way to the refrigerator.

"Don't you think you're being a bit harsh?" she asked as she poured thick batter into the hot waffle iron.

Missy pulled out a pitcher of already cracked eggs. "He seriously asked me if I had evidence that water was getting in. There was rust everywhere! Does that sound like I'm being harsh?"

"Okay. That's not so bright," Perse said while her phone vibrated on the counter. When Missy turned her back to make the scrambled eggs, she read the text from Stef, laughed quietly, then typed her response. When Perse finished her message, she continued to stare at the screen. When she looked up, Missy glared at her intently.

"Spill it!"

"Spill what?"

Missy walked toward her, armed with a spatula. "Spill whatever has you grinning like the village idiot."

"It's really nothing." Perse lifted the waffle iron's lid and checked for crispness. "Ow!" she cried in pain and rubbed the spot on her ass where Missy swatted her.

"Spill it! Or the other cheek gets it." Missy slapped the spatula against her open palm rhythmically. When Perse continued her silence, Missy drew the utensil back to strike again.

"Fine! It was a text and picture from Stef. Happy?"

Missy lowered her weapon. "Partially. Let's see the pic."

Perse reluctantly retrieved her phone and showed her the selfie Stef had taken during their hike. "It's no big deal. It's just—"

"That's the most adorable picture I've ever seen. Look at you! You're all shy and she's . . . she's cute! Older than I expected, but cute. Why would you hide this from me, you big jerk?"

Perse returned to her waffle duty. She needed any task to take her mind off the situation she couldn't articulate well. "I don't know. It's like I'm trying to focus on work—which has been great—and then Stef walks into the picture and . . . she's like no one I've ever met. She's fascinating and genuinely understands me." Perse smiled brightly as she remembered a random fact from their hike. "She has a smallpox scar that's shaped like a heart. She had to get vaccinated against it when she was called in to do a biodefense thingy."

Missy staggered like a toxic nerve agent had been released. "You just used the word thingy."

"So?"

"So, Dr. Thesaurus, I have never seen you like this. Not even with dickhead or bitchface. You really, really like this woman."

Perse wanted to deny the obvious, but she couldn't. "I'll admit to you, and *only* to you, that I haven't connected with someone like this in a long time. It's . . . nice. Also, you have to do that part where you actually scramble the eggs."

"Mommy!" Alec and Dandy came flying into the kitchen.

Missy used her spatula to turn and break up the massive yellow pool in the skillet. "What is it, Alec?"

"Grammy and Poppop are in the driveway. I came in to tell you just like you told me to." The small boy ran back out of the kitchen to greet his grandparents. However, Dandy stayed to beg for bits of veggies and shredded cheese.

Perse put her hands together in prayer. "Please don't say anything about Stef. It's just a casual thing and you know how Mom gets."

Missy shook her head and gave her loyal beagle a piece of bell pepper. "I won't say anything, but you need to know right now that this thing you and Stef have isn't casual. For her, at least."

"Of course it is."

Missy shook her head. "No, no, no. Stef's all about these levels, right?"

Perse nodded. "It's eccentric, but I respect that she has come up with her own method for dating."

"How can she be so smart and so stupid?" Missy asked Dandy and then looked at Perse. "Do me a favor, take a step back and look at the whole picture. Why is Stef doing this whole level thing?"

"Because she never wants to get divorced again." Perse caught Missy's amused, yet serious look. "She wants to get married?"

"Bingo! Stef is thinking *way* beyond dating. She's thinking long-term." Missy went to the sink and rinsed Dandy's slobber from her fingers. "That is the complete opposite of casual."

Perse hoped that was not the case. But then again, her sister's opinion was just that. Her opinion. "You don't know that for sure. She might like to date here and there for fun without the purpose of advancing to the next level. The dating level, which I'm currently in, could technically last forever."

"She doesn't want that, and you know it. Stef's not looking for a one-night stand or a date to the summer university fundraiser. She is looking for someone who wants a commitment, and if you can't give that to her, you should step away now before you hurt her. I know you don't want to do that."

Perse considered Missy's words and leaned heavily against the counter. Missy could be right. She had detached herself from relationships for so long, she hadn't admitted to herself that she could be on the verge of entering one—if this wasn't casual for Stef.

The kitchen's walls started closing in.

"You'll be okay," Missy said calmly and dried her hands on the tea towel. "I know it's been a long time since you've put yourself out there like this, so you're probably scared, but the good news is that it sounds like you're enjoying spending time with her, and you get to move slowly."

"I do like her. I just . . . When Anthony left me, it hurt more than my heart. It broke me."

"I know," Missy said with sympathy in her eyes. "I was there and remember it well. Hell, I still have the bridesmaid dress in the closet."

"Why would you keep that?"

"Because I look fucking hot in it, *and* when I see that nondescript dry cleaner bag hanging there, it reminds me of what you've been through and I shouldn't be such a hard ass when your life choices piss me off. I really do understand that you're scared, but sometimes we have to get over that hurdle to see how much good can be on the other side."

Missy diagnosed her fear correctly. She never wanted to go to that lonely, empty place ever again. "This Stef thing has me feeling so weird. Just wanting to see someone again . . . This is so new for me."

"New can be a good thing," Missy said and rubbed Perse's arm. "Although, I'm still curious what'll happen once you realize she won't sleep with you anytime soon. That'll be hilarious from my perspective," she said over Dandy's frantic barking and her children's excited voices. "Now, go say hi to Mom and Dad while I finish in here. They miss you."

"Just so you know, I can control myself," Perse said in a harsh whisper as she backpedaled into the living room and had four arms wrapped around her before she had the chance to say hello.

After everyone caught up with the basic small talk about the drive and the brunch menu, Missy insisted everyone help set the table before they ate or they weren't going to.

Once they all had their meals in front of them, Perse observed the subtle changes in her family. Her father exuded a calm she hadn't recalled. He was growing out his crew cut and allowed his stiff posture to relax ever so slightly. She supposed his retirement had finally sunk in. Her mother still maintained the same sunny aura, but she became tired easily and her arthritis prevented her from playing piano as often as she liked.

Since she'd moved out, Missy's family hadn't changed much. When she'd first moved in with them, it had shocked her to learn that Gary's thick, blond hair had started thinning in the back, Alec spoke in complete sentences, and Liz had grown to almost adult-size. Missy had even changed, which she'd thought impossible. While she was still supermom, she had taken a step back and vowed that she would take more time for herself.

Perse wondered what changes her family saw in her.

"I'm so glad you could be here, Perse. Paulo and I have missed all of us getting together outside of the holidays."

Her father nodded his agreement at the head of the table. "Do you like CBU?"

Perse had known her time in the unofficial sharing circle would come once the talk of soccer games, upcoming summer vacations, and fishing events finished. "I love it there. It's a special place with so many different opportunities that I didn't know existed."

"That's wonderful," Olivia said. "You look happy."

"Almost glowing," Paulo said. "You're not pregnant, are you?"

"If you are, you're not showing yet," Gary commented wryly, who in return received a loving slap from Missy and a cackle of her laughter.

"Are you pregnant, Aunt Perse?" Liz asked intrigued.

Alec gasped. "How many babies will be in your litter? I hope four."

"I don't think she has to worry about that right now. That comes later in the levels," Missy happily explained.

"I'm not pregnant, kids," Perse said while she glowered at her sister.

The kids' shoulders slumped and they returned to tossing food to Dandy.

Paulo cleared his throat, and it stopped Perse from throwing eye daggers at her sister. "The people there are treating you well?"

"Very well. Every day I seem to need help with something, but the whole department is willing and able to get me settled in."

"So," Olivia drawled, "tell us a little more about these wonderful people you've met."

Perse summarized her interactions within the department and what each faculty member taught. The information was more for her father's benefit than anyone else's. He was particularly impressed that her boss was *the* Christopher Jackson, since he recently finished the historian's latest book.

Paulo smiled proudly. "I still can't believe you work with him."

"Neither can I, really. If I can be half as successful as him, I'll be happy. Timera Vasquez is really on her way up too because of her web series. CBU is definitely not lacking accomplished faculty."

"Have you been able to meet anybody else?" Olivia asked. "You know, more socially?"

Perse peered up from her glass and involuntarily tensed. She knew that tone and what her mother was fishing for. She hoped she hadn't given anything away, but the answer could be navigated easily without her mother growing suspicious. "Actually, yes.

Someone in the biology department, a mutual friend of Gillian and Timera's."

"That's nice," Olivia said from behind her coffee cup. "Hopefully, you'll be able to get some breaks from all of your hard work and have some fun."

"I'm sure she'll find a way to have social fun with this person from the biology department," Missy commented.

Perse sent her another death glare.

Olivia quietly chuckled and smoothed the napkin on her lap. "Thank you for that lovely meal, Missy. Why don't you all enjoy some fresh air while Paulo and I do the dishes?"

"Thanks," Gary said and stood. "Let's finish those swings, Alec."

"Yes! Come on, Dandy," Alec said and ran outside.

Missy gulped the last of her bloody Mary and looked at Liz. "You don't want to help? Your dad said you're a natural at figuring out the diagram."

"I would, but Aunt Perse promised me a piano lesson."

"That's right, I did. But after that I have to leave. I didn't do the apartment hunting I promised myself I would do yesterday."

Olivia placed a hand on Perse's shoulder. "I understand, but I wish you could stay longer. I feel like we're getting to know you all over again." She tucked Perse's hair behind her ear. "You've changed so much."

***

Missy sat with her mother and Dandy on the deck and watched her father and husband take turns pushing the kids on the completed swings. Her family was in a happy place. Especially her mother. She had been especially positive and energetic once Perse had left.

"Your sister seems happy."

"Yeah, she's in a really good place." But Missy wasn't. She wanted to flee from the questions she knew were coming.

After a long pause, her mother said, "Perse met someone in the biology department."

Missy turned to her mother who smiled innocently in return. "Uh huh. That's what she said."

Olivia bumped Missy's shoulder playfully. "I know you know more than that. Who is he?"

Missy rolled her eyes.

"Oh, it's a she!"

Missy sighed loudly. "I really don't want to talk about it. It's not my place."

"I just . . . outside of Perse's academic accomplishments, I feel like I hardly know her."

"Most of that's because she's a walking resume, not because she doesn't want to tell you. However, she is afraid if she tells you too much, you'll blow it out of proportion and make things awkward."

"That's ludicrous."

Missy staggered into her seat for dramatic effect. "She brought Isabella to Christmas Eve dinner and you said you were starting a wedding fund because of it."

"I was joking and had no idea that would cause such . . . turmoil. Or a panic attack! Thank God Gary kept the paper bag the cookies came in. He's excellent in a crisis."

Missy sent a sideways glance at her mother. "You and I both know that she's *really* sensitive about jokes like that. And she has good reason given that Isabella broke up with her the day after your 'joke.' What made matters even worse was that Anthony was her rebound." She gave her mother the chance to let that sink in. When a guilty frown appeared, Missy continued. "When it comes to Perse, just *please* let her tell you when she's ready. If she's not, she'll run away. That's what she does." Or at least, that's what Perse had done in the past.

Olivia wrapped her arm around Missy's shoulder and kissed her temple. "I just want both of my girls to be happy."

"We are, Mom, but you have to remember that we have our own paths—levels, even—to happiness."

CHAPTER NINE

PERSE'S MIND WAS anything but relaxed as she laid on her back during corpse pose. Her mother's words had resonated with her for days. She hadn't changed that much, had she? It was true that her new job excited her and offered stability, but she still liked the same things, had the same philosophies, and, unfortunately, the same anxieties.

Anxieties.

That brought her to Stef. She thoroughly enjoyed her company, but she didn't want a serious relationship. She couldn't have anything serious right now. But Stef understood her situation and hadn't pushed after their second date for a third. In fact, the most Stef had done was send a text the day after their hike to ask if Perse's legs ached as much as hers. And also to tell her that Harry beat her at mini-golf.

That was completely casual.

Dammit Missy! She'd put those paranoid relationship thoughts in her head and now they wouldn't leave. *Why did she have to do that?*

The soothing voice of the yoga teacher entered into Perse's consciousness. Perse listened to the instruction and slowly rolled onto her side while she kept her eyes closed. After the prompt, she gradually brought herself to a seated, cross-legged position along with the rest of the class. After an *om* resonated throughout the room, everyone gave a short bow, whispered *namaste*, and quietly began rolling their mats.

"I think I fell asleep at the end there," Thom said and readjusted the bun in his hair. "Sorry if I snored."

"I thought you were just doing intense breath work."

Thom laughed and handed Perse her mat bag. "Do you have to run out immediately again? My schedule's free if you'd like to get a drink."

Stef never said anything about not seeing other people early in her levels. The first level was very casual. And nothing said casual dating more than dating multiple people. "I think I'd like that."

***

"You've been all over the world," Thom said with wonder.

"Most of it, but believe it or not I've never been to Australia." Perse sipped her iced tea and tried to shake off the feeling that something felt wrong, even though clearly everything was fine.

"Australia's such a great country. I think Auckland was my favorite place to visit when I was there."

Perse furrowed her brow. "Auckland, as in New Zealand?" Thom nodded vigorously while he sipped from his reusable straw. "New Zealand isn't Australia."

"Really?" Thom shrugged. "I was never that great with geography."

While Perse found his answer problematic, she let the mistake slide. She wasn't great with math, Thom wasn't great with basic geography. "What do you excel in?"

He bit his lower lip as he thought about her question and then launched into a summary of his accomplishments in hydroponics, pottery, and vegan baking. He was cute, but a walking cliché: not that bright and dreadfully boring.

". . . and then I discovered walnut butter. That was a real game chan—"

"Thom, I'm sorry, but I just remembered I'm supposed to be meeting a colleague for dinner."

"Oh," he said, dejected. "But weren't you just at work before you came to class?"

"Yes, but this is interdisciplinary work, and different departments have different schedules."

He looked more confused than when she corrected his geography of the Pacific.

"It's about the plague."

He went on alert. "Is there an outbreak?"

"Maybe. That's why we need to have a meeting." Perse placed some cash on the table and grabbed her yoga bag. "I'll see you in class next week."

Part of her felt bad for lying to get out of what had become one of the worst coffee dates of her life, but she mostly wanted the guilt she felt for comparing him to Stef the entire time to vanish. Stef was the complete opposite of Thom. A literal genius who played rugby, made her laugh, and understood basic global geopolitics.

Once in her car, Perse texted Stef: *Are you free to do something?* She dialed up a soothing playlist for her ride home while she waited for a response. This was a new experience for her. She was the one actively pursuing someone. Was she the one who wanted a relationship? Before she could dive into that question, her phone beeped.

I wish you'd texted 15 min ago. I just started painting.

"That's right," Perse groaned to herself. Stef had mentioned that her spare room renovations had started. Regardless, it was a reason to see Stef. *Want some help?*

***

Perse felt uneasy walking into someone else's home, but Stef had given her permission. "Hello," Perse called out in the empty living room.

"Back here," Stef said loud enough for her voice to carry down the hall. "I put some paint clothes in the bathroom for you."

Perse walked to where Stef was and stopped when she reached the doorway.

Stef was mid-way through rolling gray-lavender paint across the rear wall.

"Do I get a kiss before you put me to work?"

"Of course you do." Stef placed her roller in the tray and came closer but held her hands up. "I don't want to get paint on your yoga clothes."

Perse leaned down and closed the distance between them. "I really like the color you chose," she mumbled against Stef's lips before they both went for more. She felt Stef smile and knew she made the right choice by coming over.

"I'm glad you like it, because you'll probably end up wearing some of it."

She noticed Stef's worn running shorts and CBU t-shirt already had paint splotches on them. "I'll get changed. Then I want to hear all about what you've been up to."

Perse went into the bathroom and looked at the clothes as she began to undress. Apparently, the paint uniform was running shorts and CBU STEM t-shirts, all of the Stef-sized variety. She put them on and looked at her reflection. The t-shirt was painted on like a bright-red second skin and the shorts were just long enough to cover her butt cheeks. Had Stef done that on purpose? Or was it an innocent mistake? Given Stef's reaction when she'd taken off her shirt, it was best to check.

Perse cracked open the bathroom door. "Hey, Stef? These clothes are on the small side and don't cover much."

"I'm sorry about that. Do you feel uncomfortable?"

"No. I just didn't want to shock you."

"I'm sure you're fine. Remember, I go to the university gym, and some of those outfits do not cover very much."

"Okay then." Perse left the bathroom and returned to the spare room. "Where should I start?"

Stef turned toward her, and then Perse watched her mouth go slack as paint dribbled from the roller.

"You're dripping—your paint roller is dripping."

Stef followed Perse's eyes to the roller. "Dammit!" She placed the roller back over the tray and cleaned the mess with a rag. Her mouth curved deviously. "You look very appropriate for painting."

"I think I look appropriate to go to a nerdy dance club."

"Do they have those? I would totally go to that!"

Perse grinned. She needed the levity after the stresses the past few days had thrown at her and the catastrophe with Thom. She looked around the half-painted room. "What can I do to help?"

"Can you paint the top edge of where I just finished rolling? Step stool is there."

She picked up the smaller paint tin and stepped up beside Stef. The extra helped, but she still needed to stretch, causing her shorts and shirt to ride higher. She could feel cool air on her exposed lower back and abdomen. She glanced down at Stef who gawked at her. "Yes?"

"I'm a stupid, stupid person."

"Just think: I haven't even done the bottom edge yet." Perse heard a small sound of anguish below her, which caused her to break out into full-fledged laughter. The first real laugh she had since the weekend. "So, tell me, how have you kept busy this week?"

"Oh, boy. Where to start?" Stef asked rhetorically and reloaded her roller with paint.

Stef described her workout and rugby antics with Gillian and Timera. Apparently, the rain showers from earlier in the week had created poor footing conditions, which explained Timera's slight limp on Monday. But, as a bonus, the match was closer to Harry's senior apartment complex, so he had driven to watch the match.

"That's really sweet," Perse said as she focused on avoiding the blue painter's tape as much as possible. Based on Missy's soccer mom history, Perse had a clear picture of what this scene looked like. "Did Harry have a lawn chair on the side of field, ready to hand you orange slices too?"

Stef laughed. "No, he didn't. Like most uncle figures he paced the sideline to follow the action."

Perse was not only struck by how Stef referred to Harry, but also by her loving tone. "And let me guess, with the pacing came yelling at the ref for a blown call?"

"Pretty much. Although, in rugby the field is a pitch and a ref is a sir."

Perse skewed her brow. "What if the sir isn't a man?"

"I don't think it matters. You know, if you want to learn or watch a match, you're more than welcome to come to the field . . . where it might be muddy, ninety degrees, and there's no shade. Never mind, that sounds terrible."

Perse stopped painting so her laughter didn't mess up her clean lines.

"There's also a British pub downtown that shows rugby matches," Stef said, "so if you ever wanted to have a pint and learn, that's an option. Of course, you can also have a pint and ogle the thigh muscles. That's what Timera does."

Curious, Perse turned to view Stef's legs. As she rocked back and forth with the paint roller, the shadows from the definition in her thighs, hamstrings, and calves twitched. "Or I could ogle the muscles right here."

Stef's smiling face whipped around. "Oh, someone's saucy."

"What?" Perse said innocently. "It's observational, and per your rules, that's allowed."

"I'm glad to learn you've grasped the concept well."

Stef's praise gave her comfort, but there was a part of her that wanted to learn just how strong Stef's legs were. Could Stef carry her to bed while her legs were wrapped around her? Or could she keep one leg hooked around Stef's waist while Stef maintained their balance and fucked her against a wall?

Blood rushed to her sex at the idea. She had to get away from those thoughts fast. "Tell me about work. Any successes this week?"

Stef explained, in layman's terms, the research she hoped to present in a few weeks, but Wayne had provided a few obstacles.

Perse listened to Stef rant about him. She kept her opinion to herself, but she didn't believe that moving a box to a shelf Stef couldn't reach was necessarily intentional. Or that using the same equipment she wanted to use was a lack of professional courtesy. It seemed that Stef just really hated Wayne.

"It seriously makes me wonder how he can have a PhD. Bradyn even suggested he found his degree in a cereal box along with a decoder ring."

Perse halted her painting. She couldn't recall ever hearing that name before. "Who's Bradyn?"

"She's my most promising graduate student. There was a mild issue with lab safety last year, but now she does this twisty thing with her dreads to keep her hair back in the lab. It's really cool. Anyway, she's doing some really interesting antibiotic research, mostly amoxicillin."

Perse instantly shuddered.

"Are you allergic?"

Perse laughed whilst being mindful not to paint the molding. "That's putting it mildly. When I was younger, I took it and then got this whole-body rash. Mom only let me stay home from school a day, so when I went back it was still visible. That did not help my piano geek, library-staying, nerd vibe I already had going on. Which, come to think of it, I still have."

"Yes, you most certainly do."

Perse feigned shock. "That was cruel."

Stef stopped painting and directed all of her attention to Perse. "I mean this with every fiber of my being. That vibe of yours is hot, and I'm a scientist, so you know I can only state facts I have ample evidence to support. I can't say things like that all willy-nilly."

Perse appraised what Stef said. It was a sweet compliment that was uniquely Stef. "Thank you. And I like your vibe of using 'evidence' and 'willy-nilly' in the same statement."

"I have a way with words." Stef took a look around the room. "Wow. We're practically done."

"We make quite the pair." As soon as the words left her mouth, the air rushed out and the panic set in. "Like a team. I didn't mean it like . . . you and me and . . . Oh, God."

"It's okay," Stef said in a slightly amused voice. "I get it. We work well together. Plus, I primed the walls yesterday. Laying a good foundation is very important," she said in a sage tone.

Perse was grateful for the save and finished the edging as Stef put on the final touches with the roller.

They removed the rest of the painter's tape, shared the bathtub's faucet to clean the roller and brush, and then soaped their hands to wash away any stray paint.

"You missed a spot." Perse pointed at a large smudge on the inside of Stef's bicep. "How did you get paint there?"

Stef tilted her head to get a better angle. "I don't know, maybe it dripped down?"

"That's quite a drip." Perse was tickled by how Stef could have that much paint on her and fail to notice.

"You're one to talk."

"Where do I have paint?" Perse playfully demanded to know.

Stef retrieved a washcloth from the room's linen closet and ran warm water over it. "You have some right here." She removed the paint from Perse's cheekbone with a delicate scrub. When Stef had finished, she kissed the spot. "You may also have a little bit on your leg."

Perse saw a gray blotch on her outer thigh, right at the shorts line. "Could I please get some assistance, keeper of the washcloth?"

"I wouldn't mind helping a lady in distress." Stef kneeled down, cleaned the spot, and pressed her lips the newly washed area. When she removed her lips from Perse's damp skin, their eyes locked.

Something inside of Perse fluttered as she watched Stef do such a simple gesture with so much care. It was intimate.

She felt a mild panic rise, but concentrated on the sensation of her heels rooted to the ground and was able to stop it from snowballing. Like Missy said, a relationship was new and scary, but over that hump could be a thousand more moments like the one she'd just experienced. A loving touch after an afternoon of laughter. Perse wanted more of that.

She was willing to take the chance with Stef.

Stef cleared her throat as she stood. "Before you came here, I ordered a pizza for delivery around seven. Do you want to stay for dinner? Maybe sit outside on my new glider and have a drink while we wait?"

At least it would be more enjoyable than the drink she'd had a few hours before. "That sounds great."

As Stef mixed margaritas, Perse took her spot on the glider. The sway provided a gentle breeze and the chirps of a few frogs that found a home in Stef's water feature added even more to the summer ambience. It was nice, but Perse felt troubled. She needed to be honest with Stef, but part of her feared she would fly off the handle or break into melodramatic sobs. Perse realized both reactions were extreme, but her brain created the scenarios anyway.

Sometimes she hated her creativity.

"I need to tell you something," she said as Stef came out with an elaborate tray of a pitcher, two glasses, quartered limes, and a plate of salt.

"Shit, I'm sorry. I just assumed on the rocks would be okay. I can make yours frozen if you want."

"No, it's not that." Stef grinned happily and gestured to the salt, to which Perse nodded. "I want to tell you something and it leads to a question."

"Okay. Shoot," Stef said as she edged a glass with a slice of lime. Then, she inverted the glass into the salt.

"After yoga, a guy in my class asked me if I wanted to get a drink, and I went."

"Oh." Stef paused the motion of the lifted pitcher, but then continued to pour. "Did you have fun?"

Perse stifled a laugh. "No, it was terrible. It's actually why I wanted to come over here."

Stef handed her a margarita. "It's not that I'm not happy you feel comfortable enough to tell me this, but . . . why are you telling me this?"

It was a great question. One that Perse wished she had a good answer to. She took a sip and the taste pleasantly surprised her. Stef did not use mixes. "That's delicious."

"I have many hidden talents and only drink top-shelf. But you were starting to explain how you basically went on a terrible pseudo-date with a yoga-guy before you came here," Stef said and took a seat beside her.

"Right. Well, I think I went because I wanted to prove to myself that what we are doing is casual, but it felt wrong, and not just because he was dumb and boring."

Stef snorted into her margarita. "What a catch. Why did it feel wrong?"

Perse sighed with relief. Of course, Stef would be mature about her admission. "To be honest, I kept comparing him to you. Eventually, I reached a point where I realized it was really stupid to spend any more time with him when I could have been here with you, so here I am now, trying not to be stupid, yet acknowledging that I probably sound like a complete ass," Perse said in one breath. "I'm sorry. I think my anxiety is getting a little worked up."

Stef leaned over and kissed her softly on the cheek. "I don't think you sound like an ass. I think you went out for a drink with someone you thought was more interesting than they were, felt guilty about it, and then wanted to spend time with someone who is more your speed."

It was eerie how quickly Stef summarized her perspective, and the insight helped Perse's breathing returned to normal. "Thank you for understanding."

"You're welcome. While the story started off rocky, it ended in flattery for me. I'm more interesting, smarter, and I'm assuming more attractive . . ."

"Yes. Much more attractive, and the man bun was a bit of a turn off."

Stef laughed and rubbed Perse's bare knee. "Is there anything else you'd like to get off your chest?"

"Actually, yes. I need this dating level we're on more well defined."

Stef sipped her drink with her brow pinched. "How so?"

"Well, dating itself has many different levels, right? For instance, at one point in the relationship process, it ceases to become a 'date' and instead is assumed time together."

Stef shook her head.

"You don't agree?"

"What? No! I completely agree. I'm kicking myself for not creating sublevels." She took another drink. "I should make an outline. That'll capture the hierarchy of events more efficiently."

Stef's brain and eccentricity shined. "I'm glad you agree, but why I brought it up—why it's relevant—is because I don't know when exclusivity becomes a factor."

"Hmm. That's an excellent question. Do you need an answer right now?"

"No. I'd rather receive a thoughtful answer than a quick one."

Stef nodded and grinned. "This discussion appears to have relaxed you. Your shoulders aren't in your ears anymore. Do you feel better?"

"I do. When it comes to people and relationships—especially new ones—my anxiety takes on a mind of its own."

Stef sipped her drink with an inquisitive look. "You've mentioned that a few times now. I was wondering how you coped with it."

"Yoga helps with the day-to-day because it teaches me about breath control and relaxation, but when I know something is coming and will really get to me, I use CBD edibles."

"Cannabidiol? Really?" Stef sounded shocked. "Why not Valium?"

"Honestly, I think that my gummies are safer and they give me less side effects. Plus, now that the laws have changed, I don't have to bother getting a prescription."

"But why gummies?"

"Practicality sake. You can eat them anywhere." Perse giggled slightly. "The day we ran into each other at the cultural center I had taken one."

"You didn't seem . . . under the influence."

Stef's comment struck Perse as odd. Not because she had never been told that before, but because the remark came from Stef. "That's because I wasn't. There's no THC in them. Plus, it's not about getting high, it's about taking the edge off so I feel my brand of normal." Based on Stef's shifting facial expressions, she could tell Stef had several questions. "If you want to know something, you can ask."

"Well, do I make you feel normal? I mean, do you get anxious when you're with me?" Stef asked tentatively.

Perse had only seen Stef's vulnerable side once before when she spoke of her family. The minor quake in her voice and hopeful eyes had touched Perse. "Spending time with you is easy. I get the impression you're always being yourself and reacting honestly."

"Yeah," Stef said quietly and started to play with a loose thread at the bottom of her shirt. "Some people don't like that."

Perse lifted Stef's chin and they shared the same intense look as when they'd cleaned off stray paint. "Well, I do like it. There're no guessing games with you. And while I think you analyze everything, you do speak from your heart. That's something I wish more people did. So, don't ever change that."

Stef looked down and cleared her throat. "I . . . um. Thank you. That was a very kind thing to say." She laughed with a slight nervous twinge. "Wow, that was a strong batch of margaritas. I'm going to go in and get some water. Would you like some?"

Perse could already sense her limbs loosening and thoughts becoming hazier. "Please."

Stef took the tray and went inside. And thank God she did. Perse couldn't believe she had opened up to Stef the way she had, and that Stef had responded maturely and in a way that comforted her. Ditching Thom and seeing Stef was the best dating decision she had made since turning down the city guide's advances in Oaxaca.

Stef emerged from the sliding glass door and handed Perse a tall glass. "Water on the rocks."

"Thank you. That was a delicious margarita, but hard liquor goes straight to my head."

"You should stay away from the punch at Christopher's Fourth of July party then."

"He just sent the e-vite for that. I was a little nervous when I saw how many people were on the list, but then I realized it was primarily for the department, and I've pretty much met everyone. Have you crashed his party in the past?"

"Usually, I go as Timera's plus one, but this year I'll make an exception if someone else wanted to bring me."

"I am allowed to bring a date." Perse reached for Stef's hand. "Interested?"

Stef shrugged. "Maybe. But do you think we can plan a date that far in advance? That'll break our streak of knowing a day or a few hours beforehand."

Perse smiled and moved her thumb in slow circles over Stef's skin. "You're a real smart ass, aren't you? But yes, I do think we can plan ahead. You could even add that to your outline, 'plan dates more than a week in advance.'"

Stef looked down to where Perse continued to stroke her hand. "I actually don't think I can outline right now. I'm starting to feel pretty dumb. Not yoga-guy dumb, but pretty brainless nonetheless."

Perse arched a brow and kissed Stef's knuckles, then grazed Stef's fingertips over her lips before kissing the pads. Stef reacted by sliding her free hand to the nape of Perse's neck. Stef guided her closer until she possessed Perse's mouth with her own.

Perse craved to taste every drop of margarita left on Stef's lips and tongue. She leaned in until she covered Stef's body.

Stef started to writhe beneath her as they each sought more contact. She lightly ran her trim fingernails outside of Perse's thigh, then reached under the back of Perse's borrowed shorts and gripped her ass. She licked Perse's ear and whispered, "You are so incredibly sexy."

Perse was in a complete role reversal. Usually, she did the seducing. She turned her partner into the bumbling idiot. She made the other person squirm with need. Now, she was defenseless to Stef's wiles and loved every second of it. Perse parted her legs more, allowing Stef's thigh to rise. The blatant sexual contact only escalated Perse's lust, and then Stef pulled away with a mischievous grin. Perse liked that grin. "Are we taking this inside?"

"We don't have to." Stef returned to her spot on the slider and sipped some water. "We can still talk out here."

They were finished? How in the world could passion like that be turned off like a switch?

Stef looked at her quizzically. "You look . . . annoyed."

Perse pushed herself from her elbows and sat again. "Confused is more like it."

"Why are you confused?"

"Maybe because you grabbed my bare ass and added some frottage? I'm getting conflicting signals here."

"I don't follow."

Perse put her palms on either side of her head, then placed them together in a prayer-like position as she spoke. "Stef, I like you a lot. You've really respected my space and I thoroughly enjoy spending time with you. But we need to talk about the physical nature of our relationship in more detail. Clearly, I need to understand your boundaries more and you need to understand that I have none."

Stef scoffed. "What do you mean none?"

"I mean what I said."

Stef looked genuinely baffled. "You mean to tell me, if it were all up to you, we'd be on our way to having sex right now?"

"Yes."

Stef staggered away.

Perse approached her and gently held both of her hands. "I haven't really stated this before, but here it goes . . . I think you are brilliant, funny, and gorgeous. I'm very sexually attracted to you."

"Same. But . . ." Stef pursed her lips and sighed. "But I thought you understood my levels."

"I thought I did! But, like the dating level, there's a lot of gray area when it comes to orgasm. You can't have that without the sex which starts in the first level."

"That's . . . interesting. Maybe I should rethink certain elements. Add it to the outline, even." A sharp knock at the door interrupted their standoff. "Want to talk about sex over pizza?"

"Yes! But I'm changing back into my yoga clothes first."

When Perse emerged from the bathroom and into the dining room, the pizza box lay open in the center of the rectangular glass table. One end had her water glass and an empty slate gray plate, and at the other end Stef feverishly wrote in a notebook.

"Are you getting started on your outline?"

Stef looked up surprised. "How'd you know?"

"Lucky guess." Perse sat at the table and her mouth watered at the sight of the crisp ham and charred pineapple. "I love Hawaiian pizza."

"Please, help yourself. I just want to finish this thought."

Perse removed a slice. The cheese stretched over the edge of the box and onto her plate. She thought about waiting, but who knew how long Stef would be? She began to eat the flavorful slice and wondered what Stef could possibly be writing, especially once she ran out of room and turned the page.

It was more of a manifesto than an outline.

As Stef wrote, an idea suddenly struck Perse. One that could ease her anxiety and add clarity. "Stef, are we in a relationship?"

Stef stopped writing and looked up. "I'd say we're in the beginning stages of one, yes."

"I agree. So, shouldn't we make these sublevels together?"

Stef paused on her way to getting her pizza. "Why?"

113

Perse snickered. "Because in a relationship, the larger decisions should be made together. There's compromise. I'm not saying your main levels should change, but the gray areas of the current level should be decided by both of us."

"Okay." Stef took her slice. "I'm listening. What would you like to add to the dating level?"

"Sex."

Stef sighed. "I'm starting to think you're a little obsessed with sex. It's not that important."

"And I disagree. Sex can be just an act where it's pretty much an activity to pass the time, but for some it's also a pathway to emotional intimacy."

Stef shook her head, but smirked. "I don't buy it. I think you just want to have sex with me."

"Yes, that's true." There was absolutely no point in denying it, so why bother? "However, that doesn't make what I said untrue."

"Yes, it does! Sex can't just be a pastime activity *and* a pathway to emotional intimacy for the same person."

"Yes, it can!"

"How?"

Perse almost laughed, but she kept her composure. She was grateful for the conversation because she and Stef had very different views on what sex could be. "Much of it is state of mind, and the other comes down to logistics. Are you maintaining eye contact? Is it a rush to orgasm or are you taking your time? Is it comfortable once it's over?"

Stef sipped her water and then tapped her chin. "I reluctantly see your point, but that still rearranges the levels. Love comes before orgasms."

"Remember there are two people involved and real life is not some fairy tale where those two people fall in love with each other at the exact same moment. Not to mention the fact that some people can't admit they've fallen in love or don't even know that's what it is they're feeling. I see those two levels as co-levels."

Stef chewed her pizza thoughtfully. "So, in this scenario, the emotional aspect is very subjective, especially if the other person isn't sharing their feelings. We have to include more objective information in our sex sublevel."

She had a point. Ambiguity was the enemy they needed to defeat. "Underwear and bras stay on, and no hand-on-genital contact until . . ." Perse tapped her crust against the plate as she pondered different timelines. But it was impossible, her brain didn't work this way.

"Until we agree to only date each other and each have test results, hopefully negative, to an STI panel. That takes care of the exclusivity and my paranoia about disease transmission."

"You're sure?" Perse asked skeptically. "Only those two things?"

Stef nodded slowly. "Like you said, a relationship has compromise, and while not ideal, I can live with that because I wouldn't get my test until I was ready for full intercourse, which, by the sounds of it, will be later than you."

"That's probably true." Under any other circumstance, Perse would have lied through her teeth, but honesty was key. And, so far, it had worked to her advantage. "I also think it's better to find out sooner rather than later if we're sexually compatible."

"What do you mean?" Stef asked and reached for another slice.

"For example, I assume based on some of your characteristics that you're a top, and I like that."

"Prepare to be disappointed."

Perse's loins whimpered. "You're not?"

Stef laughed. "No, I totally am. I just wanted to see how you'd react."

Perse smiled and internally cheered. "That was mean."

"Just keeping you on your toes," Stef said and drank from her glass. "This has been a very productive conversation. What else can we add to the outline?"

"How much ink do you have in that pen?"

CHAPTER TEN

WHEN MISSY'S PROJECT manager was fired, joy filled every pore of her body. When Missy watched him fight security while they escorted him out of the building, the scene entertained her. And when Missy overheard people in the break room discuss replacement candidates and her name was mentioned, she almost yelped in surprise.

But none of those events were more joyful, entertaining, or surprising than when Perse explained the sex conversation she'd had with Stef. Missy's little sister certainly had found a worthy foe in the battle of wills.

Missy sat in her car at the streetlight and pondered what she'd heard. "So, to summarize, neither of you can have downstairs fun—even if there's no big o-moment—until you've both provided test results to an STI panel and you cease dating other people. Am I forgetting anything?"

"Oh! I made the point that some need physicality to feel a more emotional connection."

"Come on, jackass!" Missy honked her horn at the car in front of her when it refused to move. "And by some, you mean you. I knew you'd pull something to try to jump into bed sooner."

"There was no pulling! It was a mature conversation where I was upfront with my needs. I was even able to broach the topic of sexual compatibility."

Missy laughed. "You are such a bullshitter."

"It's an incredibly valid point. I confirmed she's a top and I asked her to think of her favorite partner-based sexual activity or position and then imagine never doing it again for the rest of her life."

Missy nodded. "Okay, I'll admit that was a good one. What did she say?"

"Oh my God, it was so cute. Her face turned crimson and then she admitted that scenario would be unfortunate."

Weaving in and out of traffic, Missy laughed again. "You must *really* like her to go through all of this."

"She's special and she challenges me, but in a way that I enjoy. It's strange to have that kind of dynamic with someone who isn't you. I've never had that kind of energy in a romantic relationship."

Missy's jaw dropped from Perse finally using the 'r' word, but the sound of a siren became louder and flashing, colorful lights in her rear-view mirror caused her face to contort into a grimace. "This is fantastic to hear, but I gotta go. Fuzz just got me." She hung up the phone and pulled over. She turned around to see Alec in the backseat still in the appropriate position with his hands covering his ears. She gave him a thumbs up.

The young boy dropped his metaphorical earmuffs. "Why can't Aunt Erse have fun downstairs? She used to live there."

Missy dug out her registration and blew a sharp breath between her lips. "You have no idea, buddy."

***

Perse chuckled at her sister's lead foot and went to her next task of scheduling her blood test. She hated blood and needles with a passion, but she had to admit this particular hoop of Stef's was reasonable and worth the risk of passing out.

She hoped Stef scheduled her test soon.

Perse was about to call for her appointment when a baritone throat clear caused her to look up to see Christopher taking up the majority of the space in her doorway. This was his first office pop in. Immediately, she went on alert. "Hi! Would you like to come in?"

Christopher waved away the seat she offered. "I can't stay long, I just wanted to wish you luck teaching your first class this afternoon. Do you feel ready?"

"I really do. I have what I hope is an interesting approach to the content. I just hope my students can take six hours of it per week for the next six weeks."

He smiled and it made his bushy beard puff out more. "I also came over to tell you that I was happy to see that you'd RSVPed to my party for two. I'm assuming the second is Stef Blake."

"Yes. The rumors are true." She smiled, then sipped her tea.

"I thought so. Of course, it was a dead giveaway when I saw her new relationship status this morning."

Perse nearly choked on her earl grey. "I'm sorry," she wheezed and then coughed.

"Better clear those lungs before you teach. You can't lecture dead." He laughed as he left her office.

She calmed her traitorous lungs and then called Stef. Her blood test call dropped from her priority list. She was relieved there was an answer on the first ring. "Stef, it's me."

"I know, but I think this is the first time you've ever actually called me," Stef said with a loud whirling in the background. "This must be good if you didn't text."

"We *have* to talk."

"Okay, but can I call you back in like three hours? I'm in the middle of an experiment and I need my hands free."

Three hours wouldn't do. "Can't you put me on speaker?"

"Well, in theory, but I don't know what you want to talk about, and my lab constantly has my students coming in and out of it so they'll overhear. Plus, I would think listening to the air flow from the cabinet would be annoying."

"Um." Perse got up and started pacing her office. "Can I come to you?"

"Now?" she asked surprised.

"Yes. This conversation really can't wait."

There was a long pause on the other end. "Okay, but you better bring a hair tie and closed-toed shoes."

She looked down at her pink toenails peeking out from her sandals. "Alright. See you in a few minutes." Perse hung up, grabbed her keys, and ran to her car. The campus was so large, it would take almost half an hour to walk there.

She parked in front of Stef's building—one of the newest on campus—and took out her muddy hiking boots, which were always in the back. She slapped the soles together to bash off the caked mud. The shoes didn't go with her outfit of a wispy skirt and fitted tee, but at least they were now clean-ish.

This was the first time she had been in Stef's building, and the differences between hers and those of the history department were striking. Hers felt like history. Brick walls with black-and-white photographs. Stef's had polished white floors and walls with the occasional brightly colored photograph of fluorescent microscopy. Or at least that's what the captions said.

Perse took the stairs and walked into Stef's lab. She saw a student wearing goggles, blue gloves, and she had her hair held back in an intricate braid. Based on the description she was confident the younger woman was Bradyn. She would know where Stef was. "Hello, sorry to interrupt, but I'm trying to find Dr. Blake."

"She's in the cabinet right now. It's to the right and down the row of benches." The student started to walk away but turned back to her and dug into her pocket for a hair tie. "She'll get mad if your hair isn't tied back. Safety is very important to her."

Perse took the tie and pulled her hair back into a quick ponytail. As she trod back to where Stef was, she hoped she wasn't leaving a trail of dirt. That would mar the lab's pristine level of cleanliness.

She saw Stef seated with her forearms inside and underneath the glass of the safety cabinet. As Perse came closer she could see dozens of small plastic tubes and a plastic tray with easily a hundred tiny holes. In Stef's grasp was a device she seemed to be activating using only her thumb. Perse immediately regretted making the trip over. "That looks really complicated."

"It's not that bad. For the moment, I'm just pipetting water." Stef smiled, but when she looked up to Perse she frowned. "Your hair needs to be tied back more. You have sexy tendrils. There are no sexy tendrils in the lab."

"Oh, for God's sake," Perse grunted and redid her ponytail. "Happy?"

"Very. Now, what do you need to talk about?"

Perse pulled a stool over and sat beside Stef. "Christopher came to see me and told me you have a new relationship status."

"Yeah," Stef said with a shrug and continued to dispense miniscule quantities of water into the plastic tubes.

"And what is that status?"

"That I'm in a relationship."

Stef's nonchalant answer astonished Perse. "With me?"

Stef giggled. "Well, yes, but I didn't name you specifically." When she made eye contact with Perse she put her thumb-pushing tool down in the stainless-steel cabinet, removed her blue gloves, and tossed them into the orange biohazard trash. "Let's talk over there. But I only have ten minutes."

Perse followed Stef into a small windowless room with a few microscopes. Stef shut the door behind them, and then reached for one of her hands. Perse felt the residual cornstarch from inside her gloves. "Okay. Tell me what's on your mind."

Perse didn't know where to start. "Why did you do that? Change your status, that is?"

"That's what people do now. So, after we both agreed we were in a relationship, I changed my status. But I also did it because I've had a few people hit me up for dates lately. People who aren't you."

"You said you weren't on dating apps now."

"I play rugby. I don't need a dating app."

That made complete sense, yet Perse had never once thought about the influence of social media. "Okay, I see your point. However, I would have preferred it if you had told me that you were going to post your status, and not hear the update straight out of my department head's mouth."

Stef crossed her arms and nodded. "That's fair. I'm sorry that's how you found out. Although, if we were 'friends' you could have learned that way too."

The last time Perse had been in a relationship social media had been in its infancy; the new 'rules' hadn't been established.

She got out her phone and sent Stef a friend request. "I don't want to make this a big deal, but my mother would completely overreact if she saw that I was 'in a relationship', so I would prefer holding off on changing my status for now."

"Out of curiosity, what would your mom do?"

Perse took a calming breath. She couldn't do full disclosure, but Stef deserved some kind of answer. "In the past, my mom has scared some people away with her exuberance for the relationships I've been in."

Stef's face showed she didn't get it.

"My mom pushed up the levels before I, or the person I was with, was ready."

"Oh! Totally get it now. Yeah, I don't want that to happen. Although, speaking of your family, now's probably a good time to tell you that your sister sent me a friend request about a week ago."

"What?" Perse shrieked.

"Don't worry. I didn't accept it. That seemed to be a little much, even for me. But now . . . Does your sister react like your mom?"

Perse sighed. This would keep Missy's questions at bay for a while. "You can accept, but please don't engage her. That's something I'm not ready for either."

"Also fair. What if she engages me?"

Missy knew how this new adventure in her life had challenged her; she wouldn't do anything to make it more difficult. "She won't. She probably just wants to snoop around."

"Got it. Now, is there anything else I can help you with before I get back to my experiment?" Stef asked in her most professional voice.

"No. And thank you for taking the time to see me on such short notice. I appreciate your flexibility."

As they left the lab, Bradyn frantically ran over to them. "Dr. Blake—"

"Is something on fire or did anything splash in your mouth?"

"Um . . . no."

"Then, I'll get to you in a minute." She walked Perse to just outside the lab door. "Thank you for the visit, Dr. Teixeira. I found it very informative and I hope you learned a few things too."

"Yes, it was very educational," Perse said and looked down bashfully at her boots. "You know, since Christopher's party is in the evening, I wouldn't be opposed to having dinner before it starts."

Stef's expression morphed in disappointment. "I'm sorry, but I already promised Harry I'd take him to see that new World War II movie. I probably won't get home until just before the party starts."

A dull tinge of disappointment landed in Perse's gut. "That's nice of you to take him. I'm sure you'll have a great time. Should I pick you up at seven, then?"

"Actually, Gillian offered to drive so you might want to talk to her first. I'm still suspicious of her reasons to be the designated driver, but I'll go along with it."

"I'll make sure I talk to her in the next few days about it then." Perse didn't want to leave without some kind of parting gesture. A handshake would do nicely. "Thanks for taking the time to speak to me. I'll let you get back to you research."

"And you need to head back for your first class. I know you'll be great." Stef picked up her hand and kissed the back of it. "Until next time, Dr. Teixeira."

Perse held her breath as she watched the romantic act, then cleared her throat. "See you soon, Dr. Blake," she said and turned to leave the building.

Which was not in the direction she thought it was.

She'd been so panicked about the conversation with Stef when she'd come in, she hadn't paid any attention to basic landmarks. Without any guides, the halls were a labyrinth, and she did not have time to go exploring. "Excuse me," Perse asked a staff member with a square jaw and muscular arms before he unlocked a room, "which way is the fastest exit to the side parking lot?"

"Hmm. From here . . . probably hanging a left by the study lounge."

"And where is that?"

He chuckled softly. "How about I show you? It'll probably be faster."

Perse fell into step beside him and passed several pictures, and a large indoor palm, that she hadn't recalled seeing before. "I appreciate you showing me the way. Normally, I don't get lost easily, but I was in a hurry when I came in and didn't notice my surroundings."

"It happens. Why did you come in such a hurry?"

Perse glanced at his inquisitive face. "I had this idea and I wanted to share it with Dr. Blake."

"Oh, Stef is great! I work with her. I'm Wayne, by the way."

Wayne! It had to be the same Wayne Stef hated with every fiber of her being. Her nemesis. "Perse, pleased to meet you."

"Likewise. Yeah, Stef's a brilliant scientist. I felt really bad when they gave me tenure last year and not her. We both deserved it." He stopped in the hall and pointed to the far end. "That exit sign is what you want. Hope to see you around, Perse," he said and went on his way.

"You too," she said timidly and with mild confusion. Based on Stef's description, she was expecting Quasimodo with the temperament of Cinderella's stepmother. She wondered why on earth Stef would make him out to be so unlikeable.

123

Once at her car, Perse switched her boots for her sandals again, and then her phone rang. She sighed. The past thirty minutes had been insane; she did not need to talk to her sister. But then again, she may have called to wish her luck. "Calling to wish me a great first lecture?"

"Oh shit! That's right! Um, sure, break a leg, Sis."

"I can feel the support, thanks. But since I have you on the phone, why in the hell did you send Stef a friend request?"

"That's why I'm calling! She finally accepted it and holy shit. Her page is ridiculous."

Perse's heart dropped into her stomach. Was she off the political deep end? Obsessed with goats? A fanilow? There were too many possibilities. "What did you see?"

"She has a lot of rugby and 5K pics. I can't believe her abs, and that ass is incredible. It must be driving you crazy not to be able to tap that!"

Perse bit her lip and counted down until her annoyance quelled. "You seriously called me to say that Stef has a hot body? I know that. And yes, you're right, it is driving me crazy, but I'm dealing. Was that the only thing you wanted to bring to my attention?"

"No. The other part is about her family."

"What about it?"

"Does she not get along with them anymore or something? None of these pictures look recent except for a Carol."

"That's because—God, this is sad. It's because they're all gone. They're . . . dead."

Missy stayed silent for several seconds. A rarity.

"Are you still there?"

"Yeah, I'm here. It's just . . . surely she has a grandparent? Or a cousin in jail like everyone else?"

"No cousins. Her dad was an only child and her mom's only sibling was Carol. She and Stef's uncle never had children."

"Grandparents?"

Perse winced. "Two cancers, a suicide, and a heart attack."

"Jesus! No wonder she wants to get married."

"You lost me. What does Stef wanting to get married have to do with her deceased relatives?"

Missy's silence held for even longer.

"*Missy*," she drawled in warning.

"I don't know how to tell you this without freaking you out, but think about it. What does someone gain when they get married?"

The phone almost dropped from Perse's hand as her heart broke. "A family."

CHAPTER ELEVEN

"IT'S A SHAME your husband couldn't come to the party," Perse said from the backseat of Gillian's car. "I was looking forward to meeting him."

"His company keeps him traveling quite a bit, but I have a feeling if he had a job where he came home every night our relationship wouldn't work as well as it does. I like my space," Gillian said as she turned into Stef's neighborhood.

"And if you live like me, you get all the space you want. All the time," Timera added. "I never argue about what show I'm going to watch. Can you say that about your perfect marriage?"

"That's not the point. I'm merely trying to say that no marriage is identical, and what Ian and I have works for us," Gillian said as she parked in front of Stef's house. "Timera and I will debate the finer points of partnership and television while you get Stef, but if you're not out in five minutes—"

"Ten minutes," Timera corrected.

"If you're not out in ten minutes . . . we're leaving."

"I think we'll be able to control ourselves," Perse said and bunched her sundress before getting out of the car. She had almost changed clothes, thinking maybe her level of cleavage was too bawdy for a work party, but both Timera and Gillian had insisted it was appropriate. That fashion tip came after they had seen her apartment to verify the rumor that she essentially lived in glorified student housing.

Perse knocked on the door and her excitement quickly shifted to concern when she saw Stef's bloodshot eyes.

Stef gripped her hand and frantically took her down the hallway. "Sorry, I need a few more minutes. I can't decide on what shoes to wear."

Perse allowed herself to be pulled along and found herself, for the first time, in Stef's bedroom. The last time she'd visited Stef's home, the door had been shut. Now, not only was she in the room, but she'd sat on a forest-green comforter that draped over her bed.

For an older house, the room was generously sized and decorated to fit the theme of the rest of the home. A framed landscape photograph and an abstract print added personal touches to the room, which also featured a cherry furniture set. The only item that stood out of place was a stack of aged envelopes bundled with a rubber band on her dresser. The new location was just enough of a surprise to temporarily distract Perse from her worry.

Stef paced in front of and gestured to her closet. "I can't decide which color goes best with my outfit. What do you think?"

Perse's eyes traveled from the mail to Stef, then to the floor in front of the closet where four different pairs of sneakers had been neatly laid out. Stef always matched her shoes to her shirt. This shouldn't have been a difficult decision.

Perse ignored Stef's question and guided Stef to sit beside her. "What's wrong?"

"Nothing's wrong." Stef held her gaze, but quickly shifted her gaze from Perse's skeptical frown to the ceiling.

There was no way Perse could know what had occurred, but she knew Stef fairly well now. Something so surprising and awful had happened; either there weren't words to articulate her emotions yet or she didn't feel comfortable enough to share. In either case, Perse wouldn't push. She would wait until Stef came to her.

"I was hoping it wouldn't be noticeable," Stef said after several moments of silence. "Something happened today that put me in a little bit of an emotional tailspin, but I'm cool now. Everything's fine."

Perse refused to agree or disagree. She wouldn't patronize Stef by giving her empty words, but she could offer support. She could utilize her own techniques for decreasing her anxiety with Stef. She slid her fingers through Stef's so their palms touched. "Focus on this connection. The gentle pressure, the warmth. I'm here for you."

Stef's brown eyes began to glisten as she squeezed Perse's hand before she put her arms around her.

Perse wanted Stef to trust her enough to confide in her, so she continued to follow Stef's lead. She reciprocated the hug and placed a small kiss on her temple. "I'm here, sweetie."

Stef leaned into the comfort Perse offered and hugged her more tightly.

When Perse felt a cool wetness on her shoulder, she gently rocked Stef. While the emotional barrier was partially gone, Perse's empathy for Stef soared. She wanted more than anything to heal her wound. But she couldn't.

"I can do this," Stef whispered into her neck.

Perse wasn't sure if Stef was speaking to her or was providing self-encouragement, but she knew Stef needed a response. "You can do anything," Perse said in a hushed tone. "You're amazing."

She felt Stef nod into her shoulder and then remove herself from the embrace. While Stef looked in the direction of her shoes, Perse used her thumb to wipe away a stray tear. Stef returned her gaze to Perse's.

Their eyes locked upon one another. The moment was more than intimate. It was powerful.

Perse wanted to kiss her. Wanted to stare into those brown eyes as she touched her to reassure Stef how much she would be there for her. But that wasn't what Stef wanted. That's what *she* would have wanted.

She lowered her hand from Stef's cheek to her shoulder and offered a small smile.

Stef wiped at her eyes, then gave a forced laugh. "So, how about those shoes?"

Perse knew that Stef wasn't finished letting her emotions out, but let it go. "I'd go with the red pair. That'll complete your patriotic color scheme."

"I was thinking those." When she'd finished tying her shoes, Stef looked at more than Perse's eyes. She studied Perse from head to toe like she was a floor-to-ceiling work of art. "You're absolutely stunning. You have the sexy tendrils again, and with your hair up like that it really shows off your neck and um . . . dress. It's neat how the color fades like that. It's like a red, white, and blue tie-dye, but classier."

Perse looked down at her dress's generous scoop. "Are you sure it's the color your eyes are drawn to?"

"Pleading the fifth on that one."

"It's okay. Those shorts really bring out your shapely pockets."

Stef giggled and the sound erased the glum atmosphere in the room. She traced Perse's jaw with her fingertips, stared into the depths of her eyes, and kissed her.

This kiss felt different. It was more than body parts coming together. There was an emotional weight that hadn't been there before, but a horn blast from outside caused Perse to reluctantly back away. "I guess our time is up. Are you ready? But if you're not feeling up to it, I can tell Gillian that you—that we—aren't coming to the party."

"No, I'm ready. But I don't think I would have been without this. And I don't think anyone else could have helped me like you just did. Thank you."

The hug Stef initiated didn't surprise Perse, but the genuine gratitude in her voice did. Was there no one else in Stef's life that she felt comfortable being that vulnerable with? The idea saddened her and caused her to hold onto Stef more tightly. "You're welcome, sweetie."

***

The drive to Christopher's house was educational. Mostly because Perse learned about Gillian's motivation for acting as the designated driver. At the last faculty party, the friendly game of Corn Hole had turned into a tournament that took an ugly turn. Fueled by too much alcohol, bets had been made, mild trash talk had turned personal, and accusations of cheating had soared.

"I'm gonna stay sober so I can get my money back from Patrick, that cheating huddy," proclaimed Gillian.

Perse was curious about the word 'huddy' and the circumstance. Corn hole was literally the simplest game in the world—gently tossing a pellet-filled sac at a wooden board with a hole in it. "How does one cheat at corn hole?"

Timera laughed, and Stef whispered to Perse, "Don't go there."

"He goes beyond the line and insists on using his own sacs, which I know are not regulation!" Gillian explained with passion.

"So, you see, Perse," Timera said, "it has everything to do with sacs and nothing to do with the fact that they were drunk last time."

"You'll see that I'm right at the end of the night," Gillian said as she parked her car on Christopher's front lawn, which served as a parking lot for the fifteen or so vehicles representing the CBU history department that had already arrived. And that of Christopher's editor.

Once Timera and Gillian were out of the car, Stef asked, "Do you need one of your gummy things? There's a lot of people here."

Perse grinned. It was sweet that Stef was on the lookout for her. "I know everyone here. I should be fine, but I do have them just in case." She reached for the door's handle.

"Hold on. One more thing."

Perse turned to Stef who suddenly looked very intense.

"I wanted to ask you before, but I got distracted with the . . . you know."

"What it is?"

"People know I'm your date, right?"

The question struck Perse as odd. "Well, people who asked me know, but I didn't announce it to the department. That would have been a little awkward. Besides, I think people know based on general gossip."

Stef didn't react immediately, but eventually shrugged. "That's fair," she said and opened the car door.

Perse was bewildered by Stef's question. "Hold on a second." Stef turned to her with the car door open. "Why did you ask that?"

"It's nothing, really. Just my neurosis getting the best of me. We can talk about it later, okay?"

"Alright." Perse trusted Stef to help her understand later, adjusted her dress to climb out, and walked with Stef to catch up to the rest of their group.

***

Christopher finished a bout of laughter and looked to the foursome as they strolled toward him. "Ladies, welcome to the party!" Then he directed his attention to Stef. "You just had to find another way to get invited to my departmental soirée," he said and winked at Perse.

"Just because I work on the other side of campus doesn't mean that I don't appreciate history," Stef stated dryly. "In fact, I saw *Fox Hole* earlier today. I have no doubt the movie was very historically accurate in its portrayal of Nazi evilness and subsequent ass kicking."

"Sounds like a very reputable depiction." Christopher chuckled again and gestured to the other side of the yard with his pipe. "Go get yourselves some refreshments and have fun. But don't have so much fun you miss the fireworks. Gillian and Timera, I'm looking at you two."

The small group was greeted with waves and hellos as they toured the grounds to get a sense of the party. Timera broke off once she'd filled her cup with punch, and Gillian left for Corn Hole redemption.

Perse and Stef headed to the hors d'oeuvres and dessert table. As they grabbed their drinks and filled their small plates, Perse engaged in more conversation with several colleagues and confirmed that Stef was her date.

Bjorn and Jin were especially happy to learn the news.

"Sorry if I was a little weird in the car," Stef said as she added a bacon-wrapped fig to her plate.

"I did find that a little peculiar. Care to elaborate regarding what that was about?"

"The last time I saw you, you weren't too pleased Christopher knew about us. I guess part of me was afraid you wouldn't want to be *out* with me. That I'd be a secret."

"I wouldn't do that, and I'm sorry if what happened before made you think that. I'll admit I didn't handle Christopher knowing very well, but you're not a secret."

"I'm glad to hear that, because I've been there, done that, got the t-shirt, and then donated it to charity because it didn't fit anymore."

Perse laughed heartily. Stef's humor continued to surprise her; however, her laughter came to a halt as she realized Stef's joke was a defense mechanism. "Have you felt like a secret before?"

"Yeah, I have. Actually, it's why family meetings are before cohabitation in my levels. Mei, my ex, and I lived together before I met her family. That's when I found out just how unaccepting they were of our lifestyle, and it caused a lot of problems. I would have rather known that ahead of time. And, unfortunately, that's just one example. So, I'm just trying to learn from my mistakes."

Perse wondered if she had learned from her mistakes as well. The detailed discussions she and Stef had had about dating and sex made an impact with her. Knowing and understanding what lay ahead decreased her anxiety. Although, the mention of family meetings upped her stress levels again. Either her own family or that of her partner's had been the common denominator in all of her relationship failures.

Families couldn't be controlled.

"Are you okay?" Stef asked with a gentle hand on Perse's upper arm. "You just got real introspective."

"I'm just thinking about my own past," she said with a faux smile. "Families make things difficult sometimes."

"Do you want to talk about it?"

"Not here." *Or ever.* "Let's focus on the party."

Stef nodded her understanding.

Perse took a relieved bite out of a puff pastry while she scanned the grounds. Christopher's Victorian-style home was enormous and overlooked the bay. "They either pay really well at the full professor tier or writing has been very lucrative for him."

"I'm pretty sure it's the latter, but the TV appearances help, too. Once we're done snacking, I can give you the grand tour."

"You don't think he'll mind?"

"Oh no. He told me to in a DM." Stef grinned innocently.

Perse listened as Stef shared some of the facts about the house. Christopher had lived there twenty years and recently renovated from the profits of his latest book success to incorporate green elements. Stef was particularly fond of the motion lights.

After they mingled a bit more and finished their first cocktails, Stef started the tour in the impressive dining room. Both admired the custom crown molding and wainscoting that surrounded the room, which featured an immense dining table made from a reclaimed courthouse door. From there, they walked on polished, herringbone-patterned floors through the sunken living room to an instrument that had Perse practically drooling the moment she saw it.

"Oh my God. That's the most exquisite piano I've ever seen in someone's home. He never told me he had this!" Not even her mother's baby grand was of the same caliber. Perse's fingers were itchy with the desire to play.

"Go ahead," Stef said. "You know you want to."

Perse ran her finger over the closed fallboard lid. "I do want to but I should ask Christopher first. It's probably closed so people won't play it."

Stef pouted and kicked imaginary dirt. "Damn. I was really hoping to hear you play a real piano." She really did have a child-like streak.

"How about I ask Christopher the next time I see him and we go from there?"

"I'll take it!" Stef said with a broad smile, but then her mouth formed an O, as if she was alarmed. "I hope you don't think that I didn't appreciate it when you played your keyboard for me. That was nice. It's just that this seems more authentic to who you are."

"And who am I?" Perse asked dramatically.

Stef led her down the next hall. "You are a modern Renaissance woman. You strive for knowledge and collect it in your own style. You make and appreciate art. Despite your fancy scarves and dresses, you have a rugged, rough-and-tumble nature about you. And I know there're many more wonderful things about you that I don't know, but I can't wait to learn."

Perse had never heard more beautiful words directed toward her. It was impossible to believe that Stef already knew her that well. Yet, she did. She wanted to say something back about how wonderful Stef was. That she was sensitive and thoughtful. Sexy, yet adorable. Both youthful and wise. But the words stuck in her throat. She simply followed Stef to the topmost floor of the home.

Along the way, they passed a photograph of Christopher and his late wife taken in the American southwest. Despite the desert landscape and their clothes dampened by their post-hike sweat, they were exuberant for the camera.

Stef groaned. "The scenery reminds me of my conference. I'm not ready. I mean, I have the stuff I'm supposed to have, but I really wanted to wow them with some extra statistics. Maybe have an infographic with cilia."

"I'm sure you'll be great. When do you leave for the airport?"

"Early Sunday morning, which means . . . shit. Between finishing my poster and helping my students organize their work while I'm gone, I won't have much time for us. Which has already been non-existent over the last week."

It gave Perse a small flutter to know Stef already regretted their missed time together. But it wasn't as though she could make many accommodations. "Now that I'm teaching, I can't really swing by for a lunch date during the week."

"This might sound boring, but how about dinner at my place on Saturday? Warning, you might have to help me pack."

Perse pretended to think about the proposition. "Do I get to fold your underwear?"

"We'll see," Stef said as she opened a door at the end of the hall. She flipped the switch and, as they entered the room, turned off the motion light, thus keeping the room as dark as nature would allow. "Welcome to my favorite room."

Through the skylights and large windows, the cloudless sky let the star- and moonlight to pass through, allowing Perse to see the room's details. Wall space featured books packed to the brim, the farthest corner held a telescope, and in the center of the room, facing away from the door, was a chaise lounge with an end table on either side: one table for a decanter of liquor, and the other for his pipe.

Perse watched as Stef walked to a window and looked skyward. The extraterrestrial light illuminated her peaceful grin. Stef was an angel, and suddenly Perse knew why she had been experiencing such intense feelings and flutters.

She was in love.

But it was far too soon for her to feel that way. She and Stef had only known each other since May. In all of her other relationships it had taken much longer for her to feel anything close to love, and she knew how well those had worked out. There had been so much regret. So much pain.

Too many feelings she couldn't process.

Stef turned from the window to her and cocked her head. "What's wrong?"

As the realization of her emotions and Stef's awareness sank in, Perse's heartbeat increased rapidly and her breathing came in short, uncontrolled bursts. Soon, it was as though an invisible pillow had been placed over her face.

"Perse?" Stef asked with concern.

This was the worst attack she'd had in over a decade. She couldn't breathe. She could hardly even form words. "Can't . . ." she wheezed.

Stef rushed to her and led them to the chaise where Stef sat directly across from her. "Mime my breathing."

Perse did as instructed. It was a clear physical cue she appreciated.

"Good. Nod if you need an epi pen. Shake if you don't."

She shook her head. This was anxiety, not an allergic reaction.

"Um . . . Well, that's good, so just keep breathing. Ah . . . clear your head of negative thoughts. Feel your chakra . . I think. Imagine all of those calming yoga words."

Perse continued to follow Stef. As her chest rose and fell with Stef's rhythm and she thought of yoga words, her heartbeat eventually slowed and her ability to form words returned. "I think I'm better now."

"Let's do a few more, just to be safe."

Stef was right. She wasn't out of the woods, but with each subsequent exhale the walls around her opened and the pressure on her chest lessened. "Okay. I think I'm actually better now."

"Was that like a full-on anxiety attack?"

"Afraid so. You did a good job of keeping me calm and making sure I didn't pass out. That's been known to happen—mostly with seeing blood though."

"Do you know what caused it? I mean, you were fine and then we walked in here and—Oh! It's the pipe smell, isn't it? That got to me, too, the first time I came in."

Perse decided that was a better suggestion than to admit her feelings. "Yes. That scent invokes such powerful memories of . . . stress. How'd you guess?" Perse scooted back into the fluff of the chaise. She waved Stef in to join her.

Stef kicked off her shoes and cuddled into her. "Pipes give me happy memories of my dad. He was a Civil War reenactor, and whenever he'd come home from his 'battles' the smell would hit me. The first time I smelled that cherry-tobacco scent after he died was when I met Christopher, I told him about the reenacting bit, and that was how we initially bonded."

Instead of feeling emotionally and physically trapped by Stef lying partially across her body, Perse felt safer. Stef's thigh rested over hers. Stef's hand rested over her heart.

Perse started to embrace the idea that maybe she could love Stef. But there was no way, even given the perfect room, that she could tell her. For one, it was too soon. Plus, Stef had given no indication she felt the same way, and, even worse, Stef might think she was saying it just to get into bed with her. This was a feeling she couldn't be honest about yet. It was best just to move on.

"Is this your favorite room because of the tobacco?"

"No." Stef pointed to the stars overhead. "Those are why. I thought about going into astronomy when I was kid, but the subject didn't seem practical, nor did it fit into my plan."

"Imagine that. You doing something practical and with a plan." Perse nudged her playfully.

"Sounds like you're getting to know me pretty well too."

They lay still in companionable silence until Stef lifted her head and sat more upright. In addition to the shift of position, Perse detected a change in Stef's mood, which was confirmed once Stef bit her lower lip and rubbed her forearm.

"You still don't have to tell me anything from earlier if you don't want to."

Stef laced their fingers together on her lap. "That's the thing, I do want to, and I think it's important that you know."

Perse gripped Stef's hand more surely.

Stef nodded and took a deep breath. "Something happened when I visited Harry today. You know how I said my aunt used to live in the same complex as him?"

"Yes. Your aunt Carol and Harry were friends."

"Right. Well, someone found a shoebox of stuff in my aunt's old apartment and it made its way to Harry so he could to give it to me." Stef's eyes began to well up. "It was full of unopened mail from colleges addressed to Will."

Even Perse felt that ache. "No wonder you're upset."

"I . . . I buried the feeling so I could have a nice movie day with Harry, but then when I got home and starting really looking through them . . . It just hit me like, 'Here's Will's future in a box.' But the thing that my mind keeps coming back to is that I'll never know why my aunt kept them. I hate not knowing."

Perse held Stef more closely. She wasn't even sure whether it was to comfort Stef or herself. "I can understand why the not knowing is the worst part."

"Right? I hate that! And I can't ask anyone."

"Would Harry know?"

Stef shook her head. "Maybe. But . . . I didn't think to ask at the time. I was too . . . I don't know."

But Perse did know. "You were thrown." She tilted Stef's chin so she could look into her eyes. "You're allowed to not always have the perfect strategy or plan right off the bat. Is that how you would handle a question in your lab?"

"Hell no! I would gather all of my evidence, go to source materials, look at my resources, and go from there. Why did I . . . why couldn't I see that before?"

"Sometimes emotions prevent us from seeing the obvious."

"And when we wear a fake grin it doesn't help matters." Stef gave Perse a bittersweet smile. "I think Harry may have thought something was wrong, but I don't like being sad in front of people, so I did the stiff upper lip thing."

"Let's make a deal. When you're with me, you're allowed to feel however you like. Okay?"

Stef nodded. "I feel like I want to open the letters. Or is that weird? I think he got into all of the schools, but it seems wrong to go through his stuff."

"It's not wrong at all. I did that with Missy."

"You did not!"

"I did," Perse said with a chuckle. "I didn't think she'd get into her number one school, so I opened it hoping I could rub the rejection in her face, but she got in."

"That bitch."

Perse smiled, but then grew serious again. "I think whether opening the letters is wrong or not, it's all about intent. What do you hope to learn and what will you do with the information?"

As they sat together in each other's arms, Stef took a moment to think. "I'd like to tell him. I'm not religious at all, but I go to their headstones on New Year's Eve every year to talk to them. I can give them my year in review and tell him if he got in."

Warmth flooded Perse's chest and traveled through her whole being. "You're a beautiful person, Stefanie Blake."

Their kiss was more than their lips coming together for reassurance or pleasure. Perse, a polyglot who struggled with saying the words of how she felt, had to show Stef.

A round of applause and piercing wolf whistle from the doorway interrupted her display of affection. They quickly released each other and turned to look over the chaise.

Gillian winked at them. "Sorry to interrupt the girlfriend snogfest, but the fireworks will be going off soon. Then again, you kind of have your own going on in here, so maybe you'd rather stay."

"We'll be down in a few," Stef answered.

Gillian turned to leave, but stopped. "Oh, I won my money back, but Timera definitely had too much punch."

"I guess we'll be taking her home first," Perse said as she struggled to get out of the chaise's deep cushions. She stood and then turned to see Stef's stunned face. "What?"

"You didn't correct Gillian's use of the g-word?"

Perse grinned. Their relationship outline had prepared her well. "You're right, I didn't, because I knew this was coming. If memory serves, 'girlfriend' was the sublevel after people knew we were a couple. Now that we've conquered that, we have assumed weekend dates, even if that means takeout and falling asleep on the couch watching a movie. How am I doing?"

Stef beamed. "Your memory is spot on."

"I paid very close attention. Besides, you trusted me enough to share some very personal thoughts and feelings. Based on that alone, I'd say we're girlfriend-appropriate."

"Glad that's settled then." Stef smiled sweetly and led them out of the room. "Come on, I want to watch fireworks with my girl-friend."

***

"Thanks again for driving me home," Stef said as she unbuckled her seat belt.

"Thank *you* both for helping me get Timera back into her house!" Gillian said while she looked at her in the backseat. "That was a genius idea to put crackers right in front of her."

Perse shrugged, still a bit intoxicated herself. "I have some ex-perience."

"Hear that!" Stef yelled. She didn't have quite the Timera-level of alcohol in her system, but she was more than tipsy. "My girl-friend is experienced!"

Gillian gave them both a patient nod. "Perse, please see that your half-sloshed girlfriend gets into her house and has water by her bed."

Perse was more than happy to see that Stef was safe and had everything she needed at her bedside. "I can do that. Out of curi-osity, how much time do I have to accomplish this task?"

Gillian rolled her eyes. "You have ten minutes."

Perse giggled along with Stef all the way to the front door where Stef unlocked it quickly, and then turned to Gillian to give her a comical thumbs up.

Without warning, Stef pulled her inside and, once the door was shut, pinned her against it and devoured her. There was nothing gentle about her touches or kisses. Stef desired every inch of her.

The feeling was very mutual.

While Stef kissed, licked, and sucked the most sensitive skin at her neck, Perse took the small amount of cognitive ability she had left to relish what had turned out to be a spectacular evening. She and Stef had gone to a place beyond steps and outlines. They'd laughed, cried a bit, and their emotional connection had initiated a need inside her that was more powerful than simple sexual fulfillment.

Without warning, Stef backed her into the couch until she fell with her dress near her waist and Stef between her legs. Of course, Stef grabbed under her knee and hooked her leg up to drive their bodies closer.

Perse's brainpower teetered on empty while her hormones surged.

Stef stopped kissing down her cleavage and slinked back up to whisper in her ear, "I'm going to think of you when I'm in bed later."

Now that there were more clear boundaries, Perse liked Stef the Seductress. She was a tease of what Perse's future hopefully held. "What specifically about me are you—"

Gillian's horn blared from outside.

"No!" Perse groaned in frustration. "That couldn't have been ten minutes. I want a recount."

"It was, unfortunately," Stef said with her head hanging in defeat and in Perse's cleavage. She climbed off Perse and fell to the floor. "I might be a little tipsier than I thought."

Perse pushed her dress back down and stood. "That's why it's good we didn't drive and stopped canoodling when we did."

"Right? Things got super hot. Probably a good thing Gillian interrupted us too, or I'd be on my way to going dow—"

Gillian's horn blared again.

"Shit. You should go."

Perse mindlessly walked to the door as she imagined Stef following through with what she had suggested. Her laying on the couch, dress hiked up, and looking down to see subtle motions of a blond head between her thighs as Stef's tongue stroked her.

"I had a wonderful time tonight." Stef gave her a final, chaste goodbye kiss. "Sweet dreams."

"You too." Perse staggered back to Gillian's car in a sexual daze. She got in the passenger seat and stared ahead until Gillian started laughing. "What?"

"Look in the mirror."

Perse flipped the visor down and took her reflection in. She had the perfect just-been-fucked look without the actual sex.

"Did you at least make sure Stef got her water?"

"Um . . ."

"Bloody hell," Gillian murmured and drove her home.

CHAPTER TWELVE

PERSE READ THE same answer three times, and the words still didn't make sense. The answer wasn't poorly written, completely wrong, or possibly plagiarized from a nonsensical source. She just kept thinking about Stef.

The passionate goodbye they'd shared after Christopher's party resonated with her. It was both a blessing and a curse Gillian gave them limited time. There had been such tenderness, but the passion was undeniable.

Aside from their growing physical attraction, she knew the significance of the intense emotions she felt, which was still something Perse struggled to come to terms with. After a solid ten minutes of imagining different scenarios where she did or did not share her feelings with Stef, Perse closed her office door and called the relationship expert. "Hey! I have a situation."

"The beach was fun, thank you for asking," Missy said dryly. "Self-centered much?"

"You're right. I'm sorry. Tell me about your vacation."

"Gary and Alec have matching sunburns. Liz read every single moment we were there. And I went to the spa every other day where they had this drink called a fuzzy mimo, half-fuzzy navel and half-mimosa. It was fantastic. Now, this must be an emergency if you had to call me at work,"

"I always talk to you at work."

Missy whispered, "I just had to say that so people could hear. What's going on?"

Perse took several deep, cleansing breaths before she confessed. "Do you remember why Raquel broke up with me?"

"Of course I do. You poured your heart out when you had lunch with her and her sister. Then, she dumped you in the most terrifying way possible. My foot is still itchy from never being able to kick her in the ass. Why are you bringing Raquel up?"

"I love Stef."

"Holy shit! Really?"

"Yes. It hit me like some divine truth, but I don't know if Stef feels the same way, and I can't have a repeat of what happened with Raquel. I just can't."

"Divine truth? Where do you come up with this?" Missy asked rhetorically. "Look, even if Stef doesn't feel the exact same way, I bet she'll get there soon enough. And, unlike Raquel, Stef doesn't sound like a narcissistic, impressionable dipshit who would freak out. You can't let that one incident—"

"Isabella didn't handle it well when I told her either, but at least she somewhat got over it before Mom scared her away."

Perse certainly did have a tragic past with relationships. "She deserves a junk punch too. Anyway, my point is, you shouldn't let a few assholes sour your experience with Stef. Plus, you're a different person now. You want different things. Better things, if you ask me."

Missy's pep talk helped ease Perse's worries. "There's something else too. Stef and I had a really intense talk at a party, and, well, she is officially my girlfriend. And yes, I know I sound like a teenager."

"You do, but I know that's a big step for you. Mom will be ecstatic at the next brunch."

Perse groaned. "Why can't I just enjoy this time without endless questions and pressure from Mom? And don't roll your eyes, because I know that you're doing it."

"It's eye-rollable! When you love someone, even if you can't tell them that, it's a cause for celebration. Mom and Dad want to know that you're happy and keeping this from them is hurtful. It makes them—okay, Mom—think that you don't care enough about them to share your life."

Perse sighed. Missy always had the family perspective in mind. "I don't agree with that, but I'll take your point into consideration. This is something I need to ease into." The reminder alarm for the appointment she'd set began to ring.

"What's wrong? Did your burning bush catch your office on fire?"

Perse began to hurriedly get her bag. "In a way. I forgot about my blood test appointment. God, I hate needles."

"Yeah, you do. Try not to pass out."

***

Perse collapsed into her office chair after her three-hour class. She didn't think the culprit was her mild blood loss from earlier in the day, but she was willing to blame her phlebotomist anyway. Her low energy instantly rebounded when she saw a text from Stef.

I know you're teaching right now and probably won't read this until later, but I'm coming over to your office at 5:30.

Perse checked the time: 5:15. She thought about calling, but knowing Stef, she was already on her way to account for extra time spent navigating around a possible closed street or student stopping her along the way. Stef always planned for incidentals. Even if Stef's previous planning had never once included a visit to her office. And the fact that Stef didn't ask her permission first made it out of character.

At 5:30 sharp, a cup of herbal tea was paused at Perse's lips when she heard a light knock at her office door. She saw Stef's guilty grin and a large paper to-go bag with the logo from the Vietnamese place she had been dying to try but hadn't visited yet.

The pop-in was bizarre, but Perse still rounded her desk to give Stef a brief kiss. "You're up to something."

"I might not be."

"You have never once visited my office. Yet you are here, rather unexpectedly, with pho." Perse took off her glasses and leaned back against her desk. "What's going on?"

Stef's eyes lowered to where the bandaid at the crook of Perse's arm was. "So, you went?"

"What can I say? I know the rules. But I don't think checking my arm is why you came here."

"No, it's not. I got a call and it affects our plans for Saturday," Stef said with a grimace.

"No dinner on Saturday?" Perse asked with a whine that surprised even her. They were going to have a delicious meal, and then she was going to surprise Stef with a video of her favorite piano recital from college, and then fool around until the verge of orgasm. It was a good plan.

"Unfortunately, yes, but that's why I brought this." Stef gestured to the bag.

Perse hiked up her big girl pants—as Missy would say—and came to the conclusion that Stef must have a good reason. "What happened?"

"I thought a portion of my news would be best delivered face-to-face. Or at least, that's what Timera and Gillian advised me because of the . . . Well, how you might take some of the information."

"Timera and Gillian know?" Perse asked surprised, and much louder than she intended.

"Leave us out of this!" Gillian hollered in the distance.

Usually, Perse considered it a perk that her office was so close to the break room, but not at that moment. She'd have to keep her voice down.

Stef reached into the bag and gave Perse a pink box that was on top of the broth container and its separate fixings. "Here's some strawberry shortcake for you too."

Perse squinted suspiciously. No one randomly gave someone their favorite dessert. "Thank you. But I think I'll wait to eat until after you tell me what's going on."

Stef placed the bag down and began to gesticulate. "Here's the thing. The head coordinator for the conference called me and asked if I would co-lead a breakout session since the other person had an emergency. I said yes, so I need to leave earlier to meet with my co-presenter so we can discuss the logistics of everything."

That was far from the news she thought Stef was about to deliver. "You really had me going there. I mean, I'm disappointed I won't be able to see you, but this sounds like a pretty big deal. Do you know who the other presenter is?"

"It's my ex-wife, Mei."

"Oh," Perse said and crossed her arms.

"That's . . . unexpected."

"It is, and that's why I wanted to come and tell you in person. A text that read, '*I'm canceling our date to talk endotoxins with my ex in a hotel*,' could be misconstrued easily."

Perse nodded her agreement. Given her feelings toward Stef and her paranoia that Stef may not feel the same emotional intensity, a text like that would have driven her mad. "When do you need to leave?"

"Tomorrow afternoon. And because of your class and me needing to prep Bradyn to supervise the lab, I don't see us being able to see each other at all before I go. I'm really sorry, but I can't—"

"Pass up the opportunity. I know, and I understand. Trust me, I do. I just . . . I was really excited. I was going to bring the recital I was telling you about. The one where you can hear my mom and dad talking about making out to Led Zeppelin in the background." She was sure Stef's disappointed expression mirrored her own from a moment ago. "Don't worry. We can watch it some other time."

"Pinky swear?" Stef asked. When Perse extended hers, Stef locked her pinky in place for the unbreakable promise. Then Stef took her phone from her back pocket. "Can I get a picture of you before I go? Maybe with your glasses? You looked so studious and hot when I came in—Not that you don't look hot now. I just . . . I'd like to have some pictures with me when I'm gone."

Perse felt herself finally smiling from Stef's visit. "Anything that helps you remember your girl back home. But I might be able to do you one better." She knew so little about Stef's split from her ex-wife she had to ensure that if there was competition, she would win. Perse opened the lid to her dessert. "There's a lot of whipped cream in here."

Stef asked her to pose with books, a cardigan, and the whipped cream. When she suggested she lick her spoon in a sultry manner, Perse laughed and reminded Stef she was in her office.

"What in the hell are you two doing?" Gillian demanded to know from the door. "I have a student crying in my office. The laughter is distracting from the sadness."

"Sorry." Stef turned to her. "I'm getting pictures of my girl-friend so I don't forget her while I'm gone."

Gillian harrumphed. "You know, most people don't take pictures when they say goodbye to their burd. You have two minutes." Then, she reached in for the door handle and shut them in.

***

Missy peered out her office window in victory, like she had been since first thing that morning when her boss gave her the office. So long, cubicle! This was where she was meant to be. It even had its own thermostat.

She couldn't believe that the day before she'd had to pretend there was an emergency so she could talk to her sister.

Oh, what a difference a day made!

She returned to her desk and dialed in to start her last conference call of the day. No beeps indicated that no one was on the line. To make the best use of her time, she opened her internet browser to check out the latest in social media. "What the fuck?" She hung up the conference call and called her sister. "Why am I reading that Stef just checked into the airport?"

Perse sighed. "She had to leave early, but it's actually a good thing for her. They want her to help *someone* with presenting material."

Missy narrowed her eyes. She knew that annoyed, defeated tone. "What do you mean 'someone'?"

"Her ex-wife."

"No!" Missy immediately went to Stef's friend page. "Do you know her name?"

"Mei Ling. Why?"

"No reason." Missy conducted a search of her target. It was the same process she used to research the other soccer moms when Liz wanted to sleep over at a friend's house. In those cases, there was usually a woman in ill-fitting jeans. Now her search resulted in a stunning, yet fierce woman in a power suit staring her down. "Shit!"

"What's wrong?"

Missy scrolled through all of the different, but all gorgeous, profile pictures. What was the best way to tell her insecure sister that her current girlfriend's ex used to be Ms. Santa Barbara? "Nothing's wrong. I only went to Stef's page is all."

"Did she post those pictures she took of me?" Perse asked franticly.

"No," Missy answered with a laugh. "And what kind of pictures are you taking, young lady?"

"Nothing too risqué. It was an office photoshoot. I also got a couple of her too."

"I see," Missy said absently as she scrolled through more pictures. Mei receiving a science award. Mei being handed the keys to her new BMW. Mei wearing an outfit of only straps in a dance competition. "You might want to send Stef a risqué pic."

"Are you serious? Why?"

Was Mei's hair made of silk? "No specific reason. Now, I have to go. They like it when I do things at work."

"Wait! Can you do me a favor? I want to show Stef my favorite recital, but I think you have the tape because your bridal shower is also on it."

Missy sighed. The bridal shower she had on video, but the bachelorette party was what she wanted. "Yeah, I know exactly where it is."

"Great! Can you make a digital copy somehow? I want to show Stef when she gets back."

Missy knew the exact performance Perse meant. In it, Perse exuded sex on stage. That would definitely get Stef's attention. "Tell you what. I'll send it to you tonight."

"Wow . . . Um . . . thanks! Maybe Stef and I could watch it together as a long-distance activity?"

That would be weird. But, then again, so were academics. "That's a great plan!"

*　*　*

Perse knew her sister supported and cared for her, but she had no idea how much until she opened her email only a few hours later to see that Missy sent her a link to the recital. Between the piano performance and an additional picture Perse had taken of herself—not in her office, but definitely featuring her glasses—she hoped she could make Stef pine for her from afar.

At the agreed upon time, Perse called from bed, and Stef picked up after the first ring. "You wouldn't be waiting for a call, would you?" Perse asked in her deepest, sexiest voice.

"I was, but now that I'm talking to you, I think I'll stay on the line. I'd hate to be rude to . . . caller ID says you're Dr. Feelgood?"

Perse broke character and cackled into the phone. "It does not."

"It doesn't, but now I'm seriously considering changing it. How was your day?"

"Class went as well as I thought it would. But the highlight was that Missy did an absolutely wonderful favor that you may enjoy. How about you?"

"Nothing exciting to report. Typical flight and hotel check-in stuff, but my room here is really impressive. Full desk, chair with ottoman, squishy king-sized bed."

"Sounds very chic. Bathroom?"

"Also above average. But enough about my amenities, tell me about the favor. You've piqued my curiosity."

Perse already had her computer propped on her lap and the email cued. She clicked send. "I just sent you an email about it to your personal account."

"Hold, please."

Perse heard ruffling in the background, then the clicking of keys.

"I wonder what could be in my personal email that you wouldn't send over CB—Hello!"

Perse smiled victoriously from receiving her desired reaction for the picture. It featured herself from sexy smirk to torso, shirt unbuttoned to her bra with a pair of glasses hooked at the center. "I thought you might enjoy that."

"This is easily the best thing my eyes have seen all day. I'm sorry you don't have any pics like that of me."

"Oh, I do. I took one when you were walking away." She waited for Stef's laughter to cease before she moved on to the next item of the email. "Next on your list of entertainment: I want you to click on the link." Perse went to the public video site as well. She wasn't happy that anyone could view it, but at least Missy hadn't named her. Perse would have to live with *Nerdy Sister Unplugged.*

"Oh my God! Is this what you were going to show me?"

"It is. I was talking to Missy about it, and in true Missy fashion, she found a way to make it happen."

"Can I watch the video with you now?"

The pure enthusiasm in Stef's voice made Perse's heart melt. "I'd love to. Press play on the count of three so we can be in sync."

As they started the concert, Perse noticed the audio was poor and Alec running across the scene quickly followed that observation. *"Go play outside. But keep Dandy off the swings!"*

Both Perse and Stef laughed at the interruption. Now, Perse knew how the footage had been captured so quickly.

As they returned to their viewing of the classic rock-themed recital, Perse hoped that Stef was transfixed by the rock persona she'd created while on stage. She wore torn jeans, a Nine Inch Nails tee, and high, lace-up boots.

"You wouldn't by any chance still have that outfit, would you?" Stef asked innocently.

"I definitely have the shoes. I might have the shirt if Missy bothered to give it back to me, but those jeans are long gone. Even if I had them, I don't think they'd fit."

Stef uttered a *humph*. "I think you look better now. You look healthier."

"I do eat better and exercise."

"You weren't always health-conscious?"

Perse laughed. "Oh my God, no. In college, I lived off fast food and illicit substances just like most undergraduates."

"Really? You did a lot of drugs?"

"I don't know if I'd say 'a lot', but I did my fair share and experimented with ways to manage my anxiety."

"But you don't do that anymore, right?"

Perse cringed at Stef's judgmental tone. "I do when it makes sense. I used drugs or alcohol as a tool when I was researching abroad. They were of great ceremonial importance, and since participating made me much less of an outsider, they were a way for people to talk to me in a way they don't with others. I have to say it led to some of my more well-received papers."

"Interesting," Stef whispered. "Which drugs have you done?"

Perse blew out a quick exhale. She didn't know where to start. "It's probably easier just to say I've stayed away from anything manufactured or intravenous."

"You've used cocaine?" Stef asked in a pitch much higher than normal.

Perse hated this, but the truth was important. "Not in the 'doing lines off a mirror' sense, more in the 'medicinal and spiritual' sense of drinking tea from the leaves."

Stef muttered something that Perse couldn't decipher. "But now that you're not traveling, you won't use anything, right?"

She knew Stef couldn't see her bobbing her head back and forth as she considered her options. "When I'm in the states I stick to marijuana and mushrooms—possibly peyote—and only with people I trust."

"How about since you've been back?"

"Missy and I ate pot brownies for her birthday. Don't worry, we didn't eat the entire pan. Her neighbor makes them and sells them individually. Most of the ones she bought are in her freezer."

Stef's mute state on the other end of the phone troubled her.

"Stef?"

"Oh, I'm here. I was listening and trying to figure out the song but there's a lot of background noise. Wait . . . is your family talking?"

The change in subject relieved her and she was more than happy to tell Stef the story of the recital. In the surprise visit, her mom and dad had flown across the country and Missy had taken the train for the event. They revealed themselves at the post-recital party, customarily reserved for the performers and stage crew. She didn't learn until later that her family had watched her do a spirited performance of 'Stairway to Heaven'.

A performance, based on the sighs and gulps, Stef found sexy.

"You are so much more fun to watch than Led Zeppelin," she said dazedly. "Think you could play that for me sometime? Maybe wearing your glasses?"

Perse grinned slyly. "Do you want me to only wear my glasses?"

"You're the artist, and I respect any way you choose to conduct your performances."

"Nice save."

The performance came to a close and Stef gave her a round of applause.

"So, you liked watching this? It wasn't too boring?"

"Are you kidding? It was awesome, and watching it with you like this was fun. Easily the best part of my day."

"It wasn't seeing Mei?" The question was petty, but Perse needed to know.

"You can't see me cringing, but I am. It was . . . weird. I just don't understand her. She's engaged to the director of the conference, which is why I was called to begin with. She recommended me! Anyway, I don't see how she could go from being married to me to essentially marrying Harry."

"Do I sense a bit a biphobia?"

"Not phobic. I just don't get it."

"Well, emotions aren't rational. I know when I've"—she couldn't say love—"been attracted to others, it's the person, not the gender."

"That's something I've been waiting to ask. I've brought up my exes here and there, but you've never mentioned anything about your past relationships."

Perse wanted to bring the conversation about drug use back. Anything was better than talking about her exes. "No, I guess I haven't, but there isn't much to say. They all ended. They all hurt. But I moved on."

"Aw." Stef sounded genuinely sorry for her. "How many would you say were serious?"

"Three: Raquel, Isabella, and Anthony." She didn't want to disclose any more details, but maybe if she opened up gradually, she could stave off what otherwise would lead to an anxiety attack. "I'd probably feel better if I was the one who ended any of them."

"They all broke up with *you*?" Stef asked, amazed. "Just how stupid were they?"

"You sound like Missy—except without the threats of violence," Perse said with a sad smile. "The last one, Anthony, was really, really tough to move on from."

"You must have really loved him."

"Um, actually . . . that wasn't the reason—I mean, I did love him, but . . . it wasn't why the end hurt so bad." Even now, Perse thought she sounded pathetic.

"You don't have to talk about it anymore if you don't want to."

Perse looked up and praised the powers that be. "Thank you. I can already sense that I'm on the verge of a cold sweat."

"It's okay. You can tell me more whenever you're ready." Stef really was too good to be true.

"How about you and Mei? What's the story there? If you feel comfortable telling me."

"It's no problem talking about it. I was a post-doc in her lab. Kind of scandalous in retrospect. Despite some red flags, we got married, and a few years later, when my uncle died and Aunt Carol needed help, I made a decision. I filed for separation and left."

"What were the red flags?"

"She was always choosing work, her friends, or her competitions, over me. I got to the point where I realized we were never going to be the family I wanted us to be. Of course, it didn't help that her family never accepted me."

Perse remembered what Missy had said about Stef wanting a family. "It's true that when you marry someone you marry everything and everyone they're associated with."

"Yep. And her family never liked me, or at least they didn't like that I was a woman. Now, I guess Mei won't have that problem."

A silence fell between them. Perse could sense that Stef had accepted the events but had never really gotten over it. They had more in common in that regard than she had thought.

"I kind of made a joke about it when we were at Christopher's party, but it hurts when someone you care about is, in some way, ashamed of you," Stef softly said. "It really means a lot that people at work and your sister already know about me. About our relationship."

Perse was glad she wasn't standing or else she may have wavered from the emotion in Stef's voice. "I'm glad you feel that way. Missy's my best friend, so I have to share with her what makes me happy. You fall into that category."

"That's . . ." Stef inhaled deeply. "I should let you get to bed."

While it wasn't her favorite topic of conversation, the abrupt stop concerned her. "Are you okay?"

"Yeah, it's just been a long day, and it's even later where you are. You probably want to hit the sack since it's a school night."

Perse smiled. "I've actually been in bed with you this entire time."

"Really? I suppose this is our first time in bed together. No, never mind. I forgot about the time before Christopher's party when you sat with me in that sexy dress."

"If it makes you feel better, I'm wearing much less clothing than I was then."

"You know . . . funny thing. We never established any rules about phone sex."

Perse laughed until her sides hurt. "Very true and an interesting point. How do you feel about phone sex, Dr. 'I'm-going-to-think-about-you-later-when-I'm-in-bed'?"

"I didn't think I said that out loud."

"Oh, you definitely did, because it's what I thought about when I was in bed later." There was a long pause on the other end. "Stef?"

"I'm here. It's just that I went to a very special mental place for a moment."

Perse smiled. "I'm *very* sorry my story was so boring you had to daydream. Would you like to share with the rest of the class what you were thinking about?"

"I think that maybe I'll share later because doing so right now might create more . . . tension."

Perse's smile turned into a satisfied smirk. "Well, you know what's good for tension, don't you?"

"Yoga?" Stef asked unsurely.

Perse burst into laughter again. "Yes, yoga is very good for relieving tension." She shook her head in amusement at their behavior. She didn't want to end the call, but she knew she had to. "A good night's sleep also helps."

"Are you trying to get us out of the hole we dug for ourselves?"

"Pretty much. I also want you to be well rested to impress the crowds with your research."

"You're right," Stef said with a heavy sigh. "Sleep well, Perse. Goodnight."

"Goodnight, Stef."

CHAPTER THIRTEEN

THE THREATENING CUMULONIMBUS cloud in the distance reminded Perse of herself. Inside her was an accumulation of energy so powerful, she felt the crackling and potential for electricity about to burst from her center.

She stopped at the light on her way to Stef's and gripped the steering wheel with white knuckles. She took a calming breath, followed by a drink of water. She had lasted two months without sex. She could last another two. She was not an animal. It didn't matter that her STI test came back clean and Stef knew. There would be no full-on sex until Stef was ready.

She respected that.

It just would have been helpful if every random moment in the past week hadn't reminded her of sex. A mattress squeak. A hip-opening yoga pose. A sexy song.

Perse reached for the power button and shut off the radio. The slow, steady beat of the R&B station did not help her cause to calm herself. To refocus her energies, she pondered the emotional aspects of their relationship.

No sex thoughts allowed.

During their week away from each other, the text messages about classes, posters, and life in academia were sweet and safe. Perse discussed her search for a new apartment. Stef reported that everything at the conference went better than expected. She even believed she would be contacted in the future to collaborate on a few papers, which should ensure a tenure position in the next cycle. During that conversation, Stef fessed up about her mild jealousy over Wayne, but Perse held her tongue.

Tongues. Tongues had so many uses.

She took another swig of cold water, even though what she really needed to do was pour it over her crotch. However, that would only lead to her needing to take off her pants, and that defeated the entire point of trying to keep her clothes on. She hadn't even given in when Stef had started to steer their late-night talks into something sexual. They veered away from phone sex, but they were not without innuendo or provocation. A reference to the pay-per-view porn at the hotel. An extra-long shower that was hot and steamy. And, Perse's personal favorite, a stylized, black-and-white selfie of Stef in her business suit with her hair mussed and tie loosened.

She wore a fucking tie.

Perse didn't think Stef was actually trying to kill her with that one, but her breath was taken away. And that was the only reason she sought revenge. So, for their date, she wore an outfit that, according to Missy, was sure to get a reaction.

Perse parked under the carport and completed one final item on her to-do list: she put on her glasses. When she stepped out of her Jeep with a bottle of chilled wine, the wind swirled around her, which placed her perfectly arranged updo in disarray.

After she knocked, Stef's muffled voice and running steps made Perse smile in a way she hadn't since Stef had left town. The loud approach also caused Perse to stand straighter, so the snug tee was presented well.

A little teasing was allowed.

Stef opened the door. "Hi, y—woah."

"I thought you might like this outfit." Perse giggled as Stef took in her outfit of black, lace-up boots, fitted jeans, and an aged Nine Inch Nails shirt. Perse marveled over how adorable Stef was when she was rendered mute. But she understood Stef's predicament, because Stef had chosen a perfect outfit of a burgundy halter and jean capris to showcase her sexy, girl-next-door attitude. "In order to start our evening, you kind of have to invite me in."

"Sorry about that. You look really hot," Stef said as she moved to the side and gave Perse a small kiss as she crossed the threshold.

"There're a few things I need to tell you before our evening commences."

Stef's tone was serious. Perse put the wine on the nearest table and went to her.

Stef took Perse's hands in her own and brought them to her chest. "I was thinking this morning about us and how patient you've been with some of my ridiculousness, including, but not limited to, my levels, and rather bawdy texting while I was gone."

Perse's brow raised in delight. "As long as you admit they were edging into forbidden territory. Especially that picture! As far as the levels, we've talked about it. I understand and accept. Besides, I'll be the first to admit that not having certain . . . distractions when we're together has allowed me to get to know you much better."

"And you still like me? Even after getting to know me better?"

Love would be the more appropriate word, but she wasn't going there. "More and more every day."

"Likewise," Stef said and kissed Perse.

What started as a few brief, playful touches of their lips turned into firmer contact, not just with their mouths, but their whole bodies.

Stef's hands snuck just underneath Perse's t-shirt and brought her closer. As Perse felt trim nails over her skin and Stef's tongue enter her mouth, her body temperature rose and her wetness began to build. She could handle some sexual frustration at the end of the night, but not for the entire date. She moved her hands to Stef's waist and subtly added distance between them. "Stef, I think we . . ." She couldn't make it sound like rejection. "I feel . . ."

"My test came back negative and I'm very ready to have sex if you are."

"Yes. Please. Now." Perse seized her lips while Stef crushed their bodies together against the wall. Considering Stef was the shorter of the two, she used her leverage well. The pressure of their intertwined legs caused Stef to gasp and Perse to moan.

This wasn't gentle discovery. Stef seemed to need her as much as she needed Stef. Months of flirting, weeks of yearning, and days of building sexual tension snapped inside of her—and apparently Stef—at once.

A flash of lightning and almost simultaneous thunder went ignored. "Bedroom?" Stef mumbled into Perse's lips while her hands cupped each ass check to drive her closer.

"Please," Perse said breathlessly.

Stef guided Perse by her belt loops out of the small foyer and to her bedroom.

Perse's arousal increased as Stef asserted herself as the sexual aggressor. She really was a top. Stef's fingers inched under her shirt and up her ribcage before pulling it up and off. Perse's heavy breaths caused her breasts to strain against her bra.

"Just gorgeous." Stef openly admired her chest.

Perse used the distraction to strip Stef of her halter. She moved down to kiss the top of Stef's breasts while she squeezed each and rubbed her thumbs over Stef's hardened nipples. Perse felt slight tugs to her hair and her updo fell as her mouth teased Stef.

"You have no idea how much I want you." Stef moved her hands from Perse's thick hair to her belt.

"You can have all of me," Perse replied as she was steered toward the bed. She hadn't even noticed that her bra was unclasped and jeans were already undone when they fell into a heap of tangled limbs.

Stef was efficient. And that was something Perse appreciated.

"Tell me if I'm going too fast," Stef said from above her before she slid down and pulled Perse's nipple into her mouth.

Perse gasped and fumbled to throw her own loose bra to the side. Something hard in Stef's pocket ground against her throbbing sex while she watched Stef's tongue circle around her darker skin. "Fast is good. We can have slow sex later," Perse said and made short work of Stef's bra.

"Glad to hear we're on the same page." Stef traveled lower to remove Perse's boots. After several jerks, Stef grunted in frustration. "Are these triple knotted?"

Perse already felt as if she would explode. Her skin was on fire and, before her, Stef kneeled in all her toned, topless glory. She couldn't wait for Stef to untangle her laces. "Don't worry about it. Just get my jeans."

Boots still on, Perse lifted her hips as Stef pushed down her jeans as far as they would go and then stood to remove her own. Perse didn't care if she looked ridiculous with her pants around her ankles; she sat up and pulled Stef onto the bed, then rolled them over.

Stef's body writhed beneath her as Perse ground her hips into Stef's center, licked her neck, and caressed her stomach and thighs.

It wasn't nearly enough.

Her thumbs hooked under Stef's burgundy bikini briefs and paused. Was this what Stef really wanted? But Stef used Perse's brief moment of reflection to flip their positions. "How did you do that?" Perse panted, turned on even more by Stef's strength and agility.

Stef grinned devilishly and lightly traced the teal-blue ouroboros hip tattoo that peaked above and below Perse's thong. "Leverage," Stef whispered and kissed her again.

Lips, tongues, and teeth. Perse poured all of herself into the kiss. Instead of her first time with Stef, the energy and passion felt more like their last. She was desperate for more and couldn't wait any longer. "Please," Perse begged and guided Stef's hand under the small triangle of fabric.

Stef licked along her ear and slid her fingers through her. "You feel amazing. I've wanted to touch you for the longest time."

The light strokes against her sex caused Perse to raise her hips and bring Stef's mouth to hers. Stef surrounded her, but she wanted more. She wanted Stef inside, filling her with powerful thrusts. The thought alone made more blood rush to where Stef's skilled fingers focused, and what had been a rhythmic throb quickly turned into a slight tension.

Perse recognized the sign immediately. She was seconds from orgasm and hadn't even had the chance to touch Stef. She tried to dial back her physical sensations by focusing on a smudge on the wall, but the surprise pinch of her nipple brought the drumming of her loins back. She a needed time-out. "Please . . . I want . . . Oh—oh!" Heat radiated from where Stef touched her and her back bowed off the comforter as an involuntary and deep moan started inside of her and left her mouth in a quick release as she climaxed.

Stef stilled her hand but kept it in place. "Wow," she drawled in amazement.

Completely mortified, Perse hid her face, which knocked her glasses askew. Premature orgasm had never happened to her before. She hadn't even known it *could* happen. She would have considered running away had her legs not still been bound by her jeans. "I'm so sorry. I was just so turned on and I've been thinking about this for months. It just snuck up on me."

Stef was still wide-eyed but removed her hand from inside Perse's underwear. "Please don't apologize." She took Perse's crooked glasses and put them on the nightstand, and then leaned down and gave Perse a comforting kiss. "Yes, that was unexpected, but it was still super hot."

"Really?"

Stef nodded enthusiastically.

"But I didn't even have the chance to touch you."

"I'm still here and I have nowhere to go."

The sound of torrential rain came through the window and a patient, lovely, and mostly naked woman was leaning on her elbow and looking down at her adoringly. Any remaining embarrassment disappeared when Stef lowered her body onto Perse's and kissed her again.

"Nowhere to go, huh?" Perse traced the area where Stef's panties met the skin of her hip. She pushed the garment down until they were just underneath Stef's buttocks.

Stef took the liberty of removing them and went to the bottom edge of the bed to attempt to remove Perse's boots once more. "If I'm naked, you're naked. It's only fair."

"I'll do one shoe if you do the other." Perse sat up and her fingers took on the task of unknotting her shoes. The first came off easily. It wasn't that hard since she had longer fingernails. *Shit.* "We may have a logistical problem. I wasn't expecting this so I didn't trim my nails," Perse admitted while Stef removed her jeans and socks.

"No worries. There are lots of other ways." Stef hooked her fingers in Perse's underwear but didn't move any further. "If you weren't expecting this, why'd you wear a thong?"

"I usually wear thongs."

"You just keep getting hotter," Stef said and removed the tiny article of clothing from her body. "So fucking sexy," she murmured and began to kiss Perse's calf. Then, moved up to her knee.

Was Stef about to do what she thought?

"Stef, I want to touch you too."

"I promise you will . . . eventually." Stef grinned as she kissed farther up Perse's inner thigh, causing her legs to spread farther apart.

"Not that I don't want you to, it's just you should get a t—Oh, God!" Every nerve ending woke up as Stef's tongue licked a path between Perse's legs.

"Does that feel good? Or are you still too sensitive?"

"Um." With Stef's hot breath on her she could barely think. Not to mention that not even fifteen minutes ago she was sitting in her car trying to curb her libido. There was so much happening so fast. And words were still very hard to form.

Stef continued to kiss her thigh and use her short nails to lightly scratch at Perse's knees. "Do you not like oral sex?"

That was a terrible thing for Stef to think! Perse found her voice. "Oh no! I love it!"

"Good," Stef murmured, "because that's one of my top three fantasies." Then, she flattened her tongue against Perse.

Perse shuttered from the heavenly sensation between her legs and surrendered to her desire. "Then I'd hate to deny you the opportunity . . ."

***

The vision before Perse's eyes as she woke was leagues better than what she would have seen driving to family brunch. Although, she did feel bad for Missy that brunch was cancelled because of a tournament.

Before her, Stef still slept peacefully. Her blond hair stood out against the evergreen sheets like a halo. Her eyelashes began to flutter as though she were dreaming. Maybe that was why Stef also had a small smile on her lips.

Perse contemplated that idea as Stef's eyelashes suddenly stopped their movement and slowly opened. She smiled and lazily reached up to stroke Perse's cheekbone with her thumb. "Good morning . . . again."

Hours earlier Perse had woken to answer the call of nature; however, her attempt to crawl back into bed undetected had failed. Stef had demanded that Perse make amends for abandoning her and for disrupting a dream where she told off Wayne. Perse made up for her absence in spades, which caused them to fall asleep in each other's arms for a second time.

"Think we'll actually get up this time?" Perse asked with a grin.

"Do we have to? It might not be that late." Stef shot a quick glance to the bra-covered alarm. She moved the garment in question to reveal a blinking *12:00.* Stef gasped. "Our sexual union was so powerful, we were able to knock out the power. We're biological weapons! Sexy, biological weapons."

Perse never recalled laughing so much or being so at ease the morning after a first time. Stef had such a playful spirit, but there were moments when everything around her fell away so she could have laser focus.

It was so easy to love her. And so difficult not to tell her, especially after Stef had given her the present from Phoenix, late last night.

After Stef had had her first orgasm of the evening, Perse had left to get wine and two glasses. When she'd come back into the bedroom, Stef had been digging through the jeans she'd discarded and had pulled out a palm-sized box.

Perse unwrapped a polished azurite necklace. It wasn't the most lavish piece of jewelry, but Stef explained when she'd seen the disc of blues and greens swirled together, she'd known it was meant for Perse. Apparently, such a beautiful stone should be worn by a beautiful woman.

Now, Perse touched the stone that lay between her breasts and watched Stef drift to her thoughtful place as she lay next to her. She lovingly tapped the freckle at Stef's temple. "What's going on up there?"

Stef's stomach rumbled. "What she said."

"I guess our dinner of cheese crackers and grapes didn't really provide enough calories given our activity level."

"For the record, I offered a fancy dinner, and you declined." Stef lightly touched Perse's nose to make her point.

Perse grinned. "Well, I think breakfast now would be a good idea so we can fuel ourselves up for later."

"Very logical," Stef said and gave her a kiss before getting out of bed. Her perfect ass walked away to her chest of drawers and Stef took out several items of clothing. "While naked kitchen fantasy is in my top ten, I do want you to be comfortable."

Perse sat up in bed and chuckled to herself.

"What?" Stef asked with a grin as she pulled on a new pair of underwear with a wiggle.

"This morning is very different than how I thought it would be yesterday. It's much, much better."

"Better than brunch?"

"Without question."

Stef leaned down and gave her a kiss. "Speaking of food, get dressed and meet me in the kitchen. I'm starving."

Perse raised her hand in a small salute. When Stef left the room, she pushed her well-rested body out of the bed and stretched her arms, enjoying the warmth and looseness that followed. The best night's sleep she had in ages had come to a close and it was time to start a new day.

They both pattered about the kitchen in oversized t-shirts as they worked as a team to prepare breakfast. Stef was on toast and egg duty while Perse sliced a cantaloupe. Perse lamented over the juice that ran over the cutting board when her phone rang.

"You look sticky," Stef said. "Want me to get that?"

"Let it go to voicemail. Probably a robodial."

After her phone rang again, Perse relented. "Okay, would you mind telling me who's calling?"

"Sure." Stef walked over to the ringing phone. "No name is showing up, it's an unknown cell phone number."

She knew no one with a new number. However, there was one unfortunate possibility. "Do you mind answering it while I wash my hands? The call could be someone I know being held by immigration."

"Seriously?" Stef asked alarmed.

Perse nodded.

Stef answered the call in her most professional voice, "Hello, this is Stefanie Blake answering on behalf of Persephone Teixeira. Who may I ask is calling?"

"Um, that would be Persephone's sister, Artemis Teixeira-Manners. Am I on her list of people she'll accept calls from?" Missy tiny tin voice asked with clear joy.

Perse rolled her eyes as she dried her hands.

"I'm going to let Persephone answer that." Stef handed the phone to Perse and whispered, "It's Missy."

Perse took the phone. When she it to her ear, she heard Missy cackling on the other end. "You have a new phone number. That's exciting."

"You are *so* not changing the subject. I just spoke to your girlfriend. A girlfriend that I'm guessing, based on the time of day, you may have slept with. Oh, the kids can't hear anything: get over it."

Perse ignored the fact that Missy spoke at full volume in, what sounded like, a soccer stand and focused on the fact that her sister had spoken to Stef. They'd shared words. Perse sat on the couch before her breathing became even more irregular. "Is that why you called me? To find out if we did . . . that."

"No! Although, that is a definite perk. I called you initially because I wanted you to have my new mobile work number, but I called you a second time because I didn't leave a voicemail saying it was me and also that soccer is torturous. Oh, it is too!" Missy sighed dramatically. "Sorry, *someone* disagrees with me."

Perse used a mental image of jagged cliffs along a shoreline as a focal point and found the rhythm with her breaths. "Well, now I have your new number. Thanks for call—"

"No, no, no, wait! I was given a work cell because, since I'm the PM, I'm going to be doing site visits, which includes one near you in two weeks. I'll be there for like three days. We have to get together for dinner, and you should definitely invite Stef along."

Perse glanced over her shoulder to see Stef meticulously arranging the breakfast table. "That seems soon."

"For Christ's sake, this isn't China pattern selection with Mom and Dad, it's dinner and drinks with your best friend. I think you're at a point where that's acceptable."

The look Stef directed at her from the kitchen was so full of delight she had no choice in her answer. "Fine. But if this goes south . . ."

"It won't. Now, stop being such a pussy and ask her."

Perse dropped the phone from her ear. "Stef, would you like to have dinner and drinks with my sis—"

"Yes!" As if her answer wasn't clear enough, Stef also smiled and nodded.

Perse heard Missy laugh again. "I guess you heard her answer."

"I did and I'm so excited. Oh, and I also need to tell you because of Dad's fishing trip next weekend, we're just going to do the next brunch in August. Got it?"

"That works for me." Perse watched as Stef bent over to pick up a dropped napkin. "I'm sure I can think of something else to do that day."

"I bet you will. Oh, and Perse, I told you she'd like that outfit."

CHAPTER FOURTEEN

PERSE HAD SHARED meals with her sister literally thousands of times as adults. And she had now shared some of the most intimate aspects of herself with Stef. Individually they both made Perse comfortable. But the idea of the three of them together caused her fine sheen of perspiration to develop into a full on sweat.

Stef was about to meet not only Perse's best friend, but also her sister. Her family. No one she was involved with had met her family since Anthony abandoned her all those years ago. Perse tried to play down the significance but couldn't. This casual meeting of drinks and dinner brought back the shame and humiliation from over fifteen years prior.

Perse stood inside the entrance of the bayside restaurant and regretted not taking something stronger than a gummy. The experience overwhelmed her, but she reminded herself that she was physically and emotionally closer to Stef now. She had to go through with dinner. It would hurt Stef too much not to, and maybe it would work out?

"This will be so fun!" Stef bounced as she said it. "On the off-chance things get weird, I can make an early exit."

Perse took a deep breath and promised to keep positive thoughts. Stef was lovely and Missy could keep a conversation going with a corpse. Plus, Missy had snagged an outdoor table on a gorgeous evening. Everything would be fine. "You're right. I'm being silly. Nothing to be nervous about. This'll be great."

"It will!"

As Perse walked onto the restaurant's deck, she felt most of her stress melt away. The air she breathed was salty and clean. Small yachts and powerboats skimmed the sea in the distance. A heron flew and then dove for a fish. And the breeze helped tame the August heat.

The natural beauty of the scenery helped tame her anxious thoughts.

Missy was at one of the dozen teak dining tables. She wore her typical dark sunglasses and sat peacefully while she sipped her water and admired the view.

Perse waved with her hand held high. "Missy!"

Missy turned in the direction of her name and immediately rushed toward them. "Ladies!"

Perse received the first enthusiastic hug. "Thanks for meeting us down here," she whispered into her sister's ear. "Please, be nice."

Missy wasn't as concerned with volume. "Of course I'll be nice. Stef, would it be weird if I hugged you?" she asked and then wrapped her arms around Stef. The hug evolved into a small dance. "Sorry if I squeezed too hard. You just have no idea how happy I am to meet you in person."

Stef was grinning. "Likewise. You can only learn so much about someone while stalking their social media page."

"So true!" Missy laughed, which caused the last of the tension Perse felt in her shoulders to relax. "Well, let's get some liquid refreshments." Missy waved the drinks menu in front of them. "This is a catalog of entertainment and bad decisions. I love it! Is there any one drink you're a fan of, Stef?"

"They infuse their own vodkas, so the martinis are very good, but they're also strong."

Missy scanned the bar menu. "Good to know since I have to be at the site at seven tomorrow morning. The contractor couldn't get the calendar invite for the meeting correct. Such an idiot, do you know what I mean?"

"Oh, I know. There's this guy Wayne and—"

"Oh boy," Perse said. "Fasten your seat belt, Missy. You're about to hear quite the legend."

"Uh," Stef said, disgusted. "He's not a legend. He's the bane of my existence."

"I'm just saying . . . maybe you should give him another chance," Perse suggested.

Stef snorted in obvious disagreement.

Missy shook her head with a sappy grin. "You two . . . Wow."

"What?" Perse asked.

"Don't worry about it. Stef, tell me about Wayne."

"At best, he's a mediocre researcher who was given tenure over me last year just because he inflates his students' grades so he gets better evaluations. And don't even get me started on his poor planning or his golfing bromance with the department chair."

"Tell me more," Missy said and hesitated. "About the bromance. The other stuff doesn't seem as juicy."

Perse could tell through Missy's body language that she thoroughly enjoyed Stef's summary of her nemesis. The conversation of CBU led to martinis and a larger discussion about the current college experience versus their own. Stef described her move to California for undergraduate. And Missy took the wheel to talk about her and Perse's weekend visits when Missy had been at college in New York.

Missy sipped her drink. "I haul my ass all the way down to Philly because I think she's been caught with pot or is pregnant. Maybe even both."

"God, this is embarrassing." All Perse could do was find solace in her spiced martini.

"So, I go down there, in winter mind you, to find out what the hell is wrong because she was so vague and kept changing the subject on the phone. So, she meets me at the train station, we go back to her dorm room, and the answering machine is blinking. She presses the button to play her message, and that's when I heard it." Missy sat up straighter, excited by her own story. "I'll never forget this perky voice saying, 'It's Tash. I have the house to myself this weekend. Come over and let's fool around.' And that's how I found out Perse was into ladies too."

"Wow," Stef drawled and looked over to Perse, who hid behind her large martini glass.

"I know!" Missy slapped her armrests.

"What did you do?" Stef asked Missy.

"I screamed, 'You're not a total dork!' or something like that and gave her a hug. Then I asked her all kinds of questions—some might say inappropriate questions, but I'm inquisitive. The end."

"Aw." Stef rubbed Perse's knee. "That's sweet—the supportive sister bit, that is. I don't care for this Tash very much," Stef added with mock seriousness. "Now, on an unrelated note, I'm off to the ladies' room." She stood, turned to Perse, and placed a hand on her shoulder. "If our server comes by, can you please get me the crabby BLT and a water? I'm feelin' the wobbles."

"Sure thing, sweetie."

Missy watched until Stef turned the corner, then took off her sunglasses to expose the smile that reached her eyes. "Oh my God."

Perse fidgeted nervously. "What do you think?"

"She is perfect! I adore her. And you were right, she does have the most perfect ass on the planet."

Perse breathed a huge sigh of relief. Not only was dinner going as well as it possibly could, but Missy had also given her seal of approval. "I thought you would get along with her, but there's always that seed of doubt. I'm really, really glad you like her."

"Not like, love. She's different from the other people you've been serious about. She's much less pretentious."

"I don't go for pretentious."

"Ha! Whatever, Dr. Vanilla Cardamom Martini."

Perse thought of the three past loves of her life and how the outside world could have perceived them. "Fair enough. I agree that Stef doesn't fit that mold."

"Right?" Missy exclaimed. "She obviously has taste and is crazy smart, but she doesn't rub any of that stuff in. Unlike Mr. I-Play-First-Chair-Clarinet or Ms. Harvard-Wind-Farm. No! Sorry, it was solar power. I remember when she went on and on about PV cells when all I wanted was for her to pass the salt at dinner."

Perse sipped her martini. Some of Stef's quirks were completely ridiculous but in the best of ways: her need to use timers for almost every task, the fact she had an emergency veterinarian's number on speed dial, just in case she stumbled upon a hurt animal, and Stef's insistence she have all of Perse's favorite snacks and teas available for when she stopped by or, more recently, slept over.

"Oh, look at you in your faraway land of happy rainbows," Missy said in a cartoonish voice. "You have it so bad! Just tell her that you love her already so I can start my diet to be your maid-of-honor."

Perse coughed on her martini. She stared at Missy in horror while her throat burned. "What? No. That's . . .You're . . . No. I am not ready for that kind of conversation. I just want to enjoy this time."

"Of hot sex and no commitments?"

Missy's bluntness had a way of turning Perse's stomach. "Don't say it like that. I'm too afraid to make it more than girlfriend-level right now. Once we've been together another few months, I'll start considering it."

Missy shook her head. "I don't get you. You'll plan to be with her, and only her, for the rest of the calendar year, but won't take that next step? That will hurt her and you know it." Missy leaned across the table. "I know you've built those emotional walls inside of you so high that they won't allow you to be happy, but you *have* to start eroding them, or else they will destroy any possible future with Stef."

Perse lowered her head. "I know and I'm trying. She knows some of my past, but it's so hard to get all of it out in the open. I feel like if I tell her she'll understand their reasons or think I'm a headcase for blowing it out of proportion. I don't know how to tell her everything."

"Well, maybe Stef can help you figure that out. And speaking of Stef, look who's back."

Stef sat down with an exaggerated flop. "What did I miss?"

"Oh, not much except that Perse's back teeth are floating. Right?" Missy asked while she stared at her sister. "Isn't it sweet that she didn't want to leave me alone?"

"I don't mind keeping Missy company," Stef said with a pleasant and tipsy grin. "Go ahead."

Perse glared at her sister and stood. "I guess I'll be right back." She kept her cool as she walked into the restaurant. She should have expected Missy to pull a stunt like that, but it was a blessing in disguise. She really did have to pee.

She found a vacant stall and shook her head at her own behavior. She didn't understand why she allowed herself to become so worked up. She knew her sister well enough that she wouldn't tell Stef her secrets. Missy was a vault once she knew something. Of course, once she was given permission to talk, she was a volcano of truths.

Stef could explain herself if Missy asked something too personal. She was a rational person and Perse trusted her to provide rational answers. Plus, Stef and Missy had hit it off immediately. They were the same age. They were both STEM-minded. And they both loathed incompetence.

Perse washed her hands and then headed back. She heard Missy from several tables away. "And I'll tell you something else, I put my foot down at two hundred bucks for soccer pictures."

"I see that you're ranting about that again," Perse said with humor as their plates were set down. "Did I miss anything other than soccer complaints?"

Stef shook her head. "Nothing unexpected."

Perse darted her eyes to her sister. "You threatened her?"

"Just a little bit." Missy smiled and popped a chip into her mouth. "Hardly counts. Remember what you told Gary?"

"I was eighteen! And it wasn't a threat."

"What did she say?" Stef asked enthusiastically.

Missy tilted her bead back and cackled again. "Okay, I agree with Perse that it wasn't a threat, but it still scared him shitless. She"—Missy took a moment to compose herself—"quoted some obscure poem about love."

"Shakespeare's sonnets are not obscure."

Stef sat straighter. "Do you remember what you said?"

If I should think of love

I'd think of you, your arms uplifted . . .

Perse remembered the sonnet well, but to quote it was too close to reciting the line to Stef. "I don't remember which one."

Stef skewed her mouth in disappointment, but quickly recovered and asked Missy, "How did you and Gary meet?"

As they ate their dinners, Missy was more than happy to recount Gary's persistent, but not creepy, courting efforts. Perse filled in the gaps of their fairytale wedding since Missy had been a nervous wreck and didn't remember most of it. Which was not the same reason why she had no memory of her bachelorette party. To complete the story of the Manners' family, Missy proudly opened her wallet to show pictures of their two children.

Missy reached across the table and handed last year's school portraits to Stef. "That's Liz, and she is a carbon copy of Perse and me at that age. Except, you know, she has my eyes instead of blue ones." She glared at Perse. "I always hated you for that."

"You got Mom's nose," countered Perse.

"True. I do have a much cuter nose."

Stef studied the picture. "The three of you . . . it's uncanny. What's Liz's personality like?"

"Most definitely Gary's. Very quiet, but when she does speak it's profound, and she's insanely responsible. Hopefully, that'll continue into the teen years. I don't think I could handle raising a teenage me."

"Is Alec more like you?"

"Maybe. It's still hard to tell since four-year-olds are supposed to be clumsy creatures. He starts kindergarten in a few weeks, so that will give us some insight into how he can handle structure.

And once he's a little older we'll know more. Oh! You should come to his birthday party!"

Perse gathered more salad on her fork. "Of course I'm coming to his party. I'm his aunt."

"Not you, dumb ass. Her!"

Stef mumbled around her food, "Me?"

Perse choked on her salad.

The soothing backrub Stef provided was not effective at dislodging the romaine from her trachea. Missy had just invited her girlfriend to a family event two months in the future. There had to be another way to play it. "Missy, no offense, but I don't think Stef would want to spend most of the day traveling to go to a five-year-old's birthday party."

"I would love to come! Is there a theme?" Stef asked, while Perse became speechless.

"Right now, he's into dinosaurs and Ninja Warrior, so it's a toss-up. It really would be great if you came. The neighborhood parents are boring. ll they talk about are coffee and taxes."

Perse thought of another out. "But what about Mom and Dad? I mean, I plan to tell them about Stef and me at the next brunch—"

"Good! But you don't need to worry. Dad already told me they entered another fishing tournament that weekend, so they won't be able to come. It really will be us hanging out like this, except at my house with insanely bright-colored cupcakes."

Did Perse see herself still dating Stef in two months? The answer was yes. Did she plan on telling the whole family about their relationship at brunch? Also, yes. Was Missy's proposal of bringing Stef to the party strange or inappropriate? She supposed not. Once the annoyance Perse felt toward her sister waned, she asked Stef, "So, do you—"

"Yes!"

Missy cackled. "Excellent. Now, what are you two crazy kids going to do to fill the time between now and then?"

CHAPTER FIFTEEN

"PLEASE DON'T TELL me grading papers actually makes you happy," Gillian said when she peered into Perse's office.

"You clearly weren't spying on me an hour ago. This student had a clear, well-supported thesis statement, and it's my last paper for the course. Now, I just have to input the grades."

"A congratulations is in order, I suppose."

Timera joined the duo, coffee cup in hand. "Why are we congratulating Perse?"

"I just finished grading my finals."

"That *is* good news," Timera said, then took a sip. "I still can't believe the summer's almost over. I'm going to have absolutely no time to edit my film from later today."

"Oh, is that today?" Gillian asked. "I forgot about that."

"Where are you going?" Perse's interest piqued. She had wanted to learn more about Timera's process for her web series but hadn't had the time to ask.

"I'm interviewing a group of local Vietnam vets to discuss their homecoming experiences for my Modern American History course."

"Would you mind if I came along? I promise to just be an observer."

Gillian and Timera shared a look.

"I don't know if you'd feel comfortable. My point-of-contact is Captain *Harold Riley*," Timera said seriously.

Perse had no clue why that individual would make her feel uncomfortable. Or why she spoke of him with that tone. She had never heard of him. "Why are you saying his name like that? Is he a war hero?"

"You're kidding, right?" Gillian asked.

"No," Perse said, and then watched her colleagues share the same look again. "Who is he?" she asked with less patience.

"He's *Harold Riley*," Timera answered. "And I don't know if I'd say 'war hero', but he certainly made an impact when he came back to the states."

"Okay," she said with a shrug. "Why do you both look so uneasy?"

"Well," Gillian begin, "it's just that you said you get anxious around crowds. So that, plus, given who he is . . . I figured you'd be nervous."

"I mean, it's true that larger groups make me feel on edge, but it's different here. I'd just be watching. It doesn't really matter that Captain *Harold Riley* will be there."

"You're sure?" Timera asked.

"Absolutely."

"Okay! And since you're tagging along, you're welcome to ask questions, too. I'm sure they'd have some cultural insights you'd be interested in about when they were stationed overseas."

Perse leaned back in her chair. That could be very enlightening. "When are you leaving?"

"I was going to leave after I finish my coffee, but I can push it back a little. Do you want to come too?" Timera asked Gillian.

"This isn't really up my alley of monarchies and castles. Plus, I have a couple of incoming freshmen who want to meet with me." She looked straight at Perse. "You'll be great." Gillian turned and left.

Perse arched her brow. Her colleagues were very concerned about her comfort level. "Thank you."

"I'll come get you in a half hour. Give you some time to process," Timera said with a grin and left.

***

Perse barely had time to create a list of topics and questions in the thirty minutes between learning about the outing and leaving for the community center.

"I'm glad you decided to come," Timera said as she drove.

"Me too. I'm hoping this will give me some ideas on how I can do my own research, now that I won't be traveling as much." She noticed they were quickly approaching a mini-mall off to the side of the business highway. A pit stop was in order. "Do you mind if we stop at Almost Havana?"

"You want to buy cigars?"

"Yes. It's a nice gesture and it will help grease the wheels a bit."

Timera nodded her approval and turned into the plaza. "You know, if you got one for me, I wouldn't mind."

A hundred dollars and thirty minutes later, they entered the drab community building. The finger paintings in primary colors that hung on the wall didn't add cheer to the room that smelled like stale coffee. The plastic chairs arranged in a circle were the definition of forced and awkward conversation.

It was a sad set-up.

As Timera unzipped her camera bag, Perse observed the ten vets who joined them. Men and women. All races. Based on the hats and t-shirts, she assumed all branches. And based on the rainbow pins on a bag, she supposed all orientations.

But none of them spoke, not even to each other.

Perse walked over to Timera and hesitantly asked, "Are your groups normally this quiet?"

"Not really. I hope I can get them to talk. Otherwise, this is going to be hell to edit to make interesting."

The wheels started turning for Perse. She didn't want to step on Timera's toes, but at the same time she knew her questions would start off light and gradually dig deeper into their experiences. "Feel free to say no, but would you like me to ask some questions first? It might help break the tension."

Timera scanned the crowd for herself. "You might have a point there. Okay, you can be my warm-up act. Want the camera?"

"Absolutely not. It'll make me even more nervous and I don't think they'll be honest."

Timera nodded. "Okay. See that black guy with the freckles and ball cap?"

"Yes."

"That's our guy. Introduce yourself and tell him your plan. He'll the gather the troops, so to speak."

Perse headed over to the older gentleman who stood as she approached. "Captain Riley, my name is Dr. Persephone Teixeira."

Captain Riley smiled, which exposed a gleaming, silver filling, and then vigorously shook her hand. "It is such a pleasure to meet you. I have to say, this is a surprise. I had no idea you'd be joining Timera."

"I was a last-minute addition. I hope you don't mind."

He looked positively floored. "Are you kidding? I'm meeting *the* Persephone Teixeira. This is fabulous. But, enough of that, you looked like you might have a question."

Perse was awestruck by the fact that she had a fan. Her work had been well received in academia, but she didn't know she had done anything that layman would know. Maybe she was closer to Christopher's status than she thought. "Well, in addition to coming over to introduce myself, I also had a suggestion. It's my understanding that some of you have never met, so I'd like to ask a few general questions about your experiences overseas. I'm hoping if we find elements in common it may help everyone feel more comfortable."

"Sounds like a great idea." He rubbed the gray stubble on his chin. "Something wrong?"

Perse finished scanning the room. "Do you think it'd be okay if we took the chairs outside? It's not too hot and this is . . ."

"Depressing," he said then laughed heartily. "Hey, everyone, grab a chair if you can. We're taking this outside to enjoy the sunshine."

"Thank you," Perse said warmly.

"Anytime, Dr. Teixeira," he said with a smile and a tip of his hat.

Most of the vets took advantage of smoking their cigars outside as they answered Perse's series of questions.

Over her years of learning about different cultural groups, Perse had found that the essence of understanding who the group was came down to the simplest parts of life: how people celebrated love and death, what caused a community to gather, and the food they ate. When she limited her questions to their experiences in military camps or ships, they provided the expected answers, but when she asked what their experiences were like when they were no longer under the watch of their commanding officers, the conversation took some very interesting turns. This segued nicely into Timera's more formal group interview that followed.

Even Harold Riley thought so.

"I thought I had heard everything, but I was wrong," he said once the other vets were out of earshot. "You ladies really knew what buttons to push to get them to sing."

"Hopefully I wasn't too invasive," Perse said.

"No, just invasive enough. In fact, you made me remember a few things I didn't want to share with the group. Some things are just too personal, you know?"

"I do." Perse noticed that he started stroking his chin with that ponderous look again. "Would you like to discuss it?"

He bit his lip. "I trust you two, so I think I would, but not here. How about we continue this conversation over a glass of bourbon at my apartment? I have some good stuff from real close by that I've been waiting to crack open."

"You mind?" Timera asked Perse.

It was unexpected but sounded oddly familiar. Despite that, she was willing to roll with the plan to learn what he wanted to share. "I think that sounds great."

He clapped. "Alright, then. You can follow me, but it's real easy to find."

***

His apartment building appeared more like a hotel. Although, once they were in his place, there were touches of home: mismatched furniture, a small kitchen table with crocheted seat cushions, and dozens of photographs on the wall. Many were of him and, she assumed, his wife, and four children.

Harold served Timera and Perse each a generous glass of bourbon neat. "That first one by the window was taken about two years after I left the service. You can tell by the afro."

"What year did you finish?" Perse asked.

"1983. To our health." He clinked glasses with the two women.

Perse took her first sip and expected to have to suppress the urge to cough from the liquid fire, but she found the liquor smooth. Whatever bottle he had was very top shelf. Stef would approve. "And what did you do after you retired?"

"Believe it or not I became a journalist."

"That's interesting. You're the second person I've learned about recently who went into journalism after the war."

"Really?" he asked, pleasantly surprised.

"Yeah," she answered with a grin. "Out of all of the different fields out there, what made you choose that?"

His explanation of how he got into journalism slid nicely into the few stories he didn't want to share with the rest of the veterans. They were darker stories of heroin, PTSD, and sexual assault; stories Perse knew existed, but had never heard about from a direct witness.

Timera was especially interested to learn how he coped with that knowledge once he was in the States. His answer was that he had tried to forget. But that hadn't been enough, so he'd volunteered with different Veteran organizations and had tried to include the topics into his journalism pieces when he could.

For such a serious turn of conversation, Perse found him compassionate, intelligent, and courageous. She was disappointed when their conversation came to a close.

"Let me see you two fine ladies out," Harold said and took their glasses.

Perse stood and felt the bourbon—and water she'd drank to chase it—about ready to leave her bladder. "Do you mind if I use your bathroom before we leave?"

"First door on the left."

As Perse left she heard Harold and Timera speak in hushed tones, which continued the entire time she was gone. When she came back into the living area, a new photo grabbed her attention. It was of an older white woman, and Stef. Perse's breath was immediately taken from her.

Harold was Harry. Stef's Harry. Stef's uncle figure and the only family she had left.

"Everything alright?" Timera asked.

Rather than speak, Perse sat in the nearest chair and gripped the seat under her. She closed her eyes, felt the stability beneath her, and pictured an open sky above her. She would not drift away. She would not be smothered. She would be fine. Perse pointed to the photograph. "Your Stef's Harry."

He furrowed his brow. "You didn't know that?"

Perse shook her head.

"How could you not know that?" Timera asked, shocked.

"You called him Harold the whole time and I . . . I didn't connect the dots." She felt like such an idiot. But it did explain why he was so excited to meet her, why he had heard of her, and why Gillian and Timera had been so surprised that she didn't find meeting him to be a big deal. "I'm sorry."

"Don't apologize," Harry said. "I loved this! I love the fact that you didn't really know who I was."

"Really?" This time it was Timera who asked.

"Yes! I liked meeting you this way better."

Perse lifted an eyebrow. "What other way was planned?"

"Uh-oh," Timera muttered and walked to the window.

Harry waved off her negativity. "Nothing really planned, but ever since Stef met Missy, she's been talking about the three of us getting together. But those meet and greets are always so forced and inauthentic. By you getting a little mixed up with my name, I had the opportunity to see who you are—completely unfiltered.

"Every time I met one of my kids' girlfriends or boyfriends it was always, 'Yes, sir' and 'Please, sir' while they were on their best behavior. But this wasn't like that." He chucked deep into his chest. "You handed me a cigar and asked me about street food and brothels. None of the people my children dated or married have ever done that, but with you I loved it because it was interesting, and I learned more about you from the way you responded."

With each passing word that came out of Harry's mouth she began to see his perspective more and more. However, she was left uneasy knowing Stef had been planning a meeting without discussing it with her first. They hadn't had the conversation related to that level yet, and Stef probably assumed since she'd met Missy, that meant Perse was ready. Stef's levels were equal opportunity things: if she got together with Stef's family, Stef would assume she could get together with all of hers.

She wasn't ready for that. She was far from ready. Families were conflict-inducing extensions of relationships. Perse had to be 100% certain her family could take the news of Stef calmly before she traveled down that road.

But Harry couldn't haven't known that.

Perse looked at his kind face and settled her emotions. "You're right, I would have acted much differently had I known. This was probably one of the best ways I could have met you. Although, it does still freak me out a little."

"But you're okay now?" Harry asked.

Perse nodded even though the situation had put a knot in her gut and made her slightly woozy. "I'll be fine, but do me a favor and don't tell Stef about this. I'll tell her later, because I'm not ready for that conversation now."

Harry pursed his lips as though he were in deep thought. "I can't do that. Do you have any idea how mad Stef would be if we kept this a secret? Plus, it's really not a big deal."

"But for me it is! You're like an uncle I accidentally met, so then Stef will want to meet mine. I'm not ready for her to meet my uncles!"

"Who said anything about that?" Harry asked, confused, and then looked to Timera.

"Perse, Harry," Timera said with a tone far gentler than Perse had ever heard, "how about I just call Stef and tell her what happened? Nobody has to go into the details, and she'll know. Deal?"

"I'm good with that," Harry said.

Perse didn't like the idea, but she hated the thought of giving Stef the news herself more. She nodded her approval.

"Good. Now, I'm going to put it on speaker." Timera took out her phone and placed it on the table where they had only a few minutes earlier had their drinks. The hollow ringing on the other end of the phone filled the small room.

"Hey," Stef said. "I have class in five minutes. Can I call you back?"

"I promise this will be really fast," Timera reassured. "Remember how today was the day I interviewed the vets?"

"Oh, that's right. Did you tell Harry I said hi?"

Perse smiled from the sweetness and enthusiasm in Stef's voice.

"Yes, and he says hi back," Timera answered. "But at work I was talking about the meeting and referred to him more formally as Captain Harold Riley a—"

"Seriously?" Stef asked, annoyed. "I hate it when he insists on that. We're civilians."

Perse grinned when she saw Harry's offended expression.

"Well," Timera continued, "long story short: Perse came along not knowing Harold was Harry, but Harry knew who Perse was, and they hit it off really well, but then Perse learned who he really was and freaked out because she was *not* ready for that introduction. And that's basically been my afternoon. Did you catch all of that?"

"I think so," Stef said. "Perse met Harry?"

"Yes."

After long pause Stef yelled, "That's awesome! I mean, not the Perse feeling freaked out part, but that they met and got along. I can't wait to talk to them about the three of us getting together!"

"Yes, that will be very exciting for you, but you should probably give Perse some time to digest it all. Okay, gotta go, Gillian's calling me. Bye." Timera disconnected the call and looked at both of them with a cocky grin. "Done."

So it was. Perse did appreciate the addition of Timera giving her time to digest.

"Well, this turned out to be a more interesting day than I had planned." Harry took the bottle of bourbon off the table and handed it to Timera. "My thank you for organizing the day and getting me and my peers to tell our stories in a way that made us feel so comfortable."

"That's very kind of you," Timera said as she looked down at the bottle. "You ready, Perse?"

"Yes, I am." She held her hand out to Harry. "I'm sure I'll be seeing you again."

"I surely hope so," he said with a gentle shake. "And again, thank you for the cigars."

Perse was relieved he didn't pull her in for a surprise hug and gave him a final goodbye wave as they left his apartment. She followed Timera down to her car and it wasn't until Perse pulled on her safety belt she spoke. "Missy's not going to believe me when I tell her about this."

"I really am sorry about that. Swear to God, I thought you knew."

"I know," Perse said with a sigh. "Has Stef been talking about me meeting Harry since she met my sister?"

"She may have mentioned it a few dozen times. Meeting Missy meant a great deal to her, so it was big news and got the wheels turning for you to meet him."

Perse knew Stef had enjoyed meeting her sister, but had no idea the dinner held the significance it did. "It was a big step for me too." She leaned her head back on the headrest and heard Timera move beside her.

"Here." Timera handed her the bottle of bourbon. "I think you've earned this, in addition to your professional interview credits today. Plus, I like my drinks fruity."

Perse took the bottle and placed it between her feet for the ride home. "My dad will certainly appreciate this."

Timera started their drive back to the school. "Since we've weaved in some personal and professional stuff today, can I ask you a personal question? It's about something Harry said."

"Why not? Let's just get it out in the open."

"Would the idea of meeting Harry in a traditional meet and greet have freaked you out?"

"Absolutely. He means so much to Stef—he's her family. She's said as much. And I don't have a very good track record with other people's families."

"Okay, fair enough. How about this? Does the idea of Stef meeting your parents freak you out?"

Perse looked over with what she knew was a terrified expression.

"That bad, huh? Can I ask why?"

"To put it simply, families, mine or others, aren't the best for relationships. I have a rather Pavlovian response."

"Ah. You hear family, you sense the end," Timera stated. "Well, as one of Stef's closest friends, I'm going to ask that you do your best to resolve that issue."

"I'm working on it. My family has brunch next Sunday, and I'm going to tell them about Stef and me then. Once I do that, I probably won't be able to talk because I'll be so overwhelmed with all my mom's questions, so Missy will have to fill in the gaps."

"It's great that your sister has your back like that."

"She definitely does. Even if sometimes I think she's there to push me over the edge."

CHAPTER SIXTEEN

"ARE YOU EVEN paying attention to me?" Missy asked impatiently. "You're falling asleep at the cutting board over there!"

"Sorry, I didn't sleep well last night." *Or any of the nights in the past week.*

"That explains the bags. Okay, let's try this." Missy held her whisk aloft. "Repeat after me, 'Mom, Dad, I'm in a relationship.'"

"This is stupid," Perse whined as she diced vegetables.

Dandy circled at their feet, hoping for scraps.

"Yes, it is, but I think it'll help."

Perse calmly stared at her sister. It was easier to be relaxed with a gummy in her system. "Mom, Dad, I'm in a relationship."

"Good. What is that?" She counted off on her fingers. "Six words? You can totally do it. I have all the confidence in the world in you. What's Stef said about today?"

The better question was what hadn't Stef said about it. Her excitement over Perse's willingness to break the family meeting level into subphases yielded numerous questions: When did she think meeting her parents would happen? Where would they meet? How many people in the past had met her parents? Why so few people?

Normally, Perse loved Stef's inquisitive nature, but here each question or comment added stress and fear about what Stef would learn that would drive her away. The incessant questions were also why she hadn't wanted to tell Stef about accidentally meeting Harry. Perse was completely astounded by this family-crazed version of Stef. Even Missy agreed that Stef's enthusiasm would go out of control if she learned about the Harry meeting.

Missy also told Perse to focus on the first hurdle: telling their mom and dad.

In a surprise move, Stef had understood Perse was nervous and suggested she wear her necklace so Stef could be with her in spirit, since her physical body was at a three-on-three basketball tournament with Gillian and Timera.

Perse felt the weight of the necklace lying on top of her shirt and Dandy's paw batting at her leg. "Stef is exuberant about today and"—some of the anxiety she had chemically repressed rose—"is eager to hear how Mom and Dad respond."

"Great! The important thing is that she's supporting you and that I'm supporting you. It's not like you're accidentally coming out to them. Getting caught making out with what's-her-name was the best thing that could have happened to you in that department."

Missy was right. It wasn't as though she were making an announcement that would stun them. She was simply going to state that she was in a relationship, and if her mother pressed for details, she'd be honest about her feelings. If she needed her to back off, it was up to her to communicate that need.

"Now," Missy said, "I want to you to say the mantra."

The mantra was something Missy had invented when they were kids to help Perse through her anxiety. Missy understood her challenges and tried to emphasize that its power was inside Perse's mind.

This request would have seemed silly to an outsider, but it had been strangely effective through the years. Perse started the small speech she had memorized since she was eleven. "You're an invisible jerk. You're only real because I'm giving you the power to exist. I'm done with you!"

"Very nice. I really liked the cadence on that one."

"Thanks. And I promise you, Stef, and myself, that today is the day." She wished she sounded more confident, but at least she was able to say it. Sometimes even that was an obstacle.

Missy eyed her sister skeptically and took the chopped vegetables from her. "Keep that promise, because I'd hate for you to be saying instead, 'Stef, I know you're probably in love with me as much as I am with you, but I can't tell my parents about us because of no justifiable reason.'"

"I think I'd throw up." The moment she said it, it became reality. She huddled over the sink and took deep, cleansing breaths to will her nauseated state away. As the feeling cleared, she looked up from the sink and out the window.

Alec ran across the yard, up the metal slide, and swung across the monkey bars. Liz dramatically pushed a stopwatch when he finished.

"What in the world are the kids doing out there?"

"Alec's decided to become a Ninja Warrior." She added with pride, "Liz has decided to be his trainer."

Perse watched her niece and nephew laughing. They would most likely be sitting at the table too when she shared her news. What kind of questions would a girlfriend elicit from them? She had never mentioned anyone romantically significant in their lifetimes. "What if I can't do it?" she asked in a cracked voice. "Everything changes—everyone leaves me—once families get involved. Anthony's brother, Raquel's sister, and Mom's overreaction to Isabella; they all led to the same thing."

Missy rushed over, brushed away one of Perse's tears, and placed her hands gently on each of her shoulders. "I met Stef. She's not like those dipshits from the past. She's the real fucking deal, and if you *don't* tell Mom and Dad, it *will* hurt her. I know you don't want to do that." She held her sister tightly. "Now, we can practice the power of positive thinking while you help me with the fruit. Those strawberries aren't going to sli— What the hell is he *doing* out there? Hold on, I'll be back once I'm convinced Alec isn't going to jump off the monkey bars and into the kiddie pool."

With Missy gone, Perse dried the rest of her tears with the bottom of her shirt and gritted her teeth. Come hell or high water, she had to do this. She couldn't look Stef in the eyes and say that she was still a secret. To make sure she followed through, Perse rushed to the freezer, dug behind the bags and boxes of frozen vegetables, and pulled out the box that said *facial mask*. She quickly unwrapped one of the plastic-wrapped brownies and threw it on a plate for a thirty-second zap in the microwave. She rocked impatiently on her heels while she alternated looks between the chocolate square slowly spinning and Missy, who appeared to be lecturing Liz while Alec sat in the empty kiddie pool.

When the microwave beeped, she grabbed the brownie, tested its temperature, and shoved it into her mouth. She chewed and hoped her anxiety would be gone by the time she finished the brunch prep work.

* * *

"I showed them my figures from my site visit and they still didn't believe me. So, you know what they did?" Missy asked her family. "They went and built it anyway."

"Did it work?" Paulo asked.

"Of course not! They ran out of materials before the project was even half completed. And that's how I got an even better office."

"Excellent work!"

"Well done and, as per usual, Missy, that was delicious!" Olivia beamed at her oldest daughter as she sipped her mimosa.

Missy also drank from her flute. "Thanks, Mom, it really wasn't that difficult to make. Plus, I had Perse here to act as my sous chef. Isn't that right, Perse?"

Aside from answering questions when directly asked and politely requesting others to pass food to her, which was often, Perse hadn't added much to the conversation. "All I did was make everything smaller," Perse said as she studied the bubbles in the flute nearest her. Their journey from the bottom of the glass to the top entranced her. It was like an invisible elevator took them all to the bubble penthouse where they could coexist as a single community. It was beautiful.

"What are you looking at?" Alec asked his aunt in a curious whisper.

"Bubbles. I've never really thought about them before. There may be worlds that lie inside of them."

Alec tugged on Missy's short sleeve. "Mommy, can I have a bubble world?"

"What are you ta—? Perse, can you help me in the kitchen? Now," Missy said sternly.

Perse followed her sister without complaint, but when she reached the kitchen, she was surprised to feel a force from behind her head, which caused her to stumble forward. She stared at Missy in pure amazement. "Was that your hand? How did it move so fast?"

"You are higher than a fucking kite," Missy reprimanded in a whisper.

Perse leaned into Missy's ear. "Is it obvious?"

Missy gripped the counter behind her with white knuckles. "What did you take?"

"A birthday brownie."

Missy gasped and staggered backward. "I ran out of those a month ago. You ate one of the newer—and stronger—brownies."

"Oh. That explains why I feel so . . . chill."

"Jesus Christ, Perse, this is important!" Missy tapped her foot and inhaled deeply. "Okay, this is what we're going to do. We're going to go back in there and you're going to act like Dr. Persephone Teixeira, sober adult and girlfriend of Dr. Stefanie Blake."

Perse was confident she could play the role of that person. "Who are you going to be?"

"I'm going to be Ms. Artemis Teixeira-Manners, mother, wife, daughter, and sister to the biggest pain in the ass on the planet. Do you understand?"

Perse nodded and followed Missy back to the dining area where Gary and Paulo spoke about football and the kids snuck food to Dandy under the table.

"I forgot to tell you earlier how much I love that necklace. Is it new?" Olivia asked Perse.

"Thank you. It was gifted to me recently," Perse said in her most polished voice.

"It reminds me of when we went rock hunting on that dude ranch for family vacation. Was that four years ago?" Olivia asked Missy.

"About five and a half years." She shared a knowing glance with Gary and then looked at Alec. "Trust me."

"You should have seen Liz the Rockhound," Olivia said with a slight chuckle. "She was covered head to toe in dirt. It's a shame you missed that trip."

"I believe I was in Turkey then. The country, not the bird."

"Jesus Christ," Missy muttered into her flute.

Perse shook her head. "No, he wasn't there. Islam is the religion of the majority in Turkey."

Missy cleared her throat. "Kids, why don't you go outside with Dandy and do your warrior training? We need to have some adult time."

Liz shrugged and left, while Alec jumped out of his seat and hustled out of the room. "Come on, Dandy!"

The beagle listened to his young master and kept pace.

"You have such wonderful children," Olivia said with a smile. "Just like me."

Missy took Perse's empty champagne flute and refilled it with orange juice. "We are pretty great. Hey, Perse, I've been doing most of the talking here. Why don't you fill Mom and Dad in on your latest university news?"

"Of course." Perse drank from her newly filled glass. "I am well respected and addressed as Dr. Persephone Teixeira."

Paulo and Olivia scrunched their faces. "Well, I would hope so," Paulo said, "but we haven't heard how your first class went, or what you're doing now. Fill us in!"

"My summer course was a proper introduction in a myriad of ways." Perse looked at Missy for guidance.

In response, Missy slowly nodded.

"The class allowed me to ease into learning about all of the campus nuances while only worrying about the one course."

"Much easier to learn than with three at the same time."

Perse forced herself to laugh along with her father. "Indeed. And I've been able to really get a sense of what my colleagues are about as well."

Missy nodded encouragingly.

"My boss, Dr. Jackson—"

"I just loved his last book. Fascinating perspective," Paulo commented. "I still can't get over the fact that you work with him."

"Not only that, but weren't you invited to his house?" Missy asked.

Paulo beamed at the news. "Really?"

"Oh, that sounds wonderful." Olivia was positively tickled. "I bet he has a gorgeous home."

"Beautiful, and right on the water. My date gave me a tour," Perse added nonchalantly and helped herself to another waffle.

"Oh. That's . . . unexpected. Are you still dating this person?" Olivia asked hesitantly.

Perse nodded while she chewed, but reminded herself that she was a professional. "We are, but don't worry. We signed the necessary paperwork. These waffles are so good, Missy— Sorry, Ms. Teixeira-Manners."

"You need paperwork to date?" Paulo asked confused.

"Absolutely. Dr. Blake was insistent that we fill out sexual harassment forms. You know, so no one gets sued."

Missy furrowed her brow. "Dad, what's wrong? You look . . . really mad."

"Do you not see what's happened?" he asked in outrage. "The paperwork, the appetite . . . and she's clearly not sleeping well. How many months, Perse?"

"It's kind of hard to keep track because of all the rules, but basically since I started."

"Dear God," Olivia squealed and went pale. "You're through your first trimester."

Missy choked on her orange juice.

Perse responded, "We do a quarterly semester system at CBU."

"Stop!" Missy commanded. "Everybody stop! What Perse is trying to say is—"

"Mom!" Liz screamed from outside, which was accompanied by the wailing of Alec and barking of Dandy.

The adults rushed outside.

When Perse got to the yard, Dandy circled nervously at the base of the slide and Liz kneeled over her crying brother. "What happened?"

Alec lifted his head, which allowed blood to stream from his nose and mouth more quickly.

There was so much blood. So much—

***

Perse slowly opened her eyes to see the serious face of Liz. Dandy licked her cheek.

"Grammy, Aunt Perse is awake and her eyes look funny!"

"Thank you, Liz," Olivia said and rushed over with a glass. "Don't move." Olivia had propped her daughter's feet on an empty planter's box. "How do you feel?"

"A little dizzy." Perse kept her head still and shifted her eyes around. Something fine, yet coarse, tickled beneath her arms. "Am I laying in the yard?"

"I'm afraid so. Alec hurt himself on the slide, and you fainted when you saw the blood."

"Is he okay?" Perse tried to sit up, but her mother eased her back down.

"Liz, can you get me some pillows from the patio furniture?"

Liz diligently nodded and scurried off.

"Alec will be fine. He tripped running up the slide and hit his mouth at the top. He's inside now getting cleaned up by your dad. Missy and Gary are trying to decide whether or not to take him to the ER."

Liz was barely visible behind the large pillows stacked in her arms. "Will these be enough?"

"Those will be plenty. Now, please go inside and tell them your aunt is awake. I'll take care of her."

Liz sprinted into the house.

Olivia directed her attention back to her daughter.

Perse did as she was told while the chain of events leading to her episode came back to her.

She'd told them about Stef and their paperwork, but then her father had become extremely angry, her mother had been outraged, and Missy had gone into authority mode. But why, she didn't know.

Perse drank from the juice cup her mother gave her. "Mom, why was everyone so mad inside?"

"Because of how this Dr. Blake has treated you. Do you want me to call your obstetrician?"

"My obste— You think I'm pregnant?" Perse exclaimed. When her mother nodded, she sat up on her elbows and thought about why her mother would assume such a thing. It was ludicrous!

When she realized why and how she had failed to do the one thing she had set out to do, she felt dizzy again.

"Whatever you're thinking isn't helping your current condition. Picture playing a song, like you used to do."

Perse hadn't used that strategy in years, even though it was one of her original coping mechanisms. She thought of one of her favorites, *Goodbye Yellow Brick Road*, and imagined striking the different keys with perfect timing. She gradually started to feel a more authentic calm come over her. "About what I said inside. About—"

"Mom!" Missy yelled, then emerged into the yard. "Can you and Dad stay here and look after Liz? Alec is freaking out about going to the ER without both Gary and me, and Liz just saw that Alec is missing teeth and decided it was her fault, so she's hysterical too."

"I'll be right inside." Olivia held the back of her hand to Perse's cheek. "How about you come with me and lay down? Once Paulo and I get Liz settled, we can talk."

Perse nodded slowly and let her mother guide her into the house, down the stairs to her former living space, away from Liz's sobbing, and to the couch.

Once she was comfortable, her mother draped a blanket over her and keeled to brush the hair from Perse's face. "Try to get some rest. You need it."

Perse nodded. It was a good plan. She just needed to relax and she could come at this again when her mother returned.

***

Alec ran through the house to the backyard. Despite the stiches in his face, he was still eager to get back on his warrior course. That boy had no fear and it scared the hell out of Missy. "Gary, can you watch him? Make sure the stitches don't open."

"Sure. What are you going to do?"

"Don't know yet." According to her mother and father, they'd taken the liberty of putting all the brunch items away before they had left, so that was taken care of. Based on the Jeep parked at the curb, Perse was still around doing God knows what. Missy had no plan.

Liz had her usual demeanor, which involved lounging on the sofa with her phone. That kid had resilience too.

"Is your aunt awake?"

"I don't think so."

She had a plan now. "Well, I'm going to fix that," Missy said and headed down the stairs into the dimly lit basement.

By the light of a small window, Perse looked so peaceful sleeping on the futon. A blanket was tucked under her chin and there was the faintest amount of drool escaping the corner of her mouth.

It was time for a rude awakening.

Missy flipped on the light. "Time to rise and shine!" she said with faux-cheer.

Perse jumped like ice water had been thrown on her and scrambled to sit. "Oh my God! Is it morning?"

"No, it's the afternoon. Also known as two hours after we left to take Alec to urgent care. Also known as one hour after Mom and Dad left."

"Mom and Dad left?" Perse asked in a panic. "But I was supposed to talk to them! They were going to stay because Liz was upset."

"What can I say? My daughter has the emotional fortitude of a Marine. She told them that she was fine and they could go home. Naturally, they hesitated because they didn't know if they should stay for you." She watched Perse stand and start pacing. "I convinced them that your behavior was not because of pregnancy, but because you were so fucking nervous to tell them about your relationship that you dosed yourself."

"You didn't?"

Missy held her arms out in exasperation. "What else could I have possibly said that wouldn't have come back to bite us in the ass? Or scare them? You already fessed up about Dr. Blake, so it's not like that was a secret."

Perse stilled her movements. "Did you tell them anything else about Stef and me?"

"Not really. I've been a little too busy to get into the details of you and your girlfriend. In case you forgot, I've spent the past few hours tending to my son who ripped his face open and knocked his teeth out on a sliding board!"

Perse covered her mouth in response. "Oh my God! Is he okay?"

"He's fine now, but the Novocain still hasn't worn off."

"That's good. That's—fuck!" Perse glanced at her phone. "Stef just texted me asking how it went. What the hell am I going to say?"

That was an excellent question. What could Perse say to soften the blow of incredible disappointment? "Call or text Mom and Dad and tell them about Stef. That way at least you can say you told them. Then you can call Stef and tell her the truth."

Perse nodded along to the instructions. "Then what?"

Missy shrugged. "You really fucked this one up, Sis. A lot depends on if you can actually have a conversation with Mom and Dad."

"I can't tell them like this!" Perse said frantic.

She didn't need her sister to pass out and crack her head on a table. "Okay, sit down."

Perse continued to stand with a deer-in-the-headlight look.

"Sit down!" Once Perse complied, Missy continued with her advice. "If you don't at least tell them *again* that you are one, not pregnant, and two, in a relationship with Stef, Stef will never forgive you. Tell them or promise Stef that you *will* tell them when you see them while looking them in the eye."

"Okay. I think I can do that." Perse took a deep breath. "I *have* to do this and I *can* do this."

"Good!" Missy said with cheer. "Now, repeat that until you believe it, because right now you look like you're going to pass out again."

***

Perse debated which parent to call. A conversation with her dad would be much more to the point. She dialed his number.

"Perse! Are you okay?" Paulo asked urgently.

"I'm . . . better than I was." She took a deep breath. "Dad, I need to talk to you two about Stef. I didn't handle things well and I promised her I would tell you face-to-face. Is . . . is there any chance you can swing back to Missy's house?"

Perse's heart nearly arrested in the silence that followed.

"Ouch, that'd be a tough one, Pumpkin. We just got on the Bay Bridge and will probably be stuck on it for the next hour. Can't you just talk to us over the phone?"

She could, but then she wouldn't be keeping her word to Stef. "No, I promised. It's important that I do it face-to-face. Can you come to Annapolis for dinner this week? I can show you the campus too."

Over the occasional car honk, Perse heard her dad's sharp intake of breath through his teeth.

Her shoulders slumped in defeat.

"That'd be tricky. I'm speaking at a few scout meetings this week and I think your mother has Book Club."

"I'll cancel!" her mother yelled. "Are you sure you can't talk to us now?"

"I'm sure." With her parents' previous commitments and the start of the semester looming, she had to make a decision. "Okay, how about next weekend? We can have dinner somewhere, just the three of us."

Missy gave her a thumbs up and whispered, "Thank you."

"Next weekend sounds great, Perse. Just let us know when and where. Look at this asshole coming up behind us," Paulo muttered.

There was the screech of tires, followed by more honking. Missy got her driving habits from her father.

"Sounds like you should focus. I'll get back to you soon. Love you."

"We love you too," her mother shouted.

With a sad grin Perse hung up and looked at Missy.

"One down, one to go," her sister said ominously. "You can do this. You *have* to do this."

Perse exhaled a controlled breath through tight lips and grounded herself. She dialed Stef.

"What happened?" Stef asked mid-way through the first ring.

"Well, a lot happened, actually, but Mom and Dad know about us."

"So, they took it well?" she asked hopeful. "Were there hugs?"

Perse knew this was where it would get dicey. "No hugs because I was either sleeping when Missy told them bits and pieces or they were stuck in traffic when I told them we were in a relationship." There was silence for several seconds. That wasn't good. "Stef?"

"I'm confused. Your parents never came to brunch?"

"They did." At this point, she knew she was being vague because she couldn't get herself to just say the words. She loathed her inability to say simple, honest words.

Stef continued their guessing game. "And you fell asleep?"

"For a little bit. It was after I passed out. Alec was bleeding."

Missy sent her a pointed look.

"What the fuck happened there?"

It seemed Stef was done with giving her ways to stall.

Perse pinched the bridge of her nose, took another controlled breath, and launched into the entire chain of events.

Missy sat beside her while she relived the entire ordeal, added comforting pats on her back when necessary.

To Stef's credit, she didn't interrupt. Although Perse did hear the occasional exasperated sigh. Especially after the pot brownie.

"So, let me know if I'm understanding this," Stef began. "You were so freaked out about telling your parents that you took drugs, then, high as a kite, caused your parents to believe that a colleague got you pregnant, but you didn't get a chance to correct them before your nephew hurt himself, which caused you to pass out, and then while your body detoxified itself during your nap, your sister told them about us instead? Did I get that right?"

"Unfortunately, yes. Do you want me to come over so we can talk about this together?" Perse asked timidly. "I can be there in a few hours. It'll give you time to sort your feelings."

"Are you kidding? It's going to take *way* more time than that to sort my feelings."

"So, you're mad?"

Even Missy rolled her eyes.

"Yeah, I'm mad! And I'm going to be mad until I have time to figure out my shit and you properly talk to your parents. You promised me you'd look them in the eye and tell them. Dammit, Perse! You *know* how much this meant to me!"

Missy nudged her and whispered, "Tell her about your dinner with Mom and Dad."

"I'm meeting Mom and Dad next weekend. I swear to God I'll tell them everything then."

"I was hoping we could get together with Harry next week-end!"

Perse winced. "I didn't know that."

"Because I was waiting to see how today went before I pulled the trigger on tickets for that murder mystery dinner theater place."

"I'm sorry. I didn't know."

"Yeah, I'm sorry too. Is there anything else? Because if there's not we should probably get off the phone before I say something I shouldn't."

"No." Perse sounded liked a shell of a person even to herself. "Please let me know when you're ready to talk."

"I will." Stef hung up.

Missy pulled Perse in for a hug. "You don't have to keep it together anymore."

Perse leaned into her sister's embrace and wept into her shoulder.

She had let Stef down. But even worse, she had let herself down.

CHAPTER SEVENTEEN

THE FIRST FEW days of classes went according to plan, but Perse's sleep-deprived headache hadn't left even after two days. She did everything she could to alleviate the symptom: water, eye rest, more yoga, and several over-the-counters.

Nothing worked.

She stared into her empty cup and thought maybe she could knock it out with another dose of caffeine. She strode to the department's kitchenette and almost turned back around when she saw the back of a very red head. It seemed as though the clicks of Perse's small heels had alerted Gillian to her presence.

Gillian turned to her and lifted her chin to say hello.

"Hey," Perse said with little enthusiasm.

"The beginning of the fall semester is rough on everyone. Especially the newbies."

When Perse saw Gillian pour the last of the coffee into her cup, she pouted.

"Don't worry, I'll make another. You look knackered." Gillian took the bin of grounds out of the cabinet. "Do you want to talk about it? And, just to be clear, I'm not talking about the semester."

Perse viewed her skeptically. "Don't you have a huge conflict of interest?"

Gillian shrugged. "Not as much as you'd think. I don't know much about it, but I do know that being someone's friend is not the same as being in a relationship. So, if you want to talk to someone who isn't your sister . . . I'm across the hall."

It was the most perfect thing anyone could have said to her. "Thank you."

Gillian nodded and walked into a familiar young woman as soon as she stepped into the hall. "Pardon me."

"You might be able to help me! You're both friends with Dr. Blake, right?" She pointed at Gillian. "I've seen you at the gym with her." She pointed at Perse. "And you came to the lab that one time."

"Right." Perse nodded. "And you're Bradyn, right?"

Bradyn's eyes lit up as she barely contained her excitement. "Yes! You have to help. Dr. Blake is about to do something really bad, but she won't listen to me. She'll listen to you."

Perse shook her head. "There's no way she'll listen to me right now. Gillian, do you mind?"

"Of course not. Bradyn, follow me, please."

Perse watched Gillian and Bradyn go to her office. She leaned against the wall and shut her eyes as she waited for the coffee's percolating to finish. It was impossible not to hear the conversation a dozen feet away.

"So . . ." Gillian began, "why are you worried about Dr. Blake?"

"I'm worried she might get disciplined or fired or something. She's thinking of writing a formal complaint against Dr. Malcolm."

Gillian asked the same question Perse thought. "Who's Dr. Malcolm?"

"Wayne," Bradyn succinctly stated. "I just don't know what to do. I get that he's a pain in the ass, but Dr. Blake's taking it way overboard."

"Let's go back to the formal complaint bit," Gillian said. "Tell me all that you know."

Perse listened to the conversation, at least until the coffee was made, then walked back to her office, and closed the door. It hurt too much to learn about a mess she couldn't help clean.

#

The next day passed. Classes and lunch came and went. And through the hours, any of Perse's unoccupied time was spent wondering what Stef was doing and how she was feeling.

Was she growing angrier by the day? Had she lapsed into a depressive state? The lack of information was aggravating, but she only had herself to blame. It was as if she was dragging her nails down a chalkboard. She needed to be talked down and given perspective. She dialed her sister.

Her ear was assaulted by the cackling of multiple girls.

"Hello? Missy?"

"I'm here, I'm here. Girls, can you go into the basement? I did make that entire area up for you," Missy reminded them. "*Jesus*, it's like each one is a knife in my skull."

"It's a school night," Perse stated with confusion. "Why does it sound like there's a sleepover?"

"Because I'm the hero parent who volunteered to take four pre-teen girls to see a boy band in an hour. So, how have you been? I was trying to give you some space since the semester started."

Missy did have her moments of thoughtfulness. "Semester's fine. I've met with all of my classes at least once, and no one cried when they saw the syllabus."

"Hmm. You still sound sad. Any word from Stef?"

"No, and that's what's worrying me. I have no idea how she's feeling right now, and it's making me crazy."

"Whatever you do, don't call Stef to ask her. The not knowing sucks, but ultimately that's a you-problem, and you need to give Stef space. Plus, she just started a semester just like you. She's got a ton of shit to deal with and her processing time is limited."

"That's good to hear."

"I'm glad you liked it because you're not going to like this. When you do talk to Stef again you need to tell her *everything*: why you're scared, your past relationships, and that you love her. Because you want Stef to not be pissed at you, and the only way to make that happen is for her to understand you."

Missy was right. The directive was stern, but necessary.

"What's the deal with Mom and Dad?" Missy asked while the chanting of pizza started in the background. "Hopefully, you figured out some time to meet with them."

"Dinner on Saturday at a halfway point, so nobody has to drive the entire way."

The two somber faces of Timera and Gillian at her office door took her focus away.

"Thanks for the talk, but you sound like you have a lot going on. I'll give you a call tomorrow, and you can tell me about the concert." As soon as she was off the phone her guests were already in the seats across from her. "This is an unexpected visit."

Their sorrowful faces and continued silence were the farthest things from comforting.

"What's going on?"

"It's Harry," Timera said. "He died."

A pit opened up inside of Perse so her heart could sink deeper. "Stef's Harry?"

Gillian nodded.

"When? How?"

"All I know is what Stef texted me." Timera handed her cell phone to Perse.

Perse held the device in her hands and read. The only words that gave her any sense of comfort were *in his sleep*. "She must be . . . God, she must be devastated. How is she?"

"We called her, but there's no answer," Gillian said. "Given some other things she's shared with us over the last few days, we think"—Timera nodded—"she'll pick up for you."

"She needs you, Perse," Timera said somberly and left the office.

Gillian stood as well. "As a colleague, I don't have an opinion on what you do. As Stef's friend, it would be great to know her girlfriend reached out to make sure she was okay."

"I want to, but I can't," Perse said. "She told me she doesn't want to see me until I see my parents."

"Bollocks to that! There are exceptions to every rule, right? Well, this is the exception! Trust me when I say that her being pissed at you is now a much lower priority. She's broken and needs someone who apparently isn't me or Timera. By default, that means it's you," Gillian said and then walked out.

Once Perse was alone in her office again, she leaned back in her chair and assessed her options. She forced herself to adopt a logical perspective, because her emotions couldn't get any more complicated and confuse her decision-making abilities.

Fact one: Stef's father figure and tie to her family was gone. Fact two: she hadn't spoken to Stef in days. Fact three: Stef's friends were advocating for her involvement. They'd requested that she check in. To show that she cared.

She could do that, especially because right now Stef must feel so alone. It was worth the risk of getting yelled at, or worse, rejected again.

Perse picked up her phone and called Stef. When there was no answer, she grabbed her keys and shut the door behind her.

She wouldn't abandon Stef.

CHAPTER EIGHTEEN

STEF'S CAR WAS under her carport, but there was no answer at the door. She was home, she just pretended not to be. It was a pleasant summer evening with plenty of people taking a post-dinner stroll. Would Stef be among them? She would probably want an evening of reflection, not one of talking with her neighbors.

Perse went to the side of the house for plan B.

Stef didn't move a muscle when Perse came in through the back fence. She simply stared at the fire in front of her. An orange flame licked around the logs in the fire pit and sap boiled out from under the bark creating the occasional *sizzle* or *pop*. When she prodded at the logs, sparks flew and rose into the sky until their light dimmed, then disappeared. After she dug away at the older ash under the logs, the base of the fire turned to blue while the coals pulsed with heat.

Watching was so much easier than speaking. Words complicated everything. That was why there were over 6,500 documented languages that could describe fire, and all words for it were different. Perse supposed the key to communicating life's most primitive emotions was simplicity.

"Hi," Perse said in the darkness, but walked closer until she could see Stef illuminated by the fire's dancing glow. The dark circles under her eyes were even more prominent than Stef's frown and brow crinkles.

"I guess they told you." Stef's voice sounded both raspy and tired.

"Yeah, Timera and Gillian came into my office about thirty minutes ago."

Perse settled into the Adirondack chair beside her and placed a squat bottle between her feet.

"What's that?"

"Bourbon," Perse said. "Want some?"

Stef took the offered bottle and tentatively sniffed, then sipped. Apparently, a glass wasn't needed. "That's really good. Better than some of that company's other stuff." Stef took another drink and stared into the glowing coals. "Thank you."

Perse took a sip of her own. The slow heat traveled down her throat and relaxed her thoughts. It was another good reminder to keep her communication simple.

"Why'd you come here?" Stef asked, breaking Perse out of her fire-watching hypnosis. "I thought my stony silence the last few days would have kept you away. Not that I'm going to kick you out. I don't want to be an asshole."

The defeat and humility in Stef's voice surprised Perse, but it was so quintessential Stef. So honest. It was time she tried to be more like her. "I came because I care for you and knew you'd be hurting. Plus, this bottle has significance and I thought you'd appreciate it."

"It's true that I like good booze. How expensive was it anyway?"

"I have no idea. It was indirectly gifted to me by Harry. He actually gave it to Timera first, but then, considering the events, Timera gave it to me as an apology of sorts. The three of us had a very good conversation that day. He was very personable, compassionate, and I can see in a lot of ways that he was ahead of his time."

Stef suppressed a small laugh while she sipped her drink. "I hope you didn't tell him that. Otherwise, I don't think his head would have fit through any of the doorways."

"No, I kept that to myself." Perse tentatively reached for Stef's hand, but then pulled it back. Remembering Stef was mad at her. "I know how important he was to you and I'm very thankful I had the opportunity to meet him."

Stef nodded. "He was a hell of a guy."

"And a great storyteller."

They listened to the hypnotic sounds of the water tricking in the water feature and stared at the fire as they passed the bottle between them.

The soothing environment was interrupted by Perse's phone vibrating. She looked at it but tucked it back away.

"I understand if you want to leave," Stef said into the flames. "I know I'm not good company."

Emboldened by the alcohol, Perse placed her palm on Stef's knee and then gazed into her sorrowful eyes. "Is that what you want? Do you want me to leave?"

"No. It's nice to have you here even if I don't know what to say. And I don't mind if you want to get back to whoever just texted you."

"That was my dad. I was curious about how expensive that bottle was too, so I asked a man who knows his bourbon."

"How much?"

Perse passed her phone over to Stef. There was a lot more than the price she hoped Stef would read.

I heard about Stef's loss. It's good that you want to be there for her even if you're in a rough patch. That bottle is about $150. Save some for the holidays.

Stef gave the phone back and stared into the fire. "I told Harry absolutely everything. He sympathized with me but told me that some things that sound easy can be really hard for some people, and while I thought I probably knew everything, I don't. Which is a real kick in the junk to hear, you know?"

Perse smiled. "It's true that you don't know everything, but that's my fault. I think that if I had been more open with you about my past it would have given you perspective and helped you understand." Suddenly, her mouth was dry and she gripped the seat under her. "I'm sorry, I thought once I made the decision to tell you it'd be easier. But . . . this is really hard for me."

Stef's eyes softened in the firelight. "I don't want you to feel like you have to tell me if you're not comfortable, and you don't have to tell me everything at once. We can baby step it."

Perse nodded. There wasn't more she could ask, especially since Stef had included herself in the process. "When I finished undergrad, my girlfriend, Raquel, and I went to tour some of the lesser-known museums in Europe. We started dating in the fall and things between us got pretty intense. We even had lunch with her sister in Marseille. It was a gorgeous evening, and I set it up to be this ultra-romantic gesture at sunset, in a train station, in Prague. I told her that I loved her. She didn't say that she loved me back, which was disappointing, but I understood. She also said that she wished I hadn't told her sister that my father was from Brazil, which I didn't understand. She kissed me discretely and then went to use the restroom. She didn't come back.

"I thought she had been abducted. So, in less-than-perfect French—because that was the only language I had in common with security at the station—I told them Raquel was missing. After thirty minutes of absolute terror, they informed me she had taken a cab."

Stef's put the bourbon down and her brows knitted together. "Wait, she left you? Just like that? No, 'here's a letter, read it after ten minutes.'"

Perse shook her head.

Stef looked thoroughly repulsed. "What did you do?"

"I cried . . . a lot. And then I flew home because I wasn't as well traveled yet and was nervous backpacking through Europe by myself." Perse exhaled a quick breath. "Then there was Isabella."

"It happened again?" Stef asked in both outrage and shock.

"This time was a little different. Isabella and I were dating for six months or so, but we had been friends for about a year before that. Her family lived overseas, so I invited her to Christmas Eve dinner. She was hesitant but came anyway. During dessert my mom made a crack about starting a registry list. Isabella broke up with me the next day."

Stef connected the dots quickly. "She broke up with you on Christmas day? That's so fucked up."

"I thought that too and firmly believed Missy would kill her. After that, I swore off romance for a while because it had hurt so much. But then I met Anthony. Things were very serious between us. In fact, do you remember—before I signed the papers—when you asked me if I had ever been married?"

Stef nodded. "You said you hadn't had the pleasure. Wait . . . what did he do?"

"He proposed and we got engaged. He didn't want to do a simple ceremony at a courthouse or elope like I did. He wanted *elaborate*. There would be an engagement party, a bridal shower, a bachelorette party . . . the whole nine yards. I spent six months eating Prozac like it was candy. Then, he stood me up on our wedding day. His brother told me the heart-to-heart bro talk the night before about commitment must have gotten in his head."

Stef's fist was clenched, and Perse knew if Anthony had been there, he'd have been on the receiving end of it.

"The only thing that was remotely decent was that Anthony's family was mortified by what he did, and because they were completely loaded, they reimbursed me for the entire wedding."

For the first time since Perse had arrived, Stef reached for her. "How did you get over that?"

"I don't think I ever did. It broke me. Thank God I had a great advisor, or I probably would have had to redo a semester in grad school." She took another sip of bourbon. "After all of that, I decided it was safer if I kept people at a distance. Traveling so much helped avoid romantic relationships, and therefore, humiliation and heartache." She gave Stef a soft smile. "But, then I met you and all those wonderful but scary feelings came rushing back to me. Every time I was with you the walls I built around myself cracked just a little bit more."

"Your insistence at going slow was a lot more than just your new job," Stef said, causing Perse to nod. "Why did you even start dating me at all?"

"Because you're . . . you," Perse said with a nervous laugh. "You've brought a type of joy into my life that I haven't experienced in a very long time. The last decade or so I've been content, but being with you makes me happy."

A log shifted down into the coals of the fire pit, causing a *whoosh* and sparks to fly upwards.

Stef looked into Perse's eyes with intense focus. "It's like I'm seeing you for the first time. I don't know what to say."

"You don't have to say anything. You've been nothing but completely honest with me and I've censored myself. I don't want to do that anymore. I want more than anything for you to know me. To trust me. I want you to trust me so I can look after you, if you'll allow me."

That seemed to shift something in Stef. Her shoulders began to shake, her lips tightened, and she buried her face in her free hand. She let out a sob that racked her body.

Perse pushed out of her chair and keeled on the paver stones. She took Stef's sobbing form in her arms. "I've got you, sweetie."

Emotion and obvious sleep deprivation had finally caught up with Stef as she completely let go in Perse's arms. Stef's hiccups interrupted her speech multiple times, making the words unintelligible.

"Shhhh . . . It's okay." Perse wiped Stef's tears away. "You can tell me anything, and there are still things we need to talk about, but you're exhausted and I'm tired too. Can we talk after we rest?"

Stef nodded absently, and with Perse's assistance, got to her feet. They placed the wire dome over the fire pit, grabbed the bourbon, and went inside, then into the bedroom.

Relief and fatigue overwhelmed Perse's system as she chose two oversized t-shirts for both of them to wear. After they changed out of their work clothes in silence, Perse lifted the bedding for Stef, then joined her on the other side.

Stef draped an arm over Perse's stomach and cuddled into her. "Thank you for staying."

Perse vowed that she wouldn't be like those who had left her and lowered her lips to the crown of Stef's head. Her chest ached from not being able to tell Stef the final piece of her feelings. "I'll stay as long as you'll have me."

"But?"

Perse shifted her head on the pillow. In the dark room she could barely make out Stef's profile. "There's no but."

Stef shook her head. "It's your voice. It's like there's something else."

"I suppose there is, but I'm afraid if I tell you it might be selfish on my part. You're hurting and I don't want to complicate our situation."

"Is it bad?"

Perse grinned. "No, it's quite wonderful, actually."

"I'd rather you just tell me, then. I could use some good news."

Perse nodded and brushed a strand of hair behind Stef's ear. Her pupils had adjusted fully and she could now see Stef's features more clearly.

"I love you, Stef."

As the words left her mouth and the sleepy smile formed on Stef's lips, Perse was reassured she'd made the right decision to tell her.

"You don't—"

"I love you too, Perse." Stef pushed herself up and then kissed her softly.

Neither attempted to intensify their affection. They needed to heal the broken pieces between them before they gave into anything more.

But they would mend those wounds together.

***

A shrill and insistent beeping came from the alarm. It was the first time Perse had woken since falling asleep with Stef's head on her shoulder.

As Perse felt Stef's head lift and her body slip out of her arms, a wave of different feelings overcame her. She was proud that she had been honest about her feelings, overwhelmed that for the first time in decades she believed someone loved her, and very unsure about how Stef would feel today, given the emotions of the previous day.

Stef turned the alarm off and rolled back to her. The arm that slung over her waist and brought their bodies closer together was at least a sign Stef wasn't craving solitude or felt she had made a mistake. "You look confused."

"I think that's because I am." The new, honest path to explaining herself was liberating. "I want to support you through this, but I'm not sure how to do it."

"Do you love me?"

In the early morning light, the golden flecks in Stef's eyes seemed to sparkle. "Yes, I do. I'm sorry it took me so long to tell you."

"How long have you known?"

"I realized it at Christopher's party. It's what caused my anxiety attack. It just seemed too soon, you know?"

"I do. I figured it out when we were on my glider and you told me you liked my true self. How you said it . . . it was so intense. I knew you meant every word of it. I wanted to tell you when I came back from my conference, but Mei convinced me not to."

Perse would have fallen over if she hadn't already been lying down. "You told your ex-wife that you loved me? And you listened to her about not telling me?"

Stef nodded, embarrassed. "In retrospect that was a mistake. But she said I'd scare you off and I didn't want to do that, so I just thought I'd keep it to myself until you said it."

"I guess that part of the plan worked."

There was something else. Stef bit her lower lip anxiously and the calm hand that had been on Perse's hip started to fidget.

"Tell me what you're thinking," Perse asked in a gentle voice.

Stef took a moment and then sighed. "Something happened on Monday—two things, actually—and they basically happened at the same time. The first was that Wayne really pissed me off, and the second was that I was asked if I was interested in a job interview by one of the people I met at the conference. Timera and Gillian convinced me not to file anything about Wayne, but I did say I was interested in the job."

Their morning conversation had taken a surprising turn. "Is it another school?"

"No, it's an organization that investigates pathogen research. The US headquarters is in Atlanta, which is where the interview is."

Stef was intelligent, driven, and not tenured. Keeping one's options open was a necessity in academia. In fact, Stef could easily use the interview as leverage for promotion at CBU.

But the thought of Stef leaving made Perse feel angry about the unfairness of it all. They had just found each other! "When is it?" Perse kept her voice gentle and the disappointment out of it. The situation might not make her happy, but if it made Stef happy, they would find a way to make it work.

"Fall break. I have to fly down the same day as Alec's birthday party." Stef sat suddenly. "I didn't know what to do. I was so mad at Wayne for putting his stupid fungus in the *Pseudomonas* incubators that I just said yes. And"—Stef wiped at her tearing eyes—"Harry told me I was making a rash decision, but I tried to explain to him that an interview isn't a job. I don't think he understood."

"I agree that sometimes the interview process leads to great connections." Perse combed her fingers through Stef's hair. "I think Harry's generation has a different way of viewing these things than ours."

"So, you're okay with it?"

Honesty. It was all about honest feelings now. "'Okay' is a good word. Let's just say a long-distance relationship with you wouldn't be ideal, but I'll take any relationship over none, especially if it means you'd be happier working somewhere else."

Stef averted her eyes and her jaw began to quiver. "I wish Harry had known that."

The emotional crack that Perse had anticipated started to widen. She wrapped her arms around Stef and, after a minute of Stef sobbing, laid her back onto the bed, and pulled the covers over them.

"Sorry, I'm a mess this morning."

"You have every reason. Yesterday was an extremely emotional day. You can feel however you need to feel, and it doesn't have to be logical."

"Thank you, but I would have liked our post-I-love-you-morning-after not to have included me crying profusely."

Perse's fantasy hadn't included tears either, but it also hadn't included the circumstances that had caused them. "I'm just glad we're together."

Stef sniffled as she nodded and pulled a tissue from the box on the nightstand. "Will you go to Harry's service? I know you didn't know him very well, but it'd be nice if you came."

"If you want me there, then of course I will. Do you have any idea when it will be?"

Stef shrugged. "I'm not 100% sure, but I'd say over the weekend. Oh—the dinner with your parents." Stef's sad eyes were now vacant. She appeared lost.

Perse kissed the crown of her head. She would be Stef's compass, tether, and anything else she needed to be to help Stef feel secure. "If they overlap, I promise I'll find a way to do both. I'm not letting you down again."

CHAPTER NINETEEN

TWO WEEKS AGO, Perse thought that her weekend would consist of unwinding from the first week of the semester with a yoga class and spending a fun, sex-filled night or two with Stef. One week ago, the plan had changed to yoga and meditating to soothe her inner turmoil.

The up-to-date plan was waking early to drive to breakfast to see her parents, drive back to attend Harry's service, and be available if Stef needed her.

Perse laid out her clothes for the day, which would be comfortable enough to sustain four-plus hours in a car, hide any spills at breakfast, and be somber enough for the funeral service. She was grateful that her parents were happy to accommodate switching dinner to breakfast, and that they were willing to drive two hours for it too.

She had Missy to thank for the breakfast recommendation. She'd said the diner's crab cake eggs Benedict was to die for.

As Perse drove, she worried that with each passing exit sign her anxiety would increase. That each progressive swallow of water would be more difficult than the last. But it wasn't. Her energy was stable and her nerves were relaxed. After an uneventful drive filled with mostly silence, Perse saw her father's truck in the parking lot. But before getting out of her Jeep, she decided to give any potential anxiety that skulked inside of her a piece of her mind. "You're an invisible jerk. You're only real because I'm giving you the power to exist. I'm done with you!" And with that she confidently walked into the diner.

She spotted her parents at the same time they saw her. They stood from their seats, and her mother rushed to hug her.

"Hi, Mom, it's good to see you too."

Once Olivia released her, Paulo placed his strong arms around her, and left a dramatic kiss on her forehead which ended with a wet *smack*. "Your mother and I can't remember the last time only the three of us were together," he said and then took his seat.

"I guess it has been ages." Perse struggled to remember but the Beach Boys' song playing overhead jogged her memory. "It was when you were stationed in Coronado and I had a twelve-hour layover in San Diego."

"Oh, that's right!" Olivia said with a broad smile. "We really should get together, just the three of us, more than once every five years."

"I'll second that," Paulo said, and held up his coffee cup.

Perse sipped her water and felt it slowly struggle down her throat.

"I want you to know that I'm not going to ask questions," Olivia said. "Missy said that something was worrying you."

Of course Missy would have said something to them ahead of time. "That helps. Missy's really helped me a lot during this . . . relationship-building period I've had with Stef. What has she told you about her?"

"Aside from telling your mother not to get ahead of herself?" Paulo asked with a grin. "Missy told us Stef is about her age, played sports in college, is down-to-earth, treats you with respect, is a bit neurotic, and hates Wayne. Did I forget anything?" Paulo asked Olivia.

"She's blond."

"How could I forget that?" Paulo asked with a slight chuckle. "So, as you can tell, we know *some* things about her, but we'd like to learn more." He stared at Perse, politely bobbing his head. "Whenever you're ready," he said after several seconds.

"Do you mind if we order first?" Perse asked. "I really need stable blood sugar levels for today."

As if the word 'order' had been amplified throughout the restaurant, their waitress was there seconds later.

After they went around the table with their orders, Perse got to the biggest issue first. "Every major relationship I have ever been in ended because of some sort of family issue. Raquel's racist sister, Isabella's reaction to Mom, and Anthony's brother's meddling. For the longest time I was done with relationships. I was completely emotionally drained. And for a very long time my work, and my work alone, kept me going. But then I met Stef." Perse smiled as she recalled the beginning of their courtship. "I resisted any relationship at first because of my new job and also working with her friends in my department. But, she's just . . . funny and honest, smart, sensitive, and it didn't take me very long to realize that . . . I love her." She took her phone out and brought up one of her favorite pictures of Stef.

Stef's capris were rolled to the knee as she waded in the ocean and waved at her with an enormous grin.

"This is her."

Olivia took the phone instantly and tilted her head so she could see with her bifocals. "Aww," she said with her hand over her heart. She passed the phone to Paulo, who simply nodded.

"Another part about Stef, a heartbreaking part, is that she doesn't have any family." Perse took another sip and paused. "When it comes to relationships, families became a phobia for me, but for Stef, family is a need. She was unbelievably excited when I accidently met Harry, who was like a surrogate uncle, and over the moon when I said I would tell you two last weekend. But my anxiety, and an extremely potent brownie, got the best of me and I couldn't do it. Instead, I scared you two and disappointed Stef. I can't say for certain if she would have spoken to me before us meeting today, but Harry's death . . . I wanted to give her space, but she needed me. A few days ago, I told her for the first time that I love her, and she loves me too."

"That just shows she has good sense," Paulo said with a slight smile. "I'm glad you're going to be there for her today."

"It won't just be me. She has good friends who are coming to the service too, so Stef will have a supportive network around her today. We'll get her through this."

"That's really good to hear." Olivia took the napkin from her lap and dabbed her eyes. "I'm sorry, it's just I'm proud of you in a way I've never been before. I can see how much you care, and even though it's such a sad day, I don't think I've seen you happier as when you talked about Stef."

An observation like that should have sent her reeling into a full-blown anxiety attack, but Perse smiled. "I can't tell you you're wrong."

"I promise I won't say anything else that . . . personal," Olivia said. "And I promise if I ever meet Stef, I'll be very mindful of my questions and comments."

Perse grinned. "I appreciate that. And I promise to be more forthcoming with my personal life. I know you want to know because you care. Plus, if I tell you, it'll give Missy a break from being the intermediary. I know that's frustrating for her."

"I see how it wears on her," Paulo said. "That and soccer. God, she hates soccer."

***

As promised, once Perse escaped the traffic and took the exit for Stef's house, she dialed Missy's number.

"You'll get it next time, Liz!" Missy yelled as her greeting— she was clearly still at the soccer match. "Hey! You're running behind schedule, Sis."

"I had to wait for the food the waitress forgot to put in for Stef."

"You got Stef food from a diner two hours away?"

"No, Mom said that Stef probably hasn't eaten a lot and insisted on buying her something."

Missy laughed. "That is so like her. Here, go have a snack so I can talk to your aunt Perse."

Perse shook her head while she pictured Missy bribing Alec to give her some space.

"So, how'd it go?" Missy asked. "Is the air clear?"

"It went really well. I didn't lay out Stef's life story to them, but I definitely gave them a substantial amount of details."

"How about the family fear?"

"Yes, I talked about my issues. Mom promised to behave herself if she ever meets Stef. And that was about it. Then we talked about regular stuff until I had to leave, which was really nice. I'm kind of worried about how much coffee Dad can drink though."

"Yeah, he can really throw that stuff back. I'm glad to hear it went so well. Are you still on schedule for the rest of your day?"

"I'm picking Stef up in ten minutes, and the service is in an hour. I should be fine."

"No! Sorry, that wasn't you. Alec is trying to give himself parasites by eating candy that fell in the grass. Have you told Stef about how breakfast went?"

"I sent her a message and asked if she wanted to talk, but she was having an odd morning—according to her—so I texted her a summary. She said that my morning gave her something to smile about. So, I'm happy I could do that for her."

"You've transitioned from a sex-centric, relationship-phobe to an emotionally available girlfriend. I'm proud of you."

"You sound like Mom."

"Hey! That's— Damn. Liz just got knocked down and seriously stomped on the girl who did it. Maybe soccer isn't too bad."

"It's nice to know we're all experiencing personal growth today."

"Oh, there's a yellow card. Dammit. Now Liz looks sad. I need to see if she's okay, but thanks for the update. I'm glad everything went well, and now you can both move on, but one bit of advice before I go: don't be surprised today."

Perse felt her brow scrunch. "I don't understand."

"You will. Love you, Sis!"

Why would I be surprised? Perse asked herself.

CHAPTER TWENTY

ONCE SHE PULLED into the carport, Perse finally understood what her sister meant. The sudden death of a loved one caused different people to respond differently. The initial shock and denial seemed to be universal. However, she had known many people who had skipped the anger and bargaining stages and had jumped straight to depression. Conversely, she remembered a classmate from graduate school who had remained angry for months after his mother passed.

Perse didn't know how Stef would handle her grief, but she would be there to listen to the injustice of another loved one stripped from her life, offer a shoulder to cry on when there were tears, or say words of comfort to soothe Stef. Whatever she needed.

Perse approached the house, sandwich in hand. The sound of cheering from the television carried through the window.

When the door opened, the emotional wreck of a person Perse expected to see was not there. Stef looked tired but composed in her gray pants and black knit tee.

The cheering was then accompanied by the ringing of a bell. Perse recognized it as a boxing movie at the same time that Stef hugged her. Perse wrapped her arms around Stef and received a kiss on the cheek. "Hi, sweetie," she said softly.

"I'm really glad you're here." Stef turned and went into the house. "I can turn off the movie."

"What are you watching?"

Stef took the remote from the coffee table and paused on a boxer's bloodied face. "Harry loved the new *Creed* movies, but he would get so pissed if someone called them a reboot. 'It's a spin-off!'"

Perse had never seen the films but followed Stef's lead and took a seat on the couch. "Movies allow us to connect in surprising ways."

Stef nodded, then stared into space before chuckling softly to herself. "Sorry. I'm mentally all over the place today. The end of the week was fine. Bradyn offered to cover my lab, and I could lecture with no problems because I had something so different to focus on, but this morning . . . I've been frazzled. I just haven't known what to do with myself. I woke up crazy early and texted Timera to see if she'd workout with me. Which she was game for, so we went for a run around the park where I saw the cutest puppy ever, a *boxador*."

Perse smiled when Stef's face briefly lit up at the mention of the puppy.

"And the entire time I was running, my brain kept going back and forth between Harry's funeral and your breakfast with your parents. I was so nervous it wasn't going to work out for you, but once I saw your text there was like this huge, gigantic wave of relief, and I ended up buying you stuff."

"You brought me stuff?"

Stef nodded. "And then I thought my mind would clear so I could focus on Harry again, which worked, but now I feel bad."

Perse was still stuck on the fact that Stef had bought presents. "Why do you feel bad?"

"Because I'm not crying," Stef said. "When everyone else died, I was a mess for weeks. I don't understand why I'm processing this differently. Harry was so important to me. I should be grieving him in the same way as I grieved for the rest of my family, don't you think?"

Perse took Stef's hand and scooted closer to her. "I think that you're a different person now, and because of that your grieving process is different. Also, subconsciously . . . maybe you've been preparing for this?"

Stef nodded. "I can see how that's true. Harry did talk about dying a lot once Aunt Carol passed. He told me he wasn't worried about his kids because they were all grown with good heads on their shoulders, and he was just killing time until he could finally learn what was on the other side."

"It sounds like he was at peace with his life."

"I think he was," Stef said, then brushed away a stray tear. "Doesn't mean I'll miss him any less. I'm just a bit more controlled about my weeping this time around."

Perse smiled even though she knew Stef's emotions would most likely change. Stef needed to find a rationale to her own reaction. To find the logic in it.

"Can you tell me about your breakfast now?" Stef asked. "I don't want today to be all about me."

Perse wanted Stef to speak about her emotions more, but Stef didn't want to talk about Harry. Perse needed to respect that. "Well, to summarize, breakfast really couldn't have gone any better."

"Really?" Stef said with such joy a small laugh escaped Perse.

"Yes. I decided at the last minute to get out the picture of you at the beach—"

"You showed them that?" Stef asked, surprised.

Perse would have thought Stef was angry had her smile not still been in place. "I did. It's a great picture of you and I wanted them to have a visual when I told them that I love you and you love me."

"You really told them that?" Stef asked innocently.

Perse patted Stef's hand, which had moved to her knee. "Yes, they know. I won't say they know everything, because there was only so much time, but they know why I was scared to tell them about us and how much I care about you. I think that's why they bought you lunch." When nothing but confusion passed over Stef's face, Perse picked the box off the table and handed it to her. "My mom said that you probably hadn't eaten real food in a while and insisted on getting you a sandwich. Don't worry, there was ice around it in the car."

Stef stared at the box.

After several seconds of watching Stef, Perse cleared her throat. "Stef, are you okay?"

"Yeah, I'm fine. I just can't believe how thoughtful this is. I couldn't tell you the last time someone did something like this for me."

"Get used to it. Now that my parents know how important you are to me, you can expect a lot of food. Probably offers of yard maintenance too."

"That's . . ." Stef gulped. "This means so much to me." She put the box on the coffee table and cradled Perse's face before drawing her in for a kiss. "I love you so much," Stef said before kissing her again.

"I love you too. And I need to thank you."

"Thank me for what?"

"You encouraged me to get everything out in the open." Perse gazed into Stef's soulful brown eyes and smiled. "Talking to Mom and Dad about you today wasn't only liberating, I also really enjoyed it."

"Really?" Stef beamed.

Perse nodded and reached for Stef's hand, which still rested on her knee. "They respected my wishes and didn't pry. They just let me talk—which is something Missy never lets me do—and it turns out that talking about my relationship with you is something that brings me great joy."

"All of this is really amazing. I . . . just don't even know what to say." Stef leaned forward and kissed her again.

Perse felt her bottom lip gradually become enveloped in Stef's mouth. The kiss was more than a brief, physical reminder of how much Stef cared for her. This kiss was stimulating, and when she felt Stef's tongue slip past her lips, Stef's intent was clear.

She pulled away, and as a result Stef frowned.

Perse sighed and looked at Stef, whose vulnerability had peaked. She needed to be honest and compassionate with why she stopped them from going further. Stef didn't need the sting of rejection added to her list of growing emotions. "The way you were kissing me. I stopped because . . . I'm not one-hundred percent certain, but I think you want more and I'm not sure if that's really something we should do right now"

"I do want more, and it's something I need now." Stef grazed her thumb over Perse's cheek with the gentlest of touches. "You've given your family a chance to *really* know me. You're not ashamed of me or hiding me away. I've never had that, and it's the best gift I ever could have asked for. I want to take a moment with you to celebrate that. I want everything else in the world to fall away so it can just be us. I want time to freeze so I can feel you love me."

Stef's words cut through Perse's reluctance and went straight into her heart. "I'll never be ashamed of you, and I can show you how much I love you." Perse pressed her mouth and body against Stef's. She wanted—needed—for Stef to feel all the love she had for her.

Perse didn't want the first time they made love with such emotional weight to have a deadline. She wanted the experience to last for hours, but the way Stef pulled her on top of her and wrapped her legs around her waist told her that Stef couldn't wait.

The intensity of their feelings also gave rise to a shift in their physical dynamic. Because of the levels and their default preferences, Perse had never been in the dominant role. Even when Perse had initiated sex, Stef had taken the lead.

But now, Stef wanted to be taken, and Perse wanted to give that to her.

Perse roughly pulled off her own shirt and dove back into Stef's lips while she sought for the edge of her knit tee.

Stef pushed herself slightly off the couch, giving Perse the space to rid her of the shirt.

Perse saw the wanton passion in Stef's features, and gently lowered herself again. Perse's thigh between Stef's legs added a spark to the fuel already on the verge of combustion. She knew what Stef craved, because it was the same thing she did.

Perse wanted them to burn together.

A shudder ran through Perse as Stef's tongue slid across her lips, and she lightly scratched at the skin of her thighs under her bunched skirt.

"I need you," Stef whispered. "All of you."

"Soon," she murmured. Perse dropped her mouth to Stef's neck, inhaling the sweet scent of her lavender soap, and teased the skin between her ear and jawbone with her lips and tongue. "Feel how much I need you too," Perse said as her hands went under Stef's arched back and unclasped her bra. The feel of Stef's naked back against her fingertips stoked the flames inside of her. Perse wanted to cherish the moment, but her need to feel all of what Stef was giving her was greater.

Perse's hands went to the straps at Stef's shoulders and slid down her bra until it fell loosely from her arms. As one palm cupped and teased Stef's breast, Perse's mouth trailed from Stef's neck, to the muscles of her upper chest, to the swell of her breast, to her other nipple. Perse felt the clasp of her own bra release the same time she felt Stef's nipple harden against the surface of her tongue.

The sensation of her naked chest against Stef's amplified Perse's desire. She felt heat radiate off her skin, and Stef's hands on her buttocks drove her thigh closer.

Stef was finished with foreplay, but Perse wasn't.

Perse began a steady rhythm with her hips, grinding into her, as she kissed Stef's lips, neck, and breasts. When Stef began to writhe beneath her, Perse went to the button and zipper of Stef's slacks and hastily pushed them and her bikini briefs down.

"Please," Stef said in a shaky voice. "I need you."

"I know, sweetie. I promise you'll have me soon." Perse kissed Stef and moved her hand from the outside of Stef's thigh to the inside where brown, wiry curls tickled her palm. Perse's eyes traveled up from her hand to Stef's chest, which rose and fell in a quick rhythm, to her closed eyes. The sight was undeniably arousing. "Open your eyes for me," Perse softly requested.

Stef did.

The look they shared was beyond sex. It was trust and love at the deepest level possible. Now, Stef could give herself to Perse in ways that she hadn't been able to before. Perse watched every nuance of Stef's face shift as she pushed her fingers inside her and was embraced by Stef's wet heat. It was the most intimate moment Perse had ever shared with another person.

Perse kept her rhythm strong. She noticed every touch, moan, and sigh, as she gave Stef everything she had. Soon, Stef's eyes shut again, her breathing quickened, her short fingernails dug into Perse's back, while her other hand moved from Perse's breast to grip the couch cushion beneath her.

The walls surrounding Perse's fingers began to gradually squeeze in a vice-like grip as Stef's orgasm built slowly. Stef released it with a powerful sound that was more scream than moan.

When the sharp feel from the nails in her back disappeared, Perse slowly withdrew. She kissed Stef gently and then smiled down at her awestruck face. "That was new."

Stef absently nodded like the whole world was out of focus, but then the hazed look in her eyes cleared. "I love you."

"I love you too." Perse looked down their bodies, amused by the skirt that was now at her waist and pants that still clung to Stef's ankle. She smoothed down some of Stef's wild hair and saw the time. Hesitantly, she lifted herself off Stef. "I wish we could cuddle, but we have to leave soon."

"Leave . . . ?" Stef looked at her watch. "Shit!" She stood and pulled her pants back up. She thoughtfully stared at the couch while they both put on their bras and shirts.

"What's wrong?"

"I was just wondering if it's normal to do that before . . . you know, going to a funeral."

Perse ran her fingers through Stef's hair again. "I hate the notion of 'normal' on days like this. I think people do what they need to do to get through it all. In this case, I think you needed to feel loved."

"You're very wise, Dr. Teixeira." Stef's eyes went to the coffee table. "Also, according to that logic, it's completely acceptable that I want to devour that sandwich."

"Absolutely. You can eat it in the car, but before we go you should probably brush your hair."

Stef scrunched her brow and went to the mirror by the front door. "Ah!" she yelped. "Yeah, that could be a subject of conversation. Be right back."

When Stef left for the bathroom, Perse got her phone and sent a text to Missy. *You were right about the surprises.*

***

Perse held Stef's hand in the crowded funeral home and watched Harry's fleet of friends and family mill about before the beginning of the service. One young grandchild didn't understand the traditional hushed tones of the establishment and wailed at the top of their lungs.

Stef sniffled beside her. Perse followed Stef's line of sight to a photograph of Harry, his wife, and Stef's aunt in the corner of the room. Stef brought them closer to the picture and gestured towards it. "That was a fun day," she said between new tears. "Aunt Carol moved into their building. It was kind of like watching kids when they move into dorms."

Perse smiled as she imagined the day Stef described. The picture seemed to have a calming effect on Stef's resurgence of emotions. After Stef had finished her sandwich in the car, another wave of grief had struck her.

Stef's eyes were mildly bloodshot now she looked at Perse thoughtfully.

"What?" Perse asked.

"Do you want children?"

"Ahh," Perse drawled in surprise. She hoped she had misheard, but Stef waited patiently for an answer. "Are you sure you want to talk about this now? That's a huge question, and I think they're going to start soon. The preacher is at the lectern." It was the best stall Perse could think of.

"I know, but with the baby crying and kids in college, it just came to me. And I'd be lying if I said it hadn't crossed my mind before now."

It had crossed Perse's mind as well. She knew Stef wanted a family, but what that family specifically comprised of, she didn't know.

"So, what do you think?" Stef persisted. "We should discuss it, especially as we might be on different sides of the fence."

"I agree, but this is already a tough, emotional day for you. If we do feel differently, I don't want to make it worse."

Stef skewed her face. "Not worse, just . . . more informative. I like facts. You know that."

Perse saw the determination on Stef's face. She would not let the question go unanswered. "No, I don't want kids."

Stef audibly sighed. "That's a relief."

"Really?" Perse said a few decibels too loudly for the room full of mourners, and then sheepishly led them to two vacant seats in the back. "That really surprises me," she said in a whisper.

"Well, I used to think that I might, but I see the work it takes and I'd much rather focus on my existing loved ones and myself. Plus, I'd rather have dogs, like that boxador. Much cheaper, more loyal, and less time consuming."

"I completely agree," Perse said with restrained enthusiasm. "Plus, I feel like I saw a different side of motherhood when I lived with Missy. You should see the laundry! I don't know how she does it."

Stef smirked and opened her mouth to respond, but a tap on her shoulder caused her to look behind her. She stood and accepted a hug from Timera. "Thanks for coming, guys."

"The least we could we do," Gillian responded and leaned down to Perse. "How's she doing?"

Perse watched Stef and Timera chat in hushed tones, but Stef had a ghost of a smile. "All things considered, I think she's doing well."

Gillian nodded and gestured to the front of the room. "Preacher's starting. I'm going to grab a seat. We'll catch up after."

The service started with a song and prayer, during which Perse instinctually closed her eyes and recited from memory. Religion wasn't something she and Stef had spoken about at length. Perse appreciated and respected different views of the world, but for the first time she wondered if her family would be as accepting to learn that Stef was an atheist. It wasn't as though they were strict in their beliefs. Her father was Roman Catholic and her mother was Methodist, and somehow they had formed a compromise and raised her and Missy Episcopalian.

As Perse listened to the preacher speak about Harry's life, family, and friends, the man who had been Stef's friend came more into focus, which caused her to see several parallels between Harry and her own father. She delicately dabbed her eyes when the tightly folded American flag was presented to Harry's eldest.

When the last song had been sung, the group of mourners stood row by row to see Harry one last time. For Perse, the saddest part of saying goodbye was watching others do it. The raw emotion that came from their throats and dripped down their faces was almost too intimate to bear witness to.

"Do you want to go up?" Perse asked at the same time a woman's sob carried through the room.

"I have to say goodbye."

The strength in Stef's voice surprised Perse. She looked back to where Timera and Gillian sat and gave them a tilt of her head to indicate that she and Stef were going to the front.

There was no way for her to know what Stef thought as she approached the casket. Once Perse saw his slightly waxy-looking face, she heard Stef stifled a small laugh. "What?"

"Seems like he'll be buried with his ball cap after all."

When Stef moved forward and Perse followed, she saw the black and bright orange cap. It clashed with his red paisley tie, but she still liked it. Perse refocused to say a silent prayer that he was at peace with his departed family, then walked with Stef and the others to the coat closet.

"I don't want a viewing when I die," Stef said seriously to her support system.

"Okay, what do you want?" Timera asked.

"Just put me in the ground and plant a tree. Let nature sort it out."

Perse nodded patiently. She was uncertain how Stef would react after the service, and while death was a natural topic, she wasn't sure if Harry's family would appreciate the conversation. "Do you want to go to the burial?"

"That's family only. How about we get a drink? You guys good with that?"

Gillian scoffed. "It's like you don't even know us."

***

Midway through their second round of cocktails—Stef's third—at the waterfront restaurant, Perse found herself truly enjoying the dynamic between Stef, Timera, and Gillian. She had seen a hint of it at Christopher's party a few months back, but now they were all more comfortable with one another. They could joke. They could take a good-natured jab. And, for Perse, there was no anxiety about asking a question that had weighed on her mind for months.

"So, Stef said that she came up with the levels while on a cruise with you two. I was wondering if you could tell me more about that?"

"There's not much to say about my flawless, brilliant system," Stef said with a cocky grin. Her cheeks were beginning to flush from the liquor in her orange crushes.

Timera laughed heartily. "I disagree. It all started with this waitress—what was her name?" she asked Gillian.

235

"Lea! She was a real looker."

Stef sighed dramatically. "The only part to the story Lea's relevant to is that she brought me a pen and paper so I could write down my initial thoughts."

"Sure," Timera drawled. "The part where she pinned you against the rail of the cruise ship and started making out with you in front of everyone is completely irrelevant."

Perse turned to Stef with an amused smile. Who knew her rule-following, level-loving girlfriend was into risqué deck antics? "And just what did you do about that?"

"I turned down her sexual advances because she would not go on a date with me to the popcorn snack shack. I knew anyone worthy of my love would respect my levels. And I was right!" Stef punctuated her exclamation with a kiss on Perse's cheek.

Perse's phone beeped.

"You two are just so cute," Gillian said and pointed to the phone, partially covered by the napkin the breeze had blown over it. "You might want to check that."

Perse moved the napkin and saw that Missy had texted her. "Just my sister. I can get back to her later."

"Missy! She is so awesome," Stef said to Timera and Gillian, and then turned back to Perse. "You should call her! Family is so important."

Perse looked to both Timera and Gillian, who both gave her go-ahead nods.

There was no way she was winning that battle. "I'll be right back." Perse took her phone and a water with her to the furthest edge of the outdoor dining patio.

"Shit," Missy said. "I didn't actually think you'd call me."

"I was encouraged to by the rest of the table. Honestly, I just think Gillian and Timera want to tease Stef a bit about us now that she's drunk."

"You guys went out after the service for some drinks? I take it Stef's doing alright, then?"

"I think she is." Perse leaned against the wooden railing and watched the table where Stef used wild hand gestures to explain something. "Her emotions are not what I expected at all. She's had moments of sadness and has cried a few times, but she's happy now, and before the service . . . Well, she was very excited that the breakfast went well, and we . . ."

"You had sex, didn't you?"

How did she know that? "We did, but it was different."

"Different how?"

"Missy, I don't think you need to know that."

"I told you when Gary and I broke the recliner because of reverse cowgirl."

Perse bit her lip and shook her head. "And I didn't need to know that. But to briefly answer your question, the sex was more intense."

"That makes sense. Emotions are hitting her from all angles, so being a weepy mess might not be on the cards today."

"But the laughing?" Perse watched Stef listen intently to Gillian and then burst into giggles again. There was also a fresh drink in front of her. Perse hoped that would be it for the night.

"You're probably too young to remember that during the viewing for Poppop, Mom laughed hysterically."

"I don't remember that. Well, I remember the grand piano in wherever the viewing was held."

"Of course you would. It's always about a fucking piano with you. The point is, I asked Dad what was wrong with Mom. He just said that nothing was. She had a lot of memories and feelings, and they were going to come to her at different times and she would express them in different ways. Nothing is wrong with Stef. She's just processing her emotions as they come to her."

Now, for whatever reason, Stef looked introspective and pointed to the open water.

"She's definitely not lacking emotions." Perse came to terms that she would essentially be spending time with a one-woman soap opera for the evening. "What you are doing tonight?"

"Having a me-night! Gary is camping with the kids since I did that concert. I have a quiet house, an R-rated movie, and mudslide fixings. I am good to go!"

"You deserve more nights like that. I'll let you get to it."

"Thanks, but text me if something crazy happens. Like if Stef wants to start picking up hitchhikers or something."

Perse really hoped that wouldn't be the case. "I promise. Have a good night. Love you."

She walked back over to the table to see Timera signing a bill and Gillian nodding along to Stef's explanation of brain chemistry and attraction.

"Perse!" Gillian said. "Thank God you're back."

"I was only gone for two minutes."

"Yet it seemed so much longer," Timera said and closed the bill fold. "You can get it the next time out, Perse."

That was a pleasant surprise. "Thank you. Are you both heading home now?" Perse asked.

"And so are you," Gillian said, and then added in a whisper, "Stef is very excited to go home all the sudden. She's also very drunk."

"I'm tipsy," Stef corrected and finished her drink.

With the bill settled and Perse grateful she had been given stingy pours of pinot grigio, she and Stef waved goodbye to Timera and Gillian and headed back to Stef's home.

"Did something happen that made you want to leave so suddenly?"

"No! Well, yes. I had such a good time with the three of you. My best friends and my girlfriend all together, getting along. Oh! And you talked to your sister, so at one point it was like she was there too. Man, I can't wait for someday the five of us to get together. That'll be something else."

Perse passed Stef the water bottle in her cup holder. "Maybe the next time Missy comes to visit, I can ask her."

"That would be the best!" Stef took a sip and turned in her seat so she could look at Perse more fully. "I told Timera and Gillian I love you, and that you said you loved me. I know I should have asked you if I could do that, but I couldn't help it. It was like something had removed a filter inside of me."

"Could it have been the vodka?

"No," Stef said with a laugh. "Well, maybe. You're so smart. Also, you're talented, sexy, and a fashionable dresser."

For the next ten minutes, Perse experienced the greatest self-esteem boost of her life as Stef went into detail about all the elements of her personality. Of course, all good things come to an end. Perse pulled into Stef's driveway just as Stef finished the bottle of water. She put her car in park, and glanced over Stef. "Okay, let's get you inside."

"That's what she said." Stef giggled at her own joke all the way to the door and dropped her keys after attempting to insert the key into the lock. Normally, Stef didn't have problems with depth perception. But, then again, she also didn't normally have four drinks in an evening.

Perse's way of being there for Stef had translated into providing a hand to hold, a shoulder to cry on, and being the designated driver for their surprisingly fun, post-funeral drinks and dinner with Timera and Gillian. She laughed along with Stef at the obstacle the deadbolt presented. "Just let me do it. You're drunk."

"I'm not drunk. I'm tipsy." Stef found her keys behind a potted plant and successfully opened the door. "Ta-da!"

Perse leaned down and kissed her inebriated girlfriend, who then grabbed the lapels of her jacket and pulled her in for a deeper, more enthusiastic version.

Perse pulled away from the kiss with a loud *smack*. "That was quite the celebration for just getting the door open."

"I'm excited to show you something. I was going to wait, but the timing is too perfect." She pulled Perse down the hallway and into the bedroom.

"I have a feeling I've actually seen what you want to show me."

"I can promise that you haven't."

Perse scrutinized Stef. She didn't want Stef to feel that she was in any way abnormal for being cheerful, but at the same time she didn't want Stef to put on a false smile. "May I ask why the timing is perfect?"

"Sure!" Stef said as she bounced slightly on the bed. "It's because I love you, and did you know that this is the first time we've really hung out with Timera and Gillian as a foursome?"

"You may have mentioned that in the car," Perse said patiently.

"I did?" Stef furrowed her brow but then waved her arms about. "Doesn't matter. The point is that you get along with my friends so well and they really like you too. And it just makes me want you in my life more. So, if you wouldn't mind, open that top dresser drawer."

Perse played along. Her hands went to the two knobs on either side and she pulled. Inside there was a box of green tea, the latest Pulitzer Prize-winning novel, and lounge pants of the softest cotton. Perse turned to Stef, eyes wide and mouth agape.

"Do you like it?" Stef practically shouted.

Perse stared at the contents. "This is . . . Oh, boy." Perse couldn't finish her thought with her blood pressure dropping so quickly. She knew exactly what it was. What it meant. But to say it out loud was too much. She sat on the bed to steady herself and chose to focus on the logistics. "When did you do this?"

"This was the shopping I did after my run this morning. I went to that Miscellaneous Everything store," Stef said with less volume. Her tipsy energy had started to wane. "This is going to sound clichéd, but the last few days I've been thinking nonstop about what makes me happy and how I want to fill however many days I have left. I know that we've only been together approximately three months and fifteen days, but I know that I love waking up with you. When I got that text from you this morning, I decided to pull the trigger. Although, I wasn't planning on showing you tonight."

"When were you planning on showing me?"

"I was going to work it into conversation over the next month. I figured since I'm meeting more of your family at Alec's party, it made sense to start sharing more of my space with you. See what it's like."

Perse had so many questions. "Aren't you afraid you'll miss your space? I mean"—

Perse held up the novel—"this implies that I'd literally be hanging around your house reading."

"I know!" Her enthusiasm returned. "I have this fantasy where I'm watching TV and you're reading with your legs resting on my thighs and we're both thirsty but we're also too comfortable to move."

"Could I be reading because I'm waiting for my laundry to finish?" Perse asked with her eyebrow quirked. Maybe it wasn't such a frightening idea after all.

"Absolutely! I can adjust my laundry schedule accordingly. I can make a chart that shows your days and mine."

Perse put her hand on Stef's knee and smiled softly while she thought of the perfect words. It was a sweet gesture, but there were responsibilities and logistics to consider. "But what if I'm over here, and you need to leave because of a lab emergency or something. I'm so grateful for this, but at the same time I don't want to be stuck here."

Stef brow furrowed and her lips pursed. Perse knew that look. Different ideas were at war with each other in Stef's mind.

"Hold that thought." Stef scampered out of the room.

Perse was at a loss as to what Stef was up to. One thing was for certain, any more major surprises or mood swings and she knew they would both need emotional support. Perse hadn't experienced the death of a loved one, but the day was still exhausting for her too. The rustling in the kitchen and Stef's quickening steps—along with the sound of Stef knocking an end table astray—let Perse know that she would know her answer soon enough.

Stef came back with a manila envelope no larger than her palm. She took a seat beside Perse and gave her the envelope. "Seems appropriate given the conversation."

Curious to see what else Stef had in store for her, she opened the envelope and dropped its contents onto her palm. She held a key between her thumb and forefinger, with no words able to leave her mouth.

"It's to the house, and it's yours!"

A wave of light-headedness struck Perse.

Stef caught her before she fell forward and gently laid her down on the bed. She kneeled down and brushed Perse's hair off her brow. "Baby, are you okay?"

Perse got her bearings by focusing on the support of the mattress at her back. "I . . . ah . . . I'm good. I should probably stay down though."

Stef nodded vigorously and lay beside her. "I promise I wasn't trying to make you pass out. I thought the key would be a nice surprise."

"You definitely surprised me. Can I ask why you want me to have this?" Everything with Stef was about boundaries, after all.

Stef took her time to answer and laced her fingers behind her head. "It comes down to the fact that I love you and the thought of you having a bad day and going to your apartment where the only thing to greet you is the grease smell from that fast food place makes me sad."

"You said the smell wasn't noticeable."

"I lied," Stef said. "I just want you to feel welcome here. Even when I'm not around. Is that okay? Plus, now if there is an emergency and I have to leave, you can lock up with no problems."

Perse thought about what Stef was offering. Stef loved her and wanted to share her life in the most practical manner possible. It was a massive step in their relationship. Too massive. "I'm sorry, but this is too much. It feels like you are asking me to move in with you.."

Stef's brow furrowed. "You seemed so happy about the perks of coming over."

"I am, but that's when I'm already here." Perse held the key in front of her. "This gives me permission to treat your house like my house. To come and go as I please, even when you're not there. I acknowledge and appreciate the trust you have to give me this, but I don't think I can make that step. At least, not yet."

Stef scrunched her mouth and sucked her teeth. She wasn't mad, but Perse could tell she was in for a debate. "But you clean."

Perse stared at Stef's set jaw and then laughed. "No, I don't."

"Yes, you do. You use coasters and put the pillows back exactly the way they were, and I don't know why, but at some point you used my dustpan."

"There were toaster crumbs on the floor. I couldn't just leave them there. And I still don't see your point."

"You're considerate and I love you and you always smell so nice. I just want more of you."

Perse looked at the key in her palm. "So, this isn't a move-in invitation?"

Stef shook her head dramatically. "No."

"This is for my convenience and so you can see me more often?"

Stef nodded emphatically. "Correct."

"Are you're sure you'll feel this way in the morning when you're sober?"

"Absolutely! And I'm not drunk. I'm tipsy."

This wasn't sounding like a terrible arrangement. "Despite my occasional need to clean, there are no designated chores," Perse stated firmly.

Stef leaned forward until their noses touched. "Not yet. That's the true cohabitation level. We're not there yet and won't be until I meet your *whole family*. And, don't worry, Alec's party doesn't count."

The mention of Alec's party brought up a new point. "And what happens with all of this—and us—if you get the job in Atlanta?" Perse asked and immediately regretted it. "I'm sorry, Stef. This is huge issue that we probably shouldn't talk about until the morning. We've both had a long day, and—"

"The interview is mostly leverage for tenure."

"But what about the part this isn't *mostly* for leverage? The part which implies there's a part of you that's genuinely interested."

Stef's face softened as though she finally understood Perse's fear. "I have to go to Atlanta to learn about the specifics of the job; however, I do know that there is substantial travel from there back to this area. So, if I were offered the job, and on the *slim* chance I would take it, I think we still have what it takes to make our relationship work. You didn't seem crazy about the idea of a long-distance relationship, but you weren't completely opposed either, right?"

Perse was relieved to hear that her suspicion about tenure was true and understood the compromise some professions required even if she didn't like it. They were in incredibly niche fields where only weekends at home weren't unheard of. Plus, Perse had grown up in a similar way; her father had sometimes gone away for months at a time when he'd been deployed.

"Please don't worry about things that *might* happen," Stef said with a squeeze of her hand. "I would never do anything to jeopardize what we've started to build together, and I promise that if even a *tiny* part of me wants that job, I'll discuss it with you."

"You sound pretty tipy for someone who's tipsy." Perse brought her lips to Stef's and then looked back down at the key in her hand. "Did you get this today too?"

Stef shook her head. "I've had that for ages. I would have gotten you a shinier key. Do you need a shinier key?"

Perse smiled softly. "No, this will be just fine."

#

On the curb outside of Alec's elementary school, Missy handed Alec his lunch bag as she said goodbye. "Now, what do you do if that boy is mean to you again?"

"I tell him I have peanuts and I'll throw them at him because of his allergy!"

Missy gritted her teeth. "I was just kidding when I said that to your daddy, and you were supposed to be in bed. What you should do is tell your teacher fast and then tell me at home, okay?"

"Okay," he said, disappointed, and then hugged her legs goodbye.

Missy waved as he went into the school, then scrambled back into the car to dial her sister. Ever since she'd read the text from Perse that morning, she had been chomping at the bit for this conversation. "Pick up. Pick up. Pick up."

"Missy?"

"Holy shit! Stef gave you a key?"

"Um . . . yeah. Wait, I'm confused. You texted back when I told you yesterday morning. You're acting like this is the first time you're hearing about it."

Missy sighed. "Alec stole my phone and I didn't see your last text until right before I left the house. Didn't you find it weird I only responded with emojis of presents?"

"Oh, I thought you were using metaphors."

"No, Dr. Symbolism, sometimes presents are just presents. That was his subtle way of reminding you about his birthday."

"His birthday isn't for another month."

"Yeah, but in school they each had to do a birthday project where they learned about their specific month. Needless to say, he's obsessed with his birthday, and we need to get back to the point. You have a key to Stef's house! How in the fuck did that happen?"

Missy began the drive to work, riveted by the story. It had taken years for Gary to do that. "I think I might have almost passed out too. How was the next day? Did she have drunk regrets?"

"I think her only regret was the fourth drink. But I made her my hangover cure—"

"I don't think you invented the bloody Mary and eggs sunny-side up with toast, but continue."

"Well, once we'd had breakfast, and she'd started to feel more herself, we had a really great talk about everything that transpired the day before and where we want to go."

Missy parked in her assigned space but stayed in the car. "That sounds a lot like future talk."

Perse laughed. "Because that's what it was. It was nice to openly speak about what we want professionally, and also what we want for our relationship."

She gripped the wheel as though she were still driving. "And what do you want for your relationship?"

"Moving forward. It'll be a slow forward, but forward nonetheless."

It was settled. Missy would make a marriage bet with Gary when she got home. "I bet the sex after that was hot." An email notification flashed on her screen from Alec's school. "Shit! I have to go, I think Alec threw peanuts at his bully."

"What?"

"Don't worry about it. I'll fill you in later. You focus on moving up through your levels." Missy hung up, and while she knew she should call Alec's school next, she called Gary. "It's time to start the bets. I say they're married in a year."

"I can't make that bet. I haven't met Stef yet."

She hated it when he had a point. "Okay, but once you meet her, the bets are on."

CHAPTER TWENTY-ONE

AFTER THREE WEEKS, Perse still hadn't gotten used to her new Monday routine. She didn't wake up alone or on her lumpy Murphy bed, but rather in Stef's arms and on a superior mattress. The shower spray that urged her tired limbs into wakefulness wasn't a dribble of constantly changing temperatures, but rather a forceful, steaming spray shooting from a detachable showerhead. Lastly, while she ate breakfast, Stef gave her a sweet kiss goodbye and asked her to lock up as she left for the gym in her adorable matching outfit.

Timera gave her a once over in the department's kitchenette. "It's borderline annoying how perfect you look."

Gillian's gaze bounced between her two colleagues. "I'm going to say refreshed."

"I'd hope so. I spent most of the weekend in bed." She watched Timera's brow arch and Gillian stifle a laugh. Immediately, she felt a blush crawl up her neck. "Because I slept a lot."

"I believe you," Gillian said. She sipped her tea and then cocked her head. "Have you heard about any of the apartments you were interested in?"

"Yes, but most have been a dead end. Had I inquired a few weeks sooner I would have beaten a lot of people visiting for the semester."

"Well, at least the opportunity to go over to Stef's more gets you away from the fried chicken smell."

"I do consider that an added bonus." Perse left the kitchenette to start her day. While she booted up her computer and fell into her routine, she was almost disgusted by how happy she was.

Her mood turned serious when Missy's name flashed across her buzzing phone. She never called her this early in the morning. That was reserved for the chaos of getting Alec ready for kindergarten.

"Missy? Everything okay?"

"I need help."

Perse's back straightened as her body went on full alert. "What happened?"

"You know the birthday invitation I sent over the weekend?"

"Yes. Did my RSVP not go through?"

"No, it did. Along with everyone with a five-year-old in the county! I figured I'd be flooded with mostly maybes and noes, but almost everyone in his class is coming. Including the peanut bully because God forbid I exclude someone from his class. I'm going to have like twenty kids here and probably more adults. There's going to be like fifty fucking people here. Is there any possible way you and Stef could get here like an hour early to help set up? Since Mom and Dad won't be here, I could really use you, especially since you know where I keep everything."

Perse grimaced. Stef wanted to use as much time in the morning as possible to pack for her trip to Atlanta. But it did work in her favor that Missy's house was closer to the airport. "I'll have to double check with Stef, but if we do, I hope this means we get out of the clean-up guilt trip?"

"I promise: no guilt trip."

"Good. Now, since we're talking about the party, I was wondering if you could dig something out for me. There's something I'd like to show Stef while we're there."

#

Perse had been tense ever since they'd loaded Stef's bags into her Jeep. On their way to the party, they'd talked about their fall mid-terms, new workout routines, and the public's response to Timera's video about the vets. They'd spoken of everything except

Stef's interview. The philosophy of not stressing over something until there was something to stress about seemed to be working. Which was why she hadn't told Missy. In her case, there was no reason to make her upset about something until there was something to be upset about.

When Perse parked outside the suburban home, a blond head in the window scurried away.

"That's an interesting greeting," Stef said.

"Missy gives Alec the job of being on the lookout for company, even though Dandy is fairly competent in that role," Perse explained as she headed to the door holding the wrapped present.

The front door opened and Missy appeared, ready to greet. "Ladies!" She wrapped her sister in a hug while Dandy rushed to the scene with his tail wagging. "Stef! I love the superhero shirt. Come here, you," Missy said and embraced Stef with more of a hug tackle.

"Aunt Erse!" Alec jumped off of the couch where he was perched and hugged her legs.

Perse handed his present off to Stef and bent down to hug her nephew. "Happy birthday. How are those teeth coming along?" she asked as she gave Dandy belated scratches behind his ears.

Alec held his bottom lip down to show his aunt. "Ey sill gone."

"You'll get them back in no time." Perse stood and gestured to her date. "Alec, I'd like you to meet Stef."

Stef held Alec's present under one arm and waved. "Happy birthday!"

"Hi!" Alec enthusiastically waved back and stared at her facial features.

Stef shifted uncomfortably. "Do I have something on me?"

"No." He shook his head vigorously. "I heard Mommy say to Daddy that you might have Aunt Erse's lips all over your face."

"Oh," Perse said with poised surprise. "Well, do I?"

"No," he said, and then looked over to his mother. "Can I go outside now and help Liz and Daddy?"

"Please do. And tell him that your aunt and Stef are here."

Alec ran way with Dandy at his heels.

Missy shot them a sympathetic look. "Sorry about that. He eavesdrops and then repeats everything. Don't be surprised if you hear something about a beast with two backs. So, how have you two been?"

"Uh. I'm doing pretty well," Stef answered. "Thanks for inviting me."

"Don't be silly. I'm glad you could come."

Perse had expected to see the house a mess, but instead, it was clean, organized, and decorated for the party. "The house looks great, and you seem really calm considering you're going to have four dozen people here in an hour."

"Yeah, I caved and hired someone. Plus, a bunch of people canceled because there was a tainted batch of potato salad at a PTA meeting. Isn't food poisoning great?"

"It does have its perks," Stef added with a smile only to receive a disapproving look from Perse. "What? I'm not just talking about Wayne. There are many uses for botulism toxin."

"You two are such a unique brand of cute," Missy said as she smiled brightly at the pair. "Perse, before you show Stef *the thing*, I could still use a hand in the kitchen."

"There's a thing?" Stef asked.

"There is," Missy answered with a smirk. "But not until you're done with your responsibilities."

Perse fell into her usual role of chopping vegetables and fruit while Stef pushed up her sleeves and took over cupcake detailing. In terms of helping Missy set up for a birthday party, Perse was relieved to have such a simple task. Blowing up balloons and decorating cakes were not her forte.

Gary took a time out from setting up the ninja course in the backyard to introduce himself to Stef. Perse had never seen Gary so engaged with one of her partners before; he seemed to genuinely like her. He even snorted when he laughed. Afterwards, Stef agreed with Perse's description of him: he was stoic and looked like an adult version of Alec. With more teeth.

"I'm going to reserve a special cupcake just for you," Stef said to Perse.

"Can I request chocolate with blue frosting?"

"I'll make myself a red one so we can sneak out and make purple."

"You will not be making purple at my child's birthday party!" Missy said as she patted Stef on the back, which caused Stef to flinch. "I'm kidding. I'm happy in more ways than one that you're here and helping. If all you need is a little purple for your time, then go for it." She plucked a green pepper sliver off of the tray and bit into it with a crunch. "Hey, Perse. Would you mind showing Liz that piano exercise? The one where your fingers move all creepy-like over the keys? I tried to describe it to her and failed miserably."

"Sure. I can—"

"Liz!" Missy yelled out of the open window in the kitchen. "Aunt Perse is going to show you spider-hand now." She directed her attention back to her kitchen helpers. "Thank you. As a bonus, this'll give Stef and me a chance to catch up."

"Aunt Perse!" Liz hugged her with childlike enthusiasm, but then continued with the maturity of an adult. "Thanks for the quick lesson. My new teacher tries but isn't as good as you."

Perse kissed the crown of Liz's head. She was getting so tall— the top of Liz's head almost touched Perse's chin. "It's no problem whatsoever. I know you were short-changed last time I was here."

Liz nodded in agreement. "Yeah, the last time you were here you were kind of weird . . . even before you fainted."

Missy chuckled. "From the mouths of babes."

Perse knew that infamous brunch was something she would never live down and let Missy's teasing go. "Before we start our lesson, I want you to meet someone." Stef's words from earlier came back to her. Liz would make this as big of a deal as Perse wanted it to be. "This is my girlfriend, Stef. Stef, this is my niece, Liz."

Liz offered her hand. "Mom said you were coming today! It's really nice to meet you. Are you and Aunt Perse really get—"

"Hey, this is exciting!" Missy interjected. "Liz, you better get your lesson started before everyone gets here."

"Maybe you can ask me later," Stef said in a faux-whisper. "I think your mom wants to grill me now."

"I would say it's more of a sauté," Missy corrected.

Liz looked at her aunt seriously. "We should go now."

"I suppose so," Perse said skeptically. Missy's devilish smirk did not comfort her.

"I'll be fine," Stef assured. "Go teach Liz the spider-hand."

Perse walked with Liz down the hall and into the music room, shutting the door behind them. "I'm sorry to hear that you don't like your new piano teacher."

Liz took her spot in the center of the bench and lifted the fallboard to expose the keys. "It's not that I don't like her. She's nice. She's just not as good and I know you're not coming back to live with us. It's depressing," she stated matter-of-factly.

"I had no idea me moving out would make you so sad," Perse said as she poised her fingers over the keys, preparing to show her the warm up.

"Yeah, it surprised me too. I mean, like, I knew you existed before. You sent cards and showed up on holidays sometimes, but you didn't seem like a real person until you moved in with us. It was really nice having you here and getting to know you. Plus, it made Mom super happy, even though she pretended to be annoyed."

Perse's hands fell to her sides. "I didn't know that. That's . . . really sweet. I have to say I loved seeing you every day too. I liked hearing about what you learned in school or a movie you'd seen. You've turned out to be a well-rounded young lady. I'm very proud of you."

"Really?"

"Yes. I want to see you and Alec grow up as opposed to simply hearing about it, but I think you know I probably won't live with you guys again. I'm just going to have to visit more than I used to."

"I know that." Liz's serious face brightened and she waggled her brow. A move she definitely got from Missy. "Will Stef be coming with you on all of your visits?"

Perse chuckled. "I don't know about *all* of my visits. But she might be coming to more. Why?"

"I think it's neat that you have a special person. Mom said that you had a drought for a real long time, and that Stef's made you drink from the relationship fire hose. I don't really know what that means, but I just wanted you to know that I think it's cool you brought her."

"I'm glad I brought her here today too," Perse said with a genuine smile. She just hoped that Missy was somewhat gentle in her sauté. The noise in the kitchen had gotten much louder and they still had fifteen minutes before the official beginning of the party, so it couldn't be guests. "I better show you the warm up before the house is overrun with people." She hovered her fingers over the keys. "Okay, first spread your fingers apart—"

Stef barged in and shut the door silently. "You mom and dad are here!" she whispered with intensity.

"What?" Perse exclaimed. "They weren't supposed to come, right?" she asked Liz in a lowered voice.

Liz shook her head. "I don't think so. They had a fishing event thing, but what's the big deal?"

Stef looked truly ashen. "I'm not supposed to meet your grand-parents today. I knew I would eventually, but I was going to recite a casual-sounding speech about love and stuff."

Liz stifled a laugh. "You can still do that."

"I didn't write it yet!" Stef paced in a tight circle.

It was a completely new side to Stef. Perse realized that Stef was actually anxious, and the knowledge made her feel unexpectedly calmer, which was a new experience. They were in it together; they would get through it together. "I know neither of us prepared for this, but it's going to happen. It'll be fine. Do you need a gummy?"

"Um . . . I don't know."

Perse and Stef continued to stare at each other while the voices in the kitchen became ever louder.

"Plus, it's not like they don't know you two are together," Liz said. "And they're both really excited to meet Stef."

"How do you know that?" Stef asked.

"Mom never takes her phone off speaker." Liz crossed her arms impatiently, which made her resemble Missy even more. "Just go out there!"

Liz was right. "Do you want to stay in here while I go out?" Perse asked.

Stef's mouth tightened. "No. We'll go out together."

They walked hand-in-hand down the hall as they prepared to make their grand entrance as a couple. Perse could hear Missy plead with their parents to not make a big deal out of Stef's presence.

"Please, just do me a favor and get your food, get your drinks, and—"

"Mom and Dad," Perse said from behind her sister. "This is Stefanie Blake, my girlfriend."

"Hi," Stef said with a sheepish wave. "You can just call me Stef."

Missy stared open-mouthed between them all. "Liz, let's go outside with your father and brother."

Liz followed her mother, but not before she received a quick hug from her grandmother and hair tousle from her grandfather.

The spotlight was on Stef, and Perse could tell her parents were studying her. Why wouldn't they? This was the first time they had been in the same room with a significant other since the rehearsal dinner to her wedding.

Her father made the first move and shook Stef's hand. "I'm Paulo, and this lovely woman is my wife, Olivia."

Olivia playfully slapped his shoulder. "We figured we'd see Perse here, but not you. It's such a wonderful surprise to meet you."

"I'm surprised too," Stef said with a nervous laugh. "I'm also slightly terrified. Usually, I'm much more poised and—"

"Sweetie, it's fine," Perse said as she placed a comforting hand on her shoulder. "I'm sure they empathize with you, right?"

"God, yes. I remember when I met Olivia's parents the first time. You could have wrung my shirt out, I sweat so much."

Olivia laughed along with Paulo. "I felt so badly for him. They asked him absolutely everything under the sun. Luckily for you, between what Perse has told us and the school website, we already know quite a bit."

"You have a very interesting and impressive academic background," Paulo said.

"That's really nice of you to say." Stef smiled at them and then to Perse. "If you have questions I'd be more than happy to tell you all about it, but I should finish frosting the cupcakes first." Stef headed to the other side of the kitchen island. "Why don't you all get those drinks and relax outside? I'll join you in a few minutes."

"I'll be right there soon too." Perse held the door open for her parents but stayed behind. She leaned heavily on the closed door and exhaled a long breath. Her nerves were still at bay, but she could tell the day would still be a test for both her and Stef. "Are you okay?"

Stef nodded her head much more quickly than normal. "I think so. I'm a little thrown that your parents Internet stalked me, but it's okay. They just want to make sure I'm an upstanding citizen and not an evil scientist. It's a valid concern. How are you? This has got to be making your insides all crazy too."

"I'm managing better than I expected." Perse walked over and gave Stef a reassuring kiss. "Are you sure you're okay?"

"I will be. I just need some time with the cupcakes to regroup and not allow myself to be psyched out. They're nice people. They won't lecture me. Will they?"

"I promise no lectures, but don't take too long with those cupcakes. Otherwise, they'll grow suspicious." She left the kitchen with her lips tasting of Stef's lip balm, and with the sense that she had everything under control. It was a little odd.

"How is she?" Missy asked once Perse joined the group outside.

"Surprised and very focused on getting those cupcakes finished. She's taken that job very seriously." Perse cocked an eyebrow at the large glass of wine her mother pushed her way.

"You don't have to drink all of it, but it might help relax you."

"I think I'm okay," Perse said and sipped the rosé. "I'm more worried about Stef than I am myself."

"Hallelujah and praise Jesus," Missy said dryly. "You've grown as a person."

"Be nice to your sister," Paulo lightly reprimanded. "I really feel terrible we surprised the two of you like this. Had we known Stef would be here, we would have told you we were coming. Who would have thought our fishing tournament would've met the catch limit on the first day?"

The doorbell rang, breaking the silence after the seemingly rhetorical question had been asked.

Gary was across the yard still setting up the ninja course. Liz handed him orange cones while Alec tried to get Dandy to run through them.

Perse stared at Missy who remained calmly seated. "Are you going to get the door? Stef's probably covered in icing and I don't live here anymore."

Missy slowly stood and smirked. "I know you don't because you practically live with Stef." Their parents reacted to her statement with gasps and open mouths. "I've done my job. Bye!"

Perse cursed Missy's retreating form and her mother's beaming face. "It's not like that. I have a drawer. That's all."

"Don't forget about the key!" Liz shouted from across the yard.

"Oooh," Olivia drawled while Paulo whistled a long note.

"Please don't focus on that," Perse pleaded. "Stef's going to come out soon and I'd rather keep the topic light. Besides, it's more or less so I can do my laundry while she's in the lab."

Olivia grinned, but her facial muscles appeared strained, as if she were holding back a broader smile. "I see."

A boy of Alec's age rushed past them and to the obstacle course. Missy and the child's mother appeared and went into the yard. Stef came over and stood before Perse. "I'm really wishing I had worn my Ninja Warrior shirt."

"You like that show?" Paulo asked.

"I *love* that show!" Stef poured herself a glass of wine and took her seat beside Perse. "I watch an episode before I work out, because sometimes it's hard to get the motivation to work really hard. That's also why I try to work out with friends. We egg each other on."

Paulo cocked his head as if deep in thought. "Timera and Gillian, right?"

Stef gave Perse a surprised look.

Perse gently squeezed Stef's hand under the table. "Yes, they do know more about you than just your CBU profile."

Stef's O-shaped mouth softened into a smile.

"We do. I can't believe you play rugby," Olivia said with a shake of her head. "You're so small!"

"Different positions suit different body types," Stef added.

Then Paulo described his experience playing the sport. Olivia and Perse shared amused glances as Paulo, Gary, and Stef shared all of their sport's history and favorite teams, while several more parents and children arrived. Once the topic jumped to golf, Olivia whispered to Perse that she couldn't take it anymore, and excused herself to bond with her granddaughter.

Missy excused herself from the conversation she was having and came over. "Perse, can you help me in the kitchen?"

Perse checked on Stef, but she looked like she was amusing herself. "You know, I think you might need that help." Perse followed Missy into the kitchen. "Thank you. You know I'm not a sports fan."

"I try," Missy said and looked around the kitchen, apparently searching for something. "Also, I have been dying to get you solo. So, how are you feeling?"

Perse blew a quick breath out. "I'm great. Mom and Dad aren't being too invasive. Stef's charming and getting along great with them all. I'm actually really glad I didn't know they were coming. I didn't have time to stress about it."

Missy shut the last drawer and scanned the room. "Where the hell are the tongs? Oh, there you are!" She grabbed them out of the dish drainer and snapped them open and closed. "Liz told me that after your initial freak out you both held it together."

"Liz said that?"

Missy giggled and started pulling out packets of hot dogs, along with different condiments from the refrigerator. "She also told me that Stef said she wanted to give some kind of speech but didn't have it prepared. That's a shame. I would have fucking loved to have heard that. Can you grab the buns and the chips?"

Perse picked up the grocery bags from the corner of the room. "Is there anything else?"

"Now, that you mention it . . . ." Missy waggled her brow. "You haven't spoken about apartment hunting lately, and I can't help but think that's related to certain other events. Coincidence?"

Perse would have preferred a topic about golf but trying to avoid one of Missy's questions was like trying to avoid air. "I've been too busy lately to look. It has nothing to do with the fact that I have a drawer—"

"You have a key to her house! She is definitely thinking about living together."

Perse bit her lip and averted her eyes. She never should have told Missy this bit of information. Especially because...

"Oh shit." Missy put all of the hot dog fixings on the counter. "What aren't you telling me?"

"You know how we have to leave a little early because Stef has an important meeting in Atlanta tomorrow?"

"Yeah," Missy drawled dangerously.

"Well, it's a job interview."

"What?" Missy shrieked. "Where is she? I need to yell at her."

"No!" Perse scrambled to block Missy's exit route. "Calm down. I told Stef I was fine with it."

Missy folded her arms. "You know, since you asked me to get out that photo album for you, I couldn't help but flip through memory lane. And in the process, I was reminded of how unhappy you were with that dickhead assclown and the long-distance element of your relationship with him, even before he left you."

She understood why Missy was protective. "Yes, I was unhappy, but the travel didn't cause it. That relationship was doomed from the start, and that's why I wanted you to get out the album. I want to show Stef that I can be in a committed, long-distance relationship if I have to be. I think showing her will mean more than just my word."

Missy arched a single brow.

"Plus, you looked amazing in your bridesmaid dress. I want to show her that."

Missy sucked on the inside of her cheek as she thought. "That is true. I did look really hot. But I want you to really think about this, Perse. Would you be content seeing Stef for only a few days every month? And when you do, you'd still have bullshit, weekend, adult responsibilities? It won't be a vacation when you see each other."

Perse felt her face grow warmer from the anger rising inside of her. "I know it won't be a vacation! I'm acutely aware of what exactly it would be like! And no, I don't *want* to do it, but this is what people like me and Stef sign up for. Our work doesn't exist in every city. We go where we can, and when we love someone we do what needs to be done to make it fucking work!"

Missy viewed her thoughtfully and nodded. "I like how you got all passionate just now. You never showed that kind of fire with

Anthony." Missy threw her hands in the air. "Okay, fine! I will let you make your own decision, but I don't have to like it. Anything else I should know?"

"I think that's it."

"Okay, then. Let's get this stuff out there and see how long it takes to learn someone has a gluten allergy."

After the entrée of hotdogs and Alec's wish for a "dinosaur war" after blowing out the candles, the adults scavenged what was left of the cupcakes and watched the beginning of the Ninja Warrior competition.

Perse had to admit that she was entertained by the fleet of kindergarteners jumping and swinging around the yard, but after they watched Alec run through the course and set the time to beat, Perse slowly pulled Stef away from the crowd. "I want to show you the surprise thing now."

Perse led Stef down to her former living quarters. A black scrapbook album with silver trim rested on the coffee table.

Stef took a seat beside Perse on the futon and studied the album Perse held. "Please tell me that's photographic evidence of the time you played keyboards in a Cure tribute band."

"I wish." During the past week, Perse had played different ways of describing the most painful part of her past in her mind. There didn't seem to be a right way, but she figured the quicker she delivered news, the better. "This is an album Missy made when she was snowed in over a few days. It's of Anthony and me. She said that I might never feel the need to revisit my own past, but Liz could learn from my history if she ever fell for a 'personality wasteland'. She uses gentler words with Liz."

"This is your non-wedding, wedding album?" Stef asked, wide-eyed.

"Yes. And there are some things in it I want you to see."

Stef's eyes softened and leaned forward, her thumb softly stroked Perse's jaw as she kissed her. "You can tell me anything."

Perse flipped to the first page. There was a picture of her and Anthony in front of the golden statue at Rockefeller Center.

"That's him?"

Perse nodded.

"I already don't like him. He's smirking. Reminds me of the pompous, privileged face of Wayne."

"That sounds about right. He grew up very upper class and stayed there because of his trust fund. Being first chair only stretched his ego further, but it did allow me to attend performances in a few venues that I never would have dreamed of." She flipped the pages where there were ticket stubs for concert halls and arenas from New York, San Francisco, London, Rome, and Tokyo.

Stef's posture stiffened and she inhaled forcefully, then exhaled slowly. She may hate Anthony more than Missy did.

Perse turned the next page, which showcased a Platinum Member train card with silver and gold star stickers surrounding it. Missy must have felt that page deserved extra bling.

"What's that?" Stef asked.

"Something I haven't already told you was that when I was dating Anthony in grad school, he was already an established musician in New York. I would take the train to see him twice a month, and the other weekends he'd either come to me or we'd meet halfway."

"So, this was a long-distance relationship," Stef said, but not as a question.

"It was, but as I pointed out to Missy earlier, it wasn't the distance that ruined the relationship."

"Then what did?" Stef asked.

It was a great question. These days, she knew the answer. "He was fun, but there wasn't anything deep about him. What was on the surface was pretty much what you got, and he didn't seem to care about anything that was important to me or not directly related to him."

"He sounds like a dick."

Perse laughed and placed the album in Stef's lap. "That's essentially Missy's way of putting it too. His wedding no-show was a blessing in disguise."

Stef began to study and flip through the glossy pages. "Why did you want to show this to me now?"

"I didn't want our relationship to weigh on your mind during your interview. Whatever you decide to do, we can make it work. It was important to me that you knew that before you left."

"Thank you," Stef said and turned the page to see a brunette bombshell in a low-cut royal blue dress, who stood with a handsome man in a three-piece suit. "Wow. Missy and Gary?"

"They do clean up nicely. Okay, are you ready for the big reveal pic?"

Stef nodded and turned the page. Perse stood in a white, sheath gown with a modest bouquet. Stef did several double takes.

"You can tell me what you're thinking."

"I'm actually not so sure about that," Stef said with a nervous laugh. "But I will say that Anthony might be the dumbest fucking person on the planet in addition to being a dick."

"I think Missy would agree with you. Speaking of which"— Perse flipped to the last page—"what do you think of this?" In the photo, Missy and Perse were in pajamas and had cake covering their faces as if they were toddlers.

"Was that your wedding cake?"

Perse nodded. "Missy made an excellent point that I couldn't return the cake. So, once I couldn't cry anymore, we cake smashed each other before we ate it. I have to say, it was still good even though it wasn't as fresh." Perse closed the scrapbook.

Stef appeared dazed and swallowed a lump in her throat.

"Are you okay?"

"I wore a suit."

Perse cocked her head, but then understood. "To your wedding."

"I . . . didn't walk down an aisle. At the reception, we had a band that was way too loud, and I remember thinking that Aunt

Carol could have made a better cake. The honeymoon was Paris, but I wanted to go to Australia."

Perse returned the album to the table and held Stef's hand.

"I'm sorry there's no album for you to look at," Stef said. "But, after looking at yours, I think you should know those things."

Perse initiated a kiss that was soft and reassuring, but as soon as Stef reciprocated, the alarm on Stef's phone beeped, which caused Perse to groan. "God, I hate your phone."

"Feeling's mutual. We have to go."

"I know, sweetie. We can continue this when you come home from your trip."

Perse thought the family would have dispersed around the yard and they would have to say their goodbyes six different times, but for the exception of the kids, they were all seated at the table, talking and eating. Perse looked at the ninja course and saw parents standing at key places. "Did you assign people to monitor the yard?" she asked her sister.

"Yeah," Missy said with a chuckle. "I'm a great project manager. Do you two have to take off now?"

"Where're you headed?" Paulo asked.

"Atlanta," Stef said. "I have an interview tomorrow. It seemed like a good idea at the time, but"—she glanced at Perse—"I figure I can hear what they have to say."

"It's a shame we couldn't have chatted more," Olivia said with genuine disappointment. "When do you think we can get together again? How about brunch next month?"

"Do we have to do that next month?" Missy asked in a whine. "Everything on Earth is happening next month. Can't we just do Thanksgiving?"

"Then Stef should come to Thanksgiving!" Olivia declared. "Or do you already have plans?"

Perse could see the flicker of emotion that crossed Stef's features. Thanksgiving would be her first major holiday without any of her family.

"I don't have plans, actually."

"We'll have plenty of food, so please consider it. Right, Perse?" Paulo asked.

"Right." She hoped the note of apprehension in her voice wasn't obvious. "For now, though, we should get going. It was great seeing everyone."

After brief hugs from Liz and Alec, Missy walked them to the curb for the final goodbye. "I'd say that was a damn fine birthday party." Missy squeezed Perse in a hug. "With no passing out. Good job."

"Thanks. I'd have to agree it went pretty well." Perse sent Stef a sentimental grin as Missy wrapped her arms around her.

Perse strained to hear what Missy whispered in Stef's ear but couldn't. "Don't threaten her, Missy."

"I didn't threaten her! I just gave her something to think about," Missy said and slapped Stef's butt. "Have a nice flight!"

CHAPTER TWENTY-TWO

CAR KEYS IN one hand and her purse in the other, Missy slid her pumps back on to her aching feet. "Alec, I swear if you aren't down here in five seconds Santa is getting a text from me that says, 'no rock-climbing gym pass.'"

Alec bounded down the stairs with a pout. "But I don't want to go!"

Truthfully, she didn't want to sit through a basketball game after the day she'd had either—stupid contracting error—but she loved her daughter more than she hated sports. "Your daddy and Liz are already at the court, and if you don't come with us you don't get to have dinner at Pizza Palace. You'll be stuck with carrot sticks and Perse's hummus that I still haven't thrown away."

His eyes widened in true fear.

"That's what I thought. Now, get your coat on; we're already behind schedule."

Alec's speed impressed her as he donned his coat and sprinted to the car. Once he was safely buckled in the backseat, she turned to him. "Earmuffs."

He complied by placing his fuzzy, neon-green earmuffs over his head. Hands over his ears wasn't working anymore.

Satisfied that his hearing was obstructed, Missy called her sister.

Perse answered the phone with a giggle. "Hi, Missy. What's going on?"

Missy rolled her eyes. "If this is a bad time, I can call—actually, I can't call you back. This is the only ten-minute window I have so if you could ask Stef to stop tickling you, I would appreciate it."

"She's not here. I was in Gillian's office celebrating Timera's new grant. She's going national starting in the summer!"

"Very cool." Missy heard a door shut. Perse must be safe in the confines of her office. "What did you and Stef decide to do for Thanksgiving?"

"Stef really wants to run the turkey trot 5K that morning, so we're going to do a late check in. We'll probably get to Mom and Dad's around four."

"Where'd you decide to stay?"

"Oh, there's a really cute bed and breakfast that's partnered with a vineyard, so we're going to stay there for a few days."

Missy gritted her teeth at the asshat who slammed on their brakes at the yield sign when there were no cars coming. "Sounds great, just as long as you come over the next day for the beginning of the holiday bad movie-a-thon."

"Believe me, we won't miss it. Stef's very excited about the whole weekend. I think she started planning her outfits already."

The sweetness in Perse's voice made Missy break out in a sappy grin. But then she remembered an unpleasant fact. "How about the Atlanta job? Any news?"

"No news, and please be civil about that. I told her I was fine with it and I meant it, but I do wish they'd make up their minds already. I haven't brought it up in a week or so because it just introduces stress. For the both of us."

"What the hell is taking them so long to make a decision?"

"All I know is that there were several candidates. Stef probably won't know until the semester break."

"Turn signal, you jerk! Sorry, not you. So, now that we've talked shop, are you doing anything fun tonight while I'm being the perfect wife and mother?"

"Nothing too exciting. Just emailing a realtor back about seeing an apartment this weekend. If the mood strikes, I'll play some songs. Then I think I'll just read until I'm tired."

Perse's life was heaven. "You're not going over to Stef's?"

"I just spent the entire weekend there. She would probably appreciate having some personal space for a few days."

"I don't know. I think she really likes it when you're in her personal space, if you know what I mean."

"It's pretty clear what you mean, and it's true that she hasn't complained."

Missy slapped the steering wheel as she laughed. "I'll see you at Mom and Dad's on Thursday. Love ya, Sis." She disconnected the call and saw Alec in the rearview mirror. He had removed his earmuffs. "Alec! You're supposed to leave them on."

"But I could hear. Do you think Aunt Erse tickles Stefninny when she's in her person?"

"In more way than one, buddy."

***

"I've always had to dress up for the holidays. I feel too casual," Stef said while she fidgeted in the car.

"For the tenth time, you're not too casual." Perse turned slightly to look Stef's her outfit. The jeans and v-neck were completely appropriate. "But I love what you did to your hair. I didn't even know you knew how to use a curling iron." Perse blindly reached out to touch a soft curl.

Perse felt the soft touch of Stef's lips against her hand as she pulled into her parent's gravel driveway to join Gary's SUV. In her periphery, Stef stared at the home apprehensively. Perse understood the paralysis of anxiety more than anyone, but she doubted she looked as adorable as Stef did right now what she was anxious. "Sweetie, you've met them and they already like you. There's no need to be nervous."

"Kiss for luck?" Stef asked, as if she demanded a large favor.

Perse unbuckled her seat belt and tenderly met her request. "You'll be great. Oh, do you have the bourbon?" Her father always asked for one thing and one thing only—a good bourbon.

Stef pulled the bottle from her duffle bag on the back seat. "Got it. Now, Harry's here in spirit. No pun intended."

The cobblestone walkway that led to her parents' Tudor-style home wound through the well-manicured front lawn. In the distance, the creek that bordered one side of the property trickled, and on the other, a few horses meandered near the fence. It was way more scenic than the other places she'd grown up in. She was proud her parents had achieved their dream retirement home.

"We're here," Perse announced as she stepped over the threshold, "not that you didn't already know that."

Olivia rushed over and enclosed her youngest daughter in a hug. "And just how do you know that?"

"I could see you watching us through the window. Glass is see-through."

Olivia laughed. "I suppose it is. And Stef, so good to see you too."

Stef patted Olivia's back awkwardly with the hand that wasn't holding the paper bag of bourbon. "Thank you for inviting me. That was very nice of you."

Perse and Missy shared an amused glance as Stef continued to be swallowed by Olivia's fleece pullover.

"Of course we'd invite you. And I love what you did with your hair. Don't you agree, Missy?"

"She looks just darling. You also look like you need some wine."

Olivia clapped at the idea. "Yes, get some wine and go out back to say hello to the others. And while you're out there, you can check to see that your father's safe. I am slightly worried he's going to set fire to the backyard with that new contraption."

"What's he doing?" Perse asked, worried.

"He wanted to try something new, so he bought a turkey deep fryer. If you ask me, I'm leery of any food that requires a pulley system."

Missy handed them their wine and kept a third for herself. "The kids are out there waiting for disaster to strike. Gary's on standby with the fire extinguisher. It really is a unique holiday sight."

As they walked through to the backyard, they saw the poultry-based pulley system, and were greeted by a chorus of different voices, including Dandy's barking.

Alec ran to Perse in his neon-green camouflage jacket. "Aunt Erse!"

Perse bent down to hug her nephew and noticed that his wrist was wrapped in an elastic bandage. "What happened to your hand?"

"I fell off the slide again. Hi, Stefninny."

Stef smiled and returned his wave. "Hi. I'm surprised you remembered my name, but you can just call me Stef."

He shook his head with a smile. Stefninny would be staying. "Mommy said that you were coming today and that it wasn't weird."

Paulo, Gary, and Liz all shook their heads at the small boy's honesty.

Stef, fortunately, appeared amused. "I understand. It's a little strange for me too. This is the first Thanksgiving I've ever been to where I didn't have to put on fancier clothes, but your Aunt Erse tells me it's okay."

"Of course it's okay," Paulo said loudly, but then whispered to Perse, "Do I hug Stef?"

"Mom did, so I think it's okay."

Paulo hugged Stef much more gently than her mother had.

After Stef was released, she reached into the bag and removed the mostly full bottle of bourbon. "And this is for you. I know Harry would be fine with it being passed to another service member. Even if you were Navy."

"I can definitely drink to that." Paulo stared at the bottle reverently. "Thank you very much."

"You're very welcome."

Perse grinned as her father gave Stef a friendly pat on the shoulder and a smile usually reserved for poignant moments. She continued to watch him walk closer to the deep fry system: a turkey hung in a metal basket, a large metal pot halfway filled with oil, and a propane source. "This is . . . interesting."

"I think it's awesome," Stef said and received identical smiles from Gary and Alec in return. "When does it take the plunge?"

Paulo pointed at Liz who looked down at her watch. "Seven minutes," she announced proudly.

"Just enough time." Gary tousled Alec's hair. "Hey buddy, let's go check the football scores."

"You have the game on?" Stef asked excitedly.

"Of course we do! I have the TV cued up in the basement. Feel free to go in and watch with them."

"Can I?" Stef asked Perse with pleading eyes. "I haven't watched Thanksgiving football in forever!"

"Watch all the football you want."

Between that moment and dinner, Stef went up and down the stairs a dozen times to check between the scores and the backyard cooking show. On each trip, she grabbed appetizers for herself or others which only enhanced her popularity.

"She's making me tired," commented Missy, popping a cheese cube into her mouth.

Perse agreed as she sipped her wine and noshed more appetizers. "I think this experience is giving her a bit of an adrenaline rush. But I can understand why."

Missy stopped the wine glass before it reached her lips. "I don't understand. Why?"

"Ever since her divorce, she's spent Thanksgiving with only her aunt. She was diabetic and had some food allergies, so the meal was always pretty tame. Plus, Carol hated sports. Put all of that together and . . ."

"Stef hasn't had a Thanksgiving like this in over five years?" Her mother sounded appalled by the idea. "I'm even happier she came then. I just can't imagine being that young and not having any family left."

"Which is why she should join ours," Missy said nonchalantly.

Her sheer matter-of-fact manner left Perse flummoxed. "Wait. Just wait. I don't . . . really. That's too . . ." Perse stammered while she stared at her sister's cocky grin.

"Alright, Missy, stop pressuring your sister and help me in the kitchen." Olivia stood and dusted a stray cracker crumb off her pants. "You and Stef make sense, Perse, and I can see how much happier you are when you're with her. That's nothing you should run away from or be nervous about. Embrace it already. Embrace her."

As her sister and mother left the living room, Perse was left alone to gather her thoughts. She was stunned by her mother's admission. She knew that her parents liked Stef, but to hear that they were ready to adopt her into the Teixeira clan was unprecedented. She and Stef had only been together since May, there was a large question mark over Stef's future employment, and, according to Stef's levels, they had to live together first.

"Perse, get your ass out here and help me!" Missy beckoned.

She would have to reserve her deep contemplation of that issue for another time. "I'm coming!"

After fifteen minutes, every inch of the table for eight was covered with different glasses, plates, and utensils. However, the traditional Thanksgiving favorites—turkey, mashed potatoes, green bean casserole, dressing, and cranberry sauce—dwarfed all the other items on the table.

Stef took in all the food steaming and glistening in front of her. "Everything smells delicious. How did you make all of this?"

Olivia chuckled at one of the table's heads. "Division of labor. And waking up at four this morning."

"How come you don't have to do anything besides set the table?" Stef asked Perse.

"Oh, I do. I—correction—we, have to clean up." Perse patted Stef's thigh under the table in response to her crestfallen face.

"Are we ready?" Paulo reached for Liz and Gary's hands. "You know what? This is such a special occasion, why doesn't Stef lead the prayer?"

Stef continued to gawk at the calorific display in front of her, but then her line of sight went to the joined hands around the table. "Oh! So . . . about the whole God thing."

"Dad, that was mean," Perse chastised and turned to Stef. "I told them you're an atheist."

"You did?" Stef asked with sweet surprise. "You're not going to judge me?" she asked Perse and Olivia.

"You don't have to answer to us on that one."

Paulo was about to start when Stef said, "There is something my dad used to say that's kind of like a prayer. I could say that and then you can fill in the gaps."

He and Olivia nodded their permission.

Stef raised her eyes to the ceiling and quietly said. "Thank you for the food that nourishes our bodies. Thank you for the fellow-ship around the table. Thank you for all things beautiful with which our lives are filled." Stef nodded sharply to conclude her blessing.

"Amen," Olivia said softly.

"Let's eat!" Paulo added enthusiastically and commenced loading his plate.

Everyone at the table followed his lead. Except for Alec.

"Stefninny, may I have some cranberries, please?"

"You sure can and you asked very politely."

"We've been working on manners," Missy said as she received the bowl and spooned some onto his plate. "I'm guessing no one else calls you 'Stefninny.'"

"No, Alec's the only one. He's special that way." That earned a smile large enough to show his new teeth. "Nobody really calls me Stefanie either, except when I was younger and did something I wasn't supposed to do. Then I'd get the whole, 'Stefanie Blake, what did you do?' from my mom."

Olivia glanced at her daughters on either side of her. "I guess you weren't as ornery that you got the first, middle, and last name treatment like my girls did."

"Oh, I don't know about that. One time I put a snake in the bathtub to watch it swim."

"Cool!" Alec beamed and looked to both his parents. "Can I do that?"

"No!" both Missy and Gary answered.

Perse shot an amused glance at Stef and sipped her wine. "Try a new fun fact, sweetie."

Stef's brow furrowed then arched in revelation. "Okay. How about this? I don't have a middle name. Stefanie Blake is my full legal name."

Liz gasped. "I have a friend at school, and her first name is Blake. So, it's like your last name could be a middle name, and then you can have a new last name when you get married. You can be Stefanie Blake Teixeira."

Perse choked on her wine violently, spurting droplets onto the potatoes.

Stef attempted to soothe her by rubbing circles into her back.

Embarrassed for herself and also for Stef she corrected Liz in between coughs. "Stef and I aren't engaged."

Liz's brow furrowed. "But Mom said—"

"I said nothing," Missy stated quickly.

"But I heard you and Grammy say when you were on the phone."

Missy shot her a patented motherly glare and then a patient glance to Olivia. "Grammy must have been talking about someone else."

"That's right, I was," Olivia said unconvincingly.

Stef continued to rub Perse's back, and her pinkish hue started to wane. "You know, I never thought about my name in that way. That's a good idea for, you know, someday."

"I thought so," Liz replied under her breath.

Perse could see that the rest of the table tried to hide their smiles at the slip as they continued to chat about all things non-marriage. The football game from earlier. The holiday movie line-up for the next day. The mild argument about whether bourbon was appropriate to drink with pie. She and Stef gradually found themselves back in the conversation until it was time for the dishes to be cleared.

The weight in Perse's stomach let its presence be known as she played with the leftovers' spatial relations in the refrigerator, Dandy sitting expectantly close by. The chore allowed a few minutes of alone time with Stef, which she was grateful for.

There was a lot for her to emotionally unpack. She was able to sneak in some subtle grounding and breath work, but she also needed to check that Stef hadn't been scared off by any of it. "That was quite the bombshell Liz dropped on us. I'm sorry I humiliated myself when I choked."

"It's okay. I was pretty shocked too."

"So, you're not upset by how I reacted?"

"Not at all," Stef said as she scraped crumbs into the trashcan. She reached for the next plate and continued the process while occasionally throwing Dandy turkey bits.

"What is it? You're doing that thing where you get eerily quiet and then follow it up with something introspective."

"I was just thinking about Blake being my middle name. Isn't it funny that I never once thought of that? Kids have such a unique perspective. Maybe it's because they're small?" Stef hypothesized seriously and closed the dishwasher.

"Sweetie, Liz is basically the same height as you."

"Maybe that's why I have a unique perspective on life too."

"Maybe it is." Perse stole a lingering kiss. "And I love you for it. Come on, it's time for our sugar high." They rejoined the table.

"Do either of you want bourbon with your pie?" Paulo asked.

"I'm driving," Perse said to Stef as her way of answering.

"Yes," Stef replied, "because I'm in the holiday spirit."

Paulo laughed heartily and poured three tumblers. Missy also wanted in on the holiday spirit.

After ten minutes, Stef was so enamored by the combination of bourbon, pumpkin pie, and butter pecan ice cream that the question directed at her had to be asked twice.

"Do you have any Black Friday plans?" Paulo asked and sat back in his chair, swirling his two remaining fingers of bourbon.

Stef shook her head adamantly. "I avoid stores as much as possible."

Perse's coffee cup paused at her lips. "Before the movies I thought you wanted to go into town to check out paint samples and maybe price sinks that 'look expensive, but aren't really'?"

Stef swallowed her bite of pie and tapped her fork on her plate. "Hmm. I did say that, and I did notice that we passed a Miscellaneous Everything store on our way here. It'll be nuts there, but if we stick to the plan, we should make all the movies."

Olivia's interest piqued. "Are you remodeling your bathroom?"

"Just a little cosmetic work I'm doing myself to save money."

"Between the backyard you were telling me about and this . . . that's a lot of renovation. Are you planning on moving?" Gary asked as he stirred his coffee. "Oh, did you get that job in Atlanta?"

Perse shook her head and frowned.

"I did."

"What?" Perse whipped her head around and gaped at Stef. "You got it?" Her heart soared and broke at the same time. Professionally, she knew it was a huge accomplishment, but personally, she struggled to keep the smile on her face. "That's . . . fantastic. Why didn't you tell me?" But she knew why: Stef had taken it and tried to spare her feelings.

Her stomach rolled as nausea struck her hard and fast.

But Stef was there with her hand on her back. "I didn't take it," she said softly while looking into Perse's eyes. She took a sip of bourbon and cleared her throat. "I found out last week. I'm sorry I didn't tell you. I just didn't want to make a big deal out of it. I'm embarrassed I even considered it."

"So, you're staying put at CBU?" Missy asked with an arched brow and put down her butter knife.

"Yes. My interests here far outweigh what I'd have had there."

Gary grinned. "Not enough money, huh?"

"Actually, they were going to give me more than I asked for, which was a ridiculous sum," Stef said with a small laugh. "It just wasn't work I felt comfortable with, and there was *a lot* of international travel."

"What on Earth did they want you to do?" Olivia asked.

"Basically travel the world and report on certain groups I suspected were making biological weapons. Apparently, my ability to do complex work with little equipment or funding made them believe I think like a terrorist." Under the table, she found Perse's hand. "I don't want a job where I'm sent to countries that have travel advisories and then asked to look inside mystery barrels filled with a biohazardous stew."

"Is that like looking into a barrel of monkeys?" Alec asked.

"Actually." Stef cringed. "Maybe."

The surreal turn of the conversation brought Perse back. She thought she had prepared herself for the event that Stef would leave, but in reality, she never could have. She didn't want to be apart.

Perse reached for her coffee with a shaky hand.

Missy directed a look toward her that let her know everything would be okay. "I'm happy to hear you're staying local," Missy began, "but going back to what Gary said, all those upgrades sound like quite the home makeover in a short period. Are you selling it?"

The gentle hold Stef had on Perse's hand became tighter. "I am. Despite all the changes I've made, it still feels like Aunt Carol's house. I think it might be time to find a new place."

Despite Stef's hand in hers, Perse had to concentrate on keeping her composure at the revelation. She and Missy had just talked about her possibly moving in with Stef. Had Stef done other job searching she hadn't been aware of? Or had one of her old labs asked her to come back?

She stared into her coffee while her mind tortured her, but she caught Missy's eye again.

It's fine, Missy mouthed.

"When do you want to put your house up for sale?" Paulo asked then sipped his bourbon.

"Ideally in the spring, and then close in on a new place, a little bigger and still close to CBU, in the summer."

Missy tapped Perse with her foot under the table. "Remind me again, when does your chicken fried apartment's lease run out?"

"It's by the month. You know th—" Perse's eyes brightened and she quickly looked at Stef, who made a poor attempt to look innocent.

Olivia snickered and Paulo added, "Well, if you need help moving you can let us know. I might be gray, but my back's still strong as an ox's."

The reason for Stef's secrets and Missy's not so subtle reassurance dawned on her. Stef had known she wouldn't move to New York all along. Perse smiled softly to herself before turning and directing it to Stef. "Thanks, Dad, we may need it."

After their coffees had been finished and the dessert plates had been cleared, they started their goodbye hugs. Perse reassured Alec that she and Stef would be at the house to watch all the movies with him, and she reassured Missy that between movies they would have a serious conversation about everything that had happened at dinner.

Paulo walked them out into the crisp night, his arm slung over Stef's shoulder. "I'm glad you were able to come," he said as his breath fogged. "I hope you had a good time and felt welcome."

"Are you kidding? This is the best Thanksgiving I've had in decades. And allowing me to say my family blessing, that really meant a lot to me." Stef got into Perse's car.

"Well, it was important to Olivia and me that you felt included. I just love that our family circle is expanding. Now, take care of my little girl." Paulo shut the car door for her.

Perse hugged her father and giggled when she felt her feet leave the ground.

"See, I'm still strong enough to help move." Paulo finished the spin. "This is one of the best holidays I can remember having. I'm so glad you brought Stef. She fits in well."

"I still think asking her to lead the prayer was mean."

He shrugged good-naturedly. "I wanted to see how she'd react. If anything, that made me like her more. She didn't lie, and I know she's not going to rely on anything other than herself to protect you."

"I'm perfectly capable of taking care of myself."

"Oh, I know. But that one in there"—Paulo pointed to Stef rifling through her bag in the car—"will let you put your guard down. Give you some peace for a change." Paulo smiled warmly and opened the driver's door for her. "Drive safe and I'll see you both in the morning." He shut Perse's car door and slapped the roof for good measure before turning back to the house.

Perse started the car. A weight she hadn't known was there lifted from her shoulders. "I'm so glad— Sweetie, what's wrong?"

Stef held a folded square of paper and wiped away a falling tear. She sniffled and then took a deep breath. "There's nothing wrong. But there's something I want you to see."

Perse was worried and dumbfounded by Stef's actions as she watched her unfold the paper and smooth the wrinkles out on her thigh. Even without her glasses, Perse recognized that it was a handwritten letter addressed to her. "What is that?"

"I wrote this after you didn't tell your parents about us. I was so mad and needed to organize my thoughts, but I'd like you to read it."

Bewildered, Perse took out her glasses and turned on the dome light, which illuminated the interior of the car. She held the paper against the steering wheel and bit her lip.

Dear Perse,

I'm literally a genius, but I can't make sense of this. You have a whole family: mom, dad, a sister, brother-in-law, a niece, a nephew, and more. This family goes to your shows and graduations, and they take care of you. They know who you are and they love you for it. Why you can't be open with them about us baffles me. Especially when they sound so fantastic.

I hate to say this, but I don't think you appreciate what you have. I don't have any family of my own, and the last link I have to them is Harry. The most I can hope for is that someday I can be invited into another. So, I'll admit it, I'm jealous. I wouldn't admit that to anyone else, but I will tell you because I love you. I love you in that messy way that has passion and exposes you to all my faults. I've never loved anyone like that before. Not Mei, not anyone.

I want to tell you all of this right now, but I can't. I'm too hurt. I hope that we can get over this hurdle, and someday I'll have the courage to give you this letter so you can treasure your family even more and understand what you've come to mean to me. I love you more than I ever thought possible.

Yours always,

Stef

Perse didn't know when she'd started to cry or when Stef had reached out and held her other hand. The deeper meaning of Stef's words registered in her chest. The things she wanted to say were a lump between her mouth and heart.

"I meant every word, and I understand if it's a little too much. I just hope that someday you'll feel the same."

"I do, and I know your levels are important to you, but . . ." Perse tossed the letter onto the dash and felt the emotional ball in her chest free itself. "I love you so much, Stef. I want every day of the rest of my life to have you in it. I want to comfort you when an experiment goes badly and congratulate you when you meet your goals. I want to kiss you every night and every morning. And I don't want the real estate market dictating when we can have those things. I want you to be my family now."

"So, you want to skip level five and go straight to six?"

Perse wiped away another stray tear. "I want you to know that I'm ready for anything when it comes to my life with you. I want you to know that when you're ready to give this cohabitation level a try, so am I. And I want you to know that I'm ready for the next step after that. I'll stick to your pace, but I'm ready when you are."

Stef looked at her as though she were made of hieroglyphs, but then her lips gradually upturned. "Well, if that's how you feel we should discuss and outline this cohabitation level collaboratively soon."

"I wouldn't have it any other way."

Their lips came together across the car's console. The brisk November air dissipated as their closeness warmed them.

Stef was practically over the console and in Perse's lap. "I love you so much. I'm sorry that I ended up giving you the letter in the driveway of your parents' house."

"The important thing is that you gave it to me. Doesn't matter—" A loud ring came through the speakers in Perse's car. She begrudgingly touched the screen to connect the call. "Hi, Missy."

"What in the hell are you two doing?" Missy demanded to know in a playful voice. "You are seriously confusing my children." A small inaudible voice spoke. "No, Alec, Stefninny did not attack your aunt."

They shared a bewildered expression, but then turned to the house where the entire family watched from the window. Missy waved.

"Dome light," Stef said sheepishly.

Perse cleared her throat and turned off the light above their heads. "We'll fill you in tomorrow. Stef and I have important matters to discuss. Have a good night," she said, and disconnected the call.

"*We'll* fill her in tomorrow?" Stef asked with a grin.

"We're a team. Plus, after today, Missy's basically going to treat you like her sister-in-law. I hope that's okay."

In reply, Stef leaned over the console and gave her another kiss that left her breathless. She cradled Perse's face and brought their foreheads together. "I can't wait."

EPILOGUE

PERSE WATCHED THE snow-covered scenery pass by from the passenger window. She normally preferred to be the driver, but snow and ice were not something she was comfortable with. Stef, on the other hand, had driven the route from the Sweet Hill Ski Resort near Stef's hometown to the neighboring county's cemetery once a year for almost twenty years.

After Thanksgiving with her family, the relationship between her and Stef had evolved. They'd had multiple conversations about what sharing a home would entail, emotionally and logistically, which helped ease Perse's anxiety and fulfilled Stef's need for a plan. Between her relationship with Stef and finishing the end of the semester, winter break had snuck up on Perse quickly.

The schedule for break was simple. The first week would involve decompression from the semester, followed by Christmas at Missy's with their parents. Stef wasn't keen on religious holidays but was all in for that event.

Stef had bought presents for everyone. Dandy even had a new chew toy.

After work and holiday obligations had been met, Perse was officially on vacation at Stef's favorite ski resort. Perse didn't like to ski, but she did like reading in a warm lodge, hot tub soaks while sipping brandy, and snow tubing with Stef.

But the vacation included more than just the resort. Stef wanted to give her year-end review to her family. When Stef asked if Perse wanted to come, Perse was torn, but ultimately decided that Stef had spent far too much time of her life alone, and if she could give her support, she would.

The groundskeepers at the cemetery had plowed the narrow

roads. The only indications they were in a cemetery were the occasional markers that were more monuments than headstones.

When Stef parked at a bend, and Perse saw three matching headstones cleared of snow, she knew they had arrived. "If you've changed your mind and want me to stay in the car, I can," Perse said.

Stef took a moment to think about the offer, then shook her head. "I'd like you to come. This is a big part of who I am."

"Then I'll come." Perse nodded and zipped up her winter coat. It wasn't as cold as it was on top of the mountain, but she was still going to take advantage of any protection from the New England air.

Perse held Stef's hand as they walked through the shoveled path across where Stef's family lay. The snow seemed to dampen any and all sounds, causing the cemetery to be eerily quiet. As they approached, Perse could make out the markings on the headstones. Despite knowing the tragic story, the dates caused a sharp pang in her chest.

They had all been so young. Will had only been sixteen, and Stef's parents, Stephen and Annabelle, had only been a few years older than Stef was now.

"Hi guys," Stef said with more cheer than Perse expected. "I hope you don't mind, but I brought a special guest this time around." Stef looped her arm through Perse's and brought her closer. "This is Perse."

"Hello, it's very nice to meet you." In her travels, almost every culture she'd met spoke to their dead in some capacity or another. For her, the practice was no different, but this time its significance weighed heavily on her.

This was the closest she'd ever get to meeting Stef's family.

Stef looked at her with a sweet smile and then turned back to the headstones. "You missed a very turbulent year. A real roller-coaster for the ages. I guess the first big thing that happened was Aunt Carol died in February. Mom, I hope the two of you can get together again and play cards. I'm slowly getting used to the idea that she's gone, but it's tough. It took me over a month to become a functional adult again. Timera and Gillian dragged me onto a cruise ship for Spring Break; that helped me reset. It took serious convincing from them to make me go, but I'm really glad I did. On the trip I came to the conclusion that I was tired of being lonely and developed a system of levels so I could find somebody special."

She sent Perse a smile.

"So, a few more months went by. The results of my experiments started rolling in, showing a lot of promise. I didn't kill Wayne. Then, right after the semester ended in May"—Stef turned to Perse and grinned—"I met this woman in a bakery, who I could immediately tell was perfect. Will, you wouldn't have been able to speak to her she was so smokin' hot in her yoga outfit."

Perse nudged her playfully.

Stef hugged Perse's arm closer and nuzzled her shoulder.

The fresh lavender scent that was distinctly Stef tickled Perse's nose. Despite the icy landscape and nip in the air, she didn't mind the cold. What she was witnessing between Stef and her family warmed every part of her.

"Dad, she laughed at my math joke. Mom, she was particular with baked goods. In short, I think you all understand why I was smitten. And spoiler alert: this woman is Perse. I'll admit I didn't handle the initial courtship as well as I could have. Perse had just started at CBU and was working with my best friends, so there was some convincing on her part, and, believe it or not, my little system actually intrigued her."

"Still does," Perse added.

Stef smiled and kissed her cheek right above her scarf. "We started dating, and within a month I knew I loved her. I think what really sealed the deal though was how gentle and supportive she was when I was given a bunch of college letters for Will. I still don't know why Aunt Carol kept them, but you'll be happy to know that Will got in everywhere except for Stanford. Will, don't beat yourself up because, even though I went to Stanford, Harvard *did* accept you, and they rejected me.

"The beginning of the fall semester was rough, though. I went to a job interview that I probably shouldn't have, Perse and I had a fight—not because of the interview though—she's very supportive of my professional goals. And in the midst of all that, Harry died. That was weird. Not weird that he died, he was older, had a good life, but weird because of my reaction. I think I'm so used to people dying it numbed a part of me. But Perse was there for me the entire time, and it really strengthened our relationship.

"After that, Perse started coming over a lot more. She's basically been my weekend roommate since September, which has gone well. Wayne found out somehow about my interview and told the department head. I think he was hoping to drop me in it, but it's actually worked in my favor. Rumor is, they're looking at the dossier I submitted for my tenure application much more carefully this next round.

"Aside from school stuff, I met all of Perse's family. Oh, I had met her sister, Missy, who's her best friend. She's a strong hugger. Missy's kids and husband are great. Alec, the little one, is almost as accident prone as I was when I was a kid. And, I met Perse's parents. The first time it was an accident, but *so, so* different than any parents I've met before. They genuinely seem to like me."

"They do," Perse confirmed and ducked her mouth into her scarf. The beauty of the situation could only warm her for so long.

"See," Stef said. "I went to their house for Thanksgiving. You all would have loved it! Football on the biggest TV ever, with so much pie! Dad, I remembered the family blessing and gave it, so I think you'd be proud of that. Then, in Decem—"

"I think you're leaving out a big part, sweetie," Perse said.

Stef furrowed her brow and shook her head slightly in confusion until it dawned on her. "Oh, right! Immediately after Thanksgiving, like in the driveway after dinner, Perse and I decided to co-create the cohabitation level of our relationship. So, the plan for next year is to do the weekend roomie thing and house hunt together until the end of the spring semester. Perse will terminate her lease in May and move in with me until we find a new place together. That means we'll have been in a relationship for one year before cohabitation, which is very acceptable by societal standards."

Stef looked up at the leafless oak tree with her thinking face. "We had Christmas dinner with Perse's family before coming up here. I think her family expected me to propose to her in front of everyone, but I know that would have triggered her anxiety, so I didn't do that. I've learned from the key incident. I think they were disappointed I didn't pop the question. Well, Missy was, but what they don't know is that I have something planned." Stef turned to Perse with a mischievous smile. "Perse, I realized something a few weeks ago. Before marriage there's engagement, but that's not represented in the existing levels. It lies somewhere between the two levels and can last for an indefinite period of time. It's a very unique sub-level."

"True," Perse said, but wondered where Stef was headed.

"You were right when you said that we shouldn't let something like real estate markets determine our future together as a couple. It could take months or a year to find a home that works for us. So, if you're okay with it, I'd like to propose to you tonight."

"Wha . . . wha . . . what? Are you serious?" Perse's surprise was so great she forgot she couldn't feel her toes.

"Yes. I want to give you time to get used to the idea, and also avoid the chance of making the next few days and car ride home really awkward if you're not ready, which I understand if you're not, but"—Stef's eyes glanced back at her family—"tomorrow's not promised, and I'd like to move forward with you if you are ready."

Perse felt unsteady on her feet, but Stef was there to physically support her. It was so thoughtful, and so *Stef*, to give her time to process if she needed it.

After a few moments, Perse realized Stef was right. Their time on earth *was* limited. She *was* ready to move forward with Stef. "Yes, I'd be okay if you proposed tonight." Just saying it made her legs extra wobbly.

Stef smiled broadly. "Do you want to go back in the car and sit down?"

"No, I'm okay. I'm just getting used to the idea and trying to remember which dress I packed for tonight."

"You look gorgeous in anything," Stef said as she cupped her face. "Are you more used to the idea now?"

"Yes." Perse was more than okay with it. She was excited. She couldn't wait to be with Stef day in and day out. Have random and silly intellectual conversations. Read different books while still enjoying each other's company.

And make love whenever they were in the mood for it.

"I'm glad you're on board. So, next question, what if I didn't propose tonight? What if I did it now?"

Perse grinned at the game Stef had started. "Well, I would be grateful you already planted the idea in my head, because the shock might have made me pass out. Actually, the thought still makes me jittery."

"I can tell."

"But if I knew how it was coming, I could try to picture it in my mind the best I could, and that would help take away some of my wooziness before I said 'yes'."

"I can work with that," Stef said matter-of-factly. "Okay, close your eyes."

Perse did as instructed and bounced in place, but not to stay warm.

"Imagine I reach inside my jacket and then show you a jewelry box."

"What color is it?" Perse asked while she felt a single tear escaped her closed eyes.

Stef wiped it away. "Dark blue. Then, I open it to reveal a ring with a rose gold band and an aquamarine gem instead of a diamond."

"Because you know how I feel about the diamond trade and the atrocities associated with it?"

"Exactly. And then, after you see the ring and make some kind of happy gasp noise that women always make in movies, I recite an eloquent speech about love and how I want you to marry me."

"Eloquent, huh?"

"Okay, eloquent by my standards. Did you picture all of that?"

"Yes."

"Are you're okay if all that happens?"

Perse smiled and felt her body vibrate. Every nerve in her body was full of joy; it was her energy's only escape. "I am."

"Okay. Open your eyes."

Perse did.

Stef reached inside her ski jacket, pulled out a jewelry box, and opened it.

There would have been no way Perse would have stayed standing had Stef not prepared her. And that's why Stef was perfect for her. Not a perfect person. But perfect for her. Someone who complimented her weaknesses and understood her in ways that she never thought someone could.

"You didn't say that that the aquamarine was an oval cut."

"Oops, should I restart?"

"No, you're fine." Perse sniffled back more tears. "Please continue."

"If I can. This is really tough," Stef said, clearly fighting back her own emotions, and then inhaled deeply. "Perse, I'm a hot mess: I know this. I make systems where they shouldn't exist and over half of my life is tethered to a timer. But with you, I don't feel like a mess. When I'm with you, I feel collected, and even cool. When I'm with you, you make me feel as if I can do absolutely anything. But even more importantly than any of that: you make me feel loved all the time. Sometimes you look at me with adoration when others would react like they've encountered an alien. You never make me feel like a freak. You have always, *always* made me feel special and loved. I wish I knew with one hundred percent certainty that I made you feel like that too—"

"You do," Perse said, barely audible behind her sob. She

287

hadn't realized she'd had the ability to lift Stef up with a simple comment or look, but apparently, she did. "When I'm with you . . . I can be happy being me. I don't have to pretend to be anyone else, and I don't want *you* to pretend either. I love you exactly the way you are. Timers and all."

Stef wiped her eyes with her puffy ski jacket and smiled. "That's the key, I think. Perse, I want to spend the rest of my life with you, and not just a watered-down version of you. I want all of you, not just the smart, sexy, sensitive parts. I want the part that's in love with cheesy, seventies pop songs. I want the part that likes tea made out of truly terrible barks and roots. I want the part that likes to get high with her sister and watch sci-fi movies. I want absolutely all of you for the rest of my life." Stef plucked the ring from the box and held it closer. "Perse, will you enter the last level, and marry me? Oh, but please note that if you say yes, I expect to have a detailed conversation about the nuances of that level."

Perse mentally reached through the soles of her boots to connect with the crunchy snow beneath her, and stopped shaking. She smiled as she prepared to answer. "That sounds perfect. Yes, I'll enter the last level and marry you."

Stef rushed in to kiss her, something Perse was happy to return.

Perse didn't know if it was her own tears or Stef's she felt against her cheeks, but she didn't care. She and Stef were going to start the next chapter of their lives together.

After kissing for what felt like hours, Stef slid the ring on Perse's finger.

Perse looked down at the light-blue stone adorning her hand. It didn't look new or out of place. It belonged on her, just like she and Stef belonged to each other.

###

ABOUT THE AUTHOR

TO MY WIFE, You were the first person who read the initial draft of this story (whew, is it different!), but you gave me the best constructive criticism I needed at the time. My story did need "more teeth". Your support and encouragement mean everything to me. I love you.

To Eos Publishing, Thank you for giving this story a chance and believing in me.

To my editing team, First, everyone (not just me) should thank May. With May's direction you get more of the feels and, well, more of all the good stuff. Like a second sex scene. Everyone should thank Eanna at Penmanship Editing too, because commas confuse the hell out me.,,,See, I don't know what to do! Your kind words were a surprise and very appreciated as well. To Jenn, my proofreader, you have a detailed eye. Thank you for reading my almost final draft with those amazing peepers of yours.

To my sensitivity readers, AK, Morgan H., and McGee Matthews. Thank you very, very much for taking the time to give me thoughtful comments. All of you helped to make Perse a more authentic character. As a thank you to McGee, please check out her novels:

https://www.amazon.com/McGee-Mathews/e/B07Q876MLB

To Carl N., You were the second person to read my story and, in addition to telling me my original title was terrible, you also taught me the value of having interesting peripheral characters. Without your comments, Missy wouldn't be a PM or hate soccer, Timera wouldn't have a web series, and Gillian wouldn't...well, she was always pretty punk. Lastly, I'm sorry "mad rocket" didn't make the final draft. I expect the traditional greeting card recognizing my book accomplishment.

To Dame Elicia Eberhart-Bliss, You taught me the value of narrative. "It reads like a play...which isn't a bad thing, but I'd like more narrative because...." Well, hopefully you will be pleased with the narrative in this story. Your comments are also why Dandy exists. So, thank you for taking the time to read my very rough draft and provide me with feedback that helped me shape this story in a new way. If you need me to be a guest speaker who spends half the allotted time telling your students how awesome you are, I can do that.

To Mayme, You are a my most loyal beta reader next to my wife. It's very prestigious company to be in. Thank you for giving me a few extra notes about the behind the scenes, administrative action at universities. Your honest feedback about the <whispers> intimate time, was also appreciated.

To higher education, During my time in higher ed, I was a student, a lab assistant, a tutor, a graduate assistant, and an instructor. I used all of those experiences to write this book. Thank you for all you taught me in and out of the classrooms and labs. Special shout outs to Penn State and Hood College, which is how I image the CBU campus.

To Cambridge, Maryland and Chincoteague Island, Virginia, I love your towns! From Cambridge's mural of Harriet Tubman to the boats on the water, you're how I image the town where Stef lives. Chincoteague, you have ducks and geese...everywhere...and Pico Taqueria! Thank you for inspiring the taco scene. And yes, there's a little bit of Annapolis in there, but it's mostly you two.

To the Frederick Women's Rugby Football Club, Thank you for your support and letting me share a booth with you at Pride. While there isn't a lot of rugby in this novel, I thought of your matches every time I wrote about it. Also, the FWRFC introduced me to Nikki, the bestest web master ever, and a fleet of other awesome people! Thanks <insert wife's name>, for wanting to play rugby!

To me, Serena J. Bishop, I started the idea for this book in the winter of 2015. I had no formal creative writing experience, but I was determined to write a novel. As I handed drafts out to friends to read (see above), I began other projects (Beards and Dreams), and along the way learned more and more about writing. Despite all the other outlines for stories, I was determined to make my idea of two professors falling in love with some kind of obstacle into a novel. It was a long and, at times, frustrating road, but I did it. Thank you, me, for not giving up!

To the readers of this novel, There are millions of stories out there, but for some reason you choose mine. Thank you! I hope I was able to provide you an escape, tug at your heart strings, and give you a laugh or two. If you really liked this novel please consider leaving a review or tell all your friends. Maybe have a book club (questions on the next page)? Or check out my other novels? You have so many options! Also, kudos to you if you read this far.

BOOK CLUB QUESTIONS

1. How would you describe the relationship between Perse and Missy?

2. What do you think of Stef's levels? What levels would you add, subtract, or switch to find a perfect mate?

3. Do you think Perse gave in to a date too easily after Stef described the levels? Why or why not?

4. Were you able to relate to any of the relationships depicted in this novel? If so, which pairing?

5. Who was your favorite character? Your least?

6. Food and drinks were a common occurrence throughout the book. Did reading any particular one dish or beverage make you crave it?

7. How did the inclusion of Missy's perspective affect your opinion of Perse? How did Missy's perspective change the novel?

8. How did Wayne help you understand Stef? Or was his inclusion in the story a complete mystery to you?

9. When did you realize the impact anxiety has on Perse's psyche?

10. Did you have a favorite moment? If so, what was it?

11. What significance do the title and cover hold?

12. Was the setting impactful in any way?

13. Do you think Perse and Stef will live happily ever after? Why or why not?

14. From a parents' perspective, how do you imagine Olivia and Paulo feel about Perse from the beginning to the end of the novel?

15. Would the story have been more or less interesting if the novel used the perspectives of Stef and her core group of friends (Harry, Timera, and Gillian) rather than Perse and Missy?

ABOUT THE AUTHOR

SERENA J. BISHOP is an accidental author. Since she was a child, she was always engaged in some creative pursuit, but it wasn't until her laboratory equipment broke down in graduate school that she explored creative writing seriously. Since 2015, she's loved to give life to the imaginary people, places, and situations she's created in her mind.

When she isn't writing novels, she also writes an occasional blog, and goes to her day job as a scientist, where she also writes constantly. In her non-writing time, she enjoys being a nerd, surprising others with her pop culture knowledge, or finding a new beer or wine to enjoy.

She resides in Maryland, USA with her magnificent wife and precious Chihuahua. You can join her newsletter by going to www.serenajbishop.com or follow her on Instagram, Twitter, or Facebook @SerenaJBishop.

ALSO BY EOS PUBLISHING

Dreams – Serena J. Bishop

The mind has a heart of its own.

Aurora's life is perfectly mundane. She has a job she hates, an ex that ran her out of her hometown, and the highlight of her week is Monday breakfast with her best friend. That changes when Aurora starts dreaming of a woman who can't remember her own name. A woman who Aurora falls head over heels for. She knows the romance that develops between them isn't real, but the dreams make life so much better that she hurries to bed every night...until she discovers that her dream woman isn't imaginary. Her name is Leela and she is in a coma.

Aurora must risk everything—her job, apartment, friends, and her sanity—to save Leela, a woman she's only ever met in her mind. But in order to help, Aurora must convince Leela's neurologist and parents that she and Leela have a bond that transcends the physical plane.

Can Aurora fight through a progressively nightmarish landscape to wake Leela? And if Leela wakes, will she recognize Aurora as the one who saved her? As the one Leela said she loved? Their dream-relationship might not be real, but if there is any possibility of making her dreams come true, Aurora has to try.

~Dreams is a sweet lesfic romance about a love that defies the laws of physics.

CPSIA information can be obtained
at www.ICGtesting.com
Printed in the USA
FSHW022246181020
74948FS